ALSO BY L.J. SHEN

HANDSOME DEVIL

L.J. SHEN

Bloom *books*

Published by Bloom Books, an imprint of Sourcebooks
P.O. Box 4410, Naperville, Illinois 60567-4410
(630) 961-3900
sourcebooks.com

Cataloging-in-Publication data is on file with the Library of Congress.

Printed and bound in the United States of America.
VP 10 9 8 7 6 5 4 3 2 1

AUTHOR'S NOTE

This is an enemies-to-lovers, forced-marriage standalone with strong Mafia themes. It is considerably darker than other books in the series. Please check trigger warnings before reading.

In loving memory of Dr. Maria Amalia Abreu Maceo de Perez, and to every woman who ever broke a glass ceiling. The shards have painted beautiful battle scars.

To the girls who always wanted to befriend the monster under their bed. Turns out you can fall in love with it too.

"How long is forever?
Sometimes, just one second."

—*Linda Woolverton,*
Alice in Wonderland

"I have loved the stars too truly
to be fearful of the night."

—*Sarah Williams*

PLAYLIST

"Handsome Devil"—The Smiths

"The Enemy"—Dirty Pretty Things

"Search and Destroy"–The Stooges

"Fuck You"—Lily Allen

"What is Love?"—TWICE

"Turn Back Time"—Aqua

"I Luv U"—Dizzee Rascal

"Kids"—Robbie Williams feat. Kylie Minogue

"I Never Loved You Anyway"—The Corrs

"Hell in a Bucket"—Grateful Dead

"Scissors"—Slipknot

"Drama"—aespa

"Plug in Baby"—Muse

"Die with a Smile"—Lady Gaga & Bruno Mars

TRIGGER WARNINGS

All of them.
(I'm not kidding.)
If you still want the full list, please visit this website:
https://shor.by/LRhF

PROLOGUE

From: Dr. Arjun Patel, MD
(arjunpatel@stjohnsmedical.com)

To: Tate Blackthorn
(willnotanswerunsolicitedemails@GSproperties.com)

Tate,

While I understand your schedule is demanding, I urge you to pay me a visit in the next couple of weeks.

I instructed my secretary to prioritize this meeting. You are not well. I repeat, YOU ARE NOT WELL.

You have multiple disorders that need to be mitigated immediately.

I understand you prefer to liaise directly, but if this is a time constraint issue, I'd be happy to schedule appointments through your PA.

I eagerly await your reply.
Dr. Arjun Patel.

CHAPTER ONE
TATE

ROMAN BATHS OF BATH

It wasn't on my year's bingo card to contaminate the water of two-thousand-year-old ancient thermae, but life had a way of surprising me every now and again.

"Perhaps now would be a good time to stop flailing about, Mr. Boyle," I suggested stonily, my voice muffled by the plague doctor mask I was wearing.

Breathing through an upholstered leather beak was decisively inconvenient, but the Roman baths of Bath were littered with security cameras, and while severely allergic to humans, I had a feeling I was even more averse to prison food.

Plus, I had it on good authority that Boyle wasn't a fan of crows.

I always appreciated a good Hitchcockian touch.

Nothing short of polite, Darrah Boyle stopped thrashing in the shallow water upon my request, but not before hitting his head on the edge of the Roman bath's stair and splitting his forehead. The sound of bone cracking rang and echoed through the empty arena. My nostrils flared.

I despised clumsiness.

I especially hated mess.

Crimson crawled across the green-hued water, visible even in the pitch black of the night. Clenching my teeth, I tapped on the side of my right leg twice, then six times, then twice again.

I loathed going off script. This was definitely a diversion from my plan. He was not supposed to bleed. I wanted his corpse unsoiled and bruise-free.

It's not in your plans.

It's not in your plans.

It's not in your plans.

"Plans change," I said loudly, authoritatively, to myself.

Uncurling my fingers from his blood-soaked hair, I pushed up on my heels and watched as his ashen, naked frame drifted along the rectangle body of water, face down. A minute passed, then three. Because he wasn't Aquaman, he was obviously dead.

I briefly considered leaving him inside the columned bath to be found. It would look like an accident. An inebriated ex-felon who came for a late-night dunk where swimming was prohibited. Knocked his head and drowned.

But I couldn't. Wouldn't.

There were rituals to follow. A ceremony to be made.

Two, six, two.

Two, six, two.

Two, six, two.

With an exasperated, long-suffering sigh, I strode into the thermae to retrieve my prey. Water enfolded my Tom Ford Chelsea boots, soaking my Brioni pants. The fog of the spring water swallowed his body in thick mist, and I had to fish my phone out of my peacoat and turn on the flashlight.

I checked for messages, but there weren't any. Not even from my personal assistant, Gia, whom I called a half hour ago about a missing document I needed for work.

I would deal with her later.

The quiet swishing of the water as I treaded through it drowned out my slow and steady heartbeat.

Boyle's body floated toward a corner of the stairway. I gripped his hair in my gloved hand, dragging him up to the limestone pavement. I used the tip of my boot to roll him over so that he faced me. A sloppy, sodden sound rang in my ears. His blue face was splotchy, his skull distorted and slightly caved in from the injury. His lips were liver-hued.

You couldn't even have a clean kill, Andrin's voice mocked in my head. *You just had to make a mess of it, didn't you, Boy?*

I shook my head, ridding myself of his voice. It was my first kill. Practice made perfect, and I had at least two more people to help hone my craft.

See, five years ago, Darrah Boyle, along with two other inmates, murdered my father in prison over a bet. A game of cards. A reckless, meaningless moment.

My father was a powerful man. The type not to land himself in prison for anything short of murder.

As it happened, he did kill someone. *Accidentally.*

Nothing accidental about what Boyle did to him, though.

Paying with his life was the only logical outcome. An eye for an eye, a tooth for a tooth, et cetera.

I had always straddled the murky line between a businessman and a criminal.

Tonight, I stepped over that line. Hell, I fucking sprinted through it, all the way to another continent.

To track down Boyle and his partners in crime, I had to get in bed with New York's notorious Camorra organization.

The Ferrante family, who ruled the Italian Mafia in New York, was a lot of things. None of them outstanding members of society.

"I suppose you could say you popped my cherry." I reached for the inner pocket of my double-breasted coat, producing a black thorn still attached to the twig. I pressed it to Boyle's cold, purple mouth. It was an unordinary, telling detail. Black thorn.

Blackthorn. Like my last name.

I wanted his friends to know I was coming for them.

Wanted them to run, hide, beg, and bargain.

A moving target was always more fun to kill than a sitting duck waiting to be shot.

"It's been a pleasure. Thank you for participating." I stood to my full height. A thin trail of blood began leaking out of Boyle's mouth. His eyes were wide and full of horror.

Soon, this place would be swarming with police, journalists, and curious spectators.

Soon, articles would be written, TV anchors would weep, and national panic would ensue.

Soon, but not yet.

The night was an old friend, always ready to conceal me as I tended to my nefarious business.

I slipped out of the baths and into the winter night, sliding into an untraceable Alfa Romeo I'd paid cash for. I checked my pocket watch, a family heirloom dating back three hundred years.

Twenty minutes ahead of the timeline I set for myself. I smirked. Punctuality soothed my soul.

I drove back to London, whistling a cheerful tune.

Once at King's Cross Station, I tossed the Alfa Romeo's keys into a trash bin midstride and sauntered into a waiting vehicle, reuniting with my London-based driver, Thierry.

"Where is Miss Bennett?" I settled in the back seat of the Range Rover SV Carmel, plucking my leather gloves off, one finger at a time. I'd discarded the mask earlier in an open wheat field.

Thierry frowned at his watch, his eyes swinging to the rearview mirror, where our gazes clashed.

"It's one in the morning, sir," he pointed out in a French accent.

"Did I ask for the time?" My brow quirked in mocking amusement.

"No." He cleared his throat, shrinking into his leather seat. "Miss Bennett, I believe, is in Chelsea. It's her birthday today."

Was it now?

"The first night she's had off since the Taylor Swift concert in September," he rambled on, his voice drenched in pleading.

Ah yes. My assistant was mentally fourteen and consequently a "Swiftie." This in itself was a good enough reason for me to fire her.

"Where in Chelsea?"

"The Swan and the Wine."

"Off we go then."

Thierry pressed his lips together, the word *no* threatening to tear from between them. I eyeballed him through the mirror, challenging him to defy me. Some people avoided confrontation. I actively sought it.

"I think," he began, his soft tenor ridiculous for a sixty-year-old, six-foot-three man in a tailored suit. "You should allow her the night off, if I may suggest so, sir."

"You may not," I informed him flatly. "Now floor it."

Thirty minutes later, Thierry parked outside the Swan and the Wine, killing the engine. He drew in a breath, burying his face in his hands. He was fond of Miss Bennett. Most people were, for an unfathomable reason.

My gaze dragged to the back window, settling on the trendy pub. The Georgian building was painted burgundy, the pub's name in bold, golden lettering over a black background. Pots overflowing with colorful flowers adorned the windowsills and arches of the wooden doors.

Through the wide, wood-paned window, I found the subject of my irritation, occupying a table in the corner of the tavern, wearing a pink Birthday Girl sash over her sensible, pale blue tweed dress. By her side was a man I presumed was her boyfriend, Ashley, along with football sensation Kieran Carmichael, one of my business partners, Row Casablancas, and his hot-mess wife, Cal. Emphasis on the mess. There was no amount of wipes in the world to clean her verbal diarrhea.

I knew Cal and Gia were close. Kieran was friends with Row, so he was likely invited by proxy.

Theoretically, I *should* have been offended for not being invited. After all, Gia had met Cal, Row, and Kieran through me. However, I couldn't muster anything other than mild relief. I'd take drowning Irish mobsters in historical pools any day of the week over pretending my assistant's birthday was something worth celebrating.

Alongside them sat three women I presumed were Gia's London friends. I stared at my English PA as she tipped her head back and laughed at something her boyfriend said heartily. Asshole did not look that fucking funny. Clearly, her standards were low.

She shook her head, giving his chest a playful shove, then scooped her silly neon cocktail, taking a demure sip.

I pulled out my phone—my sleeves and ankles still damp—and texted her.

Tate: Miss Bennett, I asked you a question. Answer me.

Her phone lit up on the table, illuminating her face. She scowled at it, rolling her eyes and flipping it, screen down.

She was ignoring me.

An official invitation to ruin her evening.

Thank you, Gia. I RSVPed

Her boyfriend shot to his feet and offered her his hand, which she took. They slipped into their coats and emerged out of the arched double doors, carrying their drinks. Outside, they leaned against a beer garden bench. Ashley lit them both cigarettes, passing one to her.

I didn't know she smoked.

The revelation unsettled me. Not because I cared. If she wanted to expedite her demise, I was happy to fund her four packs a day habit. The world was grossly overpopulated as it was.

I did not, however, like surprises. And this was outside the confines of her personality.

My assistant was prim and proper. A smart-mouthed ice queen who was bossily kind. Not easily defined and yet entirely predictable. She wore sensible clothes with sensible makeup and ate sensible lunches. Her curly, ebony hair was always pulled back tightly in either a high bun or a sleek ponytail. She spoke softly but sternly, like a governess. Always carried useful things in her bag no one below the age of eighty should carry—paracetamol, Q-tips, pens, miniature nut packs, lip balms, tissues, baby wipes, and an extra pair of socks.

Actually, I could use that extra pair right about now.

My fingers drummed on the side of my leg again.

Two, six, two.

Two, six, two.

Two, six, two.

"Sir, please." Thierry swallowed audibly, undoubtedly guessing my next move. "She's—"

I didn't stick around for him to finish the sentence. I pushed open the back seat door and strode out, plastering on my infamous I-just-pissed-into-your-favorite-sneakers slick smile.

The moment Gia noticed me, she stiffened, her smile dissolving into a frown. The cigarette tumbled from between her fingers onto the pebbled ground. Ashley—was that the asshole's name?—wrapped a protective arm over her shoulder. Thinking he could shield her from me was pitiful. Optimism was such an absurd trait.

Though trite and largely dull, Gia Bennett was, regrettably, a stunner.

She had smooth, tan skin, a long, elegant neck, and two prominent dimples. Her naturally curly eyelashes covered sensual amber eyes, almost honey-like in color and consistency. Her soft, luscious mouth had the most distinctive Cupid's bow, and a pert nose and two graceful arches to call cheekbones adorned her delicate face.

Row and our other friend Rhy claimed Gia resembled Nara Smith, but the truth was she defied category. I didn't think there was another human attractive enough to compare her to. If God existed, which I seriously doubted as a secular modernist, he must've spent extra time on the smallest detail in creating her, because every inch of her was pure perfection.

Her years as a competitive tennis player were present in every arc and bend of her body. She was lean but firm, with narrow calves, toned arms, and bitable collarbones. She moved with purpose, with the grace of a swan in a still, calm lake.

She was, sadly, a remarkable beauty.

And that remarkable beauty was staring back at me, looking like she wanted to do very ugly things to me indeed.

"Why are you wet?" she asked, the first to break the stunned silence. No alarm betrayed her voice, merely irritation. She was the only human alive who wasn't terrified of me.

Up close, her boyfriend was tall, dark-skinned, and striking. He wore a Thom Sweeney jacket and an adequate watch, so I gathered money wasn't an issue.

Keeping his girlfriend, however, was about to be.

"You are not in a position to ask any questions." I smoothed a hand over my coat. "In fact, you should feel so lucky to keep your job after ghosting me. Come." I hooked my index finger in her direction, swiveling on my heel and striding back to the Rover. "You're needed at the office."

"*Now?*"

"No time like the present."

"I could think of a better time, and that time is not two in the bloody morning," she countered in that defiant manner of hers, which reminded me that no matter how hard or far I pushed her, how unbearable or unreasonable I was, I still couldn't, for some reason, break her.

And I tried.

Oh, I tried.

I was trying this very second, in fact.

She bent and she pretzeled—she even cracked sometimes—but she never fucking broke.

"Mate," her boyfriend groaned. "Come on. It's her *birthday*."

Grabbing the door handle to the back seat of the vehicle, I threw it open and glided inside.

I knew she'd come. She always did. What I lacked in interpersonal skills I made up for in an astronomical, $600K-a-year salary, before overtime and bonuses, a generous health insurance policy, holiday vouchers, and a Centurion card I allowed her to take for a quarterly spin.

From the curb, I heard Gia explaining to her boyfriend in a measured, apologetic tone that she needed to join me. He didn't seem too happy about it. Poor fella still hadn't realized there was no room in her life for a man who wasn't me.

In the five years and some change she'd been working for me, there'd been a string of hopeful Ashleys. I always ensured she was unavailable for them. It helped that the headquarters of my company was in New York while our second-largest branch was in London. Made tearing her away from suitors easier. Some had been easy to shake off, while others proved more difficult. In the end, though, there was always something. A Tate-made catastrophe she needed to tend to.

An emergency.

An excuse.

If I couldn't have her, no one else could. And I wanted her. Oh yes. Her body anyway.

Not that I ever gave her the slightest indication I was attracted to her.

Gia downed her entire cocktail in one go, winced, and joined me in the back seat of the car, still wearing the stupid sash under her unbuttoned coat. She knew better than to ask if she could say goodbye to her friends inside.

I scanned her face for emotions. As usual, there were none.

"*Office*," I ordered the driver.

I yanked out my pocket book of *Alice's Adventures in Wonderland* and scowled at one of my favorite lines to soothe my anger.

"I am not crazy; my reality is just different from yours."

Thierry winced. "I'm sorry, Gia."

She reached to pat his shoulder, a regal smile painting those luscious lips. "Please, Thierry. I'll hear none of that. It's not your fault."

"Did you get something nice for your birthday?" he sniffled.

"A few hours without my boss," she provided cheerfully. "Oh, and I got your flowers too. Cheers for that."

"Of course," he spluttered. "After you managed to help Annette with that insurance claim, it's the least we could do for you."

Ah yes. I almost forgot.

Gia Bennett's ice thawed when it came to other people.

Unless those people were me.

CHAPTER TWO
GIA

"How old are you anyway?" Tate impaled the silence that grew and pulsated between us like a quiet, hulking beast.

Electricity raced through me at the sudden sound of his voice. Low. Rough. Raspy.

I'd always harbored a slight, uninhibited infatuation with my boss, against my better judgment.

He reminded me of the Smiths' song "Handsome Devil." For every time I walked into a scholarly room with him, I wondered who would swallow whom whole.

He swallows you every time. Leaving no crumbs behind.

I didn't trust myself to open my mouth without screaming. He tore me away from my birthday party because of a *filing* mishap. This could have waited until tomorrow. I always worked on weekends anyway.

"Twenty-six," I managed to retort calmly, staring straight ahead at the back of Thierry's seat as the Rover weaved through the dusky streets of London. I graduated young from college, as I skipped a grade in secondary school.

"You don't smoke." Tate skipped to another subject, eyes still trained on his book. He'd been reading *Alice's Adventures in Wonderland* since I started working for him. Either he was the slowest reader on earth, or he had an unhealthy fascination with the story.

Also, who on earth was he kidding? No one could read in the pitch black.

Anyway, it wasn't a question, so I did not respond.

"Why did you take the cigarette he offered you?" Tate slammed the softcover shut, refusing to drop the subject.

"Sometimes I socially smoke," I responded finally. "Not that it's any of your bloody business."

"And that boyfriend of yours, he lives here?" he poked bluntly.

A few years ago, I'd be astonished by my boss's arrogant breach of privacy. Now, I had become desensitized to his antics. If I didn't answer him, someone else would. Tatum Blackthorn always got what he wanted and made sure to leave a string of casualties behind.

"Yes, Ashley lives here in London," I ground out.

"Shame we're returning to New York on Monday." He sounded quite chirpy. My boss wasn't usually a mercurial creature, but he did love seeing me suffer. "I'm thinking we'll stay there at least through April. We're breaking ground in the Hamptons for that gated community project."

"I will need to return to London the week after next for Mum's appointment," I said matter-of-factly. "And will probably visit here every weekend to help her carers."

My mother had early onset dementia. The first signs appeared shortly after The Accident. She was not doing well. Luckily, I could pay for the best aides and carers, thanks to my mammoth salary. The company also allotted me a medical allowance for relatives, which paid for occupational therapy. The perks and salary were the only things that kept me here.

"Bring your mother to the States." A demand, not an offer.

"I'm not changing her environment and caregivers so you can call me at two a.m. on a Friday asking me to fetch you condoms."

File under things that actually happened in my second year of employment.

"You're taking too much time off work." His voice, like his face, was neutral and indifferent.

"Let me stop you right there." I raised my palm. "Do not make me choose between my mother and my job. You will *not* like the answer."

"Very well." Tate returned his attention to the Victorian book. "Have your Centurion card returned to the bank. You just lost your shopping privileges."

I shrugged. I never used it anyway.

"I will. Can I ask you a question?"

His lips curled in annoyance. "Clearly. You just did."

"What's your fascination with this book?" I cleared my throat, wanting to break the ice. At least some of it. It always appeared as though the entire continent of Antarctica was wedged between me and my boss.

"It is the first children's book in the world without a lesson or a moral."

"What's wrong with morals?" I wrinkled my nose.

Tate looked up, eyes as dead as the useless heart in his chest. "I wouldn't know. Haven't got any."

———

The rest of the drive was spent in silence as the vehicle neared GS Properties' office in Covent Garden. I inwardly groaned. I'd been meaning to call it a night and check in on Mum. Now I'd likely have to wait until dawn.

Whenever I was in London, which was nearly every month, I stayed with Mum in our Wimbledon semidetached, but she also had a caregiver with her around the clock. I pulled out my mobile and texted Mum's carer, Jim.

Gia: Hi Jim. Terribly sorry. A work thing came up. Can I come at around 6 a.m.? x.

"Where's the rest of your family?" Tate demanded suddenly, tucking his book back into his breast pocket and examining his long, swordsman fingers. "Why can't they take care of her?"

I put my phone down after Jim replied promptly.

Jim: NP. Have fun bday girl. x.

Gia: How is she?

Jim: ...

Jim: Don't worry about it, Gia. I've got it.

She was deteriorating faster than I thought.

"I'd say the primary reason is because they're, well, *dead*." I hoped the dramatic piece of information would wipe off his bored, mocking expression, but not a muscle twitched in his face. "My father and brother died in a car accident," I hedged. "Don't you remember?"

I still had some extended family. An aunt I helped financially and some relatives I spent the holidays with.

"Why would I remember?" He shot me an incredulous look. "I'm not the one who ran them over."

I gulped down a juicy curse. "I've been taking a day off and flying out to London every year to mark the anniversary of their death since we started working together."

He turned to look at me. The hard, metallic glint in his eyes made a shiver roll down my spine. His eyes were like two silver bullets, his beauty haunting and cruel like a medieval painting.

As always, I met his gaze head-on. I'd seen Tate break people before breakfast. It was the only sport he actually enjoyed. I wasn't going to become a statistic.

"How long ago was it?" he asked.

"Seven years."

"So you were in college."

"No, I lost them the summer before college." I still had a lump in my throat every time I talked about it.

"Were you close with them?"

"Very." I swallowed hard, trying in vain to keep my voice from cracking. "They were…they were my everything. Dad was driving Elliott back from his tennis practice. Elliott was just sixteen. It had been raining like hell. They went back and forth on whether to go. In the end, Elliott's good nature prevailed. He didn't want to slack off."

The sleepless nights I had spent stewing in red-hot anger at Elliott for always doing the right thing. For never taking the easy way.

Tate gave me an oblique smirk, like we were discussing something hilarious.

"Is this funny to you?" I scowled.

"Funny? No." He yawned provocatively. "Boring? Absolutely. Be mindful of your days off, or I'll fire you."

He was loathsome to the extreme. Almost one-dimensionally villainous.

Yet I had to give it to him—he had this…*pull*. Something other-worldly and charming, an aura that made you feel important simply for being in his radius.

He wasn't beautiful, not in the traditional way at least. His lips were too thin, his expression too sardonic, and his cheekbones too sharp. But he had an angular, patrician face that resembled a marbled Roman emperor in Italian museums. His dark hair was pure midnight velvet, cut into a neat style. With light gray eyes, a carefully shaved jawline, and a general aristocratic air, he was the kind of man to make women do a double take.

Under his impeccable designer clothes were broad shoulders, a narrow waist, and an unholy sculpted body. I knew, because I had the displeasure of having him dictate entire emails to me while he did his forty-minute swim in his indoor pool every Thursday at six in the morning.

Tate found playing sports tedious and mundane. Yet he maintained his physique by having two fitness trainers at his beck and call. He worked out every morning, followed a strict paleo diet, kept three units of alcohol a week his upper threshold, and forged himself into something that was frighteningly perfect.

On the surface at least.

"Miss Bennett," he drawled. He called me that sometimes, because he knew how much I despised it.

"Mr. Blackthorn," I countered blandly. If he wanted to do the period drama rubbish, I was game.

"Where the fuck is Fonseca Islands' certificate of incorporation?"

Fonseca Islands was one of the trillion straw companies Tatum Blackthorn owned under the umbrella of GS Properties, the largest real estate corporation on planet Earth.

"On your desk," I said through tightly pressed teeth. "Just like I texted you when I left the office."

"And *I* texted back that it wasn't there," he snapped. "I fear you have to go through every single file in the filing cabinet and look for it."

"You don't fear anything."

He smirked. "I don't like cats or dogs, actually."

The vehicle screeched to a stop. We both decanted into the frigid night and walked into GS Properties' building. The twenty-four-hour security guard greeted us with a sleepy nod. We took the elevator up to the fifth floor. Once at the office, Tate strode to the filing cabinet in my open-space office and, with a theatrical flourish, shoved it to the floor. The drawers spilled, the files flying out in every direction, skating across the floor.

My breath caught in my throat. He just ruined *months* of work. Each folder was organized alphabetically, and within it, every document was filed in chronological order.

Tate leaned a shoulder on the doorframe to his office, crossing his arms over his chest.

"Time's a wastin', Miss Bennett. The files aren't going to sort themselves, and we need to find that certificate so we can open the Swiss bank account Monday morning. Ten o'clock meeting, remember."

Actually, nine thirty, you arse.

I swallowed down a chain of outrageous profanities that'd make a sailor blush. "May I check your desk first? I am certain I put the certificate on it, notarized and apostilled, prior to leaving the office this afternoon."

"Are you calling me a liar?"

"Of course not."

His eyes tapered with suspicion. He knew I didn't miss a chance to dish it out as good as I got it.

"I'm calling you much worse," I clarified. "Normally behind your back. But since you're acting especially egregiously tonight, I don't mind telling you that you're a sadist and an asshole."

"Bold of you to speak to your boss like that," he assessed, but he looked amused more than anything else.

"You're not going to fire me," I sighed, a hint of sadness in my voice. "I'm far too competent. Besides, for whatever reason, you're hell-bent on keeping me and making my life a living hell."

"I love that you think you're something special. That makes one of us." He tapped a finger to his lips contemplatively. "As I said, the certificate is not on my desk. No, you may not go into my office—my personal space—and look for it."

"Personal space!" I cried out. "I order your *condoms* for you."

"How does this invade your personal space? You're not the one I'm using them with."

True, but I was also the one to approach his hookups with an ironclad NDA and ask for their clean bill of health and proof of contraception. My boss was wildly unfond of the idea of reproducing. It was the one thing we agreed on.

His DNA should die with him. Preferably soon.

Tate used his wingtip boot to shuffle some papers around. "Go on. Start searching for it."

I crossed my arms. Every muscle in my body trembled with rage. I was about to do something foolish, and I didn't even care.

I was done being his pushover.

Yanking me from my birthday celebration was the last straw.

"Pick up the files, and put them on my desk."

No *please*. No *kindly*. He could sod right off.

"Pardon?" He arched a thick eyebrow, the sharp blade of a warning dragging through his voice.

"You heard me. I'm not one of the supermodels on your roster. I'm not going on my knees for you," I enunciated slowly. "Pick up the documents, and put them on my desk. I will not buck, Mr. Blackthorn."

"If you don't—"

"I won't," I cut him off matter-of-factly. "So I suggest *you* will. Unless you want to look for a PA first thing tomorrow morning. I heard Rebecca is looking for a full-time position." Rebecca was my replacement on my rare off days. A darling girl, but one who could definitely use honing on her organizational skills. "Go on then. Call my bluff."

He studied me for a moment, searching for a crack in my facade. Danger sizzled in the air. I knew I was going to pay for it at some point. We played a long game, my boss and I. One where he always had the upper hand. But sometimes I managed to sneak in a snake-like, quick blow to his ego. Like tonight.

Tate concluded I wasn't going to lower myself down and pick up those files. With tight, barely contained rage, he strolled over to the discarded files, righted the cabinet that buried them, and stacked them neatly on my desk. I watched him through a screen of white-hot fury.

Why did he loathe me so much?

I was a hardworking employee. Thoroughly agreeable the first year of our work together. But no matter how hard I tried, he always made sure I remembered how much he disliked me.

Initially, I thought maybe I was being *overly* friendly. So I stopped being cheerful, cracking jokes, and leaving him the baked goods I'd prepared over lonely weekends in New York City. If anything, my change in attitude made him hate me more.

My next theory was that he didn't like paying my hefty salary, but that didn't make much sense—he *actively* increased my salary each time I tried to quit.

Lastly, I suspected Tate belittled me because I was biracial. Being half-Jamaican, half white-Cuban, I was no stranger to racism. Whether it was on the tennis court or out of it, in posh events, I'd always noticed the pseudo-subtle way some people looked at me. The backhanded remarks.

And him being racist seemed like a logical personality trait for the soulless ghoul. But I couldn't find another instance where Tate was degrading or dismissive toward a person of color. On the contrary, for all its faults (and there were too many to count), GS Properties was constantly praised in business magazines and other outlets for being inclusive, diverse, and cutting-edge. Two of the handful of people Tate respected—the CFO of the company, Will, and the head of litigation, Tiffany—were Black.

No, it seemed as though Tate's problem was specifically with *me*.

When Tate was done, I shouldered off my coat and began sorting through the files. I already knew I wasn't going to find the blasted certificate. I remembered putting it on his desk after the courier delivered it.

My boss slinked into his office, probably to sip his baby-blood smoothie. I tried to ignore the ticking clock above my head as I slipped documents back into their original files, this time sealing them with paper clips for the next occasion Tate decided to chaotically rip through the office like a storm.

At five thirty in the morning, I finished shoving the last file back into the cabinet without a single sign of the Fonseca Islands certificate of incorporation. I closed the cupboard with a soft click.

"Gia," a deep voice husked behind me.

I jumped in surprise, swiveling around. Tate popped his face from his office.

"Lucifer," I answered.

"I found the certificate of incorporation." He held up the paper, his smirk unforgivingly taunting. "Silly girl. It was under my Starbucks cup all along."

CHAPTER THREE
GIA

THREE MONTHS LATER

I clasped my fingers around the familiar curve of my shell bracelet, drawing a deep breath.

Beyond the door looming in front of me was the party of the century, hosted by the arsehole of the millennium, a.k.a. my boss. I heard the music, the chatter, the laughter, the chime of delicate champagne glasses kissing.

Smoothing a hand down my lavender chiffon ball gown, I swallowed. The last thing I wanted to do was party. And technically speaking, I was not invited to this one. Only planned it to its finest detail, hired the catering, and sent out the invitations.

But I had to speak to Tate urgently.

I needed a massive favor.

A bead of sweat slid down my spine.

Snap out of it, Gia. This is for Mum. Pull yourself together.

I threw my shoulders back, tipped my chin up, punched in the code, and pushed the door open.

The seven-bedroom flat on Billionaires' Row had a mouthwatering view of Central Park. The first floor consisted of the main kitchen, living room, three large bedrooms, and four bathrooms. Upon purchasing it last year, Tate gutted the modern, futuristic design and vaguely insisted I redecorated it as I saw fit. It was unlike him not to hire the world's most expensive and prestigious interior design firm, so at the time, I had chalked it up to him wanting to make my workload more impossible and my life more difficult.

But it backfired on him. Designing his flat had been a refuge for me, a way to decompress from my hectic day job and personal woes. I had chosen bold, textured baroque wallpapers and commissioned the artist who painted the murals. I handpicked the antique pieces, Renaissance paintings, and Gothic furniture myself. Gold-framed mirrors and cathedral-like ceilings. Medieval crown moldings and elaborate trimmings. It was spectacular, harsh, and dark. It screamed Tatum Blackthorn and all he stood for.

The flat was featured in the most luxurious design magazines on the planet, hailed as thought-provoking, shocking, and exquisite.

Tate never thanked me for the project.

Taking the curved stairway up to the second floor, I felt my heart beating out of my chest.

On to the third and last floor. The grand ballroom and highest point in Manhattan's residential properties, bracketed by floor-to-ceiling windows, with a bird's-eye view of the entire city.

The room was jam-packed with couples swirling on the dance floor. Bright pastel-colored ball gowns swished the floors, and waiters plaited the throngs of people, balancing tall champagne glasses and canapés.

I spotted Cal and Row dancing together, every inch of the loved-up fairy tale they were. Next to them were Rhyland and Dylan, another couple of friends I adored. Rhy spun her around, and Dylan tossed her head back and laughed without a care in the world. He dipped his head and kissed her neck. It made me stop and smile. Dylan was a dear friend. Come to think of it, despite Tate being Satan's spawn, his mates were absolute gems, and I felt deeply connected to all of them.

But it wasn't them I was looking for tonight. It was *him*.

A pink champagne flute was thrust into my hand, and I took a large sip, letting the fuzzy liquid wet my parched throat. My eyes roamed the room, trying to find him.

And find him I did.

He stood at the very corner, the golden light of the grand chandelier burnishing the edges of his sculpted face, highlighting his striking features. He wore his suit like a second skin, his swagger and flair unmatched in a tight-fitting black three-piece with velvet trimmings. With a rich paisley-printed pocket square and his vintage pocket watch clasped in his hand, my boss looked like the darkest sin and sweetest salvation.

Tate was standing next to the Ferrantes, a new and unwelcome fixture in his life. I didn't know what brought them together. The Ferrantes were bona fide members of the New York Mafia. Dodgier than a street cart hot dog.

There was Machiavelli—Vello for short—the father and don, who looked to be in his late sixties, and his two oldest sons, Luca and Achilles. They were tall, dark, dressed to the nines, and entirely terrifying. They always showed up with enough security for five sitting presidents.

I pushed through my discomfort and hurried over to them, carving a path through the dense crowd.

I stood before Tate, waiting to be acknowledged as he spoke to the three men. His eyes flickered to me fleetingly, unforgivingly cold, before he fixed them back on Vello Ferrante.

Tate was purposefully ignoring me.

"Tate." I forced out a smile. I leaned up on my toes, touching his arm briefly and holding my breath like he was toxic. We'd never been friendly, not to mention touchy before.

He froze, his sneer smoothing out into a blank stare. "Gia." His mouth twisted around the vowels of my name. "What brings you in here? It cannot be an invitation."

He took my metaphorical white flag and set it aflame.

"I was hoping I could speak to you."

"You and every other woman on this continent." He glanced at his pocket watch while the Ferrante men turned their backs to us and started speaking in Italian to give us privacy. "Alas, you'll have to wait until Monday morning. I have an opening between nine thirty-three and nine thirty-six. I'm entertaining now, as you can see." He gestured to the busy room.

Very charitable of him. Offering me three minutes of his precious time.

"Entertaining who?" I narrowed my eyes. "You possess all the personal charm of the bubonic plague."

Lovely, Gia. You couldn't even be nice to him for five minutes.

In my defense, he deserved much worse.

"Not helping your cause." He tapped my nose without really touching it. For all his faults, Tate had been remarkably respectful of my personal space. He never touched me nor made inappropriate comments.

"This is important," I explained.

"No, *this*"—he extended his arm toward the dazzling ballroom—"is important. Me, celebrating my thirty-fifth birthday. The eighth wonder of the world. A man of many facets and virtues. Handsome. Accomplished—"

"Humble," I finished for him, no longer able to hold back my sneer.

"Humility is reserved for people who are not self-made billionaires."

The knobhead spoke as if he didn't inherit millions and an already-successful company.

"Hard to believe you're a decade older than me." I shook my head.

"Hard to believe you're still here even though I kicked you out five minutes ago."

My throat clogged up with a scream. "Can we go somewhere private?"

"Miss Bennett, please leave the premises before I have security escort you out."

The Ferrante men glanced behind their shoulders. Vello's expression reeked of disapproval. Unfortunately, my boss wouldn't cower if God himself came down to chide him.

"Tate, please." I lowered my voice, my pulse thrumming dully in my throat. "It'll only take five minutes."

"Gia, my darling." He bowed down, snatching my chin between his thumb and index finger, tilting my face up so we were a breath away from each other.

It was the first time Tate voluntarily touched me, and perhaps it was my shot nerves, but a zing of electricity zipped through my spine. My stomach bottomed. A sense of urgency, threat, and…God, yearning, yes, stupid yearning, flooded me. My mind really was all over the place tonight.

His pale gray eyes glowed with wrath. "I haven't five minutes to spare you. In fact, not even five seconds. Go away now. I will see you at the office on Monday. And if I ever have to repeat myself again, I'll simply take your defiance as an unwritten resignation letter. Am I understood?"

He didn't wait for me to answer. He turned around and swanned away to the nearest eager woman, scooping her onto the dance floor and into a waltz.

It was four in the morning when the last of the cleaners and caterers evacuated the premises. I heard the entrance door clicking shut. I'd hidden in one of his guest rooms, waiting until the coast was clear.

Yes, I was aware that he didn't want me here, but he had one thing right—if he couldn't help me with why I came here today, I might as well quit.

I was past desperate.

Positive the flat was empty, I tiptoed out of the guest room toward the master bedroom. I stopped in front of the double doors, my stomach in knots. Feminine giggling seeped through the crack under the doors. Raspy purrs of a woman—no, scratch that, *two* women—murmuring and coaxing. I decided it was futile to knock. He'd hardly invite me in.

I pushed the door open.

When I registered the scene in front of me, my breath tumbled down my windpipe, causing me to cough.

Tate was sprawled across his upholstered recliner, completely clothed (*thank God*), an elbow tossed casually on the armrest, suckling on a cigarette. He was observing two women in ball gowns—one blond and the other a redhead—stretched on the floor like toddlers, shapely legs dangling in the air, hunched over pens and papers. They were covering their mouths and giggling as Tate supervised the situation with a parental boredom. Their faces were familiar, probably because I'd shoved an NDA for them to sign at some point.

What in the bloody hell did I just walk into?

"Miss Bennett," he greeted laconically, eyes still trained on his leggy companions. "Did you ever hear the term 'no means no'?"

"I'm not forcing myself upon you."

"That's your version of things." He tsked. "HR isn't going to like this."

"What's going on here?" My gaze ping-ponged from him to them.

"This"—he pointed at them with a tumbler full of whiskey, taking another drag of his fag—"is Precious and Paris trying to solve an Algebra II equation. The first to work it out shall have the honor of sucking my cock. What do you think?"

"I think…" *You are completely, utterly, irrationally unhinged, and no amount of money in the world can justify working for your arse.* "I think I could work it out in less than ten seconds."

He tapped ash into an ashtray, considering my statement. "Why,

Gia, I am extremely flattered. Had I known you to have any carnal interest in me, I'd have let you suck my cock every lunch break."

"Wha—" My eyes widened as realization sank in. "No, Tate. I'll solve the equation in exchange for *speaking* with you. I wouldn't have sex with you if you were the last man on earth."

"Surely, that's an exaggeration."

"I assure you, it's not."

"I'm tall and have good teeth, and the future of humankind depends on us. Be a sport."

"I really don't think you should reproduce. Nothing good can come out of your DNA. If it's down to us or nothing, then sorry. Civilization had a good run."

He grinned devilishly, snuffing his cigarette on one of the women's Chanel bags and snapping his fingers. "Perry, Paisley."

Weren't they Precious and Paris a moment ago?

"Get the fuck out. I've found superior entertainment."

"But...but..." The blond bombshell blinked, hot-pink lips hanging open in surprise. She was very pretty and comically busty. "Are you seriously going to give up sex with me?" she whined.

"Darling," he purred patronizingly, the endearment rolling off his tongue with disdain. "I wouldn't remember your face tomorrow morning if you tattooed it on my fucking palm."

I was glad I'd been too nervous to eat today, because I was sure he wouldn't appreciate my vomiting all over his Calacatta-veined floor.

The women huffed and pranced out of the room, flinging hair in their wake and sending me hate glares.

Finally, it was just the three of us.

Me, Tate, and his giant ego.

Tate gestured with his hand to the equation and pen on the floor. I quietly walked across the room and picked it up, sauntering over to sit on the edge of his bed.

"Stay standing," he barked.

I stood up before my bum hit the mattress.

"Nobody touches my bed." A flush of pink struck his cheeks.

He sounded like a toddler in the throes of a tantrum. An off-character outburst for this normally blasé creature.

I placed the piece of paper on the nightstand. Still standing, I leaned down to solve the linear equation. It wasn't difficult by any means. As the daughter of a late auditor, I did have a natural knack for numbers. It occurred to me how ridiculous I looked, in full makeup and a ball gown, solving a math problem in my boss's bedroom in the early hours of the morning. But life around Tate had always been chaotic.

He pulled his pocket watch, frowning at it. "You have five seconds lef—"

"I'm done." I put the pen down and sauntered over to him. I handed him the paper, careful not to touch him. He surveyed it through sharp, critical eyes. Though his jaw was taut, I knew a smile was hiding behind it. I'd mastered reading him as one learned to move inside a familiar room in complete darkness.

"Growing up, were you fond of math?"

"I was," I confirmed. "My father was an auditor. We did mental math together on weekends when it was too rainy to go outside."

"What did you study in college?"

I was surprised he didn't know. He had hired me fresh out of college. *On a whim*, in fact. I'd always found it odd, how Tate swooped in out of nowhere as soon as I gained my degree at a relatively unknown college in Brooklyn and offered me a job I hadn't even applied to.

"Environmental economics and policies."

"What would you have done had I not offered you employment?"

"An investment adviser. Perhaps hedge fund." I hitched up a shoulder. "Those were the few positions I'd applied for after college."

He stared at me, and I knew he was planning in that twisted mind of his. Something dark and depraved, a way to punish me for simply existing in his sphere.

"I didn't know you were analytical, Miss Bennett. Although I did have my suspicion. You are too bright to have an intuitive personality." He paused. "What's an intuition anyway? Simply a draw of luck. So common. So...*random*." He knocked back the rest of his whiskey with a snarl.

Strange, strange man.

"My theory is sociologists divide us into analytical and intuitive personalities because it is politically incorrect to call the intuitive dumbasses. What do you think?"

I think you should seek urgent help.

"As much as I'd love to discuss this fascinating matter with you tonight." I licked my lips, trying to conceal my anxiety. "There *is* something I've been trying to talk to you about."

"Oh, right. Go ahead." He leaned lavishly in his recliner, crossing his long legs. He wore a chunky gold ring on his little finger. "Your five minutes start now."

Wanker.

Nonetheless, the words rushed out of my mouth at the speed of light. I couldn't waste one second.

"As you know, my mother is suffering from dementia. She is in the middle to late stages and doing quite poorly by all medical metrics. She is confused, forgetful, and suspicious. One of the side effects is poor nutrition. She lost thirty-five pounds in four years, and she was lean to begin with." I only mentioned it because I needed him to understand my urgency. "She is the only remaining living member of my immediate family. We were a very tight-knit family. Really, they were my entire world. So now *she* is my world—"

The words tumbled out of my mouth clumsily. It wasn't often I lost my footing, but speaking about Mum did that to me. I twisted my fingers in my lap.

"And this week, well, I met with her doctor. And he mentioned that there is this trial...I mean, experimental treatment here in the States. In New York, in fact, for dementia patients. It's an in-patient, all-encompassing treatment for people who are in the middle stage of the disease. There's a lot of red tape and fine print, of course, but the doctor mentioned that the initial results of people who enrolled in the program twelve weeks ago are groundbreaking. They were able to reverse some of the symptoms back to the early, mild stages and gain these people *years* more to live rather comfortably," I said breathlessly, getting animated despite myself.

If there was one thing Tate loathed, it was melodramatic people.

Tate's apathetic gaze told me he was losing both his patience and interest. He checked his watch again. "Can you cut to the chase? My trainer's coming at five thirty, and I'd like to have my bulletproof coffee beforehand."

Curling my fingers into fists to prevent myself from slapping him, I answered slowly, "I am tired of living away from Mum, of hopping between continents to see her. I would love to secure her a place in this program."

Tate elevated an eyebrow. "Is anyone stopping you?"

He was going to make me spell it out for him. *Bastard.*

"I need someone with connections. Someone who'd be able to pull some strings and get her into the program."

"I assume I am that lucky someone." He knotted his fingers together, tapping his indexes over his mouth.

My gaze dropped to my feet.

"I haven't pegged you as a rule breaker," he mused, a hint of a smile hiding behind his perpetual snarl. "First time?"

"Yes," I lied. *I've done so much worse. You have no idea.* "There isn't much I wouldn't do for the little that is left of my family."

"And what, pray tell, am I going to get in return for 'pulling some strings'?" He used his long fingers to mimic quotation marks.

I gulped. I knew we'd reach the bargaining portion of the conversation. And though I hadn't many haggling chips, I did come up with a few ideas. "I thought you might do this from the goodness of your heart?"

"I possess no such thing, and you know it." He waved me off. "Next?"

"Helping me get Mum into the program is to your financial benefit. It would ensure I'd be on top of my game. I wouldn't have to be preoccupied all the time. Wouldn't have to go to London so frequently. That's at least once a month. It would be a good investment for you."

"How tempting." He stroked his square chin. "Even so, I am afraid wasting my resources and power for the pleasure of you doing your damn job sets a dangerous precedent. See, I am, first and foremost, a businessman, Gia. This is a transaction like any other. Make it worth my while."

Now he did smile, and I almost wish that he hadn't. He looked so arrogant, so wildly pleased to see me squirming and vulnerable.

I wondered if he'd ever loved someone. A parent. A sibling. A friend. *A pet.* Likely not. To love was to relinquish control, and Tate was too fond of that particular ingredient.

"Right then." I clapped my hands together. "This brings me to my third and final offer. I would love to pay you back by working for free. I've enough money saved up, and I could do my job without any monetary imbursement if y—"

"Christ, how unimaginative." He threw his head back and groaned, shaking his head at the ceiling with a chuckle. "This is how you Brits lost an empire. What a constricted way of thinking. Shaving a few hundred thousand dollars from my company's two-billion annual expense sheet is a terrible stimulus."

"What do you want, then?" I actually stomped, losing my patience.

"*You.*"

"I beg your pardon?"

I misheard him. I must've.

"If I'm going to break the law and likely a few fucking families standing in line for this bullshit experimental trial, I want *your* life in exchange for saving your mother's. It's symbolic, symmetrical, and one of the very few things money can't buy me."

"Me, as in…?" Ice wrapped around my bones. My stomach roiled.

Do. Not. Vomit.

"You, as in you become my wife. You wear my ring. You live under my roof. You take my name. You suck my cock." He paused, examining his fingers in sheer boredom. "You bear my children. I'm thinking four, minimum. We're bound to make mistakes on the first few before we create someone worthy to inherit the company. Oh." He snapped his fingers. "Maintaining my friendships. Socializing is my least favorite pastime. Rhyland's and Row's wives seem to like you. Keep up our appearances."

He was mental. More alarming than that—he was dead serious. I could tell by the contemplative look on his face. He was looking for more responsibilities to dump on me.

"W-where is this coming from?" I forced out a weak laugh. "You hate me."

"Yes, and?" Tate's dark brows slammed together in confusion. "That is not germane to the fact that you are the perfect candidate for childbearing. You'd do nicely."

"Why would you like to have children with someone you dislike?"

"Because you are intelligent, analytical, of excellent health, and athletic. Plus, most people are too stupid to shine my shoes, let alone raise my successors. You've proven competence during our time together. I can dislike you and still acknowledge you possess all the things I'd want in a wife."

"Respectfully," I cleared my throat, "you're a psychopath."

"I prefer inventive."

"I'm too young for you."

He gave me a pitiful smirk. "Men in my tax bracket don't adhere to age-gap norms."

"I can't marry you."

"Yes, you can. You don't want to. There's a difference."

"What's the difference?" I blinked.

"People do shit they don't want to do all the time. Work, exercise, pay taxes. The ability is there."

I shook my head. "We'd be miserable together."

"We're *already* miserable together." He tucked another cigarette into his mouth, cupping his Zippo to light it. "The only thing that'll change is that you'll get your Centurion back." He gave me a slow once-over, exhaling a plume of smoke sideways. "And a few good fucks a week, which will do a world of good to your rigidness."

I didn't know whether to laugh or cry. Of all the things he could want…of all the ways he could torture me…

"That's the most deranged thing I've ever heard you say, and trust me, the competition is tough."

He shrugged, unbothered. "Money is a great opiate. You agree, or you wouldn't be here."

"I'm not going to have sex with you," I said plainly.

Tate looked at me like I was a puppy who tried—and failed—to pee on its designated pad. "Sweetheart, the only reason your cunt is not the shape of my dick is because up until now, you were too sufficient for your own good as a PA."

"And now?" I choked out. How did he know I fancied him? Even I wasn't sure of it half the time.

"Now, I've found a better use for you. It is far harder to find a bride than a secretary."

Especially when you are the devil incarnate.

"How about…" I stopped, calculating my next move. This was negotiation. And Tate was bloody good at it.

He slipped one hand into the front pocket of his trousers and seemed to be tapping the side of his thigh through them impatiently. He was waiting for me to finish my thought.

"I mean, I'd love to date you and see where this is going," I suggested feebly.

"First of all, no, you would not. And second, I don't like to be lowballed. It's marriage or nothing. Take it or leave it."

"Are you forcing me—"

"No, not forcing," he corrected offhandedly. "You're free to walk from this place right this second. You're free to walk out of my *life* right this second. Free to keep your job regardless of your answer. Free to quit it. I am merely offering you a deal, and quite a generous one. Ask your friends' husbands what kinds of deals I usually put on the table. They are never this benevolent."

Row and Rhyland despised doing business with Tate. And they were people he didn't outwardly despise. Where did it leave me?

"Well, I'm so bloody touched." I put a hand to my rib cage. "That you're altruistic enough to offer I become your whor—"

"Stop right there." He raised his palm. "Nobody gets to call my future wife a slut other than me."

"You plan to call me a slut?" I blinked fast. It was just my luck to work for a madman.

"Only in the bedroom." He sucked on his cigarette, the ember burning orange. "You'll love it."

"Do you understand?" My teeth ground together to a point of dust. "You're essentially forcing me to have sex with you to save my mother's life?"

"Miss Bennett, you wound me. I would never force myself upon you." His voice felt like the edge of a knife, cold and sharp, traveling along my skin. "You will come to me willingly. Happily. 'Tis human nature to seek warmth where one can get it."

"Warmth?" I laughed humorlessly, nauseous with rage. "You're high if you think I'd ever sleep with you. Even if we'd been married for a hundred yea—"

"Enough." He put his cigarette out swiftly. "The human race has remarkable spirit. We have survived countless wars, famine, pandemics, natural disasters, oppression, floods, and nuclear accidents. I have every faith you will survive—and *thrive*—in a marriage with a six-three handsome man worth ninety billion dollars who is fond of reciprocal oral sex and will leave you to your own devices. Your five minutes are up. Give me your answer."

I hated him. I hated him so much the hatred had a taste and a scent and a shape. It was a living, breathing thing inside me. It thrummed under my skin. Still, I knew I had no choice. He wasn't going to budge. He had all the power. All I could hope for was that this was one of our games. Something I could bargain my way out of at some point.

"Well?" Tate flicked his wrist to check his watch. It was, I realized, a tic. "What's it going to be?"

"This marriage…" I took a deep breath. "How do you envision it?"

"With a rigid set of rules," he replied. "We live in different corners of my estate. I provide you with money, security, freedom, and comfort. My means and connections would be at your disposal. You, in return, provide me with heirs, company, and arm candy for social events."

"That's all?" I frowned.

He quirked an eyebrow up. "Am I missing something?"

Yes. Friendship. Feelings. Love.

"And are you still going to be obnoxious to me?" I asked.

"Naturally." He opened up his arms, undaunted. "You're the only person I know who is foolish enough to defy me."

My disobedience being attractive to him wasn't a good thing, because I could never stop butting heads with that demon.

"I don't even know your real name," I pointed out.

I didn't know much about my boss, but the little I'd stumbled upon in *Forbes* three years ago fascinated me. He'd spent his early years in an orphanage—or a boarding school of sorts—and was adopted as a teenager, where he took on a different name. No one knew his real name. Not even his friends.

"Tatum Blackthorn is my legal name," he retorted. "Anything else?"

I rolled my tongue along the walls of my mouth. "I have rules too."

"Let's hear them."

"The results of your side of the bargain won't be immediate. It'd take time to see if Mum is getting better and the experiment is working. Therefore, no heirs the first two years of our marriage." That'd buy me some time.

Tate didn't flinch.

I continued, feeling like a heavy stone rolled off my chest. "I decide when, where, and how we consummate this marriage. You will not pressure me. There'll be no time limit on this."

An indifferent nod. He was oddly confident that I would come to him readily. His ego was bigger than Nebraska.

"I come and go as I please. I do not answer to you. And when my mother passes away, our marriage contract expires, and I get to decide if I want a divorce or not."

He scowled. "Absolut—"

I held up a hand. "This shouldn't be an issue if you plan on taking care of her. This is *my* assurance. Bear in mind that if all goes well and we have spawn, I am less likely to leave. Or at least I'd give you a fair chance." *Lies.* I would not. And there'd be no spawn. But he didn't need to know that.

Tate suppressed a grin. "Such a ballbuster at twenty-six. I want to add more rules." He stood, eating up the distance between us. He stopped a breath away from me.

My heart rioted. He smelled of tobacco, fine leather, spice, and my own personal demise.

"One, this is exclusive. You dump your little boyfriend as soon as you walk out of here. Two, you act like you don't detest me in public. Three, do not hire anyone to assassinate me. If you want to kill me, do it yourself."

I let out an exasperated snort. He remained stoic.

Oh. He wasn't kidding.

"Haven't you been married three times before?" My eyebrows slammed together.

"Yes."

"Did any of them try to assassinate you?"

"Only one that I know of, but it is possible the other two were more discreet." He sounded entirely unbothered. "I married my way up the high society ladder. I'd inherited wealth, not status. I needed the latter to make GS Properties what it is today."

"So the marriages were to make connections?"

"Yes. They knew what they were getting into. But some people get incredibly touchy about being used as a tool."

"How overly dramatic of them," I huffed. "Children?"

"They weren't very mature, but I wouldn't go that far."

"*Successors.*" I rolled my eyes, sighing. "Do you have any?"

He shook his head. "None."

Tate being thrice divorced was a positive sign. If he treated marriage like a currency, there was bound to be someone more beneficial for him in the future. He'd have to enter another union. To break things off with me.

"I agree." I choked on every word. "On the stipulation that you will secure Mum a spot in the experimental trial, fly her out here, and allow her to stay with us once she finishes her treatment."

"Acceptable," he clipped out.

"I'm afraid I won't bud—really?" My knees buckled. I didn't know if I was relieved or terrified. "O-okay then."

"Now, there's only one matter left." The feral spark returned to Tate's gunmetal pupils. "You need to prove that you can touch me without recoiling."

My mouth parched. "How is this important exactly?"

"Well, you've given yourself unlimited time to warm up to the idea of touching me. It is vital we establish you are capable of it at all." A diabolic sneer found his mouth. "As it happens, I am right here, within reach."

Panic slashed through my spine. He wanted me to touch him. *Now.* My formidable, decadent boss. The man I'd seen blackmail and annihilate people for sport.

I refused to recoil.

"Where?" I asked evenly.

He shrugged. "Anywhere. Everywhere." His voice, low and husky, licked at my skin like a smothered flame. "Surprise me."

"Close your eyes," I ordered.

"Why?" His eyes narrowed.

"Marriage is built on trust, isn't it?" I blinked innocently. "We need to start somewhere."

Shockingly, he let his eyelids flutter shut. I lifted my hand toward his face, teetering on the fine line between panic and exhilaration. I had a feeling that even though his eyes were closed, not only could he see me, but he could also see through my clothes and thoughts and feelings.

I let my fingers guide me. Tell me which part of him they wanted to explore. My fingertips fluttered less than an inch from his face, searching, contemplating, deciding…

I pressed two fingers to his mouth, surprised to feel it hot and soft against my fingers. *Human.*

I sucked in a surprised breath. He always looked so cold. Like he was carved out of stone, engraved by the sharpest scalpels. The tips of my fingernails scraped his lips apart. My head was swimming. I thought I felt the hot edge of his tongue pressing against my skin for a taste, but I couldn't be sure. What I was certain of was the terrible, desperate ache that built inside me. It felt like someone cracked an egg in me, and its contents, yolky, thick, and warm, pooled between my legs. And in that moment, I knew why Tate had not balked at my condition about taking my time consummating our marriage.

He knew.

Knew one touch would reveal my entire hand. Every single card in it.

That I was attracted to him. That his darkness always appealed to me. That it mirrored a side of me no one was privy to.

Tate's eyes snapped open, his gaze meeting mine. There was satisfaction there. Hunger too. The starvation of a man beaten, damaged, and wrecked but not broken.

His mouth spread into a grin, and my fingers fell upon his straight white teeth. He was the Cheshire Cat now. Playful and elusive.

"This'll be fun." His teeth grazed my fingers. "You know what they say. Fourth time's a charm."

CHAPTER FOUR
TATE

AGE SEVEN

It was my birthday. I was 93.6 percent sure of it.

The last time I'd seen a calendar was three months ago, in the headmaster's office. He'd left me unattended for ten minutes, enough time for me to scan each of the twelve pages and memorize them by heart. Then I went back to my room and scraped the date into the bottom of my bedframe so I could keep track of time without Andrin knowing.

Yeah. Today was definitely my birthday.

I wondered how boys with families celebrated. I imagined with cake, parents, and friends. Maybe balloons. I wondered if I'd enjoy parents and presents. I'd never had either.

It seemed cool, having a birthday party. In the same way riding a dragon seemed cool. In a faraway, pathetically fictional way.

I put my pencil down on my writing table, next to my tenth-grade algebra homework. My pet cat, Ares, strutted along my worksheets, leaving mud-stained paw marks in his wake. He thrust his head into my chin, purring like an engine and giving me a lopsided, tooth-baring smirk. I grinned toothlessly.

We weren't allowed pets at the dormitory. Ares was my secret. A few months ago, he'd emerged from the edge of the woods, missing his tail and one ear. It was no trouble at all, sharing some of my snacks with him. Every morning, I opened the window for him to go out and roam outside. I liked the idea that at least one of us was free. And he always came back in the evenings.

"It's my birthday, Ares." I scratched his head with my index finger softly.

He pulled away, walked over to the edge of the table, and spun around slowly a couple times before curling into position. It looked like he was doing a little dance for me.

I laughed. "A present in the form of a dance. I like that."

I glanced outside my window. It was pitch-black. I traced the shape of the balustrade with my eyes, the silhouette of the thick woods beyond the Swiss boarding academy I lived in. The forest stretched for miles on each side of the property. I knew Geneva was nearby. I studied the maps and burned them into memory in case I ever needed to escape.

What I didn't know was how I got here. Or why.

I'd been told a distant relative dropped me off when I was just shy of two. Other than that, I didn't know much about myself. I only knew I was an orphan and that I was American.

I was told I had no immediate family. I remembered some faces and events in a land faraway before I came to Switzerland, but I sometimes wondered if I made them all up.

A shadow passed along my window, the shape of a man. My stomach bottomed out.

It was Andrin.

It was always Andrin.

The houseparents and tutors who supervised the dorms knew he came for me every night, and still, they let it happen.

They said it was good for me. That Andrin was looking out for my future. Maybe it was true, but if a bright future meant living in complete darkness, I didn't want to live at all.

"You need to leave," I whispered to Ares, pushing the window open and placing him on the sill. "He can't see you here."

Ares gave me the stink eye and slipped out of my room just as the door opened.

Andrin never knocked.

I buried my face in my homework, ignoring his frame as it loomed over me, casting a shadow along my body. He stood directly behind my shoulder, looking over my algebra answers.

"Boy," he grumbled. That was what he called me. Boy. Never by my name.

My spine went rigid. I said nothing. Andrin was easy to anger and quick to get violent.

He was Swiss, but his English was impeccable. He made it a point that I speak each language without a lingering foreign accent. My English was American, my French, Parisian, my Italian was Tuscan, and my German was Hochdeutsch.

His long, pale finger reached over my shoulder, tapping at an equation. "You miscalculated this one. Do it again."

I grabbed my pencil, flipping it and erasing my answer with a trembling hand. I felt his breath on the nape of my neck. I wanted him out of this room. Out of my life.

"You have thirty seconds," he clipped.

Sweat dripped from my forehead to the page, burning my eyes. I forced myself to focus. Tuned out the world around me. It worked. I solved it.

Andrin made a dissatisfied sound behind me. He wanted to punish me. He came here every night under the guise of helping me become the number one child mathematician in the world. He said it would help my chances of getting adopted. But he was never happy when I did well.

"Get up." Andrin gripped the back of my neck, yanking me up.

I staggered to my feet silently.

"Turn around," he instructed.

I did.

Andrin was slim, short, pale, and terrifying. He wore his age on his skin. His skull was peppered with liver spots, his wrinkles engraved on his flesh like roads and rivers on a busy map. He had a nasty hook of a nose, no lashes, and a grimace that seemed stitched across his face.

"Have you practiced your survival skills this week?" he inquired.

My heart screeched to a stop. Please. Not this again.

"Yes," I lied.

"Good. Then you won't mind showing me."

Reaching down to grab my sneakers, I felt his hand on my shoulder.

"No, Boy. You've been slacking on your math. This time, you'll do it barefoot."

Last time I did it barefoot, I limped for a whole month.

Andrin waltzed out to the hallway, knowing I'd follow him. We walked into the woods for ten minutes. It was prohibited for students to go past the first line of trees, but we ignored it.

The icicles in the muddy ground prickled my feet, twigs slipping between my toes. I felt like a rabbit caught in a net, my pulse out of whack. When we reached deep enough inside the woods, Andrin tugged a handkerchief from his sports jacket. He wrapped it around my eyes, double knotting it so that I was completely blind.

"Ready?" he asked.

No, my mind screamed.

Two, six, two.

Two, six, two.

Two, six, two.

I tapped my side. It was a way to reassure myself. To pretend I was in control.

My lucky numbers.

I nodded, then gulped.

An ear-piercing bang rang in the air. The scent of gunpowder filled my nostrils. Nocturnal animals screeched. Wings flapped.

I started running.

More bullets followed. They chased me like bad memories, always too close, no matter how fast I went. Boots shook the ground behind me.

Andrin trained me to survive without my sight by playing a hunting game.

He chased. I ran.

I'd become an expert at living in darkness. Andrin said people like us, people who were screwed up in the head, they need to perfect the art of living like monsters, in the pitch black.

Instead of my eyesight, I relied on my hearing. I listened to his footsteps, to their pace, to the low but deadly whisper of a cocking gun, to the heavy breathing of the forest animals lurking around us. My skin tingled at the heat of another living, breathing body in my proximity, even if I didn't see it. I'd memorized the position of every tree, every trunk, every obstacle in the forest. Mapped out my surroundings in my head.

I managed to escape him, weaving between trees, jumping over obstacles, dodging low branches.

"Boy!" Andrin barked behind me. By the sound of it, he was half a pace away from me. He was getting tired. "It's your birthday, isn't it?"

My mind went blank. I gasped and tripped over a tree trunk. Something soft but firm, probably rotten wood, scraped my shins. The hot, unmistakable sensation of blood coated my legs.

I fell face down into the mud. I heard Andrin walking leisurely behind me.

Everything hurt. Most of all my heart.

A boot pressed against my palm, digging in pointedly to break the little bones. "Yes, it is your birthday. I remember. Seven is old age for an adoption candidate. Your window of opportunity is closing in."

I pinched my lips together. I wasn't going to sob.

"You lost." Andrin grabbed the back of my hair, wrenching me up. "On your feet, Boy."

I scrambled to stand up, ripping the handkerchief from my eyes. Blinking, I handed him back the piece of cloth. It was soaked with tears. I was nauseous with shame.

"Boy." Andrin crouched to meet my gaze, putting a hand on my shoulder. "Losing has consequences. You do realize that, right?"

I nodded, bracing myself for his fist. Andrin always hit me under the collarbone to avoid bruises in exposed areas and questions from his superiors.

"And you couldn't escape me. What kind of mentor would I be if I don't punish you for not practicing your survivor skills?" His eyes crinkled in fake sympathy.

I didn't answer.

"You will get your punishment, but not tonight. Tonight is your birthday. Go to bed."

I hesitated. Andrin never postponed a punishment. He always took great pleasure in delivering it. But…he just stood there, waiting for me to leave. So eventually, I did. I ran the length of the woods back to the boarding school. Into my room.

I closed the door, fell to my bed, and cried myself to sleep like a little pussy.

The tears were fast and hot, and I went down like a brick.

The next morning, when I woke up, Ares wasn't there. Shit. I forgot to open the window for him.

I stood up quickly, pacing toward the window, yanking it open. My whole body was sore, my shins and knees caked with dried blood.

"Ares!" I called out. "Come in. I'm sorry I—"

The rest died in my throat.

Ares was splayed across my windowsill.

Limp and dead.

A small note was tucked under his lifeless body.

Happy Birthday, Boy.

CHAPTER FIVE
TATE

I waited until Gia left before heading into my office. Shivers rippled across my skin. I was in the dark woods again.

Cold. Naked. Nauseous with adrenaline.

Finally, I was alone. Here, behind my closed doors, I stripped myself of the veneer of civility. Of composure. I ripped the bow tie off. Kicked off my shoes. Squirted six pumps of hand sanitizer. Read a favorite line in *Alice's Adventures in Wonderland*.

"Not all who wander are lost."

Still, I was short of breath. No amount of oxygen was enough to satisfy my burning lungs.

It had been eight hours since I last went through my rituals.

Two, six, two.

Two, six, two.

Two, six, two.

Going a few hours without solving mathematical problems, without sanitizing, without reading my favorite paragraphs, made me feel suffocated and out of control.

I cracked open a thick abstract algebra book. I grabbed a pen and started solving equations. Math soothed me. It turned off all the other thoughts swirling in my head. Usually, I concluded every waking hour of my day with at least one or two pages of equations. But that hadn't been possible today. When I didn't have my routine, I wasn't thinking straight. I made mistakes.

Which was how I ended up engaged to my fucking PA.

I didn't want to marry Gia. I wanted to ruin her. Now I could do both. After all, I *did* need a successor. Someone to inherit this empire of ruins.

I couldn't think of a better candidate than my PA.

Beautiful. Intelligent. Capable.

Insufferable.

But my reason for loathing her was entirely independent from who she was as a person. I was a pragmatic man. I could make the distinction.

Yes, she'd do. I'd simply have to get rid of her once she stopped being useful to me. Just like the others.

I'd keep the children. Get full custody.

I was too rich to contemplate any other outcome.

I finished one page. Then another. My handwriting was neat, my pen steady. The tension slowly rolled off my shoulders. As I solved math problems, my thoughts unfurled.

Why did I do that? Why did I ask her to marry me? I could've just fucked her.

But no. That wouldn't be enough. I didn't want one night with her. I wanted all her nights. Her days too. And I wanted to stop competing for her time with random fuckboys from dating apps. I wanted to finally consume her in the same way she consumed me. To drag her with me to the dark rabbit hole that was my existence. Make her pay for what she did all those years ago.

I could worship her body and disparage her soul. I would finally treat her as she deserved to be treated—another warm, willing pussy that would do anything to get my last name and access to my wallet.

The wench had always been beautiful, but tonight, she was mesmerizing. And when she solved that math problem…when she put the pen down before her ten seconds were up…

I closed my eyes, taking a deep breath. My cock stiffened in my pants.

A tree that grows crooked can never be straightened, Andrin used to say.

He was right, of course. Choosing a wife because of her math skills was a level of unhinged many assholes could only aspire to.

Now only the pesky detail of securing her mother a place in that experimental treatment facility.

"Siri, call Achilles Ferrante," I barked.

Achilles was the Camorra's underboss and the guy who got shit done.

Siri cooed her confirmation, and the line began ringing.

"It's five in the fucking morning," Achilles greeted, sounding completely awake. "Someone better be dead."

"I hadn't realized mobsters have office hours."

"Careful." I heard him lighting a cigarette. "Or you'll wake up one day with that smart mouth of yours full of explosives."

"I need you to pull some strings at Northeastern General Hospital. They have a special dementia program I want to get someone into. Highly curated."

"I thought you have no family."

"It's for a colleague."

He bristled. "Meddling in health care is high risk."

I heard a woman moan. In Achilles's case, I was sure he was murdering, not pleasuring her.

"It requires a lot of palm greasing, security breaching, and possible unfortunate accidents. What's the budget on this project?"

"Infinite."

"Good. We have special god complex fees for people who want to break Title 18, Section 1347 codes."

Fortunately, all the Ferrante men had law degrees and a few working brain cells between their ears. Working with mobsters who learned all the rules before they broke them was convenient. They weren't low-grade criminals but the crème de la crème of corruption. The men who crowned politicians and ran every street and corner of this city.

"Get started," I ordered.

"A colleague, ah?" Achilles sounded slightly repulsed. "Don't tell me you are growing a conscience?"

"Don't be ridiculous. There's a golden pussy and blackmail involved."

He laughed under his breath. "Good. Good. I'd hate to let you go."

"Excuse me?"

"I don't work with romantics. They're prone to doing stupid shit."

"Make it happen before Tuesday." I killed the call.

I was going to put Gia's mother in that facility if I had to murder someone myself.

CHAPTER SIX
TATE

"It's Tuesday." I barged into the Ferrantes' basement two days later.

Achilles was in the middle of blowing out someone's kneecap with a golf club. That someone had a burlap sack over their head and was tied to a chair.

Luca, Achilles's oldest brother and the Camorra's consigliere, leaned against a table in the darkened room, unbuttoning his cuffs and rolling his sleeves up his elbows. He stared at me unflinchingly, like people barging into their torture dungeon demanding shit was a daily occurrence.

Enzo, their younger brother, was also present. He was playing with a Swiss Army knife. I knew there was a sister in the mix too. The youngest child of the Ferrante family. Thankfully, I hadn't met her. The last thing I needed in my life was more of this fucking family.

The sound of bone cracking like a pistachio shell soaked my ears. It was followed by a scream, stifled by the burlap sack. Blood painted the tied man's knee over his pants. Achilles swiveled my way, blasé. He twisted his wrist and frowned at his Patek Philippe. "It's twenty seconds past midnight."

"As I said—Tuesday." I surveyed my surroundings, deeming the place too unsanitary to remove my gloves. "Where's my fucking spot at that dementia clinic?"

"We're working on it." Luca lit a cigarette, peering over the ledgers on his desk. As the oldest, he was also the least deranged of the three. Which didn't say much. I had studied the Ferrante family closely before we got into business. They depopulated the state of New York at a rapid speed and with much enthusiasm.

Most mobsters I knew sent their soldiers to do the killings, but Luca and Achilles had a particular taste for violence. The Ferrantes were wolves in silk clothing. I immediately found myself drawn to their pack.

I appreciated that they were Camorra and not the Cosa Nostra. The organizational structure was less hierarchy-based, more horizontal, and therefore chose its leaders based on merit and cruelty. Luca being the oldest son did not necessarily mean he was Vello's natural heir to the throne. I had a feeling Vello was going to let his sons battle it out for the don's title when he finally expired.

I was going to secure a front-row seat to that shit.

Luca, now thirty-two, was initiated into the Camorra when he was fourteen by taking the life of an enemy. He did so in spectacular fashion, subjecting the man to a Viking eagle death. He'd broken his ribs and withdrawn his lungs from the chest cavity and watched as the man died slowly.

Four years later, Achilles was initiated on the promise he would up his brother's ante.

As legend had it, when it was his turn to kill an enemy, he plucked out the heart from the man's chest and ate it raw, still connected to its arteries and beating its last pulses.

One could only imagine what Enzo had to do to match his brothers' brutality. One day, when I was in less hurry and gave more fucks, I'd look into it.

"You're taking too long." I cracked my knuckles.

"Power is like a horse, Blackthorn. You need to rein it with restraint or you lose it altogether. We're examining all angles. Speaking of." Luca gestured to the handcuffed man with the sack on his head. "We just found out the whereabouts of one of your father's killers."

I peered at the faceless bastard, then glanced around me. It was the first time I paid attention to the setting—not hygiene—of the place since their housemaid, Imma, ushered me in.

I had noticed the upstairs door was padded and soundproofed. Now that I was inside, I understood why.

The exposed gray brick walls hid the worst torturing weapons on planet Earth. An iron maiden device, an armchair of inquiries, a hanging cage, a Judas cradle, and a fucking cranium crusher.

These assholes seemed to be having way too much fun killing people. Some families played pickleball. The Ferrantes bonded over genital mutilation and skull crushing.

"Are you done with your *My Little Pony* TED talk?" I plopped down next to Enzo. "Good. Now, the clinic space is contingent on an important deal I need to execute."

"And we'll be sure to let you know when—" Luca started before another hair-raising shriek erupted from the burlap sack.

Achilles appeared to be gouging an internal organ out of the man's gut with gusto.

Luca turned to his brother. "Christ, Achilles, would you kill him already? Mama taught you not to play with your food."

"He's not even a snack," Achilles murmured around a lit cigarette, squinting. "He vomited out all the information before we even brought him to the basement. What kind of world do we live in that you don't have to extort secrets from the enemy?"

"A dull one." I drummed my gloved fingers over the table. "Is my father's second killer local?"

Luca uncrossed his arms, readjusting his holster. "Lives upstate. This guy's been providing him with a steady stream of underaged, undocumented sex workers."

Another shriek of agony punctuated the damp, cold air, coming from the handcuffed victim.

Luca sighed. Pulling his gun out of his shoulder holster, he pointed it at the man and shot him square between the eyes through the sack. The screaming ceased at once.

Achilles's sulky expression was comically boyish on his scarred, grotesque face. "Hey, I was having fun with that one."

Luca spun and tucked his gun back into his holster. "We'll get you another toy soon. I want to unburden myself of this fucker first."

Achilles prowled our way and sank onto a seat in front of me, placing his gun on the table.

"Enzo," he clipped out. "Upstairs."

The youngest brother glanced between his siblings.

"Why?" He scowled. "I'm the enforcer now. I'm good for i—"

"I'm the underboss you report to, and I'm telling you to get the fuck out." Luca snapped his ledger shut. "You can do it voluntarily or with a second asshole the shape of a bullet. Your call."

"Dude, you pulling rank on me right now?" Enzo frothed. "This is bullshit. How am I supposed to learn the craft—"

"Do I look like fucking Georgetown?" Achilles turned to Luca, motioning toward his scarred face.

"No," Luca said flatly.

Achilles turned to Enzo. "Bye, little shit."

"Vai a farti fottere!" Enzo stomped his way out in a cloud of juvenile fury. He was surprisingly golden retriever-ish for a mobster. Luca reminded me of a stray. Achilles of a rabies-infected coyote.

Finally, I had both Luca's and Achilles's attention. Somewhere in the back of my head, I realized conducting business with a dead body in the room wasn't normal, but I concluded long ago I was anything but sane.

"Tell me where you're at with our project." I rapped my knuckles on the table.

"Which one?" Achilles asked. "Dementia lady or your father's killers?"

"Hospital." My father's murderers could wait. After Boyle, they knew I was coming for them. Living in fear was far worse than being dead. I learned that from experience.

"There's no space at the trial." Luca cracked his knuckles. "Not only is the program at full capacity, but the waiting list is a mile long. Since we can't go around killing dozens of innocent people, we have to get creative. Paint a picture."

"Elaborate, Dick-asso," I ground out.

"We'll hack the database software harboring the waiting list and put your candidate at the top of it," Achilles explained. "Luca has studied the criteria they're looking for. We found a neurologist to forge the desired test results—they'll call him before offering your candidate a spot. Then, we'll relieve one actively treated patient of their life. Your mysterious dementia patient will be their first call." The mobster loosened his shoulder holster, dumping it on the table between us. Tattoos snaked up and down his forearms, his chest and neck, up to his jawline.

"So what's the holdup?" I demanded.

"Research. We needed to look into each participating patient to see which one we should off." He grabbed a bottle of Cutty Sark, pouring himself a glass. "We have an IT guy on retainer, but we'll see if accessing a government's healthcare website and tampering with its records is above his pay grade. I'm sure there'll be more fees to come, so get your Bitcoin ready."

A knock sounded from the door.

"Come in," Luca instructed.

A beefy, tan soldier walked into the basement. He wore a sharp suit and a determined expression. He handed Luca and Achilles papers.

"Bingo. The reports of the participants came in." Luca tapped the documents with his cigarette. Both brothers scanned the papers silently.

"Susan Bosshardt owes four hundred K to Frankie Ricci." Luca stroked his chin. "A local loan shark who pays us a cut. We can ask him for a favor. Less paper trail."

"Christian Sainz had three heart attacks and a stroke this year alone," Achilles countered. "He's a better candidate, if he hasn't died already by the time I finish this sentence."

The brothers looked between them, then at me. I stood up, buttoning my coat with one hand.

"I really don't give a fuck which of these assholes gets wiped out. All I care is that by tomorrow morning, you call me with good news about this trial experiment. Am I clear?"

Achilles saluted me with his middle finger.

Luca poured himself another drink.

I walked out before the stench of the newly dead corpse of a dirty pimp seeped into my nose.

CHAPTER SEVEN
GIA

ONE WEEK LATER

I pressed my forehead to the cool glass of the Bentley, closing my eyes and drawing a deep breath.

It was happening. My wishes were coming true. Mum was here with me, about to check into Northeastern General Hospital for the dementia treatment program. I didn't know how Tate made it happen, and I preferred not to ask. Knowing would consume me with guilt.

"Hey, you." I squeezed her hand in mine, ripping my gaze from the window. I no longer called her Mum. It triggered her, since she didn't recognize me. "How're you feeling?"

My mother stared out the window, appearing to be lost in her own thoughts. I gently rubbed the inside of her pale palm, which seemed to snap her back into reality. She turned to look at me, face blank and puzzled.

"Oh, it's you again. You seem to be everywhere these days, don't you, Georgia?" A lax smile stretched across her lips.

Gia, Mum. My name is Gia.

My heart shriveled and curled inside my chest like a kicked puppy.

My mother was a striking woman who took a lot of pride in

her looks. She used to wear silky, colorful dresses and handmade earrings and an eternal, dazzling smile. Her makeup was bold and her perfumes heady. She was only fifty-five. Even though she seldom remembered me, I made sure to always dress her in her favorite attire and do her makeup before we left the house so that she could at least remember herself.

"It's Gia." I smiled patiently, dying from the inside.

"Of course. Yes. Gia. Pretty name. Who are you again?" She slurred slightly. "Charles's daughter, right? From church? My, how you've grown. Such a beauty. How is he doing these days?"

I swallowed but didn't correct her. Losing a parent in a car accident had been brutal for me, but losing a parent to dementia at such a young age was worse—she was still here but not present.

Dr. Picard's warning swirled in my head, running circles like an unruly child.

"Forget about that program, Gia. I only mentioned it anecdotally. Your mother isn't doing well enough to participate. Once a brain cell dies, it cannot be revived. The program was designed for intermediate patients."

I didn't listen.

I never listened when it came to my family. I'd burn the world twice over if it meant I had the slightest chance of getting my mother back.

"Charles is doing well," I said finally. Charles had been dead for three years now, but there was no need to upset her with a detail she'd forget all about in less than three minutes.

"Good, goo—oh, this place is marvelous. Where are we?" Mum blinked at the window as we slid from Newark and into Manhattan. The hospital was conveniently located in the city, not far from GS Properties' headquarters. "Sky-high buildings. Is this East London? I want to see the Gherkin."

"We're in New York." I licked my lips nervously. "You are going to a hospital where they will treat you for your...exhaustion." I forced myself to remain perky. "I'll come visit every day. It's going to be great."

She turned to look at me again. This time, it wasn't puzzlement that painted her face. It was weariness. Terror. A rare moment of clarity. "I am dying, aren't I?"

Yes. And I am terrified of letting go.

"Why would you say that?" I mustered a weak smile.

"Everything hurts," she garbled. "My body. My soul. I can feel it. I am..." She paused. "I am gone."

Excruciating pain flowed through me. I couldn't remember the last time my mother was in touch with the present. "You'll be just fine," I said sternly. "I'll make sure of it."

"Does my husband know?" She shifted restlessly in her seat. "Why isn't Lloyd here?"

"You'll meet Da...*Lloyd* soon."

But not too soon, if my efforts were fruitful.

"I want my husband. Now."

"Don't worry," I tried to soothe her. "I'll call—"

"Now!" She growled, reaching for the door handle of the back seat, yanking it midride. The door flew open, and I tackled her, my seat belt slashing through my sternum, to slam it shut.

"Hey, hey, hey!" Iven, Tate's driver in New York, smashed the brake with a snarl, causing the cars behind us to swirl and honk. "Christ, you need to handle your mother, Gia."

"I'm not her mother!" Mum exclaimed, reaching for the door handle once more, trying to jump out of the moving car.

"Restrain her!" Iven panicked, gripping the steering wheel tightly. "Or we'll get into a car accident."

I had no choice. I unbuckled myself, scooting toward Mum, and gathered her wrists in my hands. She struggled, trying to push me away, but I was stronger. She tried to kick me, push me. I dodged while Dr. Picard's words echoed between my ears.

"You should focus on comfort care. Her systems are shutting down. To stop this, you'll need a miracle."

Oh, but I had a miracle.

I had the richest man in the world at my disposal.

My tormentor. My punishment. My future husband.

I had Tate Blackthorn.

Once we reached the hospital, Iven helped me usher Mum to the front desk. She was exhausted and back to her normal, empty-shell state.

We were greeted by a reluctant staff, which made me wonder how exactly Tate had managed to secure us this spot. A doctor and a nurse showed us to Mum's private room.

Dr. Stultz explained that a unique combination of cutting-edge medicine and physical and mental therapy would hopefully assist my mother in reversing her symptoms back to mild dementia. I allowed myself a small sliver of hope even as I assisted her in walking, hoping no one noticed how lethargic and frail she was.

As soon as we reached her room, Mum collapsed onto a bed and slipped into deep slumber. The doctor left, but the nurse stayed, watching me through distrustful eyes.

I busied myself with fretting around Mum's snoring frame. I unpacked her suitcase, put her toiletries and clothes away, and took a tour of the facilities. I had reached the cafeteria, realizing I hadn't eaten all day, when a stern voice behind me made me jump.

"How often do you plan on visiting her?"

I spun around. It was Dr. Stultz, his hands clasped behind his back.

"Every day."

He nodded curtly. "Follow me, Miss Bennett. I'll show you around."

I did, falling into step with the middle-aged doctor in a white lab coat. The hallway was vast and full of paintings donated by philanthropists.

"I'm surprised we'll see you so often." The neurologist eyed me midstride. "I'd think you'd take at least a little time off, what with your close approaching nuptials."

I stumbled over my sensible Mary Janes, flying forward and almost sailing straight across the floor. Luckily, I grabbed the wall quickly. "H-how do you know about my engagement?"

I'd tried my best to ignore my arrangement with Tate this past week.

"Your fiancé came over to assess the amenities yesterday," he explained. "He seemed…"

Domineering? Merciless? Deranged?

"Intense." Dr. Stultz's mouth ticked with a nervous smile.

I had no idea why Tate visited here—it wasn't on our shared Google schedule—but I was certain it had nothing to do with my mother's well-being and everything to do with ensuring his future mother-in-law would get the biggest room and the nurse with the biggest tits. He was obnoxiously materialistic.

Nonetheless, a deal was a deal. To access this facility, this program, this opportunity, I had to play the doting fiancée.

"Tate can come off as a bit officious." I smiled cordially. "I apologize for any discomfort he may have caused. If you ever need anything, please reach ou—"

My phone vibrated in my hand. *Speak of the devil.* My boss was calling, probably wanting to scream at me for filling his Stanley cup with Smartwater this morning rather than Volcanic.

Dr. Stultz glimpsed at the source of the sound, catching Tate's name on the screen. I cleared my throat and pressed it to my ear.

"Yes, er…darling?" I cringed.

"We have a meeting with Mayfair Bank in twenty minutes, and you're still not here." He paused. "Did you just darling me?"

I laughed uncomfortably. He wasn't on speaker, but I couldn't know for sure Dr. Stultz hadn't heard him. "Yes, of course. What else would I call you?"

"The bane of your existence," he supplied grimly. "Gru. Satan's favorite child. Cruello de Vil. Ernesto de la Cunt. To name a few from this month alone."

"Are you reading my emails?" My fake smile collapsed. I had never called him these names to his face. I *did*, however, let out some steam in a chain email thread with my college friends Alix and Sadie. Emails he wasn't supposed to be privy to.

"It's my favorite literary genre," he replied unapologetically. "As for your speculation—no, I don't have a small dick, deflowering virgins is not my favorite sport, and I do not strangle puppies recreationally." There was a pause. "The part about taking that Victoria's Secret model as a lover to rile up her husband only because he is a bad musician is true, though. To be fair, his stupid songs were played on the radio the entire year, haunting me. It was reasonable to seek revenge. I'm only human after all."

"This is a breach of my privacy."

I was so cross with him I could barely breathe. Dr. Stultz's eyebrows shot to his hairline.

"No such thing between a husband and wife. Where are you?"

"At Mum's hospital." I knew better than to hope this would make my future husband more understanding.

"Good," he said drily. "If you start running now, you'll make it to the meeting in time."

"I'm speaking to her doctor," I protested, my anger rising in a cloud of heat, settling on my cheeks.

"Her doctor can wait. This meeting can't. Oh, and, Gia?"

At least he'd stopped calling me Miss Bennett. Glass half-full. *With cyanide, but still.*

"What?" I gritted out.

"Don't forget my coffee on your way here."

I pushed open the doors to the conference room, holding his precious coffee.

Black, like his soul.

The place was empty other than Tate. He wore a charcoal herringbone three-piece suit with a black turtleneck and looked like pure dopamine poured straight into my veins.

I peered around, catching my breath after sprinting here in my heeled Louboutins. "Where is everyone?"

"I decided to cancel the meeting to tend to more pressing issues." He didn't look up from his laptop screen. "Namely, your part of our deal."

He made me drop everything, leave in the middle of an important conversation about my mother's future, for a meeting he'd canceled?

"I loathe you," I said quietly. Coolly. "I truly do. I will honor our agreement. I will marry you. But I will also make your life miserable. You'll be so unhappy, you'll regret the day you ever met me."

"The *drama*." He sat back, yawning. "I forgot the downside of a tight, young pussy is dealing with the person attached to it. Your theatrics don't impress me."

"Don't deal with me then. Cancel our deal."

"My coffee?" he asked wryly, snapping his laptop shut. He dragged a thick contract across his desk and perched it over his laptop.

I plucked his coffee order—black, filtered, unsweetened—from the cup carrier, setting it by his elbow. He set his red pen down and reached for it, bringing it to his lips. He stopped before the rim touched his lips.

"Did you spit in it?"

"No." I waited for him to take a sip before adding, "So if it tastes different, that's why."

Tate chuckled deviously, popping open the lid of his coffee and dragging the cup across the table to where I was standing.

"Go on then." A daring glint sparkled behind his pale eyes.

I stared at him, aghast. "Go on, what?"

"Spit in my coffee. You know I'm very particular about my brew."

"I was *kidding*. It was a joke."

"Well, I'm not. It tastes off. Spit in it."

"You're depraved."

"You're delectable."

"*What?*"

"Thought we were listing each other's obvious traits?" He cocked a brow.

He was being purposefully crude. Very well. I wasn't going to be the one to bow and cower out of his twisted game. He wanted to play? I'd one-up him.

I knew Tate thought of me as prim and proper. And to be perfectly honest, that was the only side of me I'd given him. But I too harbored secrets. Some of them dark and big enough to suffocate me to death.

Palming his coffee cup, I tilted my head down and spat in it. I handed it back to him. "There you go."

He took a large sip, closing his eyes and tilting his head back with a groan of pleasure. "Hmm. Much better."

His smoky, husky moan reverberated through my entire body. Was this what he sounded like when he came? When he was deep inside one of his world-famous supermodels?

"My mother is settling quite well at the hospital, by the way. Cheers for asking." I took a seat two chairs down from his spot at the head of the table. I flipped my notebook open, as I always did when Tate and I were in the same room and I knew I was about to be bombarded with tasks and demands.

"She better hang the fuck on to her life at least until I sample the goods." Tate took another swallow of his drink, giving me an appreciative once-over. "I'm certainly not doing this pro bono."

A part of me wanted to strangle him. The other wanted to shove his head between my legs to shut him up. Unfortunately, I knew he'd enjoy both options, so I settled for neither.

"Speaking of." I tapped my chin. "Why is the hospital staff so fidgety around me? What did you do?"

"I ensured our deal would be fruitful and long-term."

"How?" I pressed.

"By explaining to Dr. Stultz I will see that his department gets defunded and his license revoked if he doesn't cure your mother."

My jaw went slack. "That's wildly unethical."

"Unlike getting someone kicked out of a dementia program to make way for your ailing mother?" He arched a mocking eyebrow. "Sweetheart, don't lecture me about morals. I see through your Goody Two-Shoes charade, and rest assured, I approve of that ruthless side of you."

I was beginning to second-guess our arrangement. Tate wasn't a predictable creature. I'd been counting on him to let me go because he was thrice divorced, but what if I was the exception to the rule? What if my fighting back provided just enough challenge for him to keep pushing? I couldn't change who I was.

"Don't you dare compare us. I'm only trying to take care of my mother." I narrowed my eyes at him.

"What a coincidence. So am I."

"To get into bed with me!" I flung my arms in the air. "Which, by the way, is sexual harassment in a workplace."

"Yeah, I found a loophole."

"Enlighten me."

"You're fired."

My racing heart screeched into a halt. "*What?*"

"Can't be sexual harassment in a workplace if we don't work together. Don't worry. I found you another role in a subsidiary company in the building. More on that later."

"Are you aware that you're a psychopath who is incapable of small talk, let alone an entire range of emotions?" I spluttered.

"I am capable of small talk," he countered.

"No, you aren't. You're crude, crass, corru—"

"This is really boring." He waved me off. "Let's change the subject."

I folded my arms over my chest. "What do you want to talk about?"

"Did you know that your vocal cords are actually folds?" he drawled haughtily.

"I did not." I frowned. Was he suffering from a brain hemorrhage? One could only hope.

"Their layers of muscles, ligament, and membrane make up two liplike pink creases. They look remarkably like a vagina."

Why was he telling me this?

"What are you doing?" I squinted.

"Nothing," he snarled. "Talking. We're talking. About things that aren't my subpar personality."

"Tate, are you trying to...make small talk with me?" I blinked. For the first time in weeks, something that resembled an honest-to-God laugh threatened to roll out of my mouth.

His eyes snapped up from the contract he was examining. He looked thoroughly repulsed.

"I'm not *trying*, I'm succeeding. And it is very dull. Why do people enjoy it?"

"It builds social bonds." I bit on my smile. "It is the human equivalent of grooming each other."

"Can we lick each other's genitals instead?" He cocked an eyebrow. "Cats and dogs figured out a better way to handle their social calls."

I rolled my eyes, shaking my head. "Why am I here, Tate?"

His eyes drifted to my lower lip, and my pulse hitched. It wasn't the first time Tate's eyes lingered on my mouth.

But it was the first time he did it after blackmailing me into marriage.

"We're here for a business conference. Oh good. I see your notebook is open. Take the minutes for this meeting."

I knew Tate frighteningly well. I knew what pleased him (punctuality, order, neatness, logicality, routine), and I also knew what drove him bonkers (stupidity, inattention to detail, sloppiness).

"What's on the agenda?" I uncapped my pen.

"*Us.*"

I put the pen down. I didn't want to talk about us. Frankly, I would prefer there wasn't an us at all.

"If this is about my job—"

"Did you dump your boyfriend yet?" He turned all business.

My pulse picked up. "No, but—"

"We'll do it together then. Our first *bonding experience* as a couple. How exciting." He rubbed his hands together, pulling his phone out of his pocket.

The remainder of my composure dissolved, and I tore myself from my chair, shooting up to my feet.

"Don't you dare call Ash—"

The familiar sound of a British phone line filled my ears, two beeps at a time. Tate put the phone on speaker, sprawling back and crossing his legs at the ankles over the conference table.

How did he even *have* Ashley's number?

My boyfriend's deep tenor filled the air.

"Hello?"

Nausea took me over. I wasn't in love with Ashley. We hadn't the time for that, always on different continents. I knew he wasn't in love with me either. Our relationship had been fizzling out since my birthday. He said I was always too busy babying my boss. But I had planned to fly out to London this weekend and sit him down for a respectful breakup conversation.

"Ashley?" Tate produced his pocket watch, rolling it over his fingers like a coin. "This is Tatum Blackthorn, Gia's boss. She has something to tell you."

I refused to humiliate him. To lose in another one of Tate's games. I decided to think on my feet.

"Ashley." I cleared my throat, my voice soft. "I'm sorry for how sudden it is, but I'm afraid you were right. Maybe it's not a good time for us to date after all."

He never said such a thing, but I wanted him to have this win. My stomach was in knots. The only thing keeping my bile from spilling out was the knowledge the perverted twat next to me was probably going to add my vomit to his coffee as a creamer.

Tate's normally grim face glowed with satisfaction.

"When did I ever say *that*?" Ashley gathered his thoughts. "Also, I'm surprised and confused as to why you're breaking this to me over the phone with your boss present."

"You're right. You deserve so much better than this. Unfortunately, the reason I need to break things off is because I will be indisposed for the next few months. See, Mr. Blackthorn is suffering from an unexplained and lengthy bout of violent diarrhea. This has been going on for a while now. We are checking him into the Mayo Clinic in Minnesota to try to find a solution for his rather...inconvenient condition."

Tate's smug smirk evaporated faster than free hand sanitizer at a germophobe convention. I knew Ashley was keeping his chuckle at bay, the fine English gentleman that he was. I also knew I managed to squeeze the best lemonade out of my lemon-filled situation.

"That sounds terrible," my now ex-boyfriend muttered.

"It's been a challenging period both for him and for the people around him, as you can imagine." I heaved out a sigh. "He's always been explosive, but now it is a bit too literal for everyone's liking."

Tate stared me down, plotting my slow, grisly murder as Ashley chuckled in the background.

"I moved Mum to America so she can be nearby while we try

to fix whatever's wrong with him. Currently, the doctors believe it's simply his irritable personality taking its toll on his bowels."

Ashley couldn't hold it back anymore. He was laughing with open delight. "Oh, Gia. What have you gotten yourself into with this job?"

"I know." I smiled sadly. "I'm sorry for how hasty this is. You're a really good bloke. If circumstances were different…" I trailed off.

"Yes, I know. Well, I wish you all the best," he said tenderly. "And if you ever quit your job and decide to rejoin civilization…"

"Then she still won't give you a call," Tate growled. "You lost to diarrhea, *mate*. Get the fucking hint." With that, he killed the call, pinning me with a wrathful glare. "You really couldn't come up with anything better?"

I shrugged, smiling angelically. "I'm resourceful, not creative."

He rolled his tongue over his front teeth. "On to the next item on the agenda of *us*. As I said, you can't work directly under me any longer," he announced. "It's a bad look."

"Since when do you care about what people think?" I snorted.

"Since my lawyers tell me it'd open me to potential legal issues." He laced his fingers together. "This is nonnegotiable. You're leaving."

"You can't fire me. We'd agreed you'd let me keep my jo—"

"Firing is a strong word. I prefer relocation." He raised a palm up to stop my panicked rush of words. "I'm transferring you to the HR department, which is employed by a sister company."

"HR department?" I scowled. "I know nothing about HR."

"You won't need experience for the job I'm assigning you to do."

"Which is?"

"Terminating employees I find unsuitable."

"You're making me *fire* people?" My voice pitched high. I couldn't recall the last time that had happened. I usually prided myself on my tranquility. Said tranquility was no longer in the building.

Or the city.

Or, let's admit it, the planet.

"Yes," Tate replied tersely.

"I won't do it." I collected my notebook, pressing it to my chest. "I won't ruin people's lives just to please you."

He ignored me completely, sorting through the paperwork in front of him without lifting his gaze. "HR is on the tenth floor. Your new employee pass is being prepared as we speak. Oh." He snapped his fingers. "You'll need to find and hand over all calendars and responsibilities to Rebecca."

Rebecca was his second assistant. She had the measurements and wheat-blond hair of a Malibu Barbie and the exact same number of brain cells.

Maybe if they were in forced proximity more often, he'd start an affair with her and leave me alone.

"Not a chance in hell. She doesn't hold a candle to you," Tate said regrettably. "Even if she did, the idiot would probably set herself aflame accidentally."

Did I say that out loud? Or could this human viper read minds now?

"Tate," I spat his name out through clenched teeth. "I don't *want* to fire people. Hurt people. I don't know what you're punishing me for, what I've done to deserve this unwarranted attention from you, but if you won't stop pushing, I *will* leave."

"You won't run away from me," he said calmly. "I have something of yours you love dearly. Your mother."

He was right. I realized I had played right into his hands. Tate helping me get Mum into the program was entirely selfish on his part. A way for him to have leverage on me.

I couldn't run. I couldn't hide. I was his.

"Besides, if you do run, I will find you. And when I find you…" He trailed off, giving me one of his infamously callous scowls. "Well, it'd be a crying shame. A woman so young. So pretty."

"I'd call the police," I threatened.

"Please do," he encouraged. "You are complicit in every single thing I've done to secure your mother's spot at the experimental treatment. Would you like to know how many laws we've broken together, *fiancée?*"

I was trapped, and we both knew it.

My knees buckled, and I became lightheaded. I stumbled back, searching for the nearest wall to lean on. But I was so frazzled that I missed. I stumbled backward.

Tate stood up, moving so fast he left skid marks on the floor. He caught me by the arms, his touch cold and impersonal, and righted me against a glass wall.

"Why are you doing this?" I whispered.

He stared me down serenely. He oozed power, this unabashed male roughness that made me swallow a whimper.

"You cannot be all good, and I cannot be all bad. We have to meet somewhere in the middle for people to buy this marriage," he said, ignoring my question.

"But you *are* all bad!" I protested, balling my fists to pound his chest. It was as solid as stone beneath the rich fabric. The notebook slipped from between my arms between us.

"That's not true. I am *very* good with giving women earth-shattering orgasms. References are available upon request."

He smirked, his face still dangerously close to mine. What lay behind his eyes made my pulse quicken. Possessiveness mixed with something else. Desperation maybe. His marble cheekbones were flushed, his nostrils narrow. For a brief moment, I thought he'd lean down and kiss me. I'd let him too. Because even though I hated him, even though I *loathed* the idea of his very existence, I was curious to know what it felt like. To be kissed by a man who owned the entire world, who had infinite power, no limits, no restraints, no conscience.

My lips parted. I could feel his breath against my own. I would find a way to get him back tomorrow. To punish him for what he was doing to me. But right now, in this minute, I wanted him like air. Like oxygen.

"One step at a time." He captured my chin between his thumb and finger, tilting my head up. His mouth curled in sardonic amusement. "If I kiss you now, you won't writhe in your bed tonight, wondering what it feels like. What I taste like. How much pressure I use with my tongue. How many sensitive spots I can find on your body."

I snatched my face away, looking sideways to avoid him. He read me like an open book. What else did he know?

"Speaking of your bed," he continued, "it is currently being transferred to the guest room down the hall from me. I've arranged for your belongings to be sent to my penthouse. A moving company is making its way with them from Brooklyn as we speak."

I'd stayed in my dodgy Brooklyn flat after graduating from uni. I never thought to find somewhere more permanent in the States. I'd desperately wanted to move back to England, to the memories of Dad and Elliott, and now that dream seemed further away than ever.

"Actually." He snapped his fingers. "I had them throw away most of your junk. Hope you don't mind. Didn't peg you for a hoarder, Miss Bennett."

There was no point in protesting. In arguing. In fighting back.

He'd fulfilled his part of the bargain. Now it was my turn.

I waited for him to leave the conference room before pulling out my phone and googling vocal cords.

He was right.

They did look like a vagina.

CHAPTER EIGHT
GIA

Gia: SOS.

Cal: When and where?

Gia: Casablancas. An hour.

Dylan: Rain check. Grav is at my mom's, and Rhy and I finally have time for evening sex. You'll have to shake the very fabric of time and space to remove my thighs from his ears.

Gia: I SAID SOS.

Dylan: Is it SOS-my-life-is-imploding or SOS-my-GHD-died-and-they-don't-make-that-model-anymore?

Gia: The former.

Gia: Although the latter technically counts as life-altering too.

Dylan: Ugh. FINE. See you there.

Cal: Me too <3

"So what did you want to tell us?" Cal munched on deep-fried fish fingers at Casablancas in Bryant Park. She looked adorable in her mustard-colored overalls, only one shoulder strap done, flowery long-sleeved shirt, and red-tipped fringe. "You sounded upset in the text messages."

"Yeah, I was ready to cut a bitch." Dylan pulled her long raven hair into a messy bun. The Super Bowl was playing in the background on giant flat-screen TVs across the restaurant. "Is it your mom? Is she doing okay on the new experimental medicine?"

Calla and Dylan were my best friends. They were true crown straighteners. I'd found them through Tate, who was close with their husbands. Unlike Tate, both my friends and their husbands were surprisingly sane, not to mention delightful.

Cal's husband, Row, for instance, was a Michelin-starred chef who opened this New York joint for his wife just so she'd have a place to eat her favorite fish fingers and fries whenever she was in town. They also offered high-end sushi, though, which was what Dylan and I were eating.

People around us jumped up from their seats and cheered. I guessed someone scored in the game. I knew nothing about American football. In truth, it had no business being called football at all. They were using their hands mostly.

"No, it's not about Mum. She is doing fine, though, thank you." I flashed them a tired smile.

Dr. Stultz told me they were running some cognitive and physical tests before they put her on the drugs and were now waiting for the results. I guessed no news was good news.

"You know you can always ask us to watch over her or keep her company if your workload is too much," Dylan said.

"I know." I took a sip of my Cuba libre. "And the same goes for you two. If you ever need me, I'm here."

"Friendship is not a quid pro quo relationship," Cal pointed out. "Sometimes you'll need us more than we'll need you. You were there when Dylan's daughter was kidnapped and she went through a panic attack. We're not keeping track of who is helping who and how much. We just want you to be happy."

"Thank you." I smiled.

We tried to flag down a waiter, but the game reached its

halftime mark, and all the patrons started ordering at once. It was a bit chaotic, with semi-drunk football fans trying to grab the staff's attention, before Dylan stood on the leather bench and cupped her mouth. "Someone better come tend to this table, or *everyone's* getting fired. Calla Casablancas is in the house."

Not ten seconds passed, and a harem of waiters arrived with more sushi and more cocktails for us.

I waited for the servers to leave before I opened my mouth again. There was no good way to tell my friends I was soon to be married to the man whose voodoo doll was their last birthday present to me. Especially as I hadn't even bothered pricking it with needles. I threw it straight into a fire.

"Oh! I forgot to tell you," Dylan blurted out, her smile lighting up her face. "Rhyland and I found an amazing place on a dude ranch just outside New Haven." She snatched her phone from the table, scrolling through her gallery to try to find a picture. "It has a stable and a huge space to build Gravity a playground. It'll be great to go there on weekends."

"Well done, him. Congratulations," I exclaimed. Gravity was Dylan's daughter. Rhyland was in the process of legally adopting her, and she was the center of their lives.

"He's such a great dad." Cal put a hand over her heart. "There's nothing sexier than a man who steps up and raises someone else's kid."

"I'd say your man is sexy too, but he is my brother." Dylan made a finger-in-mouth gesture.

I giggled into my drink, immediately feeling lighter. Gosh, I loved my friends.

"I can't believe Rhyland wore you down." I shook my head, smiling. "Cal said you were anti-relationship to the extreme."

"No lies detected. And look, I'm still no man's peace..." Dylan caught the two cocktail straws between her scarlet-painted lips, sucking on her Salvador Dalí concoction. "But for him, I'll sign a congeniality accord."

Tate is going to be a terrible father, I thought grimly. Nothing like my own dad. Not, of course, that we were ever going to have children.

I promised myself I'd be as disagreeable as possible to ensure he'd want to get rid of me.

"Anyway, you were saying?" Dylan turned her attention back to me. "What's your SOS situation?"

I wiped my sweaty palms over my dress. "Yes, well, I know it's a bit shocking but—"

"Gia!" Dylan coughed out her cocktail. "Oh my…what the *fuck?*" She pointed at the TV. I whipped my head to the screen above our heads, confused.

"Holy shit!" Cal slapped her mouth. "I'm about to have a heart attack."

My blood froze in my veins.

Tate did it again.

He beat me to it.

On the screen played a commercial featuring one of Hollywood's most desirable it girls, all flawless makeup and designer clothes. She congratulated the third richest man in the world—Tatum Blackthorn—on his engagement to Gia Bennett. The ad was for a preppy jewelry store.

"Choose elegance. Choose decadence. Choose timeless perfection. Choose Citoyenne. After all." Claire Larsen sashayed felinely along row upon row of glittering jewelry, wearing a table napkin I supposed could pass as a white dress. "Tate Blackthorn, the smartest man in the world, bought his fiancée a ring here."

A doctored picture of Tate and me sitting together with my hand resting on his lap filled the screen. It was a mash-up between a picture of me smiling at an event while sitting next to my father and a picture of Tate from Cal and Row's wedding.

He photoshopped a picture of you together, looking happy and loved up, my mind screamed. *This is how you end up as an episode in one of*

Cal's true crime podcasts as a woman who got chopped up to pieces and was found inside her husband's fridge.

This was a level of toxic I didn't even want to explore.

Every set of eyes turned their attention to me.

Larsen concluded the Super Bowl ad with the words, "Citoyenne Jewelry: Because if the future Mrs. Blackthorn wears it, so should you."

Deadly silence engulfed the restaurant. Both Cal and Dylan stared at me with their mouths hanging open.

Dylan was the first to recover from Tate's... *Tateness.*

"I'm just... I..." Her jaw went slack. She closed it. It went slack again. "You *hate* him."

Cal looked like she was about to cry. "Is this...what you wanted to tell us?"

I inclined my head, my heart sinking all the way to the bottom of my stomach.

"Tell us it's a joke, G." Cal cupped her mouth.

I shook my head, holding back my tears. "It's the truth."

"And this...you agreed to this?" Dylan swallowed. Her eyes shone.

I nodded slowly. "I agreed."

"But...why?"

"It's complicated, but...yeah." I bit my lower lip. "It's true."

"He bought a Super Bowl ad to announce your engagement," Dylan cried out, trying to recover, to lighten up the mood. "This is so extra and *so* Tate. It was either that or pissing on your leg in Madison Square Garden and barking at every man who glanced your way."

"Thank you for the emotional support." I flattened my napkin in my lap, straightening my posture.

"So..." Cal glanced around, unsure. "How did it happen?"

"We struck a deal." I cleared my throat. "He helped me get Mum in that trial program, and I, in return, have to pretend to be his loving wife. He wants to ruin my life."

"I'm pretty sure what he wants to ruin is your uterus." Dylan squinted. "He's always had a thing for you."

"That's rubbish. He loathes me," I moaned, letting my head drop between my arms on the table. "He just transferred me to human resources, and now I have to fire people for a living."

"There's no other way?" Dylan went bone-white.

I shook my head. "The trial Mum's been accepted to…" I left the rest to their imagination.

Cal's eyes went soft. "I'm so, so sorry."

There was a beat of silence before Dylan piped up again. "I mean…he is superrich, handsome, and literally obsessed with the oxygen you breathe…"

My eyebrows snapped into a frown. "I'm not even attracted to hi—"

"You told me you'd fold for him like a cheap lawn chair." Dylan raised her palm to stop me. "Remember? At Alix's wedding."

"That doesn't count. I was drunk," I balked.

"Drunk admissions are always truthful."

I picked up a paper napkin, scrunched it, and tossed it at Dylan. "So what if he's hot? He's still a meanie." I felt myself smiling. It was the alcohol, surely. And the exhaustion that came with being sad all the time because of Mum.

"Have you fucked him yet?" Dylan wiggled her brows. "Does he come lava? Poison? Tar? Asking for a friend."

"No," I spluttered, actually giggling. Dylan had the uncanny ability to make light of the darkest moments. "But I moved into his bloody apartment as part of our deal. I've been doing my best to avoid him. I've actually bought individual Cheerios cups and bottled water to survive in my room."

I couldn't risk bumping into Tate in the kitchen. Not since I almost kissed him.

"Wait, isn't he thrice divorced?" Dylan munched on the edge of a fry. "Don't be so stressed. By all available data, this marriage is going to expire before a can of lentil soup."

"Those cans are good for, like, a decade." I scowled, looking between my two friends.

"Don't worry. We'll go to our husbands and pressure them to make Tate call it off," Dylan promised.

Cal nodded, nibbling on her lower lip pensively. "Row and Rhyland are both in business with him. He wouldn't want to jeopardize his work for anything. You know business always comes first for him. Let's exhaust all our options before we freak out."

I swallowed, nodding. Tate usually put his company's needs first, but he was also unpredictable, a mad king reigning an empire of thorns. A pyromaniac with a decadent taste for destruction.

And he was dead set on ruining me.

"His ears must be ringing…" Cal jerked her chin toward my phone. The screen showed Tate's name.

Stifling a groan, I picked it up. "What do you want?"

"An agreeable fiancée, for a start."

"I'm afraid I'm fresh out. Anything else?"

"Come downstairs. We have a ring fitting to attend to."

How did he know I was with my friends? Did he follow me? The thought made invisible spiders crawl along my skin.

"Let me guess, Citoyenne Jewelry?" I drawled.

"Good, you're watching the game. Who is winning?"

"Your ego."

"I'm not surprised. It's gigantic. Size matters in football. Hurry up."

"What's the magic word?" I didn't have an appetite anyway. Besides, I was eager for Cal and Dylan to go back to their partners to try to defuse the situation.

"Immediately?" he tried.

I rolled my eyes. "No."

A half-human, half-feral grumble came from the other end of the line.

"So?" I coaxed sweetly. "Magic word?"

"Abracadabra."

"Try again."

"Alakazam?"

"No."

"Hocus-pocus? Open sesame? Daimon? Voilà? Sim sala bim? Fidelio? It largely depends on the period and culture. A little guidance wouldn't hurt."

Oh God. He didn't... Surely, he couldn't...

"You don't know what the magic word is, Tate, do you?" I gasped.

"Don't be ridiculous. I know everything. What language is it in?" he huffed.

"*English*," I enunciated slowly. "It's please. The magic word is please. Have you never used it before?"

Silence. And then, "I'm sure I have, once or twice."

"Well, happy to pop your cherry. Ask me *nicely*."

This was going to be his entire life from now on. I was going to set obstacles and be obnoxiously difficult until I wrung out his will to live.

"*Please*," he enunciated sardonically. "Come downstairs."

"If you'll excuse me, I have to get my soul sucked by the ghoul I'm marrying." I stood up, bidding my friends goodbye.

"Hey, as long as it's the only thing that's going to be sucked." Dylan saluted her cocktail in the air. "Don't worry, girlie. We're on top of it."

I took the elevator down. Oh yes. I was going to fulfill my part of the deal, but I wasn't going to be nice about it. I had taken note of all the things Tate appreciated about me and made sure to hide them.

Which was how I knew he'd have a heart attack when he saw me.

I poured myself out to the frosty street and immediately spotted Tate's Ferrari Purosangue. It was the same shade of gray as his eyes. He'd parked in the middle of the street, blocking traffic. I hurried over to the back seat and popped the door open, realizing to my shock that he was in the driver's seat, not Iven.

"You have a driver's license?" I blurted out. In all my years working for Tate, I had yet to see him drive a car himself.

His eyes tapered. "Get inside."

The honking behind him intensified. I ducked my head, about to slide into the back seat.

"*Next to me.* I'm not your chauffeur."

I did as I was told, biting my tongue and waiting for the next opening to piss him off.

The opportunity presented itself not even ten seconds after the car slid forward and into busy Manhattan traffic.

"Your dress." His cold eyes flickered over my bare legs.

"What about it?" I asked innocently.

"It's nonexistent."

Indeed, it was skimpy by my standards. I made sure to purchase a new wardrobe with skirts and dresses shorter than my fiancé's fuse in order to aggravate him. This one was a rose-gold sequin mini dress that was a far cry from my usual buttoned-up work dresses and pencil skirts.

"If you think you're going to tell me what to wear—" I started.

"You can wear whatever you want," he cut me off. "What will happen to men who stare at you as a result is on your conscience, though."

"So what I'm hearing is I'll get to piss you off *and* get you arrested for aggravated assault." I crossed my legs seductively and sat back, knowing he was going to steal another glance at my thighs. "Say less."

A muscle jumped in his jaw. He kept his gaze on the road. "You will have to choose an engagement ring fit for the wife of a respected billionaire."

"I'm marrying a respected billionaire?" I lurched forward, placing a hand on my rib cage. "I thought I was marrying you."

"Hilarious."

"No, you are," I said cheerfully. "For thinking I'd let you play any role in choosing my engagement ring."

"You're a reasonable woman." His teeth slammed together.

My plan was working. I was driving him bonkers.

"Start acting like one."

"I *was* a reasonable woman," I corrected. "Now, I'm whatever you don't want in a wife. That is my entire personality."

His nostrils flared. A lick of fear ran along my spine. Tate was a dangerous man. I'd never seen him get fucked over in deals—he always did the fucking—and I had a feeling I wasn't going to like the consequences of my own actions.

The car came to a screech in front of a white, arched building in the heart of Manhattan. The entire six-story jewelry store glowed from the inside. He threw the vehicle into park and swiveled to me with his entire imposing body.

"I've satisfied my part of the transaction in good faith. I have twisted a lot of arms and broken a lot of laws to get your mother into this program in record time. Yet instead of a blushing bride, I so far have had to deal with an unruly banshee. I find that the best way to work with a disorderly business partner is to either bend them to my rules or sack them altogether."

"Sack me then," I whispered.

"Oh, but you wouldn't like that." His tone, of pure gravel, caressed every inch of my body. His cordial smile held a threat.

"Why not?"

"Because you want your mother to live, and as easily as I put her in this program, I can also remove her."

Tears clogged my throat and burned the backs of my eyeballs.

I hated him. Yet I was attracted to him in the same way the moth longed for the flame, knowing it'd kill it.

He reached to me slowly, giving me time to retreat, and cupped the side of my neck. His touch was warm and rough and comforting. God, it made no sense. Why couldn't my body be in tune with my mind?

I realized depressingly that a broken egg cannot be unbroken.

A bitten apple could never be whole again. Now that I knew what Tate's touch felt like, I could never erase it from memory, could never resist it.

"Would marrying me really be the end of the world?" Tate asked silkily, fingers traveling along the column of my neck.

"Yes," I choked out. "It would. I've lost so much already. My only hope is to choose a good-hearted, faithful husband and to choose him well."

"You could be happy." His gaze dropped to my lips, his fingers still lightly caressing my neck, his thumb circling the skin just beneath my ear. "You'll be the richest out of your friends. Draped in the most lavish of frocks. I will be faithful. As long as you open those pretty legs for me anyway. You will have children to fuss over."

"Yes." I swallowed. "I'll have all those things, but I won't have love."

"Sweetheart, love is like God. An abstract invention for poor people to cling to in lieu of better, materialistic things."

"Yet that's all I want and the only thing you cannot give me," I croaked.

"I could grow to tolerate you," he said.

Smiling miserably, I shook my head. "No, you won't. You're not the type to protect, to shelter, to piece someone back together. To… to…give cute nicknames," I explained. "You're a villain."

My words seemed to sober him. "It is pointless to negotiate with you." His upper lip curved into a snarl. "I want your word that you'll behave."

I stared out the window, silent.

"You're making a grave mistake, Apricity."

"Apricity?" I whipped my head his way.

"The warmth of the sun in winter." He smirked fiendishly. "It was what popped into my head when I saw you for the first time. There'd been a snowstorm. It was freezing. And you looked…" His eyes rested on the faint pulse of my neck. "Well, *hot*."

Snowstorm?

He'd first seen me in August. More specifically, he was present when I walked into an interview for a position at Fiscal Heights Holdings, a hedge fund company, where he sat with the man I was supposed to be interviewed by, named Baron Spencer.

"My apologies, Miss Bennett," Spencer drawled, surly, not even a bit remorseful. *"My assistant forgot to inform you the position has been filled."*

"Oh." I stood there, smiling awkwardly. "No worries. I'd better—"

"But I shared your CV with my friend here, Tatum Blackthorn." He gestured to a tall, darkly handsome man who looked like a young version of him. "And he's been thoroughly impressed, which doesn't happen often. He's looking for a PA."

"I am looking for a job in finance."

"You're looking for whatever people like us are willing to give," Spencer corrected me. *"And you'd be wise to remember that."*

Was this premeditated? More than a coincidence?

When did he first see me?

Did he stalk me?

If so, *why?*

It was hypocritical of me to judge him for stalking. A few years back, I did the same thing to someone else. But still…

My thoughts scattered like marbles, running in a million directions. Tate knew me well before I knew him. I'd been the center of this man's attention long before I learned of his existence.

Every fine hair on my body stood on end.

"As I said." Tate unbuckled and yanked the keys from the ignition lock, unaware he'd given himself away in this crucial, small detail. "I haven't a chivalrous bone in my entire body. I will retaliate and twice as hard. Play your cards right, and I will give you half my kingdom. Defy me, and you'll lose everything that's dear and precious to you." He kept his little finger on my neck, relishing the rhythm of my hammering pulse, his thumb brushing my lower lip down. He stared at my mouth with those unsettling eyes, unblinking. "Do you want me to destroy your life, Gia?"

I shook my head faintly.

"Good. Now, you are going to get out of this car. I will drape you in my coat to hide those lovely legs I cannot wait to have wrapped around my fucking shoulders, and you will choose a ring no cheaper than one million dollars. There's paparazzi waiting outside, so you'll be on your best behavior. You will gaze up at me lovingly, point at different rings, and generally have a good fucking time." His voice was low, steady, smoky. "Am I understood?"

I clutched my seashell bracelet in a death grip.

You are your father's daughter. You won't cower to this arse.

"As you wish." I slammed my teeth over the tip of his thumb, desperate to hurt him back.

Tate grinned, placing his thumb in his mouth and sucking off the little blood I drew.

"Now that's a good girl."

CHAPTER NINE
TATE

Three days later, chef Ambrose "Row" Casablancas almost tore my door off of its hinges, galloping into my office. Even without looking at him, I sensed the blistering waves of anger pouring out of his massive body.

He was a basic creature. Like a fish, but with the ability to make a decent omelet.

"This is bullshit." He slammed a piece of paper over my desk, splintering the wood with his paw.

"You finally learned how to read." I didn't raise my gaze from the bylaws I was skimming. "Congratulations. You're almost ready for a big kid bed now."

"This is my letter of resignation from La Vie en Rogue, effective immediately. I'm selling my shares and washing my hands of the restaurant completely if you don't let that poor woman go."

I sat back, weaving my fingers together and staring at him drily. The man was as philanthropic as a lethal injection. My guess was he didn't give half a shit about Gia's well-being. His wife twisted his balls, and he sang whatever tune she fed him. Row was pathetically pussy-whipped.

Row and I co-owned a two-location restaurant chain called La Vie en Rogue in London and Edinburgh. Business was booming. So was his voice when he didn't get any response from me.

"Seriously, Tate, what the fuck is wrong with you?"

I sighed. "Neither of us has time for that exhaustive list."

Speaking of royal fuckups, I spotted Rhyland, Row's best friend and his sister's husband, from the corner of my eye through the glass wall. He was skulking his way to my office, ignoring my lip-biting, horny employees that eye screwed him. He flung the door open and slammed it behind him, pinning me with a glare.

"Who let you both in?" I asked calmly.

"The person whose life you're ruining," Rhyland retorted.

I scowled. "You're going to have to be way more specific than that."

"*Gia*," both men exclaimed in unison.

I wasn't sure why, but her mere name falling from other men's lips made me want to kill them in a creative and highly torturous way that'd make the Ferrante brothers blush.

"Release her from this agreement." Rhyland braced his arms over my desk. He had biceps the size of watermelons, but I could take him.

"No." I stacked my feet on my desk. "She's mine."

"You blackmailed her, knowing she wouldn't turn down an opportunity to help her mother." Rhyland decided to state the fucking obvious.

"*She* came to *me* wanting to strike a deal," I clarified. "We negotiated, and she accepted my terms. Not that I owe you any explanation."

Row and Rhyland were each damaged in their own way. But me? I was ruined. Beyond redemption. A normal relationship was not in the cards for me.

"She is a *child*," Row growled.

"She is twenty-six," I snorted. "An adult in every single state."

"You're bullying a *woman*. A young woman who is here on a visa. Have you no limits?"

"None whatsoever," I assured him. "I always collect my debt, regardless of gender, race, or creed."

"That debt is about to pile up into a full-blown bankruptcy if you don't let her go. You know La Vie en Rogue won't survive without me." Row grabbed the back of the leather chair in front of my desk, hulking over it. He wore a black bomber jacket and combat boots and looked every inch of the bad boy chef persona that earned him millions of dollars a year. I doubted the asshole could flip a burger better than anyone else. He just looked good making food. "I'm the face of your restaurant."

It was terribly cute, how he thought I gave a shit.

"Are you gonna let her go?"

"No. La Vie en Rogue is not even pocket change for me." I flipped my pen between my fingers, itching to solve a few equations or tap my thigh rhythmically. "If you want to send your career up in flames, I won't stop you. Hell, I might even bring some graham crackers and marshmallows to make some s'mores while you burn."

Row's eyes glowed with wrath. I guessed it was Rhyland's turn to try to convince me to let Gia go. Was this their little attempt at playing good cop, bad cop?

"Look." The good-looking motherfucker raised his palms in surrender. "Your business with Row is a little passion project, I get it. But you actually have a lot of stock in App-date." App-date was his idiotic, albeit successful, dating app. "I'll make sure the board turns on you if you don't let her go. I'll turn it into something very public and very ugly."

I tipped my head back and laughed. "Go ahead. Bruce is going to annihilate you on my behalf if you mess up his business." Bruce was his business partner and the man holding the almighty dollar of the operation. "There's nothing you can do to sway me from a good business decision. And marrying Gia Bennett is a damn good investment."

The two men shared a wordless glance.

"Tate…" Rhyland licked his lips.

I held my palm up. "You can go and tell your little wives you tried your best. I'll confirm that statement. However, I'm not letting her go."

"Why?" Rhyland pushed a hand into his blond mane, exasperated. "You always adhere to logic. Why not now?"

A question for the ages. Why Gia Bennett? Why not any other willing woman? They were practically waiting in line.

My brief marriages aside, I'd had plenty of cold arrangements with women before. Brilliant, classy, beautiful women. I paid their rent and gave them monthly allowances. In return, they were available to me a few times a week, where I dropped by unannounced, bent them over the side of their couch, and fucked them mercilessly. All of them would have gladly given me an heir. Hell, some would have agreed to give me a kidney.

Why not them? Why my annoying secretary?

Because I want to keep her close. Because she is the last thing I have left of him.

Row shook his head. "You're fucking obsessed with this woman."

"She should be so lucky."

"If we can't convince you to back out of this disastrous idea, I want some reassurances." Row worked his jaw back and forth, palming it. Probably to keep himself from biting my head off.

I decided to humor him, for the sole purpose of hearing what my hysterical bride-to-be thought I'd do to her.

"Yes?" I asked.

"You're not going to hurt her."

"Physically? No. Mentally? Probably." I wasn't known for my people skills. "Let's admit it. It's nothing she isn't used to from working with me."

"You're not going to force yourself on her," Rhyland continued.

I snorted. That douche had some nerve to play the knight in shining armor role with his history.

"Noncon is not my style."

"Are you sure?"

"Yes. If someone is dumb enough not to realize my worth, I'm not going to bother."

Row rolled his eyes. Riling them up was actually kind of fun.

"You will not restrict her liberty," Row said.

I shook my head. "She is welcome to walk out of this deal any minute of any day of any hour. She chooses to stay because I pay her mother's way through one of the most expensive experimental programs in the world. Because I burned down the world to secure her spot there. This is a tit-for-tat arrangement. Now, anything else?"

They both shook their heads.

"Very well." I pressed the panic button under my desk and smiled. "Security will usher you outside in about..." I checked my pocket watch. "Five seconds."

Two burly men entered my office and grabbed my so-called friends by their jackets, hurling them out to the hallway.

Good riddance.

CHAPTER TEN
TATE

Kieran: Is it true what they say?

Tate: Yes.

Tate: TBF I don't even think 9 inches is that big a deal. I think it's the girth that made me such a legend in certain female circles.

Kieran: You're forcing Gia to marry you?

Tate: For the last fucking time, no one is forcing her to do anything. I offered her a deal. She took it.

Kieran: Why couldn't you help her from the kindness of your heart?!

Tate: This is not a serious question. Next.

Kieran: You ghoul. Don't bother inviting me to the wedding.

Tate: Suits me. The city hall is not big enough for your ego.

———

The rest of the week unfolded like a multivehicle car crash on a burning fucking bridge.

It started with Gia's replacement, Rebecca. She was barely passable as a part-time PA. Now that Gia wasn't there to clean up her mess, my schedule was in shambles.

My calendar was chaotic, my coffee tasted like sewer water and disappointment, the filing was disorganized, tasks took ages to be completed, and meetings went unrecorded. Many errands were done poorly or forgotten altogether. Everything had to be explained five hundred times. And I had to patiently decline a blow job offer if I got her and her friend good tickets to *Hamilton* ("Before you brush up on your history, learn to use an Excel sheet").

I craved my structure with Gia. Her razor-sharp punctuality. Her ability to predict in advance my schedule commitments, needs, and wants.

But not enough to pardon her from her fate of firing people for a living.

If I couldn't kill her body, at least I'd kill her soul.

I peered on from my office with a scowl as Gia taught Rebecca the ropes with the patience of a saint and the cleavage of a nymph. Yes, she was still getting back at me by wearing next to nothing. I had already fired three men who looked at her the wrong way.

One of them wasn't even my employee.

Trying to teach Rebecca the craft of running a billionaire CEO's life was akin to trying to teach a monkey how to perform open-heart surgery while blindfolded.

While Rebecca's uselessness annoyed me, Gia's elusiveness downright enraged me.

The only time I'd seen my future wife was when she came up to my floor from her new office in HR to help Rebecca extinguish the fires she'd started. I was aware she was living in my penthouse. I had surveillance cameras monitoring the main door. But whenever she was home, she didn't leave her room at all. It infuriated me that this average, ordinary woman didn't make peace with the idea of marrying a handsome fucking billionaire.

Sure, a murderer and an asshole too, but she didn't know about all that.

Fine. She knew about the asshole part.

Hey, no one was perfect.

She could only avoid me for so long. We were scheduled to marry at city hall in two days, come hell or high water.

Rhyland and Row seemed to be giving me the cold shoulder over extorting an innocent woman into marriage. That was rich coming from an asshole chef who fucked his waitress in the kitchen after hours and a gigolo who decided to settle down only after sampling the entire female population of New York.

Tate: You are formally invited to our wedding.

Row: You're fucking high if you think I'm going to stand there and encourage this charade.

Tate: This is foul. I gifted you an Andy Warhol original when you got married.

Row: Yes. Because it was to a willing woman. I didn't hold a gun to her head.

Rhyland: I think you just unleashed an untapped kink for me...

Row: DON'T YOU FUCKING DARE.

Rhyland: I'll come.

Row: The hell you will while pointing a firearm at my sister's head.

Rhyland: I MEAN I'LL COME TO THE WEDDING.

Rhyland: (but now that you've mentioned it, I'll ask her if she is game for the other thing.)

Row: Why?

Rhyland: Because I am an advocate for women's rights and because my sex kinks are none of your business.

Row: No, dickwad, why are you going to the wedding?

Rhyland: Oh. We need to protect Gia at all costs. This wedding is happening whether we approve of it or not. We must monitor him.

Row: You've got a point.

Tate: We've got no wedding registry, but we're partial to dressage Olympic horses, summer houses on the Amalfi Coast, and Amedeo Modigliani art pieces.

Rhyland: You should be happy if I gift you a $20 Amazon GC.

Row: You should be happy if I DON'T gift you a punch.

Last but not least, I received inconvenient news from the Ferrante family.

We were sitting at a round table in a discreet gentleman's club in the bowels of Brooklyn, playing a high-stakes game of Caribbean poker. And by high stakes, I mean Achilles just won a fifteen-year-old undocumented Italian girl. She was weeping in the corner of the room, clutching her wobbly knees to her chest.

"What do you mean, *'shit got messy'*?" I ripped my gaze from my cards, fixing it on Achilles.

"What part of the sentence didn't you understand?" Achilles rolled the tip of his lit cigarette between his fingers, eyes still fixed on his cards. "I can repeat it in Italian or Latin, but if you're dumb, you're dumb. Ain't no cure for that."

The sobbing intensified, grating on my nerves. A slew of teenagers lined the walls here for trade. All from Europe. All the spawns of people who betrayed the Camorra, were indebted to them, or both.

"I thought you said Boyle was unaccounted for. No family, no relatives." My jaw tightened.

I got out of my first kill unscathed. Britain had railed for a few weeks, but the outrage died down when the media found out Boyle was, among other things, a mobster, a rapist, an ex-con, and a shit stain in human form.

"That part's true. What we didn't know was Boyle was the Callaghans' cartel operation driver. He moved shipments around the East Coast," Luca explained, palming a handful of chips and tossing them into the center of the green table. "I raise."

"Who the fuck is Callaghan?" I squinted.

The weeping increased into incontrollable shrieks, and finally, Achilles turned his attention to the corner of the room. "Basta!" he roared in Italian. *Enough.* "No one wants to fuck your ass, least of all me. No. You'll work the kitchen or the stables. No harm will come to you unless you continue giving me a headache, in which case I'll sell you to the Bratva. They will make a rag doll out of you before selling all your internal organs on the black market."

That shut her up quickly. She bit into her arm, squeezing her eyes shut and forcing herself to stay quiet.

Achilles returned his attention to me. "Where were we?"

"Callaghan." I knocked my whiskey back. "Who is he?"

"*They* are the second largest Mafia organization in New York," he provided, spitting his still lit cigarette into the ashtray. He dragged a few towers of chips to the center of the table, matching his brother's raise. "Irish. Capable. Violent. They sent Boyle to England to cool off for a couple months after a few run-ins with the law. He was supposed to come back to oversee a large-scale drug trafficking route."

"Well, that ain't happening anymore," I said dryly. "Why do you allow others to operate in your zip code?"

"Carved out a deal in the early 2000s, and everyone seems to benefit from it. We gave them the rough neighborhoods, so the NYPD can periodically arrest and prison some of their soldiers," Luca explained. "The DA has to hit a certain organized crime quota. Works for both the Irish and the Camorra. They get territory, we get peace of mind."

"Sounds like they're under your rule. Tell them to fuck off."

"It's a gray area. We stay out of their business unless they butt into ours. If you were a camorrista, we'd have more weight to throw. But you're an outsider. Merely a client. And there's another issue. Turns out the rest of your father's murderers are also from the Irish Mob."

"I see a big recruitment day in their near future." I matched Achilles's and Luca's raise with my own chips. "Because I'm not stopping. They'll all pay."

"They know it's you." Luca dragged a rough palm over his stubble. "And they know we're feeding you their names and addresses."

"This a problem for you?" I put my cards down, covering them with my palm. We all had our sleeves rolled up to our elbows, since every single man at this table was a brazen cheater.

"No, asshole. It's a problem for *you*."

"The father, Tyrone, is levelheaded. Used to keep his soldiers on a short leash," Luca explained around a cigarette in his mouth. "But his son, Tiernan, is running the show. He's yet to find a war he didn't want to take part in."

Vello, who was also sitting at the table, tossed his cards to the center of the table. "Fold."

He'd been studying his two sons, trying to gauge who showed more authority and leadership.

"The Irish have been trying to venture out of Hell's Kitchen for years, and they need us content and unbothered. Politics, after all, is the art of the possible. You're another story, though." Achilles snatched a waitress who strutted in his periphery, cementing her into his lap with a slap to her ass. "Tiernan would love nothing more than to add your skull to his collection."

"We all have dreams and aspirations," I drawled. "Underestimating your enemy is a great recipe for getting killed."

Luca scanned me ruefully. "They're a sizable organization. And they have connections. The daughter, Tierney, is friends with First Lady Francesca Keaton."

"How does that give them an edge?" I pleated my brow.

"Tierney's the type of social butterfly that makes shit happen, and Keaton is a sitting president. You could be blacklisted out of most places if she decides to be petty."

"He won't be blacklisted," the brawny errand boy who gave Luca and Achilles the documents the other day said simply. Filippo was sitting next to Achilles, but he did not play. "They'll try to kill him. It'll give them street cred."

"Agreed." Achilles jerked his chin. "Offing a rich, powerful guy? Fucking jackpot. The news would be all over it."

"I have security up the wazoo." I gestured to the two bodyguards manning the door, who were standing very close to the Ferrantes' own security detail. "Doubt they have the stamina to jump through all the hoops necessary to reach me."

"And you don't care much either way," Vello observed in his thick Italian accent.

"No," I agreed. Life was a temporary inconvenience. Though I enjoyed good food, good liquor, and good pussy, I didn't fear death.

"But you have a future wife to think about now," Vello pointed out. "She'll need security too."

"My future wife has nothing to do with this."

Luca shook his head. "Once she becomes your family, she is fair game. You need to make sure she is secured twenty-four seven. We can assign Filippo as her bodyguard. He's our best."

A better man would relieve Gia of her commitment. Let her go. Set her free.

Too bad I wasn't that man.

Nonetheless, I could think of plenty of ideas I liked more than pairing her up with a six-five Italian stud. For instance, ripping out my own testicles and using them as a shower cap.

"No, thank you."

"I'm gay," Filippo said, reading my thoughts. "She'll be safe with me."

"I never pegged her to be dumb enough or you suicidal enough to cross that line." I offered him a mocking smile. "Fine." I tossed an impatient hand. "I'll have her guarded by Filippo and your men. I want them around my building, around my apartment, around her room, *inside* her room. I want them every-fucking-where she goes. Understood?"

They exchanged wry looks.

"Are you catching feelings, Blackthorn?" Luca asked.

"Au contraire." I snarled. "I know how much she loathes the idea of marrying me. Death would be a punishment too light for what she did to me."

Achilles tugged the waitress's top down, examining her bare tits as you would a piece of raw steak before tossing it onto the grill. "I'd ask what she did, but life's too short to pretend to give a shit." He pushed the woman off his lap, waving her away. She didn't make the cut.

"Do you have the Callaghans' ear?" I asked.

"And their other bodily parts, if we wish to own them." Achilles smirked.

"I want you to relay this message to them." I leaned forward. "I am a man of infinite darkness and no shadow. If they so much as breathe in my wife's direction, forget touch, *breathe*, Hell's Kitchen will earn its name. Their businesses will be demolished, their women raped and slaughtered, their children sold off to the highest fucking bidder. It'll make the Battle of Towton look like child's play. I will take no prisoners. There's no red line I wouldn't cross. They better remember that."

Heavy silence fell across the room.

Achilles was the first to speak. A gleam of amusement tinted his onyx eyes. "Message received and will be conveyed. Now, enough chitchat. Let's reveal our hands."

Achilles exposed an impressive flush. Luca spread three of a kind onto the fuzzy emerald table. I took my time before I flipped my cards, unveiling a royal flush.

Vello and Filippo exchanged knowing grins.

"What are the odds?" Vello clucked.

"Did you know that there is a 0.0001 percent probability of

getting a royal flush?" Achilles's low voice skulked out of his mouth, along with cigarette smoke. "If you had that kind of luck, you wouldn't have grown up to be this fucked up."

"It's incredibly convenient," Luca agreed. "Even more so when you consider Blackthorn put his empty glass of whiskey on the credenza behind our backs before the game to act as a mirror so he could see our cards."

I offered them a sly smile but no words.

They saw through my tricks. I found more common ground with them than I did with CEOs and hedge fund managers.

"He won't admit it." Achilles studied me, baring his teeth. "Just as well. I *want* to give him his prize. I've been meaning to get rid of it for a while now."

"The jackpot is all yours." Luca gestured toward a terrified-looking pasty boy, no older than fourteen, who sat in the corner of the room, huddled with the rest of their human currency. "Fresh off an Irish boat and ready to be worked to the bone."

I took one quick glance at the child. "Throw him in a boarding school. I'll collect him when he matures. I've no use for him now."

The kid belched and hiccupped with relief.

I turned to him, raising my finger in warning. "Study hard. Don't do drugs. Do not fucking contact me unless you're bleeding out. Do you have a family?"

He shook his head hysterically.

"You can't spend the holidays with me," I announced dryly.

He nodded.

"What's your name?" I demanded.

"Brayden."

"I'll see you when you're eighteen, Brayden."

Luca tapped his chin, still mulling the game over. "That royal flush of yours, Blackthorn. Make sure it doesn't happen again. We're men of honor, and when you betray us, we become very unfriendly."

"What can I say?" I stood up, snapping my fingers. One of my bodyguards hurried with my coat, ready for me to slip into. "I'm a lucky bastard."

CHAPTER ELEVEN
TATE

I watched Gia in the surveillance camera app as she yet again slinked into the building at midnight, silent and sleek like a cat. She hugged a brown paper bag to her chest, tiptoeing her way in.

I did not like unprofitable deals.

As far as this one went, I wanted my fucking money back. Not only had I lost a competent secretary, but I saw my so-called fiancée less than ever. She avoided me like the plague. Which left me no choice but to consume her like an infectious disease.

Setting my phone down, I turned off all the lights in the apartment and waited in the shadows.

I heard the mechanical lock of my door turn. She stepped inside, careful not to make a sound.

"Only thieves and cheaters sneak up at night," my voice boomed in the complete darkness of the living room. I was sprawled on the antique settee she had purchased. "Let's hope for your sake you're neither. I'd hate for your mother to lose her child during such...*turbulent* times."

"Jesus." She jumped back, dropping the brown paper bag and a pair of heels from her hands.

I watched the industrial snacks she'd bought roll on the floor. I had four fridges, a pantry the size of Buckingham Palace, and two chefs on my payroll, and this idiot was living off prehistoric Rice Krispies from the bodega downstairs.

"Wrong man," I announced. "I won't die for your sins, but I'm happy to introduce you to some fun ones."

"What a tantalizing offer." Crouching down, she hurriedly collected her woeful dinner. "If only I were into megalomaniacal wankers."

I clapped twice, turning on the main chandelier. Light flooded the room. Gia squinted, her eyes readjusting. I stood up and sauntered over to her, taking her in. It'd been a few days since I'd gotten a good look at her. It left me feeling resentful and on edge. I'd been cracking those math equations more often than I liked to admit. My numbers fascination got so bad I started counting sand grains in an hourglass.

Her high ponytail was sleek at the front and flipped out at the end, like a pinup girl. She styled her edges in soft swirls to frame her forehead, which I itched to trace with my fingers. Her makeup was dewy and soft. She always looked like she spent her nights sleeping inside rose petals.

She wore a practical woolly office dress and a resigned expression. At least she'd stopped dressing like a call girl.

I knew she was dealing with a lot of bullshit after our surprise engagement announcement. The office had been standoffish and suspicious of her, thinking we'd kept our relationship a secret so they'd confide in her. Rumors swirled that I had impregnated her, a reason for our hasty marriage.

I was probably the last person she wanted to see, and I could not find it in myself to care.

"Care to explain what you're doing every day until midnight?" I stuffed my fists into my pockets.

Filippo and the rest of the Ferrante guards were due to arrive tomorrow morning, and I was in a prickly mood. I knew she'd buck at the new arrangement.

"Not that it's your business, but I spend time with my mother every night." She tipped her chin up, giving me the frostiest, most repulsed expression in her arsenal.

Now came the part where I was supposed to ask how her mother was doing. Not because I cared, God forbid. If she died, the deal was off.

But I had bigger fish to fry.

"Have you purchased a wedding dress yet?"

"With what time exactly?" She shuffled junk food back into her bag. "I work two jobs since you transferred me to HR and assigned me to teach Rebecca the craft."

"I'll have a wedding gown sent your way tomorrow. I'm flying to Geneva for an eight-hour meeting tonight."

"I'll pray for a hurricane."

"I'll be here in time for the wedding." I ignored her sarcasm.

"Don't be so sure. Tomorrow is never guaranteed. A lot can happen between today and Thursday."

"That's true. Which brings me to our next subject." My jaw locked. "A minor complication arose in one of my dealings. The Irish Mafia is after my throat. You'll need to walk around with security until I take care of this."

Gia's face contorted in abhorrence. "I beg your pardon?"

"Bodyguards, Gia. They're about to follow that perfect ass of yours everywhere you go. Work, social outings, gym, bathroom. You name it. It's for your own protection." A carnal need to touch her slammed into me. To bury my hand inside that perfect, naturally curly hair she always kept neatly straightened and devour that lovely mouth that curled in disgust every time I was in the same room with her.

I wanted to taste her hatred of me. To roll it on my tongue. To devour her desperation to escape me.

"Mafia, Tate? Really?" She blinked, stunned.

I said nothing.

"What have you done now?"

I just smirked. She didn't really expect me to confide in her, did she?

"Well, no." She stepped back, shaking her head. "Out of the question. I will not be babysat."

"Which part of the conversation made you think this was up for discussion?" My brows furrowed in confusion.

"The part where as an independent woman, I will not revert back to the Middle Ages because you cocked up a deal."

"You're free to do whatever you want," I said calmly. "With the exception of dying in the hands of mobsters to prove a point. See, I don't like it when a business partner fucks me over. And as far as our transaction goes, you're currently pounding into me lube-less."

"Of course it's all monetary for you," she muttered. She snatched her purse from the floor, turned around, and charged back to the door.

I had no choice but to clasp her by the waist and jerk her to me. Her ass collided with my crotch. A low growl escaped me. I was already hard just from talking to her. Now I was ramrod straight, throbbing and lightheaded with lack of blood flow to my brain. She tried to wiggle out of my touch and run to the door. I tightened my hold on her, my cock pressed between her lovely ass cheeks through our clothes.

"Now, now, Apricity. I'd strongly advise you stop squirming before my cock bursts out on its own accord and gives your ass the spanking it truly deserves," I whispered into the shell of her ear.

She froze, every muscle in her body stiffening.

I did not like scaring her.

The realization slammed into me like a freight train.

I usually took great pleasure at terrifying people.

But I needed her attention, and if that meant scaring her a little so she'd understand the graveness of the situation, so be it.

My arms circled her waist and shoulders, blocking her from escaping. I could feel her heart pounding through the fabric of her dress fast and hard.

"I hate you," she whispered.

"Your tight nipples against my forearms are telling me a different story."

"I'm scared and in shock. That doesn't mean I fancy you."

"But you do fancy me." My hand slipped from her waist and along her inner thigh, traveling up and dipping under her skirt. My thumb caressed her skin. "I bet if I dip my fingers into your pussy, I'll find it wet and ready for me," I croaked into her ear.

She shivered with anger and pleasure. She was too proud to say no. And I was too much of a fuckup to give up this opportunity.

"Hmm?" I hummed into the side of her neck, breathing her in. "Yes or no? Should we test the theory that you're attracted to me?"

"Sure," she croaked, trying to appear casual. "Your scare tactics never worked on me."

I had to bite the hem of her blouse to suppress a moan as my fingers traveled up her thighs. I wasn't going to show her how much I craved this. Not when my balls were already tight, my cock twitchy, leaking precum. I grazed her satin underwear, slipped my index finger into her, and found her hot and dripping for me. So warm. So soft. Her hips bucked instinctively, searching for more. My eyes rolled inside their sockets. It took everything in me to leisurely remove my finger from her tight pussy, raising it to her lips, clinging to my composure. "Why don't you taste for yourself and tell me what you think?"

I dipped my juice-coated finger into her mouth. Her pretty lips wrapped around it, her mouth hot and inviting, and I shuddered, pushing another finger into her mouth, filling it while imagining it was my cock.

She bit my finger until she hit bone, then pressed on, drawing more and more blood.

Groaning, I yanked my finger away but tightened my hold on the rest of her when she tried running. "*Fuck.*"

"You ridiculous twat." She laughed metallically. "You really thought I was going to fall for your broody billionaire bullshit, didn't you?"

That was it. I wrapped my arm around her throat and used my free hand to tug out my phone. I went through my photo album and shoved a picture in front of her face.

"See this?" I snarled, my finger dripping blood all over the floor. "This is what happened to the last person who fucked with Tiernan Callaghan."

The image was readily available on the internet from a news piece I'd read earlier. The man had been chopped up and scattered on tree branches.

Gia stopped struggling to free herself, sucking in a surprised breath.

"Now, if I let go, will you run?" I croaked into her ear.

Goose bumps pebbled her skin. Christ, she was responsive. I wanted to offer her something obscene to lie down and open those legs for me. But Gia was the only woman I knew whose affection could not be bought. The math equation I had yet to solve.

She was silent for a beat before murmuring, "Probably. Better you keep me constrained for this conversation. Not that the outcome will change."

She wanted more of my touch. I closed my eyes, breathing her in. Her Tom Ford perfume and a concoction of body oils she put on every night before bed.

"Callaghan wants my throat," I reiterated.

"So does the rest of the world, I'm sure," she sighed. "What did you do now?"

"Not important. What's important is that you're an extension of me now, whether you like it or not. If they catch you, they will kidnap you, rape you, sever pieces of your body, before I'll have to pay a hefty amount of ransom to get you back. You don't want that."

"There are a lot of things I don't want," she spat out, her ass inadvertently wiggling against my cock again. "You're at the top of that list, by the way. Being followed around by musclemen is a close second. If they come for me, I'll handle it. I won't live like a prisoner. Let me go."

"No."

She elbowed my ribs, which hardly left a dent, but raising her heeled foot and jamming it against my shin did the trick. I released her on instinct. She grabbed her purse and supermarket bag, stomping to the door.

"No bodyguards." She pointed at me in warning. "If they chop off a few of my limbs, you'll only have yourself to blame. Next time, don't mess with the Irish Mafia, Tate."

"You're being ungrateful."

"Ungrateful?" she choked out, enraged. "The Mafia is after me because of *you.*"

"And I'm pulling all my resources to protect you from them. Really, you should be on your knees servicing me for taking such good care of you." I lost the last morsel of patience I had for this woman. "No man I know would hire an entire SWAT team to protect a fiancée who hates him."

"No bodyguards," she repeated stubbornly, peering between the door and me.

"You walk out that fucking door," I warned, "and I'm sending both you and your mother back to Britain."

With a groan of frustration, she breezed toward her bedroom, crashing her bag against my shoulder on her way there. I followed her, tapping at my side furiously.

Two, six, two.

Two, six, two.

Two, six, two.

I didn't fucking care if she noticed anymore. She'd find out sooner or later.

"If they chop off your good parts and send them to me in the mail, I'm not going to pay ransom to retrieve you," I needled as I stalked her to her room.

"Good!" She slammed the door in my face, shouting through the wooden barrier. "Losing a few fingers is a small price to pay to relieve myself of you."

"You will never be relieved of me," I said to the door.

Since when did I speak to fucking inanimate objects? I hadn't let anyone treat me this way, not since Andrin. This transaction was taking on a bizarre path, and I was going to put a stop to this chaos.

I tapped the side of my thigh furiously, numbers and variables swimming in my head. "I will chase you to the end of the earth and beyond. No force in the world can keep me from you. I have earned your company fairly. The sooner you accept there is no way out of this arrangement, the better."

No answer.

She had won this round. Forcing her into walking around with security would push her over the edge, and I wanted to lure her back into the safe zone. To the place where she'd let her guard down, open her legs for me, and give me what she owed me—offspring. A family. An heir.

"They'll kill you." I drove my fist to the door, cracking it.

"Sounds like a plan. If I die, you're not invited to the funeral."

My jet was fueled and ready to take off in forty minutes for Europe, and I was standing here bickering with a woman nine years my junior, trying to convince her not to get murdered.

"I'll be gone for less than forty hours." I braced my elbows on either side of her door. "You're not to move out of this fucking apartment until I'm back. I'll be here Thursday, by three p.m. I'll expect you to be waiting for me in a wedding gown and with a much better attitude. Is that clear?"

No answer.

I could punch this door down. Break it. Scare her even more. I could remind her that I held the key to her mother's destiny.

I could.

But as a man accustomed to moving in the darkness, I had good instincts, and my instincts told me to stop pushing.

I turned around and stomped away.

CHAPTER TWELVE
GIA

The clock said three forty-five.

I wrung my fingers together, unfurled them, then dragged my sweaty palms along the pearl-white satin of my gown. My stomach churned with a mixture of anxiety, panic, and trepidation.

Tate was late. Very late.

Our appointment at city hall was an hour away, and he still wasn't here.

I knew my boss like the back of my hand, and though he was an arsehole of massive proportions, he was incredibly punctual.

"We can clear up all this second-guessing if you pick up the phone and call him," Cal pointed out gently, standing above me. She dragged a soft bristle brush along my scalp before repeating the movement with a hair wax stick across my dark, straightened hair. I'd had no time to book hair and makeup, so Cal watched a tutorial on how to give me an updo before coming here, because my hands were shaking too badly. She was doing a fine job at it too.

Despite resembling my fair mother quite a bit, I'd inherited my father's hair. Growing up, I often wished my hair was thinner, straighter, more manageable. Now, it felt like a gift. A way of seeing my precious, terribly missed dad who passed away too young.

"I'm not calling him." I crossed my arms and scowled at the mirror in front of me. "It's in my interest that he doesn't show up."

"I doubt he got cold feet, girlie," Dylan said behind us, breaking in a pair of white glitter pumps for me by walking across the room. "He seems like a man on a mission."

The heels were sent by Tate yesterday, along with the dress, a bouquet, and some jewelry.

I was surprised the delivery guy had made it to the door. Even though I told Tate I would not tolerate any security, I had spotted Row and Rhyland patrolling the building hourly. I'd be touched if I didn't know he was mainly preoccupied with my uterus, which he needed for producing an heir.

"I mean, he has snipers on rooftops around your building." Dylan withdrew the curtain an inch, peering through the window.

"He *what?*" I stood up, advancing toward the window. Cal stumbled back at the sudden movement. I leaned against the thick glass, my mouth falling open. Since the penthouse was considerably higher than other buildings, I could clearly see black-uniformed men in position on a few rooftops with their rifles directed at the reception of our place. "Christ!"

I grabbed my phone and texted him. I wouldn't give him the pleasure of asking when he was coming. Instead, I snapped a picture of the snipers and sent it to him.

Gia: I said no security.

His response came a few seconds later.

Tate: You said no bodyguards. This is the NYPD.

Gia: ???

Tate: Mayor owes me a favor.

I took a deep breath and bit my tongue, waiting for him to explain his delay. He didn't, of course. How could I expect decency from a man who had poison running through his veins?

As soon as I plopped back into my seat, Cal resumed tugging, teasing, and brushing my hair. I closed my eyes, fingering my junonia shell bracelet. I wasn't sure if I was angrier at him for forcing me into this wedding or because he was dreadfully late for it.

"Care to explain why you have so much security?" Dylan cleared her throat.

"Yeah. Row and Rhy have been checking on your building every hour." Cal furrowed her brow.

"Tate had a run-in with the Irish Mafia. He received a hot tip that I might be targeted."

Dylan and Cal exchanged horrified looks.

"I'm sorry, what?" Dylan paled. "That's insane."

"So is Tate," I said.

"What did he do?" Cal shrieked.

I shook my head. "He wouldn't tell me."

Cal looked ready to throw up.

"It's fine," I tried to reassure her. "I'm sure it's nothing. Tate has dealt with plenty of disgruntled people in his career."

Cal dropped her hands to my shoulders, massaging them. "Chin up. We're here. We'll let no harm come to you."

"Tate wouldn't let anything bad happen to you either." Dylan inserted a glass of champagne between my fingers. "That man can talk about how much he hates you all day, but he'd go to war for you."

I didn't disagree with her. He *was* obsessed with me. But it didn't mean he loved or even cared for me.

"I haven't slept in two days," I hiccupped, taking a sip of my champagne.

"Why?" Dylan settled at my feet, circling her arms around my thighs and perching her chin on my knees. "I thought you came to terms with the marriage?"

We'd been having daily conversations about doomsday, a.k.a. my wedding day.

"I did." Another hiccup bubbled out of me. I gulped more champagne. Alcohol was probably not a good idea, but I needed something to take the edge off. "But I can't help but feel sorry for myself that Mum won't be attending. The clinic said she is not in any condition to go somewhere new. I won't have a single member of my family with me."

"You'll have *us*." Cal squeezed my shoulders, her gaze meeting mine in the mirror. "We're your family now."

"Yeah, we're your ride or die, bitch." Dylan winked.

I reached to hold Cal's fingertips. "Thank you," I mouthed. "But it's not just that. Ever since Tate transferred me to the HR department, I've been under the weather. Even today, when I worked from home, I had to fire four people via Zoom. It was dreadful. Some of them have families to feed. One of them was a single mum." I pressed my lips together. "The single mum…I couldn't do it. I hired her myself to help me out with Mum. Running errands, doing her nails… It's not even her profession, though. She's a bloody IT technician."

"You're doing the best you can under the circumstances," Cal assured me.

"And you'll find a way to navigate through all this." Dylan plucked my heels from her feet and screwed them onto mine. "You always do."

A few minutes later, Cal left my room to go check on Serafina, her daughter. Then, five minutes after, Dylan got a text from Rhyland to come to the lower floor of the penthouse. Apparently, their daughter, Gravity, accidentally knocked over a two-million-dollar statue in the living room.

"Excuse me. I have to go make a scene." Dylan kissed my forehead, shaking her head on her way out.

For the first time today, I was all alone.

I glanced at the time on my phone. Quarter past four. We weren't going to make it to our appointment.

I didn't even want to marry the blasted man, but the sheer disrespect of it had me reeling. I stared at myself in the mirror, all made up for a clinical, sham wedding.

I tore the expensive gown from my body, the satisfying sound of fine fabric ripping filling my ears. I threw my closet open and chose the most outrageous pieces of clothing I owned. A pair of tiny Daisy Dukes I had purchased on a holiday in the Bahamas a few years ago and a tacky Disney World sweatshirt that matched my college friends from our graduation trip.

I polished off the rest of the champagne and cried myself to sleep.

"Wake up."

I knew that voice. It starred in my fantasies and haunted me in my nightmares. Husky. Menacing. Wry as an old bone.

I kept my eyes shut for the sole purpose of provoking him.

"What are you wearing?" he growled, his voice dripping disdain.

I let my eyes flutter open. Tate sat on the edge of my bed, wearing a full-blown tux, his hair freshly cut. He was so handsome he made my heart liquify.

"What's the time?" I asked groggily.

He pulled his phone out, scowling at it. "Nine thirty-two."

"At night?"

His flat gaze told me the question was stupid and beneath him.

"Oh." I sat up straight, immediately perking. "That means the wedding is canceled. Or at the very least delayed! We didn't make it. I—"

"The wedding's happening," he countered. "Thanks to your prayers and well-wishes, my plane had a landing gear issue, and we were stranded in London for a few hours. But I managed to sweet-talk the city clerk into opening the hall for us. Get up. We're late."

"What?" I rubbed my fists over my eyes, ruining my eye makeup. "Tate, we can't get married today. I'm not—"

"You have five minutes."

"That's not enough time for me to get ready." I gestured to

my outfit, ruined makeup, and hair, which I had not wrapped in a protective bonnet prior to falling asleep spontaneously.

"I see." He stroked his chin.

I nodded, exhaling in relief. "We'll have to resch—"

"Guess you're marrying in it." He stood up brusquely, buttoning his jacket with one hand. "I'll wait in the living room. Row, Rhyland, and their respective headaches are still here. Witnesses," he explained tersely.

"You can't give me a sixty-second notice and expect me to be at your beck and call."

"Can't I?" He rubbed his knuckles over his sternum. "Funny, it seems to be exactly what I'm doing right now."

Springing up to my feet, I did something I'd never done before. I raised my open palm and tried to slap him.

He caught my wrist in his big hand before it reached his cheek. Slowly, he brought my knuckles to his mouth, brushing his hot, soft lips over them, his eyes boring into my own. "My regal ice queen. Were you worried I wasn't going to come?"

"You aren't *going* to come," I said, deadpan. "Unless you use your hand. This marriage won't be consummated."

"Oh, I'll come." He dragged his straight teeth over my knuckles ever so gently, making my skin tingle and sticky warm honey pool between my legs. "So will you. Multiple times each encounter, in fact. Making heirs with you will be a pleasure."

Every functioning brain cell in my head screamed at me to pull away, but my traitorous body remained still, letting him pepper soft, feathery kisses on the back of my hand. Kisses that felt like velvety butterfly wings flapping over my flesh, all while maintaining eye contact.

"I'd have made it to this wedding today if I had to swim my way from England."

"But…why?"

"Because you're the only thing I've ever wanted and couldn't buy," he admitted earnestly. "And because I'm utterly consumed by the idea of destroying your life, sweetheart."

He dropped my hand, stepping away from me and waltzing to the door.

"Twenty-two seconds, Gia."

What?

Bollocks. He tricked me. I didn't think our conversation ate into my preparation time.

He slinked away like the night, the echo of his kisses still dancing over my skin.

CHAPTER THIRTEEN
GIA

City hall was empty other than our guests. It was ten o'clock at night, and the place felt ominous without human traffic.

"Oh, to be young and in hate again." Dylan clucked her tongue in my periphery, dabbing her eyes with tissue. "Remember when we hated each other, Rhy?"

"I never hated you for real." Rhyland kissed her temple. "And we never tried to kill or blackmail each other into marriage."

"I'm sorry your relationship is bland and boring like yourself—" Tate started, then sighed. "Fuck, I'm not even going to finish this sentence. It's a lie. I'm not sorry at all. You deserve one another."

Our witnesses included Row, Rhyland, Cal, and Dylan but also Tate's two bodyguards and all the men in the Ferrante family. Vello, Luca, Achilles, and Enzo. No doubt here to monitor, not celebrate.

Just how deep into shit had Tate gotten us with the New York Mafia?

The clerk inspected me through the thick rims of his ancient reading glasses, fluffy silver eyebrows hitting his nonexistent hairline. "My dear, are you sure you're...*prepared?*" His polite way of asking why I was wearing Daisy Dukes and a decade-old hoodie with holes in it. Tate, by comparison, was impeccably dressed, tailored to the last inch of his damn immoral soul.

"As prepared as I'll ever be." Lack of enthusiasm dripped from my voice. I'd be lying if I said I didn't derive some satisfaction from knowing it infuriated Tate to see me like this. Sloppy and unmade.

The clerk's brow crumpled further. "Miss, are you being coerced to—"

"Less talking, more marrying us." Tate snapped his fingers. "At this rate, I'll be your age by the time I wed."

We signed the paperwork, answered the clerk's questions, all the while not even looking at each other.

The wedding being lackluster wasn't surprising to me. What I didn't expect was for Tate to accept a work call *during* the ceremony.

"What is it?" I heard him ask just as the clerk was going through the final technicalities. I saw Row and Rhyland exchange exasperated glances, shaking their heads. Dylan balled her hands into fists, ready to physically assault my husband-to-be.

"We're kind of in the middle of something." I felt my face blistering with heat, still staring at the clerk. "Can't it wait?"

"No." Tate produced an AirPod from his pocket, tucking it into his ear. "It's the Geneva client. He wants to pull out of the deal. I'm going to take this." Tate pointed at his phone, pinning the clerk with a glare. "When I'm back, you'll cut through the red tape bullshit and seal the deal."

He left me standing there, shooting embarrassed smiles at our witnesses, mumbling my apologies. He strolled in leisurely twenty minutes later like nothing happened. My pulse hitched at the sight of him. I was so furious, I was surprised I didn't burst into flames.

"Where were we?" Tate tucked his phone into his pocket, glancing between me and the clerk.

"You were getting married, sir." The elderly clerk pushed his reading glasses up his nose with his middle finger. "And making a spectacle of the ceremony, if I may add."

"You may not," Tate said genially.

It took sheer resilience and all my restraint to go along with the wedding. The entire time, I reminded myself that I was doing it for

Mum, saving what was left of my family. Tate continued texting his clients in Geneva throughout, ignoring everyone in the room. I felt small and insignificant. A mere comma in somebody else's story.

And then it was over. The papers had been signed. Vows were exchanged. Consent was given. Rings slid onto fingers.

We were husband and wife.

The clerk stood up and waddled his way to the door, shaking his head. Tate turned to face me.

"Iven'll drive you home. I'm going to the Ferrantes' to play some cards."

I spun on my heel and burst out of the room before he had time to take a good look at my face.

He could have my future, but he'd never have my tears.

CHAPTER FOURTEEN
TATE

Usually runaway brides ditched their grooms *before* the ceremony.

My wife was more creative than that, though.

Gia wasn't in an agreeable mood. I followed her at a careful distance, cloaked by the night. What a pitiful creature. Not a single woman in the entire fucking GS Properties building who wouldn't be ecstatic to take her place, and here she was, making a spectacle out of both of us.

She wandered aimlessly through the frosty streets of New York in her tiny shorts and hoodie. It was relatively warm for February, but I still didn't like her chances of catching pneumonia. If she knew I was following her, she didn't give it away. My wife of ten minutes peered into bars and restaurants longingly, eyes halting on couples walking with their hands entwined.

How unreasonable of her to be mad that I was late, considering my plane was stranded. Equally unreasonable of her to expect I wouldn't take an important business call, as I'd taken board meetings while buried in women's pussies before.

I couldn't believe she made me succumb to stalking her in full wedding attire in the middle of the fucking night.

She was so much work, I briefly considered asking her for a salary with full health benefits.

Eventually, the streets converged, and she edged into Times Square, blending in with the crowd.

Smart girl, I thought with satisfaction. Gia knew she was a target, so she wanted to disappear. She purposely walked into a sea of tourists, bought herself an ice cream, and stopped to look at Broadway schedules in a well-lit corner of the street.

It was two thirty in the morning when she decided to call it a night. She walked briskly toward the street, tugging her phone out of her hoodie's pocket, likely to order an Uber. She lowered her gaze to the screen and stopped at the curb.

In a flash, a nondescript black sedan pulled in front of her, camouflaged by the darkness. No license plate. Tinted windows. A burly man wearing all black charged out of the back seat. He balled her hoodie in his fist, pulling her into the car.

My whole world turned red.

I tore off toward them, ramming into his side with my shoulder, angling myself in a way that ensured I cracked a couple of ribs. He exploded with profanities, his accent unmistakably Irish, stumbling down the pavement. Gia tripped backward while I straightened him by the collar, jamming him against the car. I could hear the driver inside speaking frantically on the phone, begging for instructions. The muscle man in front of me was middle-aged and pasty. No doubt a simple soldier.

I seized his left arm and twisted it until the sound of bone snapping echoed between the buildings, then grabbed the car's door and smashed it into the injured area, handcuffing him with one arm trapped by the door. He folded in two, delirious with pain. I kneed his chin, and his head snapped up. Blood gushed from his mouth.

I wanted only one thing more than breaking his spine in two. And that thing was for Gia's clit to rub my nose as I ate her out, which was why I refrained from killing him right in front of her stunned eyes.

"Who sent you?" I grabbed him by the hair, tilting his purple, battered face to me. I already knew, but I wanted the admission.

If this beef was out in the open, Tiernan Callaghan wouldn't be the only one doing the chasing.

The man pressed his lips together defiantly, chin trembling and dribbling blood. I opened the door that clasped his arm, gaining momentum and slamming it again over boneless, torn flesh. He let out a piercing scream that landed nowhere.

"Let's try again." I tugged his hair roughly, ripping a few patches from his scalp. "Next time you don't answer, I'll amputate your limb clean from the rest of your useless body. Who sent you?"

"*Th*iernan Callaghan!" He spat blood, falling to his knees, his arm still wedged between the car and the door. By the way he was slurring, I could tell he'd likely bitten off a part of his tongue. "Feck, who elth?" he lisped.

I wasn't going to kill him. Tiernan was going to do it anyway for snitching. Instead, I used him as pigeon post.

"Tell Tiernan next time he comes for my wife, I'll dismember every single person he ever cared about and send him their organs at random to piece together as a puzzle. Would you like that in writing?"

"N-no." He writhed, trying to squirm away from the pain. "Goddamn your thoul to hell. Let me go!"

I opened the door again, shoved him in, and kicked it shut. I banged the roof. "Send word to your boss. *Now.*"

The car careened forward, leaving skid marks in its wake.

A soft whimper sounded behind me. I swiveled in its direction, finding Gia pressing her knuckles to her mouth. She trembled, her eyes wide and haunted. I noticed for the first time that she was bleeding. He must've caught her cheek and split it open when he struggled to shove her into the car.

I instinctively put my thumb to the injured spot to assess the bruise. She sucked in a breath and recoiled. It was a shallow cut. Barely even a scratch. That realization did nothing to calm down my hammering pulse.

Two, six, two.

Two, six, two.

Two, six, two.

They fucking hurt my wife. *My wife.* Nobody touched what was mine.

"Are you hurt anywhere else?" I asked tersely.

She shook her head, hands flying to my shoulders. I caught her waist, steadying her. She was hysterical, the waves of adrenaline still crashing through her.

"H-h-he," she started but didn't finish the sentence. Her fists crashed into my chest, a sob ripping from the depth of her lungs. I'd never seen her cry before.

"I know." I pulled her by the back of her head to my chest, engulfing her with my entire body. I wanted to protect her and kill her in the same breath. I'd never met a woman so insolent, so independent, so completely unmanageable, and fuck my life, but it made me want her even more. She was categorically unattainable, even after I put a goddamn ring on it.

"What you did to him…" Her eyes ran wildly in their sockets. "It was…it was—"

"Warranted," I growled. "He tried to *kidnap* you."

Gia was too gentle, too straitlaced to witness this kind of violence. I wagered she couldn't hurt a fly. If she did, she'd probably usher it to the vet for medical attention.

She was shaking in my arms like a coin inside an empty tin. I clenched my teeth, my blood roaring in my veins. "This is precisely why you need security," I scolded her.

"Do you carry a weapon?" She tilted her face up to look at me.

"I *am* the weapon." Guns were for pussies. And irrefutably less fun than good ole spine breaking. "You, however, need security. I'm calling Achilles right n—"

"I–I can't breathe," she muttered into my chest. "I think I'm having a panic attack. Distract me."

"The hell I will. Reap what you sow. This could've ended in catastrophe," I chided her. "Starting tomorrow, you will be surrounded with enough bodyguards to last a—"

She snapped her head up and pressed her lips to mine. My brain short-circuited.

What the fuck was happening?

She is kissing you.

And you are standing there.

Scowling.

While her lips are moving against yours.

Her mouth was intense and pleading on mine, cold from the ice cream and the night. Sweet and exquisite and unbearably soft. My mouth finally snapped into action.

The entire world crumbled around us like ancient ruins, and all that was left was the pressure of our lips on each other and the sound of her ragged, desperate breaths. She opened her mouth, and the sweetness of it un-fucking-did me. Whatever scathing words I had for her were swallowed by her pretty, pliant lips. Our tongues met awkwardly, stroking and exploring one another for the first time. Then she sucked my tongue into her mouth, and my knees fucking buckled. This wasn't a kiss between two grown-ups declaring their intentions but a teenager's kiss, clumsy and desperate and all-consuming. With complete abandon.

It shouldn't feel this dirty. This dangerous. We were adults. And *married*. But it hit different all the same.

My arms wrapped around her tighter, and she sank into my frame, melting into it. I drew the tip of her tongue into my mouth, sucking it, and she sighed and moaned, and there was not enough of her. Not nearly enough. Not *ever* enough.

My shaft leeched to my thigh, my cock erect and begging for space in my tight-fitting slacks.

Two minutes ago, I wanted her like I wanted the sun. An erratic, prideful desire to own something exquisite and special. Now, I wanted her like I did my next breath. In a dull, unrelenting despair that consumed me.

The kiss deepened, becoming more frantic and demanding. I threaded my fingers along her cheeks and temples, drawing her closer. I played dirty, capitalizing on her heat and confusion. I chafed the fabric of her stupid shirt and hoodie over her nipples with my chest, making them sensitive and raw.

Gia gasped, her hands roaming my body sloppily, frantically. Precum gathered at the tip of my cock as I let her explore. She cupped my ass, ran her fingers along my back, my abs, my chest.

It was entirely possible I was going to die from desire.

A chance I was more than willing to take.

"Will you tell me your name?" she hedged, her lips moving over my own. "Your real name, so I know who I'm kissing."

Her words were a bucket of ice water, drenching both of us. I ripped my mouth from hers, stepping back. "Stay in your lane, Gia."

"Our lanes merged, you fool." She narrowed her eyes at me. "When we said our vows earlier tonight."

I stared at her from a safe distance, panting like I'd just run a marathon. Her lips were swollen and raw.

What the *fuck* just happened?

This wasn't a kiss. I knew, because I'd kissed enough women in my life to file the experience under inadequate. Something I needed to do in order to hit the home run.

This was...this was...

"Come here," I growled, rushing back to her, bending my head down, claiming her mouth harder and faster now. She gasped when our teeth clashed, when our tongues shared the taste of her ice cream and my brandy once more. Good. Fantastic. Fucking wonderful. Was this a trick? A spell? What was her recipe for this...this...

"Your name." Now it was her turn to end the kiss abruptly.

I glowered at her. "It'd take much more than a fucking kiss to make me tell you that."

Growling, she glued her lips to mine. We kissed again.

No one was privy to my real name. That boy was buried right along with my past. My hand molded over her ass, the ass I'd glared at for years when I knew she wasn't looking. Through shades. When I opened doors for her to meetings. When I berated her for no good reason at all.

"Bedroom," I found my voice somewhere in the back of my throat.

She broke the kiss breathlessly. It took me a few seconds to catch up with that fact. My faculties were scattered like clothes on a teenage girl's bedroom floor. It took another two seconds to register the cold, metallic edge kissing an artery in my neck and the fact that Gia was holding the small pocketknife I took with me everywhere. She must've fished it out of my pocket when she roamed my body.

Her eyes danced like two flames, her gaze finding my own.

Joke's on you, Apricity. Now I'm even harder.

"No bodyguards," she said evenly. "You got us into this mess, you will get us out of it. You want me to be protected, you protect me. You've shown great capability tonight. Am I understood?"

I stared, mesmerized. I'd never been this attracted to someone. To some*thing*. I couldn't wait to fuck her. To watch this strong, beautiful woman taking my cock in her mouth. In her pussy. In her ass, *maybe.*

I was sick with want.

"Well?" She applied a little pressure with the knife, just enough to tease my skin but not to break it.

"I accept your terms," I said coolly. It was the first time I'd been blackmailed in my entire life, and I enjoyed it immensely. "But I will shadow you everywhere you go. Work. Gym. Your mother's. No more avoidance, Gia," I warned. "You're mine, and you're going to act like it. Am *I* understood?"

"Crystal clear."

When I got home, I rushed to the office and closed the door. I could still feel her pulsating all over my skin. Her scent, her mouth, the knife.

I called Rebecca, the least useful creature in all of New York, other than maybe sewer rats.

"Sir?" she asked in confusion. "Is everything okay?"

Was it? A lot had happened in the last few hours.

Wedding.

Irish mobster.

Gia hurt.

Kiss.

Kiss.

Kiss.

I hadn't been this affected when, two years ago, I mounted three *Sports Illustrated* models on top of one another and fucked them from behind simultaneously, slamming into a different hole each time.

"Cancel all my meetings for today," I choked out. It was a Friday, one of my busiest days, as I chased tail ends before the weekend rolled in. But I knew I wouldn't be productive today.

I hung up, cracked open six math books, and solved equations and followed rituals the entire day to soothe myself back into breathing normally again. I needed to count sand grains and windows on skyscrapers and letters in thick books. I needed numbers to not feel twitchy and anxious and on edge.

Another one of Dr. Patel's emails popped on my phone's screen, as though he was reading my mind.

From: Dr. Arjun Patel, MD
(arjunpatel@stjohnsmedical.com)

To: Tate Blackthorn
(willnotanswerunsolicitedemails@GSproperties.com)

Subject: Re: re: re: re: re: re: Reschedule Meeting

Tate, please. You're dealing with multiple issues. I can help.

I hit Delete.

I was beyond redemption.

I spiraled into my own pitch-black mind.

CHAPTER FIFTEEN
GIA

I put the toilet seat down and sat primly on top of it, unfurling the wrapper of my chicken Caesar wrap.

Taking my lunch in the toilets of the HR department's floor was ridiculous, but I didn't have any choice. I had become a social pariah at GS Properties.

It started with the surprise announcement that I was engaged to Tate, which felt like betrayal to all the coworkers I'd been close with. They'd become enraged by my hypocrisy and left letters on my desk calling me a double agent and a Jezebel.

I'd gone from being one of the most loved employees in the company to public enemy number one overnight. Between firing people at my new position and marrying our dictator CEO, my colleagues' opinion about me changed drastically.

I could feel their eyes following me like the barrel of a gun trained on a gazelle.

Today reigned already as the lousiest workday recorded on earth, after being creepily stalked across town by my husband and then kissed to the point of toe curling by the man I hated. My lips still tingled every time I thought about that kiss.

I couldn't face the public humiliation of taking my lunch alone, at my desk, knowing everyone around me hoped I'd choke and expire on it.

Sighing, I balled the empty wrapper in my fist and smoothed out my tweed dress. I stood up, unlatching the door's lock when the clicks of Mary Janes echoed across the restroom. I stilled. The sound of compact makeup mirrors popping open filled the air.

"Ohmigod, I literally cannot *stand* her." The voice of the payroll administrator, Trisha, grazed my skin. Trisha and I used to be close. She even invited me to her bachelorette party last year.

I peered through the narrow gap of my stall's door, heart stammering out of whack. She and a recruitment consultant, Mariam, were fixing their makeup in front of the mirror after lunch.

"I'm mainly just…puzzled." Mariam reapplied her eyeliner, leaning over the sink. "I've known her for a couple years. She's always been super sweet. Why would you do a one-eighty and marry the asshole everyone hates, then take a job firing people for a living?"

"It's not for a living." Trisha snapped her setting powder container, rummaging through her makeup bag. "She doesn't need to make a living anymore. She married a billionaire. And he is obviously infatuated with her, because look at the ring. She's obviously a sadist. She was just really good at hiding it until now."

Tears pricked the backs of my eyeballs. All my hard work and reputation had gone down the drain in the past couple of weeks because of my arrangement with Tate. And still, I also acknowledged this was beyond the pale. These people had no right to speak about me like this. I could marry whomever I wanted without answering to them. I had never tattled to Tate and didn't plan on it now.

"…felt bad about not inviting her for lunch, but what she did to Jessica was brutal," Mariam sniffed. Jessica was the last person I had fired. The one I gave a job taking care of Mum.

"Don't you dare be nice to her," Trisha cried out, enraged. "Maybe if we ignore her, she'll eventually go away and pop out babies for Satan and leave us alone."

Mariam snorted. "He's awful, but low-key, I would pop a baby or two for him too."

Trisha huffed, "I bet it's been going on forever. I wonder if it's why she took the job in the first place. Did you know she studied business? Now everything makes sense."

I flung the door of my stall open and waltzed outside, catching their gazes in the mirror. I smiled casually, refusing to cower. Yes, I was kindhearted, but I was no pushover.

"Hullo!" I greeted, dumping the wrapper of my lunch into the bin and flicking the tap lever to wash my hands. "Marvelous day we're having, isn't it? It almost feels like spring."

They both stared with their mouths agape, pink creeping up their faces under three layers of foundation.

"You know, we Brits don't take this kind of weather for granted," I chatted amiably, squirting soap into my palm. "Oh, and please don't worry yourselves about inviting me to lunch. I'd rather have the company of the bog than poisonous vipers any day of the week. As for Jessica—she is settled in another job and will be starting her master's program in a few months anyway. As for my marriage—it is indeed none of your business who I shag. But just for the record, my husband gives excellent, *superb* dick. Highly recommended, if you can afford it." I winked with a smile. No shagging to speak of had transpired, but they didn't have to know that. "Finally, regarding my new role—I'm an employee taking orders from management just like any other person. I don't make the decisions. If you take issue with my performance, you can always report to human reso—oh." I snapped my fingers theatrically. "I *am* human resources. *Pity.*"

They exchanged horrified looks, giggling in embarrassment.

"Well, I suppose that settles it then." With another sugary beam, I ripped a paper towel from the machine by the sink and walked my merry way, leaving them to stew in their own nastiness.

My standoff with Trisha and Mariam did nothing to soothe my nerves.

In fact, I decided to postpone firing an intern named Kevin, who was objectively horrid at his job and so far had misfiled hundreds of documents, spilled coffee over expensive machinery, and tweeted meanly about his superiors.

Tate checked on me at least every hour, coming down to the floor I worked on, and despite my literally threatening him at knifepoint not to assign any bodyguards for me, I had spotted plenty of stoic-looking, dinosaur-size men tailing me everywhere. They never got close enough for me to feel claustrophobic, but it still annoyed me.

Admittedly, I was frightened for my safety.

Friday's encounter made me vomit uncontrollably for the rest of the weekend. Or perhaps it was my kiss with Tate.

No. It wasn't. That kiss was divine. When his lips were on yours, you forgot all your troubles.

Deciding to cut my workday short (what could Tate possibly do? Fire his own wife?), I showed up at Mum's treatment facility, armed with guava and cheese pasteles. Her favorite. I'd found a Cuban bakery where they did them just right, and the lilting singsong Cuban accents of the workers reminded me of her. I desperately hoped they'd jog her memory.

Dr. Stultz explained the delay in starting the experiment with her was due to her fighting a few infections.

I found Mum hunched over an open book, perched on a rocking chair. She didn't look at the pages. Rather, her blank gaze stared out the window, unblinking. A thin trail of saliva ran from her mouth down her chin.

"Hi, Telma." I used her name, knowing even if she could hear me, she couldn't recognize me. "I brought you your favorites."

I removed the red-and-white kitchen towel off the straw basket and revealed the pastries to her. Her pupils remained stuck on an invisible spot past the window.

I inwardly sighed and settled on the incliner next to her. The last time she spoke was in the car on our way to the facility when I brought her from London. And before that, it had been weeks.

Tossing a look at the book she was holding, I noticed it was a worn-out copy of *Alice's Adventures in Wonderland*. It gave me pause. I only knew one person who walked around with this book. And there was no way on earth he'd take time off his busy day to visit a complete, unresponsive stranger.

What were you doing here, Tate?

A nurse popped her head in the door a few minutes after my arrival. "Need anything?"

"I'm good. Cheers." I smiled politely. "I did leave some pastries at the reception if you are interested."

The nurse nodded but seemed in a rush to get out.

I hesitated, then decided to stop her. "Any update on when she starts her trial?"

She visibly winced at my question. "I'll send a doctor to talk to you, okay?"

I pressed my mouth into a grimace. "Do you think Mum could do with some fresh air? Maybe I can take her out to the gardens downstairs if you help us walk her there."

Her eyes darted to the corner of the room, and I noticed a wheelchair there, right next to a stand covered in orange prescription bottles. So. They had moved her to a wheelchair. She could no longer use her own legs.

"Thank you," I said around a lump of tears, clearing my throat. "For...thinking about her comfort."

"Yeah." The nurse bit the side of her lip. "No problem."

Around an hour later, someone knocked on the door. Dr. Stultz walked in, holding an iPad with her chart. He seemed startled to see me but rearranged his wary expression into a polite smile quickly. "Oh, Gia. Good to see you."

"Good to see you as well, Dr. Stultz."

"I actually wanted to speak to you. Join me at the cafeteria?"

I rose from my incliner and kissed Mum's cheek. "I'll be here tomorrow. I love you."

She was still staring at the same spot. I tried to remember if I saw her blink and decided that I hadn't.

My eyes darted to an annotated paragraph the book was open on.

"You may have noticed, I'm not all there myself."

My husband was a very strange man.

I hoped he'd never change.

I met Dr. Stultz in the hallway, but before I could close the door, nurses rushed in. I caught a glimpse of them mounting Mum back in her bed, setting the book aside.

"Do they take her outside when I'm not here?" I didn't like that they didn't read to her. Take her on long walks. Play her favorite music. Put on old movies she loved in the background. I did all that when we lived together, hoping it would bring her back, pull her from the dark pool of oblivion her mind drowned into.

He placed his iPad on the reception desk midstride and laced his hands behind his back, his steps brisk. He was tall and bald with thick, dark bushy brows. His crow's-feet told me that when he wasn't on the clock, he had a lot of laughter and joy in his life. Usually, such things made me happy. Now, I felt nothing.

"Gia, your mother's test results came back." The edge of his voice grounded me back in reality. "They were not what we were hoping for. The initial metrics and tests prior to accepting her into the program were much more favorable. In fact, her condition appears to be past moderate and quite severe. I don't know how we let that slip through the cracks."

I gulped. I knew Mum's situation was dire. What I couldn't figure out was how she'd passed the initial tests in the first place. The ones Tate sent her to.

Oh, but you know, don't you, Gia? Tate's gruff voice mocked in my head. *You just choose to be obtuse.*

No. Doctors operated under oath. They wouldn't fabricate test results to get her into a prestigious program.

I cleared my throat. "Where does this leave us in terms of her treatment?"

"Well, dear," the doctor said, breaking the professional wall between us, his voice saturated with compassion now. "Once she recovers from the pneumonia and UTI, we're going to slowly initiate the same treatment protocol we use for all our patients but moderated. It's going to be an interesting case study, actually. Seeing if the medicine and therapeutic program can revert symptoms of a case so advanced. But it also means that we probably won't be able to reverse her progression back to a milder case of dementia. We're going to focus primarily on her comfort and include her in some of the initial trials to see if it might slow her deterioration. So what we're doing right now is palliative, not therapeutic. You need to understand that."

Dr. Stultz basically told me my mother would never recover, never regain her faculties, never recognize me as her daughter again.

He stopped in front of the cafeteria but didn't step inside. This was where our paths would fork.

"I understand," I rasped, my voice, my knees, my *soul* weak, crumbling like a sandcastle. "Thank you for being candid with me, Doctor."

He nodded, walking off into the cafeteria. I stumbled on uneven feet to the nearest wall, collapsing against it breathlessly.

A ping from my phone impaled my miserable thoughts.

What now? I thought. I tugged my phone out and frowned at the screen.

> Tate: You slipped past security. You shouldn't have gone to your mother's without telling someone.
> Tate: I'm on my way to my Hamptons estate and can't

turn around. Enzo will personally escort you to your
new security, with whom you'll stay until further notice.

Tate: His name is Filippo, and he is both gay and sane,
so he will not touch you.

Gia: We had a deal!!!

Tate: I'm not an honorable man.

Tate: Plus, I'd go to great lengths to have you tease
me with a knife again. I still get randomly hard thinking
about it.

Gia: I said no bodyguards.

Gia: You force me to marry you. You force me to work
a job I hate. This was the only agency I had left. To live
on my own terms.

Tate: You'll get your agency back when you stop
making dumb decisions.

I slid down the wall and found myself crouched in the hallway
of the hospital, holding my face in my hands.

My father was dead. So was my brother. And now I'd been told
that my only surviving relative—Mum—was, for all intents and
purposes, gone in all the ways that mattered.

Everyone left before I could say goodbye.

My only pathetic comfort was my ironclad knowledge that
Tatum Blackthorn would never leave me. No matter how much I
aggravated him. No matter how far I'd gone to try to rile him up. But
it wasn't love that drew him to me. It was obsession.

Enzo was on his way to the hospital. He might already be
here. Tate could stay in the Hamptons for days. It wasn't out of the
ordinary for him to take his meetings there over golf.

I refused to be ignored. Not when I needed someone to make
me forget so badly. And Tate was a ghoul, but our kiss proved one
thing—he was really good at distracting me.

I scrambled to my feet and made my way to the hospital map.

Enzo would already have people in the elevators and stairwells, waiting for me to walk in. I was a woman on a mission.

That mission was to prove to Tate I could get past all his bloody security.

The map showed a far-off elevator leading to the morgue in the bowels of the hospital. I followed two transport staff wheeling out a gurney with a hidden compartment used to transport corpses to the far end of the floor. Once I stepped into the elevator with them, they shot me confused looks.

"You can't—" one of them started.

I held my palm up. "I'm on my way down to identify my gram."

"Oh." They both grimaced. "Sorry," one of them said.

Once in the morgue, I slipped out the emergency exit, slinking down and rushing to the underground parking. My heart hammered in my chest all the way to my bulletproof Cadillac. A wedding gift from Tate. The keys were casually placed on a cushion Saturday morning, under an engraved note with my parking spot number.

The underground car park was dark and empty, but I could still feel eyes on me. Whose, I wasn't sure.

I broke into a jog.

My entire body was sleek with sweat by the time I got into my car and locked the doors. I spent another full minute glancing around and turning on the flashlight on my phone to ensure I was alone in the car. Then I started driving.

I knew Tate's address in the Hamptons. Been there dozens of times before.

I couldn't wait to show up and ruin his week in the same way mine was destroyed.

Yes, he was a good kisser.

Yes, he was suspiciously good at inflicting pain on his opponents.

But we were still enemies.

As I floored it away from the hospital, I caught the sight of Enzo in my rearview mirror. He jogged out of the main entrance, long tan fingers tangling his whiskey hair. He spotted my Cadillac racing through the street. Meeting his gaze through the rearview mirror, I flashed him the middle finger and smiled.

Before I took a sharp right and lost him, I could see him stomping and yelling at his soldiers to get their cars.

1–0 to the underdog team.

CHAPTER SIXTEEN
TATE

"What do you mean she ran away?" I roared at Enzo through my phone. Beneath me was quite the ungrateful guest, thrusting and thrashing hysterically. Then again, I did have my foot pressed against his windpipe, slowly crushing his airway, suffocating him in the same manner in which he'd murdered my father in prison.

The only sad thing about killing Nolan Duffy was that I could only do it once.

"By the time I got there, she'd slipped away," Enzo muttered in disbelief and more than a little fury. "What the fuck did you expect me to do? Teleport her back to the building?"

Enzo was Vello's enforcer. He was good with a gun, even better with a knife, and had a talent for making dissident camorristi and foes either bend the knee or disappear. I knew taking this babysitter job wasn't something he wanted or expected.

He thought it beneath him to babysit a hot piece of ass who happened to be married to a billionaire who worked with them. But he wasn't going to make a big stink about it. Unlike his brothers, he wasn't a complete shit.

"She didn't use the elevators or the stairs," Enzo lamented. "Filippo had our soldiers manning every corner of the hospital. I thought she was a dumb civilian?"

"Civilian, yes. Dumb, no. She took the morgue elevator probably."

I massaged the bridge of my nose, pressing my foot harder against Duffy's throat. My gorgeous, intelligent wife. Always one step ahead. "Find her for me. After you do, you become her personal detail until further notice. Our business is contingent on you keeping her safe."

"Filippo—"

"Is just a soldier," I finished for him. "I want the best."

"You think my brothers will let you waste my time shadowing a secretary when I have an empire to help run?"

I could envision him sticking his fingers in his floppy, heartthrob hair.

"Dude, no offense, but you're just one person."

"One person is all it takes to destroy an empire."

I hung up the phone and smashed Duffy's throat with my boot, shattering his hyoid bone into dust.

CHAPTER SEVENTEEN
GIA

The sky was pitch-black by the time I arrived at Tate's waterfront estate.

A sprawling neoclassical palace boasting columns and arches, surrounded by private golf and tennis courts as well as a gigantic pool. I knew he had inherited it from his adoptive father and was immensely fond of it. He insisted on not altering a single detail about the property, which was in dire need of a fresh coat of paint and updated furnishings.

My name was registered as a permanent guest in the database of his gated community, so I managed to get through the first set of gates breezily. Once in front of the property, I punched in the main gate's password: an elaborate sequence of numbers only he knew. The Fibonacci sequence.

I knew it too.

Thank you, Daddy, for making me a math nerd.

And then I was in.

The house was dim and quiet. I peered around, wondering if he was even here. Maybe he drove back into the city? Maybe this was all a trap set by the Callaghan guy, and I landed exactly where he wanted me to be?

My heart began racing. Clutching my phone in a death grip, I moved through the vast space of the first floor without turning on the lights. If a monster lurked in the shadows, I didn't want it to see me.

Empty kitchen. Empty guest rooms. Empty study. Empty family room. The only telltale sign someone had been here was a single glass of water, half-full, sitting on the kitchen counter.

I turned toward the door, stepping over something slippery and sticky. The hardwood squeaked beneath my feet. I frowned, turning on my phone's flashlight. I grabbed the sole of my shoe, examining the smear of crimson marring it.

Blood.

I angled my phone to the floor. A path of blood led into the hallway. A straight line of minuscule drops, like morsels of candy in Hansel and Gretel's story. I knew how that tale ended, but curiosity killed the cat.

It might as well kill me too.

Why was there blood here? And what did it mean that my first reaction was to worry for my awful husband's well-being?

I followed the red trail, keeping my flashlight on it. Two sets of dusty imprints from boots marked the floor. One I recognized as Tate's Hermès loafers, but the other set belonged either to another man or an extremely robust and tall woman.

The trail led me back to the study. I'd searched here before, and it was vacant. I continued following the blood to where it stopped in front of the floor-to-ceiling mahogany shelves laden with books, certificates, and decor.

A smidge of blood sat inconspicuously on the bottom of the wooden shelving, trickling just beneath it, hinting that whoever had been dragged here also disappeared beyond the shelves.

A secret passage.

Tate was a high-profile billionaire. Having a place to hide in case intruders came in was probable. Most billionaires had panic rooms.

I scanned the rows of books, mostly business-related, wondering which one I should move to open this sesame. Initially, I looked for a book placed out of order, knowing my fiancé's affinity for structure and math. Alas, they were all primly ordered alphabetically, by surname, with equal numbers of hardcovers and paperbacks on each shelf.

I began sliding books in and out. Shifting small statues around. The figurines and bookends were all *Alice's Adventures in Wonderland* themed. The White Rabbit. The Caterpillar. The Queen of Hearts. The Hatter. The Dormouse. It was no wonder my boss was enamored with this particular artwork. It was a satirical book, penned by a don of mathematics in a Victorian era, that dealt with the tragic and inevitable loss of innocence, death, and life as a meaningless riddle.

My heart rammed against my rib cage, and bile coated my tongue. Finally, my gaze landed on two matching bronze bookends. Each had the face of a creepy, smiling cat. Their ears could be used as a lever. I yanked one toward me.

Nothing happened.

I pulled both simultaneously, and the ceiling trembled, the floor shifting beneath my feet.

The bookcase groaned and squeaked, moving slowly as it parted into a door leading to a steep, pebbled stairway.

Goose bumps shot from the base of my spine all the way to my skull.

I stepped inside before I changed my mind. The door clicked shut behind me. I took a deep breath and made my way down. Danger soaked the walls, the air, even my lungs.

Why was I here, doing this?

Because if he's in trouble, you'll help him. And if he is the trouble, you'll be able to blackmail him out of this arrangement.

It was a win-win situation, really. Unless I had just signed my own death warrant and this ended with my body in someone's trunk.

Music reverberated in the narrow, curving stairway, bouncing off the walls like bullets. It sounded like it came from somewhere deep and far. "Search and Destroy." The Skunk Anansie version. The bass danced in the pit of my stomach.

Muffled voices rose from the foot of the stairway, ribboning around my limbs like chains.

My fingers gripped my seashell bracelet. I had spent my entire life doing the right thing, always on the straight and narrow, and this was where I landed.

In the secret basement of my ruthless billionaire husband, while he did God knows what to God knows who.

Not everything you did was right. You do have one very messed-up secret.

I reached the end of the stairway. A panic room. Small and square, paneled by metal walls, and scarcely furnished.

Inside, my husband, still clad in his work suit, crouched over a dead man on the floor, surgically sewing what appeared to be a small, black thorn between the corpse's eyes.

I slapped my mouth and clamped my teeth, desperate not to make a sound, but a frightened moan escaped anyway.

Tate twisted around, expression vacant, eyes dead.

And that was when I started to run.

CHAPTER EIGHTEEN
TATE

AGE TEN

Two, six, two.

Two, six, two.

Two, six, two.

I was considered a genius student, but I did not test well.

Tests were followed by a whole lot of punishments and no rewards if I didn't succeed. I'd been trained to think of them as my enemies.

Yet the academy forced me to enter this stupid math contest. I was already breezing through the material most people who pursued a bachelor of science in mathematics were still struggling with.

I found myself sitting on a Zurich stage with high schoolers on a crisp winter afternoon, solving equations in front of an audience.

We were given little clocks they put on our tables and pencils engraved with the name of the insurance company that sponsored the competition. My fingers quaked around my pencil. I could not focus on the numbers in front of me.

Two, six, two.

Two, six, two.

Two, six, two.

My eyes traveled up to the crowd. Teachers, professors, and

family members of the contestants. The only person who came to see me was Andrin.

He sat in the front row and narrowed his eyes at me menacingly, fingers pressed together, elbows on his armrests. He didn't need to say a word for me to understand everything that dripped from his scowl.

If you don't win this competition, I am going to ruin you.

But what was left to ruin?

I was all alone in this godforsaken world. I had no friends. No family. Nothing to live for.

Recently, I'd been fantasizing about dying. The only thing stopping me was the technique of it.

I allowed myself time to research the idea. Which death would be the least painful?

Life was an ugly period of time in one's existence. But it wasn't going anywhere. I could off myself in a week, two, or even a few years.

Beads of sweat slithered down my spine and forehead.

Tick, tock, tick, tock, tick, tock.

The numbers on the page blurred into stains, splotching under the drip-drip-drips of my sweat.

Before I knew it, the clocks began to buzz, and the other contestants handed over their score sheets.

My page was blank. I hadn't solved one equation.

The drive back to the academy was silent. Andrin was no doubt plotting the best way to hurt me. I was already numb to his physical abuse.

He dropped me off by shoving me out of my seat. I hit gravel, tiny stones digging into my knees, slipping between my teeth.

I spent a sleepless night wondering when the other shoe would drop.

I'd learned my lesson since Ares. I no longer welcomed pets into my room. Instead, I went into the woods in the dead of the night and met my pet there.

His name was Zeus. He was a fox.

Completely blind and helpless.

Vulnerable, like me.

I brought him food and fresh water and made makeshift toys for him.

I never let Zeus follow me, always outsmarting him and slipping away before he could sense where I was going.

Yet when the sun slid up the sky the next morning and I stepped out of the dormitory, there he was, my Zeus, his throat slit, on the steps of the house. His expression was surprised, his neck almost completely dislocated from the rest of his body. But his eyes. They were still so kind. So hopeful. More trusting than I ever could be.

Because Andrin had taught me a brutal lesson.

Everything I'd ever love was destined to die.

CHAPTER NINETEEN
GIA

I pulled the lever to open the panic room and started running. Tate's steps boomed behind me. I charged out the main door and gained speed, headed toward the car. Then I remembered I placed the keys on the counter when I walked inside.

Bollocks.

Turning around and trying to retrieve them was the surest way to get caught.

Tate had *murdered* someone. That man was clearly dead. Why did he kill him? How many had he killed before? Somehow, I knew this wasn't his first tango. He was too calm, too precise, too comfortable in his own skin when I caught him.

One thing was for sure—I wasn't going to let him catch me.

I decided to disappear inside the woodlands adjacent to his property. The gated community boasted a natural reservoir that stretched for acres across a cliff.

A few advantages worked for me. Darkness fell with no natural or artificial light outside, so the night could cloak me. The grass was fresh and damp beneath my feet, so my footsteps were soundless. And I was a very good runner. Years of training diligently meant I could outrun most men I knew.

I bolted deep into the woods, putting more distance between Tate's house and me. I kept my arms outstretched to avoid colliding with objects. It was pitch-black. I knew I managed to lose him due to the absence of noise coming from behind me. I whipped my head over my shoulder to make sure. There was no one behind me. The forest was cold and thickly threaded with trees. My feet sank into the muddy ground, slowing me down. My muscles were sore. I needed to find my way out of these woods at some point, and I had no idea where they started or ended.

And then I heard them.

The unmistakable howling of hungry...wolves? No. There weren't any wolves in New York. Eastern coyotes. Hyenas laughed from the shadows, the sound of them seeping into my ears like they were a hairsbreadth away.

I stumbled to a stop, surveying my surroundings as best I could. My skin was ice-cold, but my body was hot and slick with sweat. From beyond a thick tree trunk, I caught a glimpse of two eyes glowing in the dark. They danced like fireflies.

The eyes moved in my direction.

Slowly. Nearer. Closer.

Lungs burning, muscles quivering, I careened sharply to the right before they could tear me to shreds.

Even as I sprinted, I knew it was no use. I couldn't outpace a coyote. But I refused to go down without a fight. I gained more speed, their barks and yowls bouncing off the treetops. I pierced through the air, racing faster, *faster*. So quick it was too late for me to order my legs to stop moving when I realized I was barreling straight toward the edge of a cliff overlooking the Atlantic Ocean and to my own demise.

No. No. NO.

My last thought was Mum. Who would take care of her? Read to her? Brush her hair?

This was where my life ended and hers too. She'd become the state's problem. Tossed into an institution—maybe back on a plane to England—to spend her remaining days alone.

An agonized scream ripped through my throat. The ground slipped beneath my feet. My legs hovered over air, nothing beneath them to catch me. My body sank, yielding to gravity. I squeezed my eyes shut, claying into stone.

A rough tug yanked me back to land. The coyotes must've gotten the collar of my coat. I covered my face in my palms, petrified, before I felt my body soaring through the air, flying. I slammed against a surface. Hot and sweaty and alive. The texture of beastly muscles vibrated between my thighs.

No. Not coyotes.

I was on top of a horse that was galloping forward.

Behind me was my husband, steering the reins skillfully, my body boxed between his huge arms. My back was flush against his torso. I could feel his heart drumming rapidly.

It was the only proof I had he was mortal. Alive.

The beast whirled around abruptly and dashed straight toward the two coyotes that chased me. They scurried in different directions, whimpering their submission. Tate tugged at the reins and straightened his legs forward in the stirrups, mindful not to hurt the coyotes. We rode so fast the wind slapped my face, making it hard for me to draw a breath.

My thoughts swam inside my head.

My husband was a murderer.

But he saved me from certain death.

And he had a chance to run over these coyotes yet left them unharmed.

"Apologies for the bareback. I had no time to saddle."

Tate's warm breath caressed the back of my sweaty neck. Each gallop reverberated along my spine. Tears rushed down my cheeks. I was petrified, shaken, and angry.

At him, for everything he was putting me through.

At myself, for not being able to escape him.

Desperate, I tried to elbow his ribs with all my strength, but he easily dodged my elbow, and I nearly lost my balance and fell off the horse. He bunched the reins in one hand, using the other to grab the back of my neck like I was a feral animal, applying pressure without actually hurting me. His mouth found the shell of my ear. "I do love a good, hostile foreplay, but you might want to wait until we make it back to my mansion."

"How did you find me?" I bit out, realizing for the first time that my mouth was full of blood, the tip of my tongue raw. Sometime during the adrenaline rush, I'd bitten my tongue and didn't even notice.

"I can see in the dark." There was no sarcasm in his voice.

"Rubbish," I bristled. "What kind of idiot do you take me for? No one is capable of—"

"A big fucking idiot indeed. It takes a special brand of stupid to run into wild woods in the middle of the night. In fact, I'm pretty sure it's the beginning of *Scary Movie*."

"I'll take any forest creature over a cold-blooded murderer."

"You're welcome, sweetheart," he said sardonically. "Anytime."

Since I'd rather chew my own arm off than say thank you, I kept my mouth shut for the remainder of the journey.

When we arrived back at his mansion, he hopped off the horse and kept me on it as he guided it by the bridle to the stables, not giving me another chance to run away.

Once he put the horse back in his stall, he caught my waist and brought me down to the ground. He led me back to the main entrance by holding my arm captive, steering me in his desired direction. I was his prisoner now.

Inside, Tate turned on all the lights and hiked the thermostat up three degrees. I was hungry and dizzy and in pain. Collapsing on the floor seemed like an attractive option right now.

"You'll sleep here tonight." He was the first to break the silence.

"Keep dreaming." I swiveled toward him with the vigor of a wounded, frightened creature. He may have saved me, but only because he probably thought death would be too lax a punishment for whatever the heck I'd done to him. "I will, however, call 911 and report the *murder* you've committed today."

"Strange way to show someone gratitude for saving your life." He strolled over to the kitchen, unperturbed.

"My life wouldn't be in danger in the first place if you hadn't blackmailed me into marriage and killed a man in front of me."

"*Gia*," he chided, opening a cabinet and taking out a tall glass. "Please. You're a smart girl. That guy was dead long before you entered the room." He filled the glass with tap water and set it on the counter in front of me. "And I already told you, I'm tying up a few loose ends, and then the Irish will leave us alone. Go upstairs."

"No." I hugged my shoulders, my fingernails caked with mud and blood. "I'm not going anywhere with you." I knocked off the water. Glass shattered everywhere.

He studied me intently. "What can I do to make you come upstairs with me?" He was brusque but not as callous as usual.

We'd reached an impasse. Either I handed him to the authorities and watched his entire empire—and likely my own life—implode, or I struck a deal with him.

"You can tell me why you scouted me when I finished college, why you stalked me beforehand, why you kept me close when I tried to leave so many times, why you loathe me so much." I held on to the wall, my knees trembling. "You can tell me who you killed, why you killed them, and how you plan on getting away with it," I continued, feeling the adrenaline slowly evaporate from my body, like mist. "And you can tell me why our lives are in danger, what you did to the Irish Mafia to make us targets. And…and your name." Pause. "Your *real* name. I want to know it. Not all of us can see in the dark, Tate."

There was barely any space between us at all, I realized. The air sizzled between us, soaked with something foreboding. I was going quite mad, I thought, when our breaths danced together, our heat and the scent of our sweat colliding. Because I longed to feel his lips on mine again. His rough finger pads peeling off my wet coat.

"And if I tell you everything, will you stay?" His gaze landed on my ivory pearl choker, and a rush of heat melted between my legs. I knew, with terrifying certainty, that I'd let him twist that choker and take my breath if it suited him.

Because I wanted him more than I hated him.

Always had.

"Y-yes."

"No name, though," he bartered. "That's nonnegotiable."

"First, promise me that I'm safe here."

Tate smiled, his hand resting on my neck, right on my necklace. My heart picked up. "If I wanted to kill you, I'd have let the coyotes do their job in the woods. Less evidence to clean, less paperwork. No, Apricity. You're safe."

I followed him up the stairs, leaving my common sense behind me.

———

Thirty minutes later, I was lying inside a claw-foot bath, the steaming water thawing my icy fingers and toes. The sensation returned to them bit by bit as they tingled back to life.

Miraculously, I found my favorite peony and blush shower oil in the en suite bathroom, a welcome surprise, and was now postponing the frank conversation that awaited me beyond the door. I tipped my head up on the edge of the bath, sighing as I stared at the ceiling.

A dead body lay somewhere on the grounds of this estate.

A soft rap came from the door. I groaned, closing my eyes.

"Apricity." Tate's voice, dark and smooth, slipped like smoke beneath the door.

"Don't you dare come in."

"You need to eat."

"I'm not hungry."

My stomach gurgled, protesting the lie. I hadn't eaten anything other than the small chicken Caesar wrap around eleven.

"Even if you weren't lying, you still need to eat. You are mine now, and I want you well fed."

I bit my lip down. I didn't want to accept his offer.

"I also brought booze."

I sighed, slinking deeper into the water so that only my head was afloat. "Put it in and sod off."

He opened the door and ambled inside, still in his suit, which was filthy from riding a horse in the woods and butchering someone. He held a wooden bathtub tray and lowered it to rest on the lips of the tub.

There was handcrafted sushi and a Tajín-rimmed margarita. My mouth watered. I was dizzy with hunger. And tired. Bone-deep exhausted.

He stood back, surveying the top of my head. I snapped the chopsticks apart, trying to ignore him. It was a bit difficult to work the chopsticks and manage to keep my sternum below water to protect my modesty.

I brought a piece of a rainbow roll to my mouth. "Did you order in?"

"No. I have a private chef who lives on the grounds."

How could said chef miss me running then? Or witness Tate's wrongdoing, for that matter?

"He lives in the pool house across the backyard," Tate read my mind.

Encouraged by the fact that I still hadn't hurled any sharp objects at him, he sauntered to a vanity chair opposite to the bath and sat on its edge, bracing his elbows on his knees.

"You can make yourself useful by bringing me my clothes," I allowed. "I put them on the radiator to dry."

"You've fresh clothes in the guest room," he said tonelessly, not offering any further explanation. "We need to talk."

"No. I need at least one more margarita in me and to finish this food before I can hear you out."

I continued shoveling sushi into my gob until the water got cold. Then I asked him to turn around and wrapped myself in a plush dressing gown.

"I'll see to that margarita while you get dressed," he offered.

"Next time you make it, bear in mind my day started with shit-talking colleagues, followed with bad news about Mum, and concluded with the realization my husband is a killer."

"I've had tax days worse than yours." Tate slinked out of the bathroom with a shake of his head.

Padding barefoot to the guest room, I pushed the door open.

I blinked, confused. All my belongings had already arrived. On the bed. Nightstands. Inside the opened closet.

My Invisalign retainer. Satin nightcap. Blue light–blocking glasses. iPad. My essential oils. Clothes. Socks. Slippers.

"When did you have time to bring everything from the flat?" I yelled to be heard through the hallway.

Tate appeared behind my back in a flash, holding a fresh margarita. He moved like a ghost, in complete silence.

"I didn't." He leaned against the wall, the soft light caressing the hard planes of his jawline. "I remembered what you use and bought replicas after our engagement. You were bound to come here sooner or later, and I really didn't need you whining about wanting your Dots for Spots."

"First of all, those things are literally lifesaving. Second, when have I ever forgotten any of *your* stuff?"

"You never forget my shit," he agreed. "But you forget yours. You have a tendency to put yourself last."

He wasn't wrong, unfortunately.

"Anyway." He scowled. "I was preemptively making sure you wouldn't run in the middle of the night to get your fucking grown-up braces or something."

"Tate, this is giving I'm-going-to-cut-you-and-make-sandwiches-out-of-your-meat."

"I'm not going to cut you." He quirked an eyebrow, giving me a once-over. "Unless you're into that kind of stuff."

"Do you realize how *obsessive* that is?"

His throat rolled with a swallow, and he looked away, at the wall. He'd catalogued every single product I'd used over the years. Paid close attention in the few times we saw each other in an informal capacity.

The peony and blush shower oil wasn't a coincidence; he bought it for *me*.

Butterflies fluttered inside my stomach.

Kill them now, Gia. Kill them with fire.

"Anything else you want to say to me?" he asked, expecting a thank-you.

"As a matter of fact, yes. Drop dead."

Slamming the door in his face, I got dressed and brushed my hair into a bun. Once I was done, I made sure my Life360 was on and tucked my phone into the pocket of my pj's. Cal and Dylan had the app. They'd track me if they didn't hear from me.

I took the stairs down to the kitchen. Tate waited for me at the table with my margarita and whiskey for himself. His lips were pressed in a grim line, his fingers flipping an unlit cigarette. He seemed quite cross to be explaining himself, and it occurred to me it was probably the first time he had to answer to someone. I could not recall him in that position before.

"Start from the beginning." I sipped my second margarita. It was almost undiluted tequila.

"What do you want to know first?" He lit up his cigarette, exhaling the smoke to the ceiling. "Why I hate you, or why I killed that man? They're connected."

I flinched at the admission he hated me. Of course I knew it, but it was the first time he confirmed it. I was also puzzled as to why I was connected in any way to this murder. Did I know the man he killed in the panic room?

"Why you hate me." I cleared my throat. "I want to know what I did to deserve the last five years."

His index finger trailed the rim of his whiskey glass, and I could not, for the life of me, stop imagining him doing the same to my nipples, which puckered under my pj's.

"When I was twelve, my late father adopted me. Up until then, my life had been hell on earth. I came to him battered and scarred, inside and out. Angry and distrustful. I was fucked up. I wet my bed until I was fifteen. Suffered from nightmares that followed me no matter where I slept. The first few years, I ran away from home every other week. I'd sleep in the woods. Graveyards, sometimes. I needed dirt on my skin, darkness in my eyes to feel at home.

"It took my dad years to peel off my roughest exterior layers. And still, he couldn't manage to take off more than the first charred coats." He knocked his tumbler of whiskey back, gulping it in one go before pouring himself three more fingers. "I was unfit to attend a normal school—too aggressive, too wild, too dejected—so he homeschooled me himself, despite being a successful businessman. He ignored my curriculum entirely, instead teaching me useful things. Latin, medieval history, and computational science. Metaphysics, advanced logic, and Eastern worldviews. Every lesson was art, every class an experience. We'd talk into the night, almost every night. When he realized I'd been sneaking out to graveyards, he sometimes followed me. Sometimes sat with me there too. He said I was like the moon." Tate's throat bobbed with a swallow. "Just because I wasn't whole didn't mean I wasn't enough."

Tears stung my eyes. His adoptive father sounded perfect. I was surprised he'd never mentioned him in the five years we'd worked together.

"I'd become an extension of him. He took me on work trips. Business meetings. Holidays around the world. I learned the ropes and the craft of his profession as a real estate mogul. I was eighteen when I realized why Daniel decided to adopt me out of nowhere. It wasn't because of charity. Not all of it anyway. He needed someone to inherit his business and had no family to speak of. And me, I was a genius child. A wonder kid. By nineteen, I had a master's degree. I served as his CFO and de facto CEO as he eased himself into early retirement. A brilliant plan, if you ask me." He smiled ruefully.

"Why did he need to retire so early?" I frowned.

"So he could focus on his first love and his greatest addiction—*gambling.*" He grimaced. "Daniel was a gambler. It was a compulsion. He had no self-control when it came to the poker table. He'd been blacklisted from most East Coast casinos. The only ones who were willing to let him play were the Ferrantes, and even they only did so because their bouncers roughened him into submission whenever need be."

Little by little, I felt my anger melting, giving way to empathy. Tate obviously went through a traumatic childhood and adolescence. No one had ever loved this man unconditionally. The only person who ever resembled a parent to him was a stranger and an addict. Strings were always attached to him being accepted. Be it his talent for his adoptive father, money for his lovers, power and connections for his friends.

"It was an artificial match, he and I, but it worked," Tate explained. "I threw him into rehab a few times, but he always went back to the tables. Still, I allowed myself to get attached to him. He was the closest person to me. Then one day, he was in the wrong place at the wrong time. He killed a man. Accidentally. The victim was found with his head smashed in. Dad explained he did it in self-defense. That the man attacked him. The jury went back and forth for days."

My blood froze in my veins.

No. No. No. *No.*

My secret, my origin, my *sin,* was Tate's personal heartbreak.

"He was sentenced to five years in prison with parole. He had an excellent legal team and no criminal record. All he had to do was stay alive. But then three of his inmates murdered him for winning a poker game and not wanting to give up his earnings." Tate's lips flattened, steel eyes clouding. "It was barely forty bucks, but Dad was always serious about his gambling. They were Irish Mafia. The Callaghan clan."

The pieces clicked together all at once.

I swallowed down bile, biting down on a scream.

Tate continued speaking. "My father, the only person I have ever cared about, the only person who showed me love, sympathy, and devotion, was taken away from me. And it all happened because of a nameless foreign student who witnessed the so-called killing in an alleyway and decided to call the cops."

A loaded beat of silence passed. I closed my eyes. A tear slid along my cheek.

"That person was you, Gia."

I was violently nauseous.

"The police had no idea who you were, but I pulled every string possible and found your name." Tate's tone was businesslike. "*Gia Bennett*. Honor student. Gifted tennis player. Goody Two-Shoes. Perfect but not enough to step forward and testify at the time of the trial. I guess you had more pressing issues than helping my father not get thrown into prison."

I'd returned to England at the time.

To be with Mum.

I was trying to take care of her and not fall apart.

I was never subpoenaed.

This explained why he first saw me in a snowstorm. The timeline put it a few weeks after Daniel's sentence.

It explained why he orchestrated an entire scenario where he'd meet and hire me on the spot.

Why he loathed me with every fiber of his body.

"You knew they searched for you," Tate said metallically. "Why didn't you make yourself known?"

"I was scared," I admitted, my voice scratchy. "I didn't want to get into trouble."

He gave me a smile so cold my body temperature dropped below zero. "No. God forbid perfect Gia would get herself into trouble. How's that been working for you, by the way?"

I looked down at my fingers, which were splayed across the margarita's base.

It all made sense. Why he insisted on marrying me. Why he did insane things that put my life in danger. I tried to avoid consequences, so he brought them to my doorstep, the fucked-up teacher that he was.

"At first, I wanted my payback quickly." Tate crossed his long legs, puffing on his cigarette. "Get you deported as soon as you arrived back in the States from your summer break. Maybe let the Ferrantes teach you a few lessons. But then you returned, and I drove to your dorms when your new school year started. Saw you for the first time. And you were beautiful. So infuriatingly beautiful." He closed his eyes, jaw tight as his throat worked around a swallow. "*Pure*. With your wide smile and dimples and knee-length pastel dresses. And I decided to take my revenge slowly. Really relish it. This is why I scouted you." He tapped his cigarette on the ashtray. "Why I never let you go. I wanted to prolong your suffering. To ensure you were as miserable as I was."

"But…" I licked my lips, frowning. "My…I…the man I met that night. His last name wasn't Blackthorn."

I remembered Daniel Hastings. He occupied my thoughts more often than I cared to admit.

"He let me choose my full name." Tate sent a ring of smoke skyward, exhaling an arrow through it. "Said in order to put my past behind me, I must independently reinvent my future."

My heart ached. Tate didn't even know the truth. Not all of it anyway. The real story behind what happened that day would make him hate me even more.

I reached across the table and grabbed his hand. He slid it away, tapping his fingers on the side of his leg.

"I'm so sorry." I let tears run freely down my cheeks. "There hasn't been one day I haven't thought about your father. It wasn't me who called the police. I swear it. I wish I could turn back time. I wish I could change the way things happened that night. If it's any consolation, I am already in my own personal inferno. I always think about that day."

He stubbed his cigarette into an ashtray, scowling at it. "Sorry doesn't cut it. Paying with your life, however, might."

Still, I could feel an invisible wall breaking between us. Fog had lingered around our animosity. Around how we ended up in each other's sphere. Now it cleared, and all that was left was the ugly truth of what brought us together.

I hadn't known Daniel died in prison. Not until now. Fresh grief filled me. It wasn't that I didn't care what happened to him, but I'd been too frightened to check, knowing the truth could destroy me.

"I won't report you to the police." I swallowed thickly. "For…for what you did to that man. I've done enough to hurt you."

He said nothing. Something in him knew I wasn't capable of handing him over to the authorities. This knowledge frightened me. What else did he see that I didn't?

"Is marrying me a part of punishing me?" I asked.

"Knowing you'd hate yourself each time I made you come is definitely alluring." He tucked his hands into his front pockets. "But it isn't just that. My relationship with my father was both manufactured and successful. I believe we can replicate that." He scowled. "With the exception that I didn't want to fuck Daniel, of course."

My cheeks heated. I nodded, feeling oddly triumphant for managing to win this man over at some point, considering he'd lost his father because of me.

And if he knew to what extent…

But I was too much of a coward to tell him.

"I will never love you." His gaze caressed mine, almost soft in contrast with his harsh promise. "But I won't abuse you. Knowing you'd be stuck in a loveless marriage is enough of a punishment. And you will be free and pampered. I will give you money and clothes and vacations. Jewelry and beautiful, well-bred children. You'll never want for anything."

"Yes, I will," I said, smiling sadly. "I will want love. And you'll never give it to me."

"This is your penalty, Apricity." He arched a brow. "You took away my only parent. Despite that, I am now saving yours."

I was willing to go a long way to atone for my sins. But there'd be plenty of time to discuss that. Tate was uncharacteristically open with me. And I needed to squeeze more information out of him before he clammed up.

"And the person I saw you with today?" I cleared my throat. "What was his sin?"

"He was one of the three men who killed my father in prison. The Ferrantes are hunting them down for me."

This explained his affiliation with the crime family.

"I have one more person to kill." He swirled the amber liquid in his tumbler. "The one you saw today, Duffy, he was the second guy."

"You can't kill anyone else, Tate. The Irish are already after us."

"I do not negotiate with terrorists. The way you react to your enemy teaches them how to behave and what to expect. If I stopped now, they'd think they could extort me. If I finish the job, they'd see they have no leverage on me."

"You said I'd be safe," I pointed out.

"And you will be. As soon as I eliminate killer number three," he said calmly. "Shouldn't take long. I'll sit down with the Callaghans and tell them I consider our feud over."

"That's ridiculous," I cried out. "We could be spending *months* in hiding."

"We'd make good use of it if you drop that saintly charade of yours and do what we've both been itching to do for half a decade."

"Which is?"

"Sit on my face." That patronizing, devil-may-care smirk returned to his elegant face.

I opened my mouth to chide him. He stopped me with a wave of a hand.

"You can cut the bullshit about not being attracted to me. Our kiss told me a different story. And no, the fact that I killed Duffy won't deter you either." His eyes bore into mine. "You've been let down by humanity before. You love the idea that your husband doesn't abide by the rules of society. That I would kill to protect you. The fact that you'll never have my heart sets your soul on fire. You've never failed at anything, Gia, but you will fail at making me love you."

I swallowed.

"But you'll still scream my name as I feed you my cock and my tongue. Settle for whatever scraps I'm willing to give you."

I didn't answer.

My face was aflame.

My knickers were *drenched.*

This wasn't me. I was the girl who needed proper foreplay. A certain mood. A good bloody meal and candlelight.

Tate continued, his voice soft as velvet. "You secretly love that I am obsessed with you, don't you, Gia? That my need for you is dirty and inappropriate, filthy in nature. A part of you has always wanted to spread those legs for me. Now the only question is whether you're going to deprive both of us much longer." He stood up, finishing his drink and slamming the empty tumbler on the table.

I remained woodenly seated, struggling to breathe properly.

"If you want to know what a six-thousand-dollar bottle of

whiskey tastes like, I'll be in my study until midnight. All this chasing you around in a forest opened my appetite." He left, his knuckles brushing my shoulder ever so fleetingly, leaving little tremors across my skin. "For your pussy."

CHAPTER TWENTY
GIA

My body was splayed against Egyptian sheets in the guest room, every fiber of it attuned to the study across the hallway.

I blamed it on the margaritas. My long day. The near-death experience in the woods. Whatever the cause, I wanted to slip into Tate's study and find out what his expert hands were capable of. Deep shame bloomed in the pit of my stomach.

I was responsible for his father's death. More responsible than he could ever know.

My eyes drifted to my phone on the nightstand. I touched the screen to check the time. Eleven fifty-eight. I had two more minutes to change my mind. My husband was a punctual creature. He wouldn't wait a second past midnight.

They say that the heart wants what it wants, but in the end, it was my vagina that made me slip out of the lace-trimmed linen and tread across the hallway. My toes sank into the plush, silken carpet that drowned out my footsteps. I stopped before his study. He left the door ajar, an open invitation for me to come in. I peeked inside, my pulse accelerating.

It was completely dark. All the lights were off. A silhouette of my husband sitting at his desk, jotting something down on a thick textbook, danced in the center of the room.

He wasn't lying. He *could* see in the dark. He was writing in the dark.

Solving equations in the pitch black.

Everything clicked. That time he fetched me from my birthday and read a book…he *truly* read it.

Tate finished the page, flipped onto a fresh one, and continued jotting. A few seconds passed before he closed the textbook and sat back.

"It's five seconds past midnight."

His voice jolted me out of my reverie, and I sucked in a breath. I hadn't realized he noticed me.

"Are you coming in or staying out?"

I stepped into the doorframe, closing the door behind me.

"Attagirl." His words slipped through a condescending smile.

"I won't have sex with you."

"If you're here for a conversation, I'm afraid I'm fresh out of patience for chitchat."

Gulping, I shook my head. "I don't want chitchat either."

"What do you want then?"

"An orgasm," I admitted. I'd never been this forward before. Not that anything was wrong with it. It just wasn't me. "I'm in knots. I want…I want…"

You.

"I will give this to you," he said, no hesitation, no judgment. "Come here, sweets."

Sweets.

The word caressed my skin, spreading a delicious sensation in its wake. He'd rarely called me anything darling. Even Apricity was tainted with derision.

I advanced toward him until I reached the edge of his desk. He opened his palm. After a moment's hesitation, I put my hand in his. Still sitting, he guided me to stand in front of him, my bum resting on the edge of his desk.

"Close your eyes."

"I already can't se—"

"Close them," he repeated.

I did, a thrill of something dangerous and decadent shooting through me. I was completely at his mercy.

What a terrible place to be.

"Keep them closed. If I catch you cheating, I will bring you to the brink and deprive you of your climax. You don't want that."

My body was as tight as a bowstring, attuned, craving his next touch, wherever it might land.

I felt his fingers wrapping around my bracelet and sucked in a breath in surprise.

"Tell me about this one," he murmured, his voice closer, his mouth a breath away from mine. His knee nudged my legs open, spreading me wide.

Heat rushed to my center, and my hips rolled instinctively, my inner muscles squeezing against nothing.

"I've never seen you without it."

His whiskey-tinted breath fanned against my bare neck, and every cell in my body awakened with desire.

I heard a drawer open to my right, and Tate rummaged for something. My throat worked as I tried concentrating on his question.

"My father made it for me." I licked my lips. "In Jamaica. We used to go on holidays there often. Whenever we could."

Tate finally picked what he was looking for and closed the drawer silently. My pulse skyrocketed. His cock was now pressed between my legs, which had opened farther on their own accord sometime during our conversation, welcoming him in. It was hot and hard and thick through our clothes.

"We used to collect seashells on the beach together. We did that for hours. When I found this incredibly rare seashell, I was delighted. The *Scaphella junonia* only washes ashore after rough storms. Juno was queen of the Roman gods, married to Jupiter. So this shell represents her and symbolizes strength and power, grace and self-sufficiency. My dad made it into a bracelet for me. Gifted it to me on our last Christmas together. It always reminded me I could get through the hard times."

"Where in Jamaica?" Tate kept the conversation going to distract me from what he was doing. His hands were nowhere on me, but he was grinding slowly against my core, which sparked fissures of pleasure all over my skin.

"Negril. Half Moon Beach, Green Island."

Christ. I didn't want to come from his penis rubbing my clit through our clothes, but I already felt my muscles quaking and tightening.

"Do you trust me?" he asked.

His mouth was now directly against my lips. I could taste his cigarette, his whiskey, his desire on my own tongue. I wanted him to kiss me. My entire body clenched in expectation.

"Y-yes," I admitted. "I do."

"Rookie mistake." He chuckled. "Never trust a sociopath."

His lips slammed against mine, and our tongues found one another. My hands impulsively moved to his face, demanding more, begging, roaming, clutching, before he grabbed both my wrists with one hand and pressed my back against the length of his desk, pinning my arms over my head. He climbed over me, his erection nestling against my pussy. I wanted him with abandon I didn't know existed in me. His teeth bit and nipped at my mouth, and I got angry, frustrated, returning his kiss with my own boldness. With demanding strokes, exploring every corner of his mouth. His free hand was fumbling all around me but not actually *on* me, and then his lips ripped from my mouth and wrapped around my right nipple, and that was when I realized I was naked from the waist up.

What the...?

My eyes flew open, but it was too dark to see anything.

I heard the ripping sound of the fabric of my pajamas.

"I was doing you a fucking favor." His mouth moved over my nipple, sucking it with insatiable greed. "That top was *horrid*."

The dagger he'd retrieved from the drawer was so close to my pubic bone I felt it lick my skin teasingly. He was still holding the weapon he used to tear my top, I realized.

"Go on then." I found his eyes in the dark, and they were gleaming with menace. "Kill me. I know you're capable of it, Tate."

He pressed the dagger—a letter opener, I realized—to the tip of my chin, nostrils flaring.

I tilted my chin up, still meeting his grinds thrust for thrust through our clothes, never breaking eye contact. "I should be on the list too," I said.

"Shut up," he snarled.

"If it weren't for me, Daniel would still be alive."

I had to push him.

I had to show him he wasn't beyond redemption.

There was something brilliant inside me, something that deserved to be loved, and he needed to know that.

The letter opener pressed harder into my skin, not yet breaking it but enough for me to feel the pinch. I swallowed but pushed through, pressing my pussy to his cock, feeling it nestling inside.

"Kill me, Tate."

"I'll do you one better, Apricity. I'll ruin you."

He tossed the letter opener to the floor, scooping me into his arms, sucking my entire breast into his mouth. Every nerve ending in my body concentrated in the rigid, tight bud of my nipple while he suckled and teased and bit it. He freed my wrists, and his hands were everywhere I wanted them. Teasing my other nipple. Caressing my stomach, my waist. Kneading my ass. Moving farther down to my panties. The base of his palm pressed against my slit through the flimsy fabric. It was wet with my want for him.

A low groan escaped his throat.

I didn't know if I could survive this man.

I didn't know if I wanted to.

His mouth slid down from my nipple to the length of my rib cage and stomach, kissing and nibbling on every inch of flesh, on my sweat and my scent. I had never been worshipped before. Splayed on an altar and ravaged so thoroughly. Tate did not miss one cell of my upper body before his tongue teased my hip bones, kissing them softly, hooking his thumbs into the junction between my center and my thighs, spreading me open and nuzzling his nose into my slit through my knickers.

I cried out, arching, grabbing the back of his head and pressing him to my core shamelessly.

"Take off my bottoms," I urged him between desperate pants.

He chuckled darkly into me but, being the arsehole that he was, didn't remove my knickers. Instead, he began nibbling me through them. Teasing with pressure and heat.

He knew it wasn't enough to hurl me over the edge but was just sufficient to drive me mental. He trailed his tongue along my labia, then sucked my entire pussy into his mouth. Flicked my clit with the tip of his tongue.

Again.

And again.

Faster.

Harder.

Until he found the rhythm that made every muscle in my body clench.

Finally, he tugged my bottoms by one leg but continued teasing me through the soaked fabric.

"Tate, Tate, Tate," I chanted, wishing I knew his real name. The boy who came before the man I hated but couldn't get enough of. "Please," I choked out. "Please, let me come."

All he needed was to move my knickers to one side. To fill the emptiness inside me.

"You want to come?" His teeth grazed my soft flesh through my underwear.

"Yes," I panted.

"What will you give me in return?"

"I...what do you want?"

"What I want is to come inside every hole in your body, nostrils and ears included. But since this is a little premature, I'll settle for making you promise you'll stop running." He growled, clutching my outer thighs, spreading me wide. "Stop avoiding me. *Stop* fighting this."

Every muscle in my body quivered. I wanted him beyond reason and logic.

"I'll stop fighting this," I croaked.

He fisted my knickers and slashed them off my body. "As soon as I tasted your cunt on my fingers, I knew I had to have my fucking fill." His thumbs spread open my folds, and he plunged his tongue inside me like a feral animal, his nose massaging my clit as he devoured every drop of want I had for him. "That small sample just wasn't enough."

He pushed two fingers into me, the invasion sudden and rough, pumping into me gently as his mouth fastened around my clit, blowing air on the exposed little nub, a trick that made me feel full and shattered me into pieces.

I cried out, spasming. It wasn't just the sensation that turned me on but also the way he ate me out. Like nothing more delicious in this world existed for him than me.

My muscles bunched, my toes curled, and stars detonated behind my eyelids.

It took me long seconds to come down from the high. When I allowed my eyes to flutter open, I glanced around the darkened room and realized I was...*alone.*

Tate slipped out of the room as soon as I climaxed, escaping like a vampire from sunlight.

I knew better than to think he went off for a wank. He was too refined for something like that, too frighteningly in control.

Carefully, I slid my tailbone off the desk and stood up. I was completely naked, my pj's and knickers gone. He stole them, I realized, for his obsessive collection.

I gingerly made my way to the light switch and flicked it on. The scent of our sweat and my desire for him lingered in the air. Embarrassment swamped me. I let an ice-cold murderer play with my body. No, not just that—I actively *sought* him out.

I returned to the desk, glancing at the textbook I'd been pressed against. The one he'd been working on before I interrupted him. It was a bit smudged from the juices my body produced, some of the ink smeared, but I could still read it.

It was all complex equations. Solved in measured handwriting. And in the margins, in neat, cursive letters, so identical in size and flair they looked like a font, one word:

Nolan. Nolan.

The name was written hundreds of times. Maybe thousands. Always identical. It looked…compulsive. Uncommonly precise.

Hypergraphia.

My heart beat faster. I rushed out to the hallway and made my way to the primary bedroom, only to find the doors closed. I rattled the door handles, unsurprised to find them locked.

"Tate!" I called.

No answer.

I slammed my fist onto the ancient wood. "Tate!"

Nothing.

This, I understood, was a statement.

My husband's way of telling me I could have the orgasms and the private chefs, the lavish luxury of his lifestyle, his expert tongue, his thick cock.

But I could never, ever have his heart.

———————

The question Tate left unanswered—what happened to the body in the panic room—answered itself rather promptly.

Ten hours after I found Tate leaning over him in the Hamptons, Nolan Duffy's body appeared floating in Lake Michigan, of all places. Bloated and splotched but identifiable. Mafia deal gone wrong, the six o'clock news speculated.

Duffy had a black thorn sewn to his forehead and words engraved on his cheek with a sharp knife.

Two down.

One more to go.

CHAPTER TWENTY-ONE
GIA

"Thank you for coming in." I plastered a forced smile on my lips as I sat in front of GS Properties' worst employee to date, Kevin.

Kevin jerked his chin in a nod, his foot bouncing at ninety miles per hour. His eyes were red, and his brown shaggy hair was a mess. He was in his midtwenties but didn't look a day over eighteen. The only way I could justify calling him in here and terminating his employment was that I'd learned he was living with his mum on the Upper West Side. He didn't have a family to feed, nor bills to pay.

"Well, uh, I didn't actually have any choice." Kevin scratched his unkempt stubble, studying me warily. "I know why I'm here. You're firing my ass."

"Actually, this is an executive decision, not mine."

"What's the difference?" he spat out. "Am I not being kicked out of the company or somethin'?"

"Your employment is still terminated," I said carefully. Jesus, this was more awkward than the drive home to Manhattan with Tate from the Hamptons. "But I've arranged for your terms to be more favorable."

I allowed myself to tweak the termination process since I was the designated person to carry out the actual sacking. If Tate had a problem, he was welcome to fire me. I'd sue him for wrongful termination and retain the best lawyers in town. After all, I was now married to a billionaire.

"Uh, can you say that in English?" Kevin blinked slowly.

"We'll be giving you a generous severance package of twenty thousand dollars as well as a two-week salary continuation."

"Oh." His eyes remained dim. "Thanks, I guess."

Kevin did not behave as though he cared about this job at all. He missed more days than he attended, arrived late, and was rarely focused.

My eyebrows knit into a frown. "Were you expecting something else? Anything that could've made the process easier for you?"

Kevin rolled his tongue along his teeth. "So...this is pretty embarrassing, but actually, my mom is going through a tough period. My dad left her for another woman." He bit down on his lower lip. "Fuck, I can't believe I'm telling a complete stranger." He shook his head, chuckling humorlessly. "That woman is my former nanny. And my parents didn't have a prenup, so my mom, who stayed home with me, definitely got the short end of the stick. Since I'm no longer a minor..." He trailed off. "Anyway, she became very depressed. Couldn't hold on to the shitty job she found. I decided to move back and have been taking care of her since. Recently, it felt like she was on the brink of something bad. Like, suicidal or somethin'. I've been watching her and trying to keep this job. I barely sleep. I eat mostly junk since I don't have the time. I just..." He rubbed his palms over his face, falling forward, elbows on his knees. "I'm tired of juggling this shit. When I first got the job at GS Properties, I thought I hit the jackpot. I wanted to work my way up to management. And I fucking hate my dad for putting me in this position. It feels like I went to Emory and busted my ass for nothing."

I reached forward and put my hand on his across the table, knowing it was against protocol and not giving a toss all the same. "I'm sorry. I had no idea."

"I started out strong here." Kevin screwed the bases of his palms into his eye sockets. "I got the hang of my job. My boss liked me. But then Dad dumped Mom, and everything fell apart. I can't just leave her like this. I'm an only son, you see. And fuck my dad for what he did. Seriously, he thinks he's some kind of a saint for waiting until I was a grown-ass man. But yeah, it screwed up my entire performance. I'm agitated and bitter and just…I don't know. *Fucked.* I feel like I'm fucked."

GS Properties was a huge corporation. We could bloody afford therapy sessions—or at least vouchers—for those who needed it. More support for struggling workers. Easier access to time off for people with special circumstances. I'd only been in HR for a short period of time, but I'd already seen enough to realize Tate ruled this place with an iron fist and screwed people out of their basic rights in exchange for adding GS Properties to their résumé.

Long, unpaid overtime. Measly days off. Draconian contracts.

My jaw tensed, and my nostrils flared. Kevin's story hit home, because we were going through similar things. I visited Mum at the hospital day in and day out, watching as she drifted further away from me, like a balloon sailing across the sky toward the sun.

"Know what?" I huffed, standing up. "You're not sacked. In fact, I have a job for you."

Kevin wobbled to his feet, scratching his head uncertainly. "You mean, like…here?"

"Yes," I said brightly. "We're going to start a workers' union. I need you to help me put together an employee survey and send it across the company, to all twelve thousand employees."

"S-start a union?" he stuttered, eyes flaring in a panic.

"Start a union, Kevin." I nodded briskly. "We deserve one, don't you reckon?"

Later that day, after reading a gazillion online articles about the process, I worked on the four-page survey for all GS Properties' employees and its sister companies in the building.

In order to start a union, I had to get most of the workers' signatures, no small feat for a company with over twelve thousand personnel. I felt positive I could do this, though. It would help people like Kevin—*everyone*, really—and I wasn't mad about the fact that people would stop treating me like the Wicked Witch of the West. If they saw I was still one of them, still fighting for what's right and what's good, they'd understand I was the same Gia.

I typed along different questions—*What would you change about the company? Roughly how many overtime hours do you work per week?*—when I caught sight of the elevator sliding open and Tate stepping out of it in my periphery.

Fumbling my laptop shut, I accidentally spilled my iced coffee all over my dress, which made me squeak.

Shoot. I forgot to visit him upstairs for our daily romp.

Two days had passed since Tate and I had returned from the Hamptons.

My husband and I seemed to slip into a routine where, sometime during the workday, he'd call me into his office, flip my skirt up as I braced my forearms over his desk, and eat me out from behind while he was on his knees. He'd make me come so hard I started bringing an extra pair of knickers to work. He always dismissed me from his office by giving my arse a little careless slap.

When we returned home, we ate dinner in silence. He did not ask after Mum, how my day was, or if the bodyguards he assigned to me—Enzo and Filippo—were doing their job.

(They were. Too well for my liking. They suffocated me with their looming presence. But they had this weird, nonthreatening vibe of two frat boys giddying up together on initiation week.)

Tate never asked for his own release. In fact, he seemed completely unfazed about not getting his rocks off, to a point where I began to suspect he wanted to fuck me just for the notch on his belt and not because he was mad with desire.

I didn't know why I was so hell-bent on not sleeping with

him. Perhaps I still clung to this one, single power I had over him. Something I could control.

The HR crowd cleared the path for him like Moses parting the Red Sea. He sauntered toward me, ignoring the coos and the greetings of people around him.

Expressionless. Cold. Frightening.

He opened my office door, closing it behind him. It was surrounded by glass, so everyone could still see us.

Enzo and Filippo were on either side of me, staring hawkishly. He gave them a curt nod, which they didn't even acknowledge.

"The fuck happened to your dress?" he bit out, examining the giant coffee stain on my garment. "Are you five now? Incapable of drinking from a straw?"

Smiling calmly, I retorted, "I'm not five, though I doubt if I were, it'd have stopped you from strong-arming me into marriage. In fact, I believe if taking candy from babies was a profitable occupation, you'd have pursued it."

Enzo looked up, trying to cover his laugh with a cough.

Tate arched an eyebrow. "What are you doing?"

I wanted the workers' union to be a surprise. The type that might be followed by a minor heart attack and send Tate to his eternal slumber.

I fell back into my seat and grinned. "Oh, this and that. Slammed with work."

"You should be slammed by *me*," he quipped, ignoring the two bodyguards next to me.

I didn't give him the pleasure of flinching in embarrassment.

"It's four in the afternoon, which means my breath should be the scent of your cunt."

"Absence makes the heart grow fonder."

"I don't have a heart, and for your reproductive health, my cock doesn't need any more growing." He sat on the edge of my desk, folding his arms over his sculpted chest. Behind his broad back, I spotted Trisha, Mariam, and the rest of the floor watching in awe as the great Tatum Blackthorn acted casual—almost human—with his lowly wife.

"Your cock is not my vagina's problem," I reminded him with a sweet smile.

Tate snatched my chin, tipping my head up to catch his gaze. "We'll be rectifying that soon. I have my tricks." Before I could sass back at him, he stood up and waltzed over to my window overlooking the busy Manhattan streets, lacing his hands behind his back. "Actually, I'm here in a professional capacity."

"Oh?" I swiveled in my executive chair. "How so?"

"It's Rebecca." He turned around to face me, a dark glower on his face. "She put the mess in embarrassment."

"There's no mess in embarrassment." I frowned.

"You should tell her that. She misspelled the word in a company email."

I pressed my lips together to suppress a smile. Karma never disappointed.

"I'd say she is stupid as a rock, but that'd be offensive to rocks everywhere. If she ever had a clever thought, it died alone and afraid."

"Rebecca is a Dartmouth graduate," I said primly. "She is extremely—"

"Disposable," he finished. "Come back."

I sat up straighter. I had no intention of coming back. I liked not having him as my direct superior.

"Whatever happened to 'people will talk'?" I smirked.

"I'll cut everyone's tongues off."

"That's a lot of lawsuits."

"I have a lot of money," he deadpanned.

I laughed. He didn't. Oh. Of course he was serious.

"She's also hitting on me," he added. "Constantly. Offering kinky sex that's depraved, even by my standards."

Smiling to hide the simmering rage bubbling beneath my

skin, I groused, "Guess she can fill in for me when I don't make it upstairs."

"In case you forgot, we're exclusive." He motioned between us. "I've no interest in other cunts. And trust me when I say you don't want to see what happens to any man dumb enough to try to touch you. Now, come back."

Standing up, I swanned over to him, stopping when I was shoulder to shoulder with him. Fine, shoulder to elbow. The arsehole was tall. We both stared out the window.

"That is a firm no, Tate. By the way, I forgot to tell you, I'm meeting Cal and Dylan after work today."

His face clouded over in my periphery, a muscle jumping in his cheekbone. "It's not safe."

"I've accepted the Ferrantes' security detail." I gestured to Enzo and Filippo, who were messing with their phones and conversing in Italian. No point in trying to get myself killed, I had an entire season of *The Bear* to catch up on.

"Enzo did a shit job tracking you down three days ago," Tate said.

Enzo's head snapped up from his phone. "She was out the building before I set foot in it. It's not my fault you can't put your woman on a leash."

"We stopped doing that in the twenty-first century." I smiled serenely at Enzo.

"Depends on your kinks." Enzo shrugged. "Though I guess Tate's vibe is staying a virgin."

"Achilles punished Enzo by fucking his high school sweetheart," Tate said without breaking eye contact with Enzo, a sadistic smile on his face. "Or should we call her *ex*-girlfriend now, Enzi boy?"

Enzo's cheerful smile never wavered.

"That's awful." I gave Enzo a sympathetic face.

"I concur," Tate agreed. "The punishment for losing *my wife* should be, at the very least, death."

Enzo rolled his eyes. "Bro, she's your wife by name only. I've seen her show more sympathy to half-eaten subs at her desk."

"Enzo is doing an excellent job," I clarified, mainly because I didn't want Tate to add an entire SWAT team to watch over my every move.

"He's not doing an excellent job keeping his mouth shut," Tate said.

"Hoo boy," Enzo smirked. "Someone got bitch-slapped by their own emotions."

"I only trust myself to keep you safe," Tate argued.

"Well, I need a break from you," I countered. "Go make plans with your mates."

"Don't have any." He turned to stare at me, looking angry and lost and...*boyish*, almost.

"Shocking stuff," Enzo muttered, playing with his knife.

"Find some." I breezily made my way to the door, opening it and jerking my head for him to leave. The entire floor was at a standstill, watching as if we were the best show in town. Not every day did they see Tate Blackthorn brought to his knees. "In the meantime, I'm busy, and you should be too. Go make us millions, stud." I winked, blowing him a little kiss.

His steadfast, unrelenting scowl melted in an instant, making way for something gentle and beautiful. Almost childlike. He wasn't smiling, but he looked...*content*.

He enjoyed when I pretended to like him. That I assumed the role of the playful wife.

He made his way out the door. When he brushed past me, I gave his arse a small slap, the way he did me when he was done eating me out in his office. "You're dismissed."

Tate side-eyed me, giving me a barely audible *woof.*

Promising to punish me for that little flex.

I couldn't wait.

CHAPTER TWENTY-TWO
TATE

From: Dr. Arjun Patel, MD
(arjunpatel@stjohnsmedical.com)

To: Tate Blackthorn
(willnotanswerunsolicitedemails@GSproperties.com)

Subject: Appointment

Tate,

I started a new email chain just in case.

Following this up to see if you'd like to schedule an appointment. I've been refilling your prescriptions, but the pharmacy notified me that you've not been picking them up. If the issue is around scheduling, we can meet virtually, or I can make a house call as discussed. I would advise keeping with the agreed upon protocol to avoid a setback.

Dr. Patel.

———————

I didn't think I had it in me to out-asshole myself, but knowing I would be deprived of my wife's pussy juices for an entire day pushed me to the next level.

How dare she have plans that didn't include my tracing the tip of my tongue around her clit? Her priorities seemed completely out of whack.

I told her mother as much when I checked up on her after I finished work.

Her response came in the form of snoring softly.

I was short-tempered and disagreeable during my spontaneous after-work drinks with Row, Kieran, and Rhyland, to the point that I considered *not* bashing their heads against the table, a remarkable testament of my altruism.

The concept of socially drinking in itself was jarring to me. The entire allure of having a glass of whiskey was to enjoy it in peace and quiet. *Alone.* Instead, I had to pretend to care about Row's restaurant woes and Rhyland's subpar child. And don't get me started about Kieran wears-sunglasses-indoors Carmichael.

"You have to see what Gravity did in art class." Rhyland made a sound of a distressed baby seal, picking up his phone and thumbing through his gallery. "She's so fucking talented. I told Dyl we have to get her a private tutor."

He turned his phone to us, exhibiting the so-called talent. Comprised of an incoherent scribbling in brown and yellow. Not much different from the result you'd get if you let a dog drag its ass over a carpet.

"Very expressive." Row fingered his chin, attempting courtesy, presumably because said child was his niece.

"Is that…a forest? Trees?" Kieran made an effort to sound interested.

"It's a bear," Rhyland deadpanned. "Obviously."

Kieran nodded enthusiastically. "Yeah. Totally. Uncanny."

"It's garbage." I tossed my drink back. "Do the kid a favor, and don't encourage her to pursue art professionally."

Rhyland's smile liquefied into a glower. "Anyone ever told you you're an asshole?"

"Easier to count the number of people who *haven't*." I stared into the bottom of my empty drink.

"That's a new low, even for you." Rhyland put his phone on the table, screen down. "Picking on a five-year-old."

"She's not here, is she?" I mock searched for the small child. "Unless she's taken after her stepdad and started drinking early."

Kieran ripped his shades off his face, massaging his eyelids. "One day, you're going to get cancelled for punching a kitten or something, and I'll suffer the fallout because I'm associated with you. I'm sure Getty Images has a few pictures of us hanging out together."

"Don't worry, lover boy. Nobody cares about soccer on this side of the pond. You're about as relevant as a fucking iPod." I patted his shoulder good-naturedly.

All Kieran cared about was his fucking image. He wanted to continue selling his jersey to doe-eyed kids all over the world. Fucker was the kind of wholesome that made me suspect he had a big, juicy secret he was overcompensating for.

"Where's your weekly arm candy?" Row changed the subject, lifting a dark eyebrow as he studied me across the sticky pub table. Since this was a last-minute gathering, they all insisted we go somewhere "down-to-earth," and we ended up in a tavern. One with mortal, unimportant people, warm lager, and chirpy country music.

I didn't like down-to-earth things.

I didn't even like *Earth*.

My jaw ticked. "What the fuck is that supposed to mean?"

"It means you normally show up with the latest Victoria's Secret sensation wrapped around your arm." Rhyland's smirk extended over his mouth like a rubber band, ready to snap back into a scowl in a flash. "Your dick has seen more pussy than a rescue shelter."

"That's rich coming from a literal man-whore."

"A *former* man-whore," Rhyland corrected, raising his left hand, showing off the thick, golden band on his ring finger.

"I'm married too." I raised my own banded left hand but erected my middle finger instead.

"My marriage is real. You haven't even *fucked* her." Rhyland grinned devilishly.

"How do you know?" Row snorted.

"I know that satisfied glow Tate gets when he ruins someone's life." Rhyland circled my face with the hand that held his beer. "I don't see it right now. Plus, Gia doesn't have rabies."

"I made an honest woman out of her before we slept together." I leaned back on the sticky vinyl couch. I was going to bathe in fucking bleach after visiting here. "Don't see the problem in that."

"A lying bastard like you can't make anything honest." Rhyland shook his head. "Not even a sweet girl like Gia."

He'd think that, of course. I screwed him out of millions of dollars while he was pursuing Dylan, his wife. After all, one man's weakness was another one's treasure.

"Does this mean you're faithful?" Row cocked his head in surprise.

I signaled for a spotty waitress with a dress far too short for anywhere other than the red-light district to get us another round, keeping my exasperation in check. I was about as fond of Row and Rhyland as I was of ingrown toenails, but Gia cared for their wives, so I guessed I couldn't add them to my hit list.

"She satisfies all my needs."

"Is that a declaration of love?" Rhyland retied his man bun.

"Love is a weakness. I do not engage in such foolishness."

But I didn't hate her anymore. Not completely anyway.

She didn't notify the authorities I murdered Duffy, and I did appreciate the honied nectar of her cunt. She was a mild nuisance now, no longer the bane of my existence.

I checked my phone for messages.

Luca: She is being trailed by Enzo and Filippo. More protected than Fort Knox.

I'd asked if Gia was safe tonight.

Tate: Send three more men to err on the safe side.
Luca: Your wife won't like that.
Tate: I'd rather have her angry and alive than pacified and dead.

Meanwhile, Row, Rhyland, and Kieran were bickering about football. Or was it soccer? Either way, I'd be bored to tears if my body could produce them. I allowed my thoughts to drift into more pressing matters. I would eat fish when I returned home. Yes, fish and broccoli. Then I'd do some equations. Count the number of tiles in my bedroom again. Read a few paragraphs in *Alice's Adventures in Wonderland*. That would relieve me of the tension of knowing my wife was out there, prey to Tiernan Callaghan. I didn't need Dr. Patel, with his intrusive questions and over-the-top diagnosis. I was fucking fine.

See? Fantastic.

My phone pinged in my fist.

I glowered at a notification from my bank. It alerted me via text every time someone made a transaction on my black card for over ten grand.

Garia Desert Collection Golf Cart x 2, $34,598.

I cocked my head sideways. I didn't remember buying—
Ping.

St. Marton Cay, Private Island, The Exumas, Bahamas, Caribbean, $13,498,229.

My jaw went slack.

Gia bought a fucking private island. On my card. What the hell did she think she'd do with a private isla—

Ping.

No Kill Corp. Animal Shelter. NYC Registered #2233, $329,000.

She was going to make the shelter a rescued animals paradise. I pressed my lips together to suppress a smile. My wife was coming out of her shell. Becoming mischievous and daring. I always knew a great warrior lived behind those demure dresses and perfect curves. I chose well. Someone the complete opposite of Andrin. Who wanted to save animals, not kill them.

Ping.

Kopi Luwak Coffee, 6 lbs., pure, unfiltered, at Café Rem, $14,998.

Ping.

Viking Tuscany Stove. <<<Dual>>>. At AJ Madison. $36,827.

Great choice. I'd wanted one of those for my Mamaroneck summer house.

My chest quaked with stifled laughter as I watched ridiculous, spur-of-the-moment charges gliding down my screen, chasing one another. It wasn't too long before my phone started ringing in my palm.

Hans.

My private banker at Lombard Group International.

What did she do, attempt to buy the American Museum of Natural History?

I slid my finger over the screen and pressed my phone to my ear. "Yes?"

"Mr. Blackthorn, sir," Hans greeted in his usual, exaggerated manner. "How do you do?"

"Fine. I'd ask the same of you, but I pay you too much interest to pretend to care."

"Fair enough." He forced out a rusty chuckle.

I pressed a finger to my ear. The pub was noisy and full of people.

"It appears someone is currently trying to use your personal Amex…"

"That someone is my wife. What's the issue?"

"Oh! My warmest congratul—"

"Yeah, yeah, get to the point."

He cleared his throat. "Well, she's attempting to purchase a Gulfstream G450."

"I'll ask again—what's the issue?"

Quiet quilted the other line. Either a cat got his tongue, or he was too much of a pussy to say it.

"Spit it out, Hans."

"She's added a special charge of an additional one hundred and three thousand…"

"Approve the transaction." In this Russian roulette of fucking with each other, I wasn't going to blink first. I wasn't going to blink at *all*. Came with the territory of embracing my own psychosis. She needed to know tiny skirts and giant bills did not sway me one way or the other, even if she didn't like the necessary extra security on her tonight.

"The surcharge is for a customization, a design." He cleared his throat.

"Right," I said slowly. "Why wouldn't she want a custom design? Do you think my wife should travel in a generic jet? Something bland and boring? Like a peasant?"

I was fucking with him, knowing he'd gladly surrender every

hole in his body to me in exchange for managing a portfolio like mine. Usually, I derived endless pleasure from taunting people.

Row, Rhyland, and Kieran slowly spun their heads to stare at me, looking like I just shat in their cereal bowls.

I didn't usually have a one-track mind, but I couldn't stop thinking about her. The way she bit my finger too hard, threatened me with knives, and tried to elbow me off my *own* galloping horse.

Her mouth. Her tits. Her cunt. Her ass. Her legs. Her *laugh*…

She never laughed for me, but whenever she did laugh, life ceased to be an endless torture of medieval fucking proportions.

"Certainly not! But the custom tail lettering…uh…" Hans paused. Gulped. "It reads *My Husband Is a Knobhead* across the empennage."

A long silence strained between us before I let loose a joyous burst of laughter. It was, to my knowledge, the first time I laughed in my entire life. I was not a laugher.

I was barely a smirker.

Row, Rhyland, and Kieran stopped their conversation again, shifting their stunned gazes to me.

"Think he's going through some kind of a nervous breakdown?" Row murmured.

"Looks it." Rhyland fumbled with his pocket, tugging out his phone. "Shit, get your phones out. We can extort him with the evidence." He pointed it at me.

"Where's your humanity?" Kieran chided, turning Rhyland's phone from vertical to horizontal. "Nobody can pull off vertical videos." He took his own phone out. "I'm sending this to Gia. Maybe it's her way out."

"Hans," I addressed my financier, who was likely unconscious from mortification at this point. "Make it *My Husband Has a BIG Knob* and approve the transaction."

"As I always say, sir, you have *excellent* taste. Understated elegance. I shall do that immed—"

I killed the call.

It was half past midnight when Gia texted me that she was heading home. Even though I'd already showered and dressed for bed, I summoned Iven to usher me to La Grande Boucherie to pick her up. I wanted to see for myself she was alive and in one piece.

Purely for capital reasons, of course.

She stood at the curb surrounded by huge, scary-looking security detail and Enzo, and for the first time in my life, something that resembled guilt speared me. I'd snatched away whatever little normalcy she had left.

One of the Ferrante soldiers opened the back door for her, and she poured inside, all smooth legs and breathless giggles. She wore a velvet burgundy dress with gold buttons. Sophisticated, rich, and demure. I was glad she'd outgrown the phase of wearing skimpy clothes to piss me off. While I was certain I could get away with three murders, killing the entire male population of Manhattan seemed like a stretch, even for a savant like me.

Her long legs folded nimbly beneath her pert ass, and she flung her head back in a fit of uncharacteristic snickers. Beneath her normal scent of sensual oils and Tom Ford perfume was a hint of daiquiri.

"Are you drunk?" I asked deprecatingly.

"Positively plastered. Is my bottom on your crotch?" She wiggled in her seat before I managed to buckle her up.

"No." I hoped I didn't look as flustered as I felt, seeing her dangled in front of me like bait, decadent and alluring, knowing I couldn't bury my dick in her even after putting a ring and—more recently tonight—a fucking thirteen-million-dollar private island on it.

"What do you reckon I'm sitting on then?" She twisted back and pulled something from beneath her. "Oh!" She snorted. "It's the liquor I bought earlier tonight."

A Bhakta 1990 Jamaican rum.

"Flattered you'd mix the two up." I scanned the 750-milliliter bottle. My dick was ramrod straight and deserved its own zip code at this point.

"Are you cross?" She sobered, rotating toward me as the vehicle slid back into traffic, the dregs of amusement clearing from her delicate features.

"Why would I be?" I asked evenly.

"For, you know, spending all your money?" Her pearly upper teeth dragged over her bottom lip.

"First of all, it wasn't all my money. It wasn't even point two percent of my money." I reached to release her lip from her teeth with my thumb, appalled by her words. "Second, it was the only entertaining thing about my evening. Did you have fun with your friends?"

Her mouth dropped in shock.

"What?" I scowled.

I thought she *liked* small talk. Would she make up her mind already?

"You've never asked me a thoughtful question. You never ask *anyone* how their day is going."

"Never truly cared."

"And you do now?"

Fuck, no. But you seem to care an awful lot about social niceties, and I'd love to skip to the part where your thighs are pressed so hard against my ears I'll be able to hear the ocean.

Before I had time to answer, she started blabbing, "It was great. Always good to catch up with Cal and Dyl. After the third cocktail, Enzo's reinforcement came along, and I got a bit upset. Cal and Dylan challenged me to take the piss by running your Amex through every available PIN card machine. We waited for you to stop us. But…you never did."

She sighed dreamily, allowing her head to plop on my shoulder.

My heart hammered violently in my chest. Sickening desire and a heady sense of danger swirled inside my gut. I wanted to push her off and jerk her closer. To ruin her and save her from me. Each sexual encounter we had ended with me spiraling into an attack of rituals. Equations. Counting. Rereading soothing paragraphs.

Still, it was worth it.

Life had been hell from the moment I was born. But for the first time, I was enjoying the dancing flames.

She began nuzzling my neck. My blood roared in my veins, pulse pumping, quicker, harder. I balled my fists to stop myself from pouncing on her.

"Someone's in an agreeable mood," I croaked, my muscles bunching painfully. "If spending a few million is what it takes to make you putty in my arms, I'm happy to make it a daily occurrence."

She sighed contently, her sweet breath fanning my face. Her lips moved down my neck, robbing me of the little sanity I still possessed.

To make matters worse for my cock, I had a conference call in ten minutes. One where I actually needed to speak.

"Apricity." I fumbled for the button to lift the partition divider between us and Iven. "I—"

"Stop the car!" she yelped.

The Rolls-Royce screeched to a halt.

Gia bolted out the door. I followed after her out of instinct. Her heels pounded the pavement, rushing toward a Duane Reade. Unless this was about her buying condoms so we could fuck our way into next month, I was not happy about this recent development.

Also—I had a huge stack of those extra-thin Japanese condoms at home.

Gia stopped next to an elderly woman in a cleaning company uniform and a tattered coat. She was holding an unholy number of bags.

"May I help you to your car with those?" my wife inquired in her crisp English accent. "They seem quite heavy."

The woman tilted her head dazedly. Her nose was red, and she looked exhausted. "Are you talking to me?"

"Yes," Gia said, her voice earnest, snatching some of the bags. "Which way?"

"I'm taking the subway."

"No, no. It's too late and cold for that," Gia insisted. "Where are you off to?"

"Yonkers."

"We'll take you th—"

"I'm calling her a cab right now." I embraced my wife's shoulders, physically removing her from the stranger before she started massaging her feet. "I'm sure this lady wouldn't want to spend an entire car ride with complete strangers."

Gia nodded thoughtfully. "Right. I hadn't thought of that."

I signaled Iven with my hand to call a cab. A taxi appeared less than two minutes later. I took the bags from Gia and the lady and settled them into the back seat of the cab. I ushered my wife back to our car and used enough hand sanitizer to drown a child.

Gia started thumbing through her phone, like the last ten minutes didn't happen.

"Are you going to explain yourself?" I asked.

"What?" She pouted, then shrugged. "I care, okay?"

"Care about a random stranger?" I pressed.

"The invisible people."

"Invisible people?"

"I mean people whose job is to take out the rubbish. Stock the shelves at the supermarket. Trim the bushes. The people society trained us to look past. *Through.* I refuse to do that. I always make eye contact. Smile. Ask them how their day is going." She fell silent. "I remember once in college, I bumped into a cleaning lady in the dorms. I asked her how she was doing, and she started laughing uncontrollably, covering her mouth. I was puzzled. I didn't think it was that odd for me to ask. Then she explained, 'This is the first time in twelve years on the job that I forgot to put my dentures in before leaving the house. And the first time in twelve years on the job that someone has actually noticed I exist.' It fills my cup, being kind to others." She gnawed on her lip again. "It makes me feel...powerful."

I studied her, in awe.

She was far too hot to be that sweet too.

"What about you?" She scooted toward me again. "Is there anything that holds meaning for you? Anything that you love?"

I thought about it, desperately wanting to care about something so I could look humane in her eyes.

"I do enjoy higher categories and operads."

She blinked. "Anything that's *not* math-related?"

"Not right now, but I'm optimistic that *something* is going to be your cunt."

"I'm warming up to the idea of allowing you to test that theory." She unbuckled and climbed over my lap, bracketing me with her thighs.

This time, I did hit the partition button, but not before barking at Iven to drive in circles until further notice.

"Wasting fuel isn't good for the environment." She wrapped her arms around my neck.

"I'll buy you a rainforest to atone for my sins." My fingers sinking into her ass, I guided her to press against my cock through my gray sweatpants.

She dragged her mouth down the bridge of my nose to my lips teasingly before I slammed my mouth on hers and claimed her tongue with a feral growl. I tugged the top of her dress and bra down, freeing her tits. She yelped in surprise when I ripped my mouth from hers and clamped her nipple, tonguing and running my teeth over the tip of the sensitive bud.

She whimpered, arching her back to offer me more of those beautiful breasts of hers. My fingers dug into the base of her skull to extend her neck before I moved my attention to her other nipple, running my stubbled chin over her perky breasts, over her neck, marking her with my scent and saliva and venom. She began grinding against my abs, begging for more.

I released the back of her neck and skimmed her body with my hands, going over all the sensitive parts: the backs of her knees, her inner thighs, under her full, bouncy tits. Her breaths became frantic.

My phone rang noisily between us.

I swore, yanking it out of my pocket. "I have a conference call."

"Video?" She buried her face in my neck again, still riding the air between us. Her panties were soaked. I could tell by the dampness of my sweatpants and the sweet, earthy scent that filled the car, making my mouth water.

I shook my head. "I refuse to see people's faces past six o'clock on principle."

"You're seeing my face now."

"You're the exception."

"Why?"

"You're my wife."

She shuddered, silently offering her tits to my mouth again. There was something about calling her that that made me feel like I'd just conquered the entire continent.

I locked eyes with her. "Would you like me to play with this pussy while I take the call, *wifey*?" I ran the tip of my finger along her slit through her panties. She shivered, her skin pebbling.

Gia nodded, biting down on her lower lip.

"What's the magic word?" I threw her words in my face.

"Immediately," she said, not missing a beat.

My chest felt funny. We had inside jokes now. I'd never formed a human connection like this one before.

"Let me help you. *Tate, please play with my pussy while you're on a business call.*" My dick was on the verge of detonating. "Come on, Apricity. Be a good girl."

I dreamed about this from the moment I saw you.

"Tate, please play with my pussy while you're on a business call." The words slid from her lips in an urgent pant. Her head fell backward.

I rewarded her good behavior by flattening the base of my palm against her pussy. She tried rubbing her clit against it frantically, whimpering in abandon.

Guess the call was going to have some background sound effects. Hey, it was better than elevator music.

I accepted the call. It was a four-way conference meeting with Beijing. A hostile takeover of a revoltingly expensive vacation resort they couldn't keep afloat. It was locked, sealed, and underway. This was my introduction meeting to the purchased company's board.

"Afternoon," I said gruffly while my wife rode my palm. I massaged her ass, tonguing the space under her tits. "Allow me to introduce myself. I'm your new boss—*and* nightmare."

Gia glided down my body, her fingers scraping down my sweatpants. She wanted to be fucked. I could not have that, if only for the simple reason I knew the minute those lips wrapped around my shaft, it'd be game over.

I grabbed the back of her neck, tugging her up and hurling her so her stomach was splayed over my lap. She was draped across the back seat now, twisting her head to look at me with those smoky feline eyes. Liquid gold and sooty lashes. Heavy with desire.

Her ass was up in the air, right in my face. Round, a little muscular, curvy. It was an offering I couldn't refuse.

"William, my CFO, is going to share the signed deed on the screen. I trust you all have it in front of you. We'll go through the bullet points. Ah, there it is." My voice didn't waver as I roughly yanked the top of Gia's dress farther down, using the narrow sleeves to restrain her arms. Her tits chafed against the leather seat. I clasped one of her nipples as though it was a precious diamond, rolling it between my fingers. Her forehead dropped to the seat, and she moaned with abandon.

"What was that?" the accountant of the Chinese company demanded.

I put the phone on speaker and tossed it onto the seat on my other side so I could play with her tit with one hand and use the other to pinch the lips of her pussy through her underwear.

"Nothing," I said coldly. "Pay attention to William's presentation."

While Will droned on about business plans, cutting budgets, and shutting down parts of the resort to manage cost, I slipped Gia's underwear to one side and buried two fingers inside her. She arched, chasing my touch with her pussy as I explored her silken, soaking folds. She was tight. To make matters worse for my leaking dick, she squeezed against me every time my fingers moved inside her, clamping around them in a death grip.

For Pete's sake, I was never going to survive this woman. Fucking her would probably be like ramming my dick into a rubber band the width of a nickel. My balls shuddered at the thought.

I slid in and out, blowing air on her tight hole softly while playing with her tits. The sounds she made seared themselves into my DNA. Doubtless it was the sound of angels singing while they opened the gates of heaven for you.

Not that I'd ever get the chance to find out.

Gia was as close to paradise as I was going to get.

I brought her to her first climax quickly, making her writhe and whimper my name, all while somehow managing to keep my dick from shooting all over my briefs. She spasmed around my fingers, and I felt a rush of liquid heat coating them. It leaked down to my knuckles, vining around my wrist.

On the conference call, Will groused, "We need to be diligent about managing costs. If you go to page three-oh-two, item fifty-six, you will see some of the cuts we've made."

Shit. Yes. Cuts. Costs. Hotels. Mini soaps. All that crap.

"I'll make the trip there myself in a couple months," I warned, withdrawing my fingers from Gia's pussy and reaching over to her mouth for her to taste them. Her lips fastened around my fingers, sucking them off. She maintained eye contact with me, and that was all it took to eradicate whatever willpower I had left in me. With a ravenous snarl, I pulled off my sweatpants. My cock sprang out, the girth thicker than her wrist. I nudged my cut crown between her thighs, tapping the bare slit of her pussy teasingly. The glistening, whitish liquid of her cum glazed her shaved cunt like cake icing.

My sweet tooth was out of control.

A thrill chased through my spine. I stopped tapping my dick against her pussy and leaned down, my face level with her asshole, and tasted her cunt from behind. Her cum tasted like syrupy innocence. It poured like a thick river of honey between her lips every time she came, dripping straight into my eager mouth.

"From this point forward, any minor change, including switching the scent of the complimentary soap, is out of your hands," I had the audacity to announce when my voice was muffled by my wife's cunt. "You run it up the chain until you get an approval from either me or Will," I continued ruefully to the discarded phone. "No detail is too small. We want to know everything."

I finally found the strength to remove my mouth from her pussy, angling my dick back to it.

Gia squirmed, eating the space between us by scooting in my direction, pleading for my cock to press home while she was still draped over my lap. I couldn't do it now. I wanted her completely sober.

And I wanted her begging.

Instead, I fisted my shaft and carefully slid the purple, angry crown of my cock superficially along her slit until it hit her clit, then began massaging said clit with the mushroom of my cock, denying her penetration.

It was a dick move, all puns intended. But that couldn't be news to her.

"I'll be vetting the higher management myself." My voice rose a decibel to drown out Gia's moans. I sounded calm and civilized as I carried on with my business call. "I'm partial to people with a minimum of eight years face-to-face customer service experience, and they must speak at least four languages."

Gia was so vocal trying to chase my cock with her pussy, I had no choice but to shove my fingers deeper into her mouth and quiet her moaning. She gagged on them a little, but when I tried to withdraw them, she clamped her mouth around them, sucking hard, flattening her tongue under their base, showing me what it'd be like.

Wife material indeed.

I slid my fingers in and out to the back of her throat, preparing her for my cock. She needed to work on that gag reflex if she was serious about taking my dick.

I wasn't being cocky. Nine inches were a lot. It pissed me off when women started tearing up and making drunk girl sounds when my dick was not even a quarter of the way down their throat.

"Everything okay over there, Tate?" Will cleared his throat. I supposed they could still hear the slurping of my cock smearing her creamed pussy as it slid up and down her opening.

"Sure."

"Are you having…reception issues?" His way of telling me everyone on the call knew I was having sex.

"None on my end," I reported apathetically, withdrawing my cock from Gia's pussy when I realized I was seriously leaking precum. I didn't know her contraception status and respected the fact that she didn't want children so soon. "Just as long as we're all on the same page about cutting costs and raising prices to turn this ship around." I killed the call without saying goodbye.

I grabbed Gia by the front of her throat and pulled her up so her back pressed against my chest, forcing her legs open so she sat on me, spread-eagle. She wasn't a petite girl and wasn't the lightest woman to ever straddle me, but I still couldn't help but think there wasn't enough of her. "You were a tennis player." It was a statement, not a question.

"Y-yes." She was still panting hard, coming down from the high of her second orgasm.

"How flexible are you?"

"Very..." she said slowly, unsure of my angle. "I take yoga five times a week. Why?"

"How about we test that flexibility? I want you to clean me up."

I pushed her down to the tip of my cock, letting my head fall against the headrest as she sucked my crown clean of my precum and her pussy juices.

When she was done, she settled in my lap, batting her eyelashes at me shyly.

I stroked her cheek and smiled down at her.

"You please me, Apricity."

CHAPTER TWENTY-THREE
GIA

"Morning, everyone!" I breezed through the double doors of Mum's hospital wing. I came bearing baked goods and sunny smiles. Just normal, perky, Goody Two-Shoes Gia.

Nothing to see here, folks.

Everything was normal.

I decided to forgive myself for letting my husband finger and play with me while he conducted his business from the back seat of his vehicle yesterday.

It was a momentary lapse of judgment. Could happen to anyone, really. I was blinded by the thrill of having just bought a private jet. Although now that I'd received all the paperwork and got a peek into the red tape of it all, I was sorely regretting the decision.

I didn't even like flying.

"Good morning, Mrs. Blackthorn." The nurse at the reception smiled warmly, standing up to rummage through the pastries I placed on the counter. She took a slurp of her massive Dunkin' iced coffee. "Dr. Stultz is in your mother's room. You can still catch him if you hurry."

"Lovely. Thanks!" I advanced toward her room and noticed the door was ajar. I'd decided to tackle this situation with Mum head-on. Yes, her condition had worsened, but miracles happened every day. Case in point—Tate actually asked me how my night had been yesterday.

Only three million and two hundred more steps until he became an actual human. *So* close.

I walked through the door to find Dr. Stultz standing next to another doctor. They were both speaking in hushed voices. Mum was folded over to one side, one leg unnaturally elevated in traction. The side of her face was completely bruised. What the hell happened? She was fine when I left her yesterday. I stepped farther in, sucking in a breath.

"What's going on?"

Both doctors turned to me. Dr. Stultz was the first to speak. "Gia. Your mother fell out of bed. Broke her tibia and two ribs." A loaded silence dominated the room as his throat worked around the next sentence. "We found her immediately after. All our flight- and fall-risk patients wear sensors to avoid this situation exactly."

"Oh, um, thanks?"

His expression darkened. "She could not produce sounds of distress."

I closed my eyes, somehow managing not to cry. Enzo and Filippo were just beyond the door.

"I…how…" I peered beyond their shoulders, itching to go to her, to scoop her into my arms. And then another, darker thought penetrated my mind.

There was nothing left to hold. She wasn't really Mum. Not the mum who cracked jokes with me and once chased me down the street all the way to the tube station because I paired a mustard-colored coat with white Mary Janes, and no daughter of hers could commit such horrid fashion crime in broad daylight. We both toppled over with laughter when she showed up with a pair of black sneakers. Then I'd ended up being thirty minutes late to a movie because we couldn't help ourselves and went to share a cookie at Caffè Nero.

Now Mum appeared to be sleeping—always sleeping these days—hooked up to monitors.

In her dressing gown and without any makeup, I saw her in

a way I hadn't ever before. Frail and fragile and out of touch with the world around her. Her collarbones and sternum jutting forth beneath papery, vein-mapped skin.

"When was the last time she was awake?" I finally found my voice.

The second doctor excused himself and scurried out of the room.

"Three days ago," Dr. Stultz said.

When I was in the Hamptons.

"And I missed it?" This time, my eyes *did* pool with tears. I couldn't bear the loss.

"You've been here every other day of the week," he said carefully.

"Well, have you been able to start the trials with her yet? At least the neuroplasticity therapies?" I wiped the tears from my face quickly. "Or…or…what about reading to her a little bit?" I asked desperately. I knew it was useless. I'd been reading to her almost every day. Her favorite classics. *Wuthering Heights* and *Sab* by Gertrudis Gómez de Avellaneda and *Of Mice and Men*. I played her all her favorite Celia Cruz songs, probably too loudly. Talked her ear off. Nothing worked. Nothing ever brought her back.

Dr. Stultz approached me, his face etched with pity. "Did you come here alone?"

The question startled me. I always did.

"Um, yes." I stood up straighter. "I mean, I have my security. Because of…you know, my husband's high profile." He didn't ask, but I felt the need to explain anyway.

"Right."

"Is something wrong?"

"You might want to ask your husband to come in." Dr. Stultz put a hand on my shoulder. "We need to talk."

No. Wrong answer. The right one was "No, everything is great. Nothing to see here."

My knee-jerk reaction was to refuse him. I'd spent the past seven years braving everything on my own. But something in his face made me shuffle to a corner of the vast reception and pull out my phone. My hands were shaking, and it took me a few attempts to unlock the screen.

> Gia: The doctor wants to talk to me about Mum. It seems serious. He asked if you could come.

I blinked at the words on my screen, knowing I'd crossed an invisible line we drew in the sand. Tate and I weren't that type of couple. We weren't *any* type of couple. Just because he ate me out a few times and flaunted his fuck-you money in my face didn't mean we were a united front. And for obvious reasons, I wasn't too keen on him seeing me at my worst.

I typed another message quickly.

> Gia: I told him it's not necessary, but he's watching, so I texted you.
>
> Gia: Feel free to ignore. I'll just tell him you have a meeting or something.

His answer came before I managed to hit Send on the last one.

> Tate: Ten minutes.

I didn't know how exactly Tate made it to Mum's floor in less than eight minutes. The office was close, but not *that* close. Then I remembered how fond he was of stalking me to ensure I wasn't kidnapped to check on his "investment." He was probably already inside the building, being his usual, creepy self.

Creepy as he might be, he looked like a sin waiting to be committed in black slacks and a matching onyx dress shirt. The effect of well-built men in sharp suits needed to be studied. Urgently. What were we putting our research money to these days? Not the important stuff, obviously.

"What's going on?" Tate breezed directly toward Dr. Stultz, a furious scowl on his face. He pinned Dr. Stultz with the looks he gave interns who spilled coffee on new MacBooks at the office.

"Mr. Blackthorn, I appreciate you coming on such short notice." Dr. Stultz visibly flinched at the sight of my husband, instinctively taking two steps back. "Please follow me into my office."

Tate led the way, as if he owned said office. Usually, I was embarrassed by his blatant show of dominance, but right now, I was grateful someone else was taking charge.

We settled in horrid green seats that I found particularly offensive for some reason. I supposed I just wanted to take my anger out on something. The walls were littered with certificates, diplomas, and pictures of Dr. Stultz with his wife and four children, smiling in faraway exotic places and during cozy Christmas holidays. Jealousy dragged across my chest like a rusty knife. A reminder of all the things I couldn't have with my own family anymore.

Dr. Stultz settled across from us, one hand hidden behind his desk, no doubt hovering over the panic button in case Tate decided to strangle him.

The last few days had dulled my senses. Now, in broad daylight, fully clothed, oozing power and malice, I saw him for who he was—a predator in Prada.

"Why are we here?" Tate demanded, laser-focused on Dr. Stultz. He'd been largely ignoring my existence since he showed up, and I was beginning to realize inviting him here was a mistake.

Dr. Stultz widened his collar under his white lab coat, clearing his throat. "I've been meaning to call you to set up a meeting, but Gia beat me to it—"

"More information." Tate bared his teeth, causing Dr. Stultz to rear his head back with a wince. "Less meaningless chitchat."

Dr. Stultz pursed his lips.

I put my hand on Tate's thigh. "Honey, please."

Tate produced a dissatisfied growl but didn't argue.

Dr. Stultz yanked a few tissues from a box on his desk and patted his sweaty forehead. "As I mentioned to Ms. Bennett—"

"Mrs. Blackthorn," Tate cut him off bitingly.

"My apologies. It's hard to keep track when I treat dozens of patients. Mrs. Blackthorn and I spoke earlier this week, and I explained to her that Telma is in advanced stage dementia. Her latest tests show a steep decline in all areas of the brain, including frontal, parietal, and temporal lobe function. It is my and my colleagues' belief that the buildup of amyloid plaques has caused extensive cell death. Severe enough, I'm afraid, to be beyond the scope of this program to offer her any marked improvement, such as it is."

Tate narrowed his eyes, and I could tell he was about to say something...*Tate-y*. I grabbed his hand and pressed. Hard. I wanted to hear the truth, even if it hurt.

"Gia." Dr. Stultz turned his attention to me, the fear on his face replaced with sympathy. "The progression is irreversible. Your mother has advanced beyond what our trial was created to treat. She's lost language processing and spatial awareness, and earlier today, Dr. Sheridan and I found her unresponsive to severe pain. She's incontinent and can no longer move on her own accord."

"It's nothing in comparison to what I'll do to you if you don't fix her," Tate muttered. His hand beneath mine began tapping his leg.

Dr. Stultz redirected his attention to him. "Mr. Blackthorn, it's out of my hands."

"Then use other fucking parts of your body," Tate enunciated slowly, callously. "Your brain, for instance."

"Tate," I breathed out, my lungs devoid of oxygen, my stomach swimming with dread. "Please, let him finish."

"We can only offer palliative care at this juncture." Dr. Stultz pulled open a drawer, taking out a brochure. "She is severely malnourished and dehydrated. Unable to eat on her own. She hasn't been fully conscious for some time. She keeps getting new infections before she finishes battling old ones," he explained, grabbing a pen and circling a phone number in the brochure. "She'll need the assistance of a feeding tube to continue living. In addition, her immune system is compromised as she's currently suffering from pneumonia, periodontal, and Lyme disease. She's going to be transferred to UC in the next hour to treat these conditions."

"What's next for her after UC?" I asked. She wasn't going to stay there forever. Hopefully.

I realized in my haze that Tate's leg tapping had a rhythm.

Two, six, two.

Two, six, two.

Two, six, two.

And then I realized it *always* had a rhythm. Every time I caught him tapping, it was always the same. Compulsive. Yet almost soothing in an abstract way.

"Since she doesn't meet the criteria for our clinical trials, her condition has advanced beyond our capabilities…" Dr. Stultz turned the brochure in my direction on the table, pushing it my way. "This is a great hospice nearby. Highly recommended. Once she's stable for discharge, she will need to be checked into an institution that prioritizes her comfort, because her decline will be rapid, I'm afraid."

His words sliced at me like knives, leaving searing pain everywhere they landed. It was well and truly over. I wasn't getting her back.

"What about…um, keeping her at home?" I didn't even look at Tate for permission. Fuck that.

Dr. Stultz shook his head. "Her health has deteriorated to a point she needs easy access to medical assistance. She might be able to be discharged and go home closer to passing away."

"This is bullshit." Tate stood abruptly, slamming his palms against the desk and towering over Dr. Stultz like a bloodthirsty hound. I'd never seen him this mad in my life. "You're supposed to be the best in your field."

"I *am* the best in my field."

"Then keep her alive," Tate commanded.

"I wish I could."

"You *can*," Tate argued. "Figure out a way if you want your career to survive."

Dr. Stultz fumbled for the button under his desk. I didn't think he was actually going to use it—who knew? Maybe he would—but I didn't leave it up to chance. I grabbed Tate's sleeve and tugged him away before he launched himself at a healthcare provider.

"Come on. Let's go." I hated the twinge of desperation that leaked through my voice.

"I'm sorry, Gia." Dr. Stultz put his hands back on the table.

"It's fine." My head was a mess, and I felt like a stranger in my own body. My entire existence was falling apart, but I kept my head high. "Thank you, Dr. Stultz. I appreciate it. Please don't worry about security. We'll be off now."

I had to physically shove Tate away from the doctor's office and toward the elevators. His body was like an ancient statue of marble, heavy and punishingly hard, refusing to budge as we stumbled into the hallway. Punching the button to the lift, I sighed and pressed my forehead to the cool wall tiles.

"Before you get any ideas, you can't divorce me until she flatlines." He got in my face, snarling.

I spun around, too shaken to understand what was really happening.

"W-what?"

"Our deal. The terms of which were abundantly clear. You can only divorce me when she dies. Not before. Even if she's in hospice," he clipped out, his eyes darkening into something terrifying. "Even if she is in a vegetative state for years. It's all in the fine print. Read it."

Sourness exploded all over my tongue.

What kind of monster did I marry? This was the time when he was supposed to comfort me. Or at least pretend to give half a shit. Instead, he was reminding me of the terms of my imprisonment. "That's what you care about right now?" I had to hold my own head to keep it from exploding. "Your precious deal?"

Tate's expression remained blank and empty. "This was always about business."

"Yeah?" I laughed humorlessly. "Well, you're a shit business-man then. Because so far, you've got next to nothing out of this arrangement."

"*Yet.*"

All the despair, grief, and hopelessness inside me had morphed into hot, white rage. Before I knew what I was doing, I slapped his cheek. Hard. The sound of it rang between us, echoing over the bare walls. He didn't even touch his cheek. Just stared down at me, hard jaw tightening, his mouth set in a grim line.

"Do it again," he ordered. "I deserve it."

I pressed my lips together, crying. I really needed to stop crying. And slapping him too. We were so toxic. I didn't like the person I was becoming with him.

"If it makes you feel better," his baritone was low, his eyes boring into mine, "hurt me. Transfer your pain to me. It's just pain. I can take it."

Just pain? Who said something like that?

"Slap me. Punch me. Kick me. Cut me." He paused. "But don't you *dare* leave me before our contract is up, Apricity, or you'll feel the wrath of a thousand fucking wars."

The lift arrived, and the door slid open. Neither of us moved. The door closed.

Tate snatched my hand and brought it to his face. "Do it."

And I remembered dejectedly that my husband's past was murky and full of dark secrets. Maybe he was used to being people's punching bag. Maybe the invincible man in front of me was forged from abuse, sculpted by brutality. After all, to become cruel, one must experience cruelty.

"No, I won't hurt you." I wrenched my hand from his hold. "I'm sorry I lost control. Regardless of your abhorrent behavior, violence is never the answer." I licked my lips. He was staring at me with odd, frantic desperation. "I need air. Don't follow me. Not you either." I pointed at Enzo and Filippo behind us.

Tate gave them a quick, jerky nod.

I turned around and pushed the door leading to the stairway, running. From Tate. From Mum. From the terrible news.

Hospice. It was only a matter of time now. The countdown had begun, and I had no way to stop it.

My vision was blurred with tears as I took the stairs two at a time. When I reached the main floor, I slammed into a hard body. I gasped, my mind immediately going to the Irish. But when I blinked the tears out of my vision, I saw Dr. Stultz.

"Gia." He clutched my shoulders, a fatherly air to him.

For a moment, I wondered if *he* was a part of the Callaghan family. I trusted no one at this point.

"I didn't want to finish the conversation on such a bad note," Dr. Stultz explained. "I hope you know we did all we could."

I nodded, the heat behind my nose warning me another wave of weeping was fast approaching. "Of course I know that."

Dr. Stultz rubbed at his cheek. "I'm going to take off my doctor cap for a second and speak to you candidly, if I may."

I sniffled, nodding again.

"I'm the first to appreciate a man who would pluck the moon from the sky for his woman, but your husband was wrong to do what he did to get your mother placed in the program. He could go to prison for a long time if his actions come to light."

My eyebrows slammed together. "What do you mean?"

Dr. Stultz studied me in surprise. "I thought you knew."

"Knew what?"

"That he managed to break into one of the most secure database servers in the world, add your mother's data to a vetted list of candidates, and then had the audacity to send someone to threaten a top neurologist at gunpoint to falsify her test results to meet the desired criteria for the program." He paused. "At least that's my educated guess, considering her state and the coincidental way stars aligned."

My mouth went dry.

Tate did that?

I was horrified, yes, of course. But also...*comforted* somehow.

It terrified me that I was attracted to this side of him. The side of Tate that craved me like I was a deadly, addictive drug. After all, what was obsession if not love's wicked sister?

Don't fall in love with him, Gia. He will never love you back.

Tate was only capable of the twisted and perverse. A relationship that allowed him a sense of complete control.

"Please don't report him," I choked out. I was too desperate for pride. "I'll make sure he doesn't act on any of his threats to you. You'll never hear from him again. Please, he's all I have."

The admission ripped from me like a snatched beggar's bag. It wasn't lost on me that first, I did not report my own husband for murder, and now I was covering him for another crime he committed.

Dr. Stultz worked his jaw back and forth, nodding wordlessly.

I threw my arms at him in a hug, sniffling into a white lab coat that smelled like isopropyl and antiseptic.

He patted my back gently. "I know he meant well. And I know you have no one else." His chest deflated. "I have a daughter your age. She lives down the street from us. I'm devastated for your loss, sweet child."

We stood in the stairway for minutes, me crying, him comforting me, before I opened the door and emerged into the main entrance of the hospital.

Tate waited for me at the front desk, his hawkish gaze trained on the door I came out of.

He joined me silently, giving me the space I needed as we walked back to the car.

When Enzo and Filippo met us, he nudged them aside with his shoulder, edging them away.

"Take the day off," he ordered. "I'll watch over her."

CHAPTER TWENTY-FOUR
TATE

I was sick with longing.

It consumed me like cholera, spreading internally, taking over my body.

Outwardly, I was a symbol of success and indifference.

I worked. I exercised. I attended meetings. Counted tiles, precious gems, and solved equations, like usual.

But nothing was normal.

Gia was doing poorly. I could tell, even with my nonexistent ability to feel empathy.

She had not left her room in four days, save for a quick trip to the kitchen. Did not visit her mother at the hospital. Didn't go into work.

She was wasting away. The catch was I had the emotional intelligence of a fucking Birkin bag. I couldn't help her if I tried.

I paced outside her room like a caged panther, racking my brain, trying to figure out how to make her happy.

She was foolish, negligent, and a complete failure in honoring our contract. I wanted to sue her for breaking every single clause in it. This was *my* time with her, *my* fucking hard-earned prerogative, and she was wasting it away by being difficult and impossible.

Our marriage was by far the worst deal I'd ever struck in my entire career.

On day four, I called Calla and Dylan. They rushed to her side with cupcakes and sweet tea—*fuck*, refined carbs, I could've thought of that myself—and resurfaced after three hours holed up in her room.

"She's grieving." Calla wiped her pink, tear-stricken eyes, closing the door softly behind her. "You need to give her time."

"I've run out of that certain ingredient, right along with my fucking patience." I bared my teeth.

Once her mother died, Gia would leave. I had to find more leverage over her.

No, you have to stop extorting people into bending to your will.

Easier said than done. Force was the only weapon I knew how to use in a relationship, *any* relationship.

"Hmm." Calla tapped her lips. "That certainly seems like a *you* problem."

"It's Gia's problem more than anything. I'll bury her legally for breaking our contract if she doesn't turn a corner."

"Okay, first of all? That's a *great* way to win a woman over." Dylan mimicked a gun with her fingers, pointing at me with a wink. "Keep doing that. You're in the right direction, Romeo."

How did Rhyland marry this woman? I knew warts more lovable than her.

"I'm not trying to make her fall."

Dylan pulled a worried face. "I wonder if you believe your own words. You let her buy a private jet and a whole-ass island."

"She did it without my knowledge."

"Yeah," Dylan snorted. "And your punishment for her was two orgasms."

For Pete's sake, women talked about *everything*. I was never going to accept the double standard of men not being able to talk about their sex lives.

"What is she saying?" I stirred Dylan back to the topic. It felt like herding cats.

"Not much." Dylan scrunched her nose. "I think she needs some cheering up, though."

"No fucking shit, Sherlock."

"There's that charm again." Dylan smiled big, resting her cheek over her hands and batting her lashes dreamily. "Tone it down a notch, or Gia will have some real competition. We'll all be vying for your affection."

"How does Rhyland cheer you up?"

Dylan squinted to the distance, giving it some thought. "Usually? Anal."

Not very helpful, considering I hadn't even *fucked* my wife yet.

"What about you?" I turned to Calla.

She pinched her lower lip. "Honey-glazed chicken nuggets. But I think Gia is a seafood kinda girlie."

I shook my head. They were utterly useless. "Get out."

As much as I wanted to berate my former PA for screwing me over, this was one of those times when I'd probably catch more bees with honey. She needed something to lift her spirits. I'd lost my parents long before I knew what it felt like to have them in the first place, so her pain was foreign to me.

I searched the internet. Some seriously idiotic suggestions popped up, but a few sparked an idea in me.

At three in the morning, I found myself driving to a storage unit on the outskirts of the city where Gia had stored her mother's belongings. I sorted through boxes full of impractical junk the majority of the night until I found what I was looking for.

At ten thirty in the morning, my work was done. I knocked on Gia's door. There was no answer.

"Gia." I braced an elbow against the doorframe, fighting the urge to kick it down. "There's something I need you to see."

"I saw it already." She whimpered, hiccupping on the other end. "And I heard what Dylan said. But you, sir, won't be getting any backdoor action with that size of yours."

My mouth quirked into a half-moon grin. Things were not so dire if she managed to crack an anal joke.

"You'll take it everywhere, Apricity. All in good time. Now, open the door."

"I'm not done sulking."

"Nobody else is coming to save you," I rasped. "It's me or nothing."

"I'll take nothing then."

Practice empathy, Dr. Patel chided in my head. *Work on it like it's a muscle you need to develop.*

"Get the fuck out."

Oops.

"Since you asked so nicely…" She trailed off, voice sweet as a peach. "*No.*"

"Out, Gia."

"No."

It was time to bring out the big guns. Probably should've started with that. I was terrible at this. But I had zero fucking experience.

"I brought macarons from Paris," I said.

"I'm allergic to almonds."

"Arancini from Sicily."

"Don't eat fried food on weekdays."

"Fluffy Yorkshire pudding. Still warm." My fist pressed into the wall so hard it started chipping. "I know it's your favorite."

A pause. A hesitation. A tick of the clock.

"With gravy and creamy garlic potatoes?" she sniffled. "And… and…Sunday roast?"

"Yeah. Row made it himself. Just how you like it."

"He makes mashed peas."

What was I to say to this? *Go marry Row Casablancas then. See if I give a damn.*

But I did. And it infuriated me.

Finally, she said, "Give me a few more hours."

No, I wanted to howl. *Already, you're not delivering your side of the bargain.*

But I had no chips to bargain with. It was the first time since Andrin where I was at a disadvantage against another human.

I did not like it.

I turned back and left.

CHAPTER TWENTY-FIVE
GIA

Stepping out of my room, I rubbed the sleep and tears from my eyes.

I'd spent the past few days steering clear and well away from my husband. Not because I looked like hell. It wasn't even entirely because of Mum.

What kept me hidden was the realization I was falling for my monster.

Craving its claws. Missing its pointy, venomous teeth. Wanting to capture its stony, unmoving heart.

Clearly, I'd fallen down the Stockholm syndrome rabbit hole. Yay me.

He was callous, forbidding, not to mention a *literal* murderer, but he was oddly loyal to those he'd chosen to entwine his destiny with, and I found myself at the top of that list.

Before making it one step, my eyes landed on the elaborate gift Tate had brought me. Cellophane-wrapped treats from all over the world—the UK, Cuba, Jamaica, Italy, France, and South Korea— individually wrapped and waiting to be consumed. There were baskets of fruits and chocolates. And something else. Something that made me pause.

No. No way. Where did he...?

My old photo albums.

The ones Mum kept in the attic back home.

Dozens of them, for me to leaf through.

Pictures of Dad and Elliott and Mum and me. Of our pets throughout the years. Trips. Birthdays. Christmases. I rushed to one of the albums and sank to my knees. Flipped through the pages hungrily, cupping my mouth, tears of joy and laughter and sadness drifting from me. Bliss poured from the pages. Nostalgia flooded me.

Smiling faces.

Goofy expressions.

Notes Mum scribbled on blank address labels and glued under every picture, lest we forget.

Disneyland 2014. Elliott was too scared to ride anything but the teacups! Claimed he had food poisoning but then ate seven waffles when we got to the hotel.

Christmas 2017. Gia accidentally set her dress on fire trying to light a scented candle. Insisted on wearing it and said the asymmetrical edges were a part of the design.

Boxing Day 2012. Dad lost a footie bet. Man U won. He had to get the result tattooed to his arm.

A rush of memories slammed into me all at once.

The way Elliott squinted in all the photos to hide what he was certain was a lazy eye.

Dad always deliberately ruined family pictures with silly faces just to make Mum exasperated so they could make up in the grossest, most adorable way.

The way Mum always tsked and shook her head whenever Nicole Kidman popped up on the telly and said, "This woman called her daughter Sunday Rose, which is too bloody close to Sunday roast."

An unfeminine snort escaped me, and I shook my head.

Pressing the albums to my chest, I tucked them in my room, where they'd be safe.

My heart stammered as I made my way toward Tate's bedroom. I stopped at the threshold.

Perched on the edge of his bed, he was solving equations in a textbook, thick brows crumpled in deep in concentration. He oozed gentle violence. This elegant, complex, Victorian creature.

His free hand tapped against the side of his leg.

Two, six, two.

Two, six, two.

Two, six, two.

I frowned, checking my Apple Watch.

Two, six, two.

Two, six, two.

Two, six, two.

His tapping was in a three-second increment exactly, just as I'd calculated in Dr. Stultz's office.

The penny dropped.

All this time, his body whispered his secret to me when Tate wasn't looking.

My husband has OCD.

He needed rituals, routines, and numbers. Soothing quotes from books he'd read and loved.

And he hid it from the world. I couldn't imagine how suffocating it was for him to keep his rituals in check at work so that I—someone who spent almost every day with him for the past five years—wouldn't notice.

Obsessive-compulsive disorder. It was right in front of me all along.

I now understood why he didn't want anyone in his bed. I'd read somewhere that sometimes people living with the disorder were germophobes.

Why he checked his pocket watch every single hour.

All the times he rushed away after we fooled around to gain back his sense of control.

The way he drank his coffee in exactly nine sips. At exactly nine in the morning.

The way he wore his Valentino suit every Wednesday, the Prada every Thursday, and the golden engraved cuff links only to meetings that were at risk of being unfruitful.

He always entered rooms with his right foot. Wiped his utensils with the tablecloth at restaurants. Only drank from straws.

I knocked on the open door softly to make myself known. His head snapped up.

"Done sulking, I presume." He clamped his teeth over the tip of his pen, looking up from his book.

"For the immediate future, yeah." I stepped inside, ignoring his jab. "Might melt down later, though."

"I don't doubt it."

Of course he'd make it hard on me.

"Thank you, for…" I jerked my head to the hallway. I knew explicitly mentioning what he did would irritate him.

"Yeah." He closed the textbook, setting it aside along with the pen. "I needed to lure you back out. Fuck knows how long this arrangement will last."

"You do realize this is not how people think, right?" I cleared my throat.

"Have I ever claimed to be normal?"

"No."

He spread his arms as if to say, *And there you have it.*

Filled with fresh compassion toward him, I let him ramble on. And on he went.

"In lieu of a functioning daughter, I hired a certified nurse to check on your mother." He stood up, waltzing over to his walk-in closet.

I followed him, realizing it didn't really surprise me that Tate did this. He did a lot of thoughtful things for me when I wasn't even paying attention.

He began undressing from his casual suit in the vast mahogany room. A freshly pressed tux hung on the mirror across from him. "You'd be happy to know your mother's pneumonia is almost gone.

The rest of her infections are being treated now. She is going to pull through."

I knew that. I had been texting with Dr. Stultz every day, getting reports from him. He made the trip to ICU to keep me in the loop. My mother was unconscious and heavily drugged. Dr. Stultz insisted there was no point in me coming in. She wouldn't know.

"Thank you," I whispered. "I appreciate your concern and your thoughtfulness."

He produced a barely human grunt.

"Where are you going?" I asked when his dress shirt sailed down his arms onto the floor. His torso was a work of the gods. Sculpted to its last inch, his abs prominent, each muscle in his arms defined and molded to perfection. A rush of heat found its way to my core, reminding me it was so very empty.

"Luca's engagement party." He unzipped his pants.

I didn't look away. A bit late to play coy.

"Oh, lovely. Sounds like fun."

"He begs to fucking differ," he muttered sarcastically, saunter-ing in nothing but his black Armani briefs toward his suit. "It's a marriage of convenience to strengthen the ties with the Chicago Outfit. As far as I'm aware, he finds her mousy and unattractive."

"Why?"

He unhooked his dress shirt from the hanger. "Because she is mousy and unattractive."

"That's not nice," I chided. I was now inside his walk-in closet, leaning against the central island, staring at him with fascination.

"I'd be pissed off too if I had to commit to an eternity fucking a woman I wasn't attracted to."

"Do you want me to come with you?" Maybe getting out of the flat would do me good.

"Unnecessary."

"I could use the fresh air."

"You won't get it in a hotel ballroom full of people."

"Do you not want me to come?"

"I do not want you to *leave*," he snapped, turning around to stare me down with fire in his eyes. "You're already flaking on this deal, and I'm tired of getting fucked over."

I ate the space between us so we stood toe-to-toe, pressing my palm to his cheek. His gaze narrowed into slits. Both our hearts galloped, beating against one another.

"I will not run," I whispered.

"I know." His jaw twitched.

"How do you know?"

"Because I run fucking faster, Gia," he deadpanned. "I'll catch you, and you'll regret it."

"Not until our contract is expired anyway." I ignored his threat, not missing his flared nostrils and the muscle jumping in his jaw. "I'll fulfill my duties to you."

"That's very charitable of you."

"I'll go put something on," I smiled.

He clasped my wrist before I could spin around, jerking me back to his sphere. "You're not coming unless I am."

"Excuse me?" My breath stuttered in my lungs.

"You heard me." He stood up, towering over me, making me fight my instinct to shrink and cower. "I've eaten you out, fingered you to oblivion, and awarded you with a hundred and thirty-two orgasms now."

A hundred and forty, actually. And here I thought he was the math genius.

"Your point?"

"You're using me, and I'm over it. You want to play wife— we fuck. Otherwise, you can stay here, and we'll resume our little cat-and-mouse game when I'm in a better mood."

My jaw went slack. "Are you telling me that if I want to come with you, I have to fuck you *now*?"

He trailed a thumb over my eyebrow affectionately. "Not

necessarily *now* now. I'll choose the time and place. But it'll be in the next twelve hours."

"Fuck you," I spat.

"*Now* she is getting it."

Yet I didn't leave. I didn't say no. I didn't argue. Deep down, I wanted it. Knew it was inevitable. And I loved the way he pulled me out of my comfort zone. How he molded me into this fearless, feisty creature. One who pressed daggers to his throat and outsmarted mobsters. He lured me into his own Wonderland, into a sink-or-swim situation, and I swam.

"Glad we're on the same page." Tate interpreted my silence as compliance, giving me his back. "Get dressed. Something with easy access, of course."

"E-easy access?"

"No tights," he explained. "Unless you don't mind them being ruined."

I was already halfway across the room when he asked, "Oh, and, Gia?"

"Yes?" I turned around to see he still had his back to me.

"Wear something modest, unless you want your dress stained by other people's blood."

CHAPTER TWENTY-SIX
GIA

The golden Mikado dress I swathed myself in had one purpose and one purpose only—to piss Tate off.

The plan worked better than I anticipated. As soon as I slipped into the limo, his gaze alone seared me into ash.

"What in the *fuck* is this?" he demanded.

"Your sweet undoing?" I pouted, giving him my best angelic look.

"I told you I'll ruin any indecent dress you wear with the blood of your admirers."

"And I'm telling *you* that gold and burgundy go exceptionally well together. Look, I even wore my Louboutins." I flung one leg in the air to reveal a rubicund-hued heel. "To be fair, it's full length and reaches past my ankles." I planted my derriere on the crème leather seat.

"*To be fair*, the strapless corset barely covers your nipples," he retorted, mimicking my English accent. "Your tits jiggle every time you breathe."

I pressed my lips together, trying hard not to giggle.

"Don't you dare laugh." He erected a finger in my direction. "Your tits will be dancing in that thing, and I'll have no choice but to kill everyone in the vicinity."

"Only when I sit down. The corset sort of rides up. Anyway, we're alone." I gestured around us. Iven was all the way in the front with his back to us. The partition was open, but that could be remedied.

"Not for long." Tate sat back with his legs spread open, reaching for his cigar box. "We're picking up Row and that thing."

"*That thing* is called Cal, and she is one of my best friends." I scrunched my nose. "Anyway, what do they have to do with the Ferrantes?"

"Row's in charge of the catering."

"I hadn't realized he offered this service."

"He hadn't either. But then a two-million-dollar offer in cash came along, and his schedule magically cleared."

I was definitely friends with people outside my tax bracket.

"Go upstairs and change." Tate bit off the edge of his cigar. "I don't like that dress."

"That's all right, darling. You're not the one wearing it." I offered him a condescending pat on the cheek. "You'd never pull it off with your ankles."

He ran his tongue over his upper teeth, sharp, sly eyes full of malice inspecting me. "Don't say I didn't warn you. Thierry." He snapped his fingers. "Start driving."

"Thierry's here from London?" I brightened up, turning toward the driver.

Since the vehicle was too long for him to catch my gaze in the rearview mirror, Thierry raised a hand in a wave. "How do you do, Gia?"

"Very well. How about you and Annette?"

The limo slid into the heavy Manhattan traffic, driving at a snail's pace.

"Better than ever. Got her hip replacement last week. Healing smoothly. Sorry to hear about your mother—"

"Yeah, yeah, yeah." Tate puffed on his cigar, sending a rancid cloud of smoke to the space between us. "Nobody really cares. She's just being nice."

Silence blanketed the interior of the car. Each of us sat in an opposite corner of the back seat. I stared out the window, wondering if he would take me here, in front of Thierry, with the partition open just to humiliate me. He wouldn't have to take me by force.

Deep down, I knew I'd let him.

Deep down, I knew I turned into a very different person where Tate was concerned. He seemed to pry the darkest, most nefarious parts of me out into the light.

And I *loved* it. All of it. Even the toxicity.

Every second that passed on our way to Cal and Row's Fifth Avenue building had the knot in my stomach twist harder until it pressed against my sternum.

We stopped outside their building, and that was when I noticed Tate had his phone angled toward his window with the camera app on, facing him.

"Would you like me to call Cal and tell her—"

"We'll go upstairs," he cut into my words.

I squinted. "Why?"

"We're being followed."

I didn't have to ask by whom. I ducked my head, trying to follow his line of vision, but I didn't have a good angle.

"And you want us to go upstairs, where we might endanger our friends? Their *daughter*?" I asked incredulously.

"There are rules to abide by in the underworld. Certain codes." He clasped my elbow. His eyes, cold and empty, dug into my flesh like a metal knife. "They won't hurt an innocent family. The Casablancas will protect *us*, but we won't endanger *them*."

He got out of the limo first, shielding me with his body as we slipped into the building. We took the stairs up, him following closely behind me, glancing down every few seconds.

Cold sweat settled over my forehead. I stumbled over the fabric of my dress, reaching to the wall of the darkened corridor. Finally, we reached their door. Tate rapped on it three times.

Row opened, surprise pleating his forehead. "What's up? Thought we're going to meet downst—"

Tate shoved past him, tugging me to his side. He strode over to the living room window.

I winced apologetically. "Sorry. We're being followed by Irish mobsters."

"*Oookay*, I'm gonna need a little more context than that." Row double locked the door and pulled on the latch. "Which one of us is calling the cops?"

"No one. I've got it handled," Tate said calmly. "They were bound to try tonight. Enzo and his soldiers are off for the engagement party."

"You brought mobsters to my doorstep?" Row blinked. "While my daughter and wife are in the other room?" He looked ready to kill my husband. I was almost certain I was going to help him if he tried.

"They won't come in here. You and your family are under Ferrante protection. You're innocent. They're not that dumb."

"Maybe, but *you* are." Row looked around us, sticking a hand into his tousled jet-black hair and messing it further. "Jesus fucking Christ, Tate. I mean, your ass is more disposable than a soiled diaper, but what about Gia?"

"Hi guys! Thanks for giving us a ride." Cal appeared from the hallway, heels clicking as she put an earring on. "Serafina's nanny just arrived, but we still need to go through her evening routine together."

Tate ignored her, hiking over to the kitchen and returning to the window with a butcher block. "Is this the eight-pound block you used for that Netflix special?"

"Yeah." Row rubbed the back of his neck. "Wh—"

Tate tossed it out the window.

"What the fuck?" Row snapped before the sound of a watermelon bursting filled the air. "Holy shit."

Tate raised two fingers to point at his eyes in an I-see-you gesture. "Don't. Your building's in an angle that makes it impossible to see where the object fell from."

Row, Cal, and I sprinted to the window, peering down. Tate'd knocked down a man waiting at the building's entrance. The mobster lay on the pavement, unconscious, blood pouring out of his head. Three men talking on the phone dragged him into a nearby truck. There weren't any pedestrians on the street, but that was hardly any consolation.

"We're in the middle of Manhattan," I pointed out. "You do realize that?"

"No security cameras on this side of the block." He spared me a look. "And I knew they'd fuck off before the police arrive."

Actually, the police didn't arrive at all. There was no one to report the incident, I suppose. We waited a few minutes in stunned silence. Cal was shaking and giving Row the incredulous look of a woman who decisively did *not* want to host a murderer in her apartment.

"D-did you just kill someone?" Cal coughed out finally.

"No. But he'll need a sabbatical to take care of that head injury," Tate replied.

"It sounded like his head exploded," Cal insisted.

"He moved," Row reassured his wife. "I saw it. I don't think he's dead." But I could see on his face he didn't entirely believe his own words.

"Stop looking so scandalized." Tate slanted his eyes in Cal's direction. "He tried to kill me."

Cal placed a trembling hand over her heart, trying to regulate her breathing. "This is…this is not okay." She was hyperventilating. "You're not okay, Tate."

An odd urge to tell her not to speak to my husband like this slammed into me. I had no idea where it came from. Objectively speaking, she was totally right.

"I'm going to give my daughter a bath, read her a story, and put her to bed." Row threw a thumb over his shoulder, then pointed at my husband. "You better not fucking kill anyone else while I'm gone." He glanced at Cal, then grabbed her by the hand and tugged her close. "And I'm taking my wife with me."

"Don't be dramatic, Ambrose. I was sending a message." Tate rearranged his pitchfork cuff links.

"Next time, use email, fuckface."

Row and Cal disappeared back into the hallway. Still shaken, I stumbled to their kitchen, grabbed a glass from the cupboard, and filled it with tap water, taking big gulps. I rinsed the glass, set it on a dish rack, and gripped the edges of the sink, drawing a breath.

Tate's arms bracketed me from either side, locking me with my stomach pressed to the counter. His mouth found my ear. "*Now.*"

His voice reverberated in the empty space between my thighs.

I knew what he meant.

Shivering with delight, my thighs parted on their own accord, thick, sticky heat gathering between them. His torso was flush against my back, and my muscles jumped reflexively at the sudden touch. He reached down under my skirts from behind, flipping the long dress over my upper body. With his free hand, he dipped his fingers into my panties, stroking my pussy, which slurped excitedly at his touch.

"No," I gasped, but even as the word tumbled out of my mouth, I kept chasing his elusive, maddening strokes. "Cal and Row will hear us."

He tugged my panties down to my lower thighs, then kicked my legs apart with his shiny loafer. "They might even catch us if they get lucky."

"Are you on some kind of an episode? I am not contaminating my friends' kitch—"

"Row fucked Calla on every surface in my Belgravia house, Mamaroneck mansion, and Mediterranean superyacht. I'm merely returning a favor. Besides, his bath and story routine with that kid? Half an hour long. *Minimum.* That kid reads sixth-grade books every night." His fingers skimmed up my ribs. "*Fuck.* You're so sexy it's a health hazard. If I don't bury my cock inside you right now, I am going to die."

I heard his zipper rolling down. No foreplay. No kissing. This wasn't the act of making love. This was him fucking me, conquering the few parts I refused to share with him until now.

"Sounds good. We never signed a prenup," I clapped back, grabbing onto the tap for dear life.

"Hold on tight." He guided the fat head of his cock into me. A dark, evil laugh prickled my skin. "Oh, and for the record, you'll never be rid of me. I'll haunt you from the grave, sweetheart."

He teased me first, taking his sweet time drawing circles with his tip around my entrance. Cal's and Row's voices rose from the hallway, only a few feet away from us. They were talking to their nanny while my husband drew circles around the lips of my pussy with his cock, dipping it an inch or two before pulling away. I chased his touch, past shame, pride, and reason. Wiggled my arse, offering myself to him. But he was drawing pleasure from making me desperate, crazed with heat.

Breathlessly, I reached for my clit and massaged it with my fingers. This set him off. He withdrew from me, grabbed my waist, and swiveled me to face him. His gray eyes darkened into two onyx pools.

"Stop defying me every step of the way," he snarled.

"I'll never stop." I tilted my head up. "*Nev—*"

He slammed into me all at once. I cried out with such abandon, I was sure not only Row and Cal heard me but the rest of the East Coast. Our hosts' voices snuffed into tense silence. God, this was so embarrassing. They knew we were *fucking* inside their house. What must they think of me?

Tate read my mind, a smug smirk spreading across his face. I could feel his lips spreading across the shell of my ear. "How about you focus on how I'm giving you the best and the only dick you'll ever have and stop worrying about people who had anal sex in my Jacuzzi three months ago?"

He pressed home again. Long and thick, he filled me a bit beyond my capacity, and I stretched around him, welcoming the slight uncomfortableness, marveling at the way I could feel the shape of him inside me. The prominent crown. The thick, curving veins. It was a shock to my system.

Before I could recover, Tate grabbed me by the backs of my thighs so my arse was up in the air, detached from the counter, tilting my pelvis just so that he'd have a good angle to hit my G-spot. His thrusts were long and controlled, steady, as he pumped into me with fierce, deep strokes. His eyes were locked on mine the entire time, in a confusing power struggle I was too pleasure-drunk to decode. My legs were languid in his rough palms as he shagged me. It was rough and punishing, wild with fury and passion, and I knew the scent of us was going to cling to the many layers of my dress. It took me a few moments—maybe even minutes—to realize Tate wasn't blinking as he glared at me.

"Are you okay?" Each of my words was punctuated by a grunt as he thrust into me.

He shook his head, his lips pressing into a grimace.

He *wasn't* okay?

"Fuck," he growled, throwing caution to the wind. He leaned to catch my mouth in a kiss that was pure tender violence, a clash of teeth and tongues, of fast strokes and slow burn.

I convulsed around him, a firestorm climbing up my spine, my muscles clutching, burning, toes curling as the orgasm tore through me like a volcano, the lava spurting in waves as I rocked against his cock, my abs tight while he still pumped into me.

My climax subsided gradually, euphoria slinking under my skin like warm milk on a winter night. Tate grunted and arched, coming hard inside me. He pumped lazily into me for a few seconds before pulling out inch by inch, arrogantly reminding me how long his shaft was.

My husband stepped aside, hoisting me over the counter, flattening my skirts against my stomach so we both had a good look at my pussy. He parted my thighs with his fingers, staring.

"Look at that pretty defiance of yours now, trickling down your inner thigh," Tate cooed mockingly. "How adorable." He trailed his index finger along my inner thigh.

I watched in fascination as he tucked his cloudy, thick cum back between my folds. Not only did he put his stringy seed inside, but he pushed two fingers, filling me to the hilt. I gasped uncomfortably when I thought he reached my actual uterus, squirming away from him.

"Be a good guest, and keep it in. Don't wanna dirty your friends' kitchen."

The haze of the orgasm completely undid me, though. If having mind-blowing sex on your best friend's kitchen counter was wrong, then I didn't want to be right.

"I'm on the pill." I slapped his hand away, slowly reclaiming my sanity. "So forget about little Lucifers running around anytime soon."

"We'll see about that." He stood back and smoothed out his suit and bow tie.

"You won't trap me by impregnating me." I frantically pushed down my dress. He seemed like the type to change your birth control into Tic Tacs.

"Gia, stop talking about leaving. It's not fucking happening. Before or after your mother dies."

"Doesn't it bother you that I don't love you?"

I had to leave because I *was* falling for him.

Because he would never love me, and I'd have to live with the tragedy of it, day in and day out.

"Darling." He bent down to give me a cold peck on the lips, patting my head. "That's a bonus."

Row and Cal swanned out of the hallway. They were both bright red.

"Are you decent?" Cal had her hand flung over her eyes.

"Yeah," I squeaked, horrified. "I'm so, *so* sorr—"

"I just want you to know, my wife's pussy is the most delicious thing I've ever eaten in your damn kitchen," Tate announced in his no-bullshit tone. "No close seconds."

Lord.

Row screeched to a stop in front of him, blowing a hot breath. They were nose-to-nose, and both looked ready to kill each other.

"You crossed every fucking line tonight, and it's not even seven o'clock," Row informed him.

Tate looked unbothered. "Send me the bi—"

"There won't be a bill. I'm burning this fucking condo to the ground after your spunk was released here. Hell, I'll probably have Cal and my daughter move to a hotel *tonight*." Row pointed at the floor, seething. "You're buying me the Park Avenue apartment we went to see together."

"That shithole's still on the market?" Tate elevated a bored eyebrow. "It's been three months."

"Still for sale," Row spat.

"It's yours." As Tate put his hand on my lower back and ushered me outside, he whispered in my ear, "Measly price to pay for the best fuck of my life."

CHAPTER TWENTY-SEVEN
GIA

The drive to the engagement party was awkward, but at least we weren't being followed anymore. The silence sat between the four of us like a ten-ton elephant.

Finally, Cal sighed. "Please, can we move on from this little oopsie? Row and I once did it on his prep station in Descartes. He was lucky he closed the restaurant voluntarily or it'd have been shut down." She bit down on her lower lip.

Row narrowed his eyes at Tate. "That was in *my* kitchen, *my* station. Tate is welcome to do whatever the fuck he wants on his property. Preferably drop dead."

"Gonna live till I'm a hundred and twenty just to spite you." Tate smirked wolfishly, one arm slung over my shoulder. "Also, may I remind you that time in my Montauk Jacuzzi three months ago?"

Row scowled. "How do you even know that? You weren't home."

"CCTV."

"You were spying on us?" Row shrieked.

"I only watched the first five seconds before I added it to a PornHub compilation as retaliation. Nobody wants to bathe in your jizz, Row."

Row unbuckled quickly, ready to pounce on him, before I yelped, "He's kidding! He's kidding."

At least I hoped he was.

The exchange *did* break the ice, because afterward, the three of them slid into conversation about how Row didn't really even cook for the event, only helmed the staff that was working there. "Taylor's handling the entire operation and pocketing fifty percent of it. The kid's a wiz," Row said warmly about his sous-chef.

My mind drifted elsewhere. A few minutes passed before I felt my husband shift toward me.

"What's going on in that hectic mind of yours?"

"If we were to have children—and we won't, but *if* we did…" I trailed off.

"Yes?" He tilted an eyebrow.

"Our kids would be biracial," I said, gnawing on my lip.

He stared at me flatly. "I'm well aware of that."

"Are you sure you're prepared for that?"

"Why wouldn't I be?"

"Because it's…well, *different*." I clutched the trimmed hem of my dress, fumbling with it. "No matter how intelligent, beautiful, well-spoken, filthy rich, and powerful they'd be, sooner or later, they'd face prejudice and difficult moments. We'd have to have the gut-wrenching, frank conversations."

"I am nothing if not fucking truthful." He scanned me, then added, "Does it bother you?"

It didn't. I was proud of my heritage and was excited for my children to be a part of it. But I wanted to make sure he knew what he was getting into. "Does it not bother you?"

"No. Then again, I've never had to walk a day in your shoes."

This simple acknowledgement encouraged me. Tate's childhood seemed far from perfect, and I knew he had a humble beginning, but he never looked different.

"Diversity is not very common in your circles," I said matter-of-factly.

"It's becoming more common than you think. Even if it wasn't, ignorance is a terrible reason not to do something." He was quiet for a moment. "Besides, they'll have you."

"One person is not enough."

"One person is more than enough, when it's the right one."

Liquid heat filled my chest, and something dangerously close to deep affection took over me. "I reckon any woman—any *mother*—of a child who is a person of color needs to come to terms with the fact that she must be a lioness. You have to advocate for them more, always have your finger on the pulse. I think, for a lot of children, evil is an abstract concept. But for children who must know history well, whose grandparents experienced atrocious inequalities, evil is just another facet of human nature. The world can be a very unkind place."

"If the world is cruel to them," he said wryly, finding my fingers across the seat, lacing them with his so I'd stop fumbling, "I will be crueler. You can quote me on that."

Row and Cal were now talking animatedly between themselves, paying us no heed. I dropped my voice to a whisper, "Do you think if we had kids, you'd be able to love them?"

He considered my words. "If I could feel love...I think I'd love the hell out of our kids."

CHAPTER TWENTY-EIGHT
TATE

The limo pulled in front of the hotel, and we poured out.

I shielded Gia until we were well inside the ballroom, not taking any chances. Vello was the boss. This Callaghan fuck would never dare touch one of his guests in his territory. Row and That Thing finally fucked off to the kitchens, and I was able to tap my numbers in my pocket, thusly calming my quick heart rate. Gia and I were immediately surrounded by ass-kissers, wishing to congratulate us on our nuptials.

I let my wife do the talking. She was good at peopling. By contrast, I was good at *un*peopling. This yin and yang situation reminded me that I needed to put a stop to the killing spree as soon as I was done avenging Daniel. This killing people shit was addictive. I half understood why Achilles, Luca, and Enzo were married to their jobs.

I still bathed in the aftermath of fucking Gia. I planned to do it at least until my dick fell off. I'd happily try to override the 98 percent effectiveness of birth control by constantly copulating.

Scanning the room for potential security breaches, my eyes landed on Achilles. He seemed in good spirits, joking and mingling with underbosses in the corner of the room. The hideous motherfucker should know better than to gloat. He was next in line, surely.

Vello was going to marry all his deranged sons off before he picked a successor.

Speaking of the big boss, Vello stood a few feet away from his son with his wife, Chiara, by his side, chatting with President Wolfe Keaton and his wife, Francesca. Not only a president but plenty of senators, congresspeople, and billionaires rounded out the list of attendees. The turnout was impressive, and I barely stood out.

Francesca had a belly full of baby under her lacey dress, and Wolfe reached to splay his fingers over the bump, stroking it absent-mindedly as he no doubt pretended to give a shit about whatever Vello had to say.

An internal fit of jealousy consumed me. What a fantastic way to trap a woman. Although by the shit-eating grin on Francesca's face, I suspected she'd be with him even if she wasn't knocked up.

Across the room stood Luca and a girl in her late teens. His expression suggested he was attending his own funeral. She held the grave expression of the coroner. Fuck, and I thought Gia and I had it rough.

Woodenly, the girl extended her slim wrist to well-wishers who wanted to see her ring. Showing the anello di fidanzamento was big at Italian engagement parties. They didn't exchange a word. I gave this thing between them one tax season. Tops.

"Wow," my wife breathed out, "Francesca Keaton is stunning up close."

Maybe she was. Sometime in the last few years, I had stopped paying attention to what women looked like. I just fucked the ones others deemed attractive while pining for my PA.

Gia and I grabbed our seating cards and approached our table. "Stay by my side, and don't go anywhere without me." I leaned down to whisper in her ear. "Callaghan won't touch a hair on your head in this ballroom. Anywhere outside it is fair game, though."

Her spine stiffened. My wife didn't like to be told what to do.

Especially when she had to live like a caged songbird because of my fuckups.

"Is he here?" she asked.

"No."

My presence here was contingent on Callaghan being disinvited. Somehow the idea of sharing hors d'oeuvres with the asshole who wanted to kill me didn't appeal to me.

We ended up sharing a table with hedge fund moguls and a congressman I'd seen frequenting the Forbidden Fruit Club. The club was owned by the Ferrantes and served as a high-end brothel during the daytime. My wife seemed determined not to speak to me more than absolutely necessary after I fucked her in front of our friends, and she instantly struck up a conversation with an elderly real estate developer.

Enzo slipped into the seat next to mine and started yapping happily. I tuned him out and found myself scanning the room again, looking for signs of Callaghan soldiers. I couldn't find any, but I found Vello and his extended family, sitting at a never-ending table.

I spotted Lila too. The mysterious baby sister of the Ferrante clan. Only seventeen.

She was delicate in her beauty. Ethereal and otherworldly. Like a Claudine painting by Marcel Dyf. Intellectually challenged, if rumors were to be believed.

She sat alone at a separate small table fitted for children, garbed in a glittery gold gown the same shade as her hair, her spine ramrod straight. She appeared to be hosting a tea party with porcelain dolls. Sprawled on the table was a British tea set, floral and vintage with carved handles. She poured air into mugs and laughed haughtily at something a porcelain doll said. How this pale-haired elfin shared full DNA with her strong-featured, ginormous brothers was a case for the FBI. She looked nothing like them. Not in height, not in build, not in color, and not in features.Her graceful pout and childlike innocence did nothing to yours truly, but I could see men clamoring for the chance to marry her. Knowing the Camorra and Vello Ferrante specifically, there was a good chance he'd marry her off despite her intellectual challenges.

He was the biggest prick I'd ever met. And I actually worked closely with Baron "Vicious" Spencer.

"Remove your eyes before I scoop them out, Blackthorn. Lila's off the table." Enzo tapped my shoulder, reminding me of his unfortunate existence.

I shot him a cool glare. "I'm a married man."

"Start acting like it, bro."

If that little shit bro-ed me one more time...

"Well, this one in front of you isn't attracted to children."

Even if she wasn't so young, I found her to be nothing extraordinary. She didn't have Gia's courage, fire, and wit. My wife's intelligence, firm values, and soft heart set me ablaze. Her beauty—while exquisite—was just a small fraction of her appeal to me.

"FYI, the exterior of the hotel is swarming with Callaghan's men." Enzo swirled his drink, giving it a sniff. "Since I'm off duty, I suggest you keep an eye on your wife."

"You think Callaghan is brazen enough to attack her during Luca's party?" I asked.

"I think he's brazen enough to set the sitting president on fire in front of the entire Congress," Enzo answered, unblinking. "Just because he's not here today doesn't mean he's not going to try to pull some bad shit. He's got a hard-on for your neck, and since you killed his proxies, he'll likely target yours."

The next hour included an endless amount of Italian food, badly crafted conversation paired with lovely crafted wine. A hedge fund dude bro, who was clearly a legacy hire, droned on about crypto to me while I pretended my full attention wasn't on Gia. I didn't let her out of my sight. Not a difficult task, considering watching her was hardly a punishment. She avoided my eyes, which got on my nerves.

Just when I thought the evening couldn't get any more tedious, the live band began playing a waltz, and Achilles appeared like a summoned evil spirit in a séance gone wrong. The wicked grin on his face looked like it'd been carved with a knife. He offered my wife his open palm with a bow. "Mrs. Blackthorn, would you do me the honor of a dance?"

He was insane if he thought I'd let his filthy hands touch her.

"Hard to pull off a waltz with two broken legs." I draped an arm over the back of her chair.

Gia's icy glare turned into a warm smile once she realized I didn't want her to dance with him.

"Mr. Ferrante, I'm pleased you asked." She placed her hand in his and stood up.

I pushed up to my feet, getting into Achilles's face. "What are you playing at?"

"Why, Blackthorn, can't a man dance with a beautiful woman at his brother's engagement party?"

"A man certainly can. But not this one." I pointed at Gia.

I had no idea where this hissy fit came from. I wasn't usually the jealous type.

"This one also has a mind of her own." Gia wedged herself between us, pushing at my chest. "And she wants to dance. Bugger off, Tate."

The smirk Achilles gave me as he led my wife to the dance floor was reason enough to break every bone in his body, stapes bone included.

Making a scene was not my style. Shocking and terrorizing people, however? Right up my alley. So instead of seething, I strolled straight over to Achilles's heel.

To the Ferrantes' unspoken weakness.

To their innocent, precious Lila.

Raffaella 'Lila' Ferrante only noticed my presence when my frame cast a shadow over her kiddie table. She stared up at me, sapphire eyes flaring in panic. She was not used to being acknowledged by nonfamily members was my guess.

"Hello, Raffaella," I said slowly, softly, as you would to a toddler. From the corner of my eye, I saw four Ferrante soldiers stand up from their seats, as did Enzo and Luca.

Her eyes immediately went in search of them, terrified and unsure. I ignored the way the chatter in the room died altogether.

"Would you like to dance?" I drawled.

She wasn't yet eighteen. I wasn't a pedophile and wasn't attracted to her, but sometimes, it really paid off to be seen as the most debauched creature alive, because then people assumed the worst about me.

Lila's eyes longingly drifted to the dance floor, but she pursed her lips, shaking her head no.

Every soldier in the room held their breath, waiting for an order. Every underboss tuned in.

"It's okay if you don't know how," I coaxed, knowing full well I was ruining the dance for Achilles and Gia, as they both stared at me for very different reasons. Even just chatting Lila up was enough to make a point. But I had a feeling I was going to persuade her. I knew want when I saw it in someone's face.

Lila's throat rolled with a swallow. Her gaze cut to her parents, to her brothers, then back to me. I didn't even know if she understood what I was saying.

"I won't let them hurt you," I added.

I could not give two shits what would happen after I made my point, but she didn't have to know that.

Finally, the frightened little creature put her bony hand in mine.

Ten men sprang toward me the minute our hands touched. Vello raised his palm, a silent order for them to stand down. They halted. You could cut the tension in the room with a butter knife. The entire ballroom watched in horror as I escorted her to the dance floor, like leading a newborn lamb to slaughter.

I stopped next to Achilles and Gia and assumed a waltz position. Lila was stiff in my arms, disoriented.

"Do you know how to waltz?" I asked.

She stared at me dumbly, blinking.

"Do you know how to talk?" I stifled a groan.

Another horrified blink.

With a sigh of annoyance, I planted her heeled feet on top of mine and started moving. She didn't know how to dance. Didn't know how to speak. But I watched the way her eyes glimmered. Her lips twitched.

She was no fool and definitely not intellectually challenged.

What the fuck was her family playing at?

Vello had his eye on us the entire time. So did every other man in the Camorra.

Achilles and Gia shuffled closer until we were almost shoulder to shoulder.

"Every Achilles has his heel," I said and grinned. "I think I just found yours."

"You've crossed the line." He bared his teeth at me.

"Impossible. I have no lines when it comes to my wife," I responded. "I thought I made that clear last time we spoke."

"She has an intellectual disability." Achilles spun Gia expertly to distract her from our hushed conversation.

Blinding, searing jealousy struck me. I was unaccustomed to that emotion. To *any* emotion. My stomach churned and twisted. I did not like what the sight of Gia in another man's arms did to me.

"She's human," I clapped back. "You treat her like a French bulldog. She wanted to dance."

"She doesn't know what she wants," Achilles sneered. That he was an ableist fuck was the least surprising thing I learned this century.

I bent Lila down, careful to cradle her head—poor girl was as arrhythmic as a pet rock, not one musical bone in that body—and spun her halfway. Her cheeks were flushed pink, her mouth parted, and she stared at me with a mix of awe and joy, like I'd plucked a particularly fanciful, glittering star and gifted it to her.

"I think she does. I think she very much wants to be treated like a normal teenager."

Achilles's jaw tightened, and Gia was now giving both of us her full attention.

I spun Lila around, stared into her eyes, and very slowly mouthed, "I'm going to say horrible things right now. I don't mean any of them. Nod once if you understand."

I waited a beat. Two beats.

She nodded.

The kid goddamn *nodded*.

"Look how happy she is," I murmured, smiling to the young woman, ready to deliver the final blow. This wasn't just to mess with Achilles. I wanted him to know he was selling his sister short. That she understood the world better than he gave her credit for. "I bet there are other ways I could make her happy. Is she promised to anyone yet? My marriage is shaky these days."

"What the bloody hell is wrong with you?" Gia ripped herself from Achilles, staring at me in abhorrence. Her fists were curled tight. "She's a *child*."

"I'm barely touching her." I continued swaying Lila in my arms with enough space for Jesus between us. Lila seemed quite happy by the way she clung to me, her arms fastening around my shoulders like I was an anchor, innocent eyes pleading for me to continue.

Achilles, like Gia, didn't like my little joke. In fact, as soon as the words fell from my mouth, he was jerked back by Luca, who left his unexciting fiancée to growl, "He's just messing with you, you idiot."

"*Tate.*" Gia stomped.

"*Gia.*"

"This is incredibly disrespectful to all of us."

"If you want me to stop dancing with another woman, just say the word, and I will."

She clamped her mouth shut.

I shrugged. "Very well."

I spun Lila again.

Tears clung to my wife's waterlines. My knees nearly buckled at the sight. Yet I couldn't stop myself. I wanted us to be exclusive. To never see her in another man's arms again.

Spinning Lila for the third time, I thought I heard a lilt of juvenile laughter. Achilles and Luca were ready to rip her from my arms, but they didn't. They saw her having fun for the first time in what I assumed was years. Maybe ever.

Gia pivoted on her red-soled heels and tromped her way off the dance floor. I finished the waltz with Lila, then escorted her back to her pitiful table, determined not to give my maddening wife any more power over me than she already had.

Plus, Lila deserved to be bidden goodbye properly. I had no idea when exactly I grew a fucking conscience, but something in me knew that normal Gia, not the one who was pissed off with my ass, would want me to treat this girl right.

Practice empathy, Dr. Patel's words echoed in my head. At the time, I didn't see a need to try.

Now, I was willing to play along. For her.

When I returned to our table, Gia wasn't there.

"Where's my wife?" I asked Enzo, who now seemed to be flirting his way into a threesome.

"I'm off duty," Enzo quipped, his eyes never wavering from the blond and brunette he was chatting up. "Ask someone who car—"

I fisted his bow tie, yanking him so our noses squashed together. "Let's try again, shall we? Where is my wife?" For the full effect, I palmed the pocket where he kept his knife, silently signaling I could easily cut his thigh if he pissed me off.

"Jesus Christ. She went in the direction of the restrooms last I saw." He wrenched himself out of my hold, elbowing me for good measure. "Please don't make me kill you tonight. I'm really looking forward to the dessert."

Ignoring the jackass, I galloped out of the ballroom. In the women's restroom, I found a few horrified ladies who shrieked when I entered, but none of them was Gia. Men's restroom—nothing but limp dick and a few lines of top-tier cocaine.

Tearing through the hallway of the ballroom floor, I began kicking doors open. Kitchen. Maintenance room. Grand suites. Where the fuck was she? I tried calling her, but my calls went straight to voicemail. Gia was angry, not stupid. She'd let me know she was okay. Would at least text.

Cold sweat formed over my brow. A foreign concept, and one I wasn't eager to be introduced to. If she was getting back at me for my little stunt, this was a disproportionate penalty.

The hotel had twenty-five floors, and we were at the top of it. There was a good chance she wasn't on the premises anymore.

A raspy cry erupted two doors into the hallway. Faint but unmistakably female. I inched to the room it came from, taking a step back and kicking the door down. It sailed and dragged across the plush carpet. I stomped over it on my way inside to find my wife pressed to the bed stomach down, her arms behind her back as a pasty, burly prick pressed his knee to her back while he zip-tied her. Another Irish soldier stood between us, advancing toward me with a knife.

Red tainted my vision as I grabbed the first guy and tossed him over his friend who was on top of Gia. They both tumbled down to the floor like bowling pins. One slammed against the wall beforehand, putting a hole in the drywall. Gia was still on the bed, motionless.

I grabbed the man on top of her by his greasy hair, yanking him to his feet. The other guy seemed in considerably worse shape, his neck fractured, by its unnatural angle. He was down for the count.

"Now." I smashed the man's nose against mine, sneering. He had heavy stubble and sharklike dead eyes. Definitely not a simple soldier. At least Tiernan Callaghan stopped sending me fucking amateurs. I was beginning to get a complex. "Want to try to zip-tie my wife again, this time to my face?"

The man pursed his lips insolently, trying to wiggle himself free of my hold.

Tugging on his hair, I angled his face to Gia, who was still on the mattress. "Does she look comfortable to you?"

No answer. Gia stared up in horror. She didn't look injured, just shaken. My current behavior undoubtedly made things worse.

"Doesn't look too comfortable to me." I tossed the guy headfirst to the mattress far enough from her. I pressed the back of his head down with my palm, smothering him in an expensive sheet. "See? The lack of oxygen. The heat on your face. Not too friendly," I said conversationally.

He flailed and writhed, squirming away from my touch. I yanked his head up.

"Where's Tiernan?" I asked.

He coughed, gasped, but didn't answer.

I pushed him down for another asphyxia session. Brought him up again after thirty seconds.

"How 'bout now?"

But he was a seasoned mobster, and despite his purple face and bloodshot eyes, his lips formed a thin line, and he gave me a cold stare. "Feck you, bastard."

I put him down again. Finally, when he was weakened but not yet dead, I pulled him back up.

"One last chance to cooperate," I offered.

His face was blue, his eyes swollen and unfocused. He wasn't gonna crack.

"His death will be on your conscience," I said to Gia, pointing at the still stoic man. "You could've prevented this if you just stayed put."

"While you copped a feel and danced with a gorgeous woman?" Her eyes glittered.

Was she jealous? I wanted her to be.

"She is a mere child, and even if she wasn't, you're the only one who can do this to me." I stepped toward the bed, grabbed her hand, and pushed it against my hardness. "The *only* one, Gia."

"You expect me to believe you don't find other women attractive?" she spluttered.

"I don't expect jack other than to stop trying to get yourself killed. Now, if you'll excuse me." I dragged the brawny man toward the window, then slammed his face against the thick glass over and over again, breaking all his facial bones in the process.

"Jesus, Tate." Gia scrambled up to a sitting position behind me. "What are you doing?"

"Throwing him out the window."

"The window's not even open!"

"That's the best part."

Thrash.

Thrash.

Thrash.

Finally, when the man was on his last few breaths, I unlatched the window's lock and tossed him out.

Silence blanketed the room for a moment before Gia opened her mouth again.

"Do you think he's dead?"

"No, sweetheart. Of course not."

He was definitely dead. And in at least fourteen different pieces. But there really wasn't any need to distress her further. I potentially killed two of Callaghan's men today. I hoped it got the message across.

Shit. Now I had to clean this entire place of her fingerprints and mine.

It just became one hell of a crime scene.

Swiveling to my wife, I found her perched on the edge of the bed, trembling. Her hair was a mess, her makeup streaked with tears. I wanted to gather her in my arms and comfort her, but I was also beyond pissed that she'd put herself in danger again.

"How did you get here?"

"Th-they took my bracelet. The one my dad gave me," she hiccupped, ignoring my question, rubbing her wrist absentmindedly. More tears slid down her cheeks, and she hugged herself. "They took my one last keepsake of everything good and happy and *normal.*"

My heart sank. Fuck knew normal and happy weren't in the cards for her with me.

"It's not what I asked," I said aloofly, feeling something… *something.* Inadequate. "How'd you get here, Gia?"

If she went into a bedroom with another man willingly, I was going to do something drastic. Not to her, but I could see myself setting the entire city on fire. When we weren't in it, of course.

She sniffled, wiping her eyes with the back of her hand. "I went to the kitchen to find Cal to vent. These two men waited around the corner in the hallway and dragged me here. I didn't see them coming. Once the door was shut, they called someone downstairs and told them to wait outside the back door."

I glanced at the unconscious man at my feet. He looked pretty dead, or at least too badly injured to answer any questions. I rolled him with the tip of my loafer and crouched to put my fingers on his neck. Shallow pulse, no reflexes.

"They came close this time," Gia whispered.

"Whose fault is that?" I tipped my head up, tapping my thigh as I counted crystal raindrops on the chandelier. Three hundred and seven. Odd number. How could they?

Gia stood up. "Only in your twisted mind is any of this my fault. You brought this on us. You and your stupid revenge plot."

"Stupid?" I arched an eyebrow. "You got my father sent to prison *and* are responsible for his death, and we haven't even properly discussed your role in this mess yet. Don't you find that interesting?"

She flinched. I knew she had apologized, but she was still cagey about the details of what happened that night. A little fucking clarity would've gone a long way.

She opened her mouth. Clamped it shut. I was surprised and

proud of her for hardly paying attention to the dying man at our feet. This was definitely progress.

Finally, she said, "You touched another woman."

"You touched another man," I countered.

She was jealous. I wanted her to admit it. To own it. To understand the implications of it.

She pinched her lower lip, staring at the carpet. "I don't want you to touch anyone else ever again."

"Done and ditto." I peered around. I was going to need a lot of fucking soap and alcohol to wipe this place out.

"No more jokes about making someone else happy either," she warned.

"Sweetheart, I'd never deliberately bring joy to anyone but you. You're the only human I can stand." The confession surprised me more than it did her.

I didn't hate her.

I didn't tolerate her.

I *liked* her.

Quite a fucking lot.

A terrible complication, obviously.

For the first time since I walked into the room, I softened, eating the space between us with one long stride. I put my hand on her damp cheek, tilting her face up. She closed her eyes.

"Look at me."

She shook her head.

I brought both my palms to her cheeks, inching my face to hers. "*Now.*"

Her eyes fluttered open. I felt my heart drilling its way out of my rib cage.

"Listen to me carefully, Gia. I am yours. All of me belongs to you. My body—yours. Brain—yours. Money—yours. Kingdom—yours. Every inch. Every cell. Every atom. Every single breath has your name on it."

"And your heart?" Her voice came out scratchy and thick, eyes glittering with tears. "Is it mine too?"

"Oh, Apricity." I plastered my forehead to hers, gathering her into my arms. "If I had a heart to give, it would be yours. Without question."

CHAPTER TWENTY-NINE
GIA

Later that night, when I stared in the bathroom mirror, I didn't recognize myself.

My nose was the same. My lips, ears, and apple cheeks all recognizable to me. But my eyes had changed shape. They'd morphed into something hard, almost sinister. They had seen my husband kill numerous people. They had witnessed blood and terror and anguish. They sent this message to my heart, but it was never delivered.

Because the bloody organ did not care in the least.

I should've been scared. But all I felt was jealousy and possessiveness that simmered beneath my skin, threatening to explode.

Watching Tate with Lila tonight unleashed something wild in me.

I found myself crossing another moral barrier, like I did when I asked Dr. Stultz not to report Tate to the authorities.

I was willing to go all in for him.

Even if I didn't know his real name.

Even if he didn't know what really happened with his adoptive father and me and finding out would probably ruin what we had.

Shaking my head, I flicked the tap on and rinsed my facecloth in warm water, moving it across my cheeks, forehead, and chin. I wet it again and reached between my thighs to wipe the dry cum that clayed over my skin before thinking the better of it. Something thrilled me about going to bed marked by my husband's sperm.

A knock hammered on my bedroom door, and Tate shouldered past it. The door to the en suite was open, giving him a direct view of me.

I rotated, leaning against the sink. "I'm not decent."

He was wearing his gray joggers again. No shirt. Not an ounce of fat on his body. My thighs involuntarily squeezed at the sight of him. His cheekbones were extra sharp under the dim light, his hair damp from a shower.

"I'm wearing my retainer and nightcap."

"I can see." He took a step closer.

My pulse skipped all over the place.

"And my nightie is horrendous." I pointed at my stripy blue pajama shirt.

"To put it mildly," he agreed ardently and placed an open kiss across the side of my neck, his rough fingers hiking my sleepshirt up my waist. "Let's get rid of it."

He pushed me against the sink, and my traitorous legs opened for him on their own accord. I grunted, clutching the vanity to steady myself.

"We can't... I have all my bed stuff on. I don't feel sexy." I plucked out my retainer, setting it on the vanity behind me.

"Well, you are." His lips crashed against mine, claiming my mouth in a bruising kiss. He thrust himself against my thigh, demonstrating the evidence of his attraction. "You've never looked sexier to me than right now. Guard down. Barefaced. Without the fancy heels and the pastel suits."

The praise warmed me down to my little toes, making me feel heady, lulled inside a dream.

"The Irish want me, not you." I tore my mouth from his. I'd had time to figure it out on our drive back home.

"I know." He trailed kisses along my collarbone and farther

south. "Collateral. They have no use of me dead. Instead, they want to blackmail me by taking the only thing I care about."

A wave of heat rolled through my body. Perhaps my husband could never love me, but he cared for me, and in time, maybe I'd learn to live with that. Maybe it'd be enough.

"This is bound to end badly."

"For Tiernan Callaghan," Tate said. "Yes. Not for us."

"Be serious. How many people will you kill to stop the Irish from kidnapping me as a bargaining chip?"

"All of them." His head disappeared between my thighs, under my nightie. His hot, wet tongue lashed at the dry cum around my pussy, cleaning me in circular, teasing strokes, a vortex of heat that kept inching toward my aching center.

"You're playing a very dangerous game, Tate." My fingers threaded in his hair, messing his perfect Ivy League cut.

"I'm very good at it," he said cockily, parting the lips of my pussy with his thumbs to reveal my clit like he was extracting a pearl, flicking the tip of his tongue teasingly around it, swirling and sucking, grinding his teeth all over it. I shuddered, my nipples puckering under the flimsy fabric.

His tongue disappeared between my folds as he began thrusting into me with it, and I clutched his head, euphoria washing over me. He massaged my clit with his tongue and feasted on my pussy, fingers digging into my arse in a death grip, and when I came all over his tongue, he slurped it all like it was water in a desert, grabbed my waist, and dragged me down to lie on the floor beneath him. I gasped when the backs of my legs hit the cold tiles, and he took advantage of my open mouth, tonguing me hard and making me taste my own desire for him.

He tugged my nightie up, releasing me from its confinements, and latched on to one of my nipples, drawing moans and soft purrs from me as I opened up before him, eager to welcome him in again. His cock pressed against my core.

Tate's lips fastened over my other nipple, and he tugged and caressed the breast he just kissed while I arched myself in offering. The way he teased me without entering me left me crazed. But I also wanted to pleasure him back. He'd been remarkably humble by not rubbing it in my face that I'd caved to our attraction in less than a month. The least I could do was reciprocate oral sex.

I pushed at his chest, and he immediately leaned back, giving me space. He propped against the cabinets, frowning. "Not good?" His voice was roughened.

Butterflies flocked my stomach. This man, whose knuckles were busted, who'd killed people with his bare hands, was so mindful of my slightest discomfort.

"No. I mean, *yes*." I crawled between his open legs, jerking his joggers down.

His cock sprang out, head purple and gleaming, veins snaking up and down his shaft. He licked his lips in concentration, grabbing his base and reaching between my thighs to ensure I was wet enough for penetration.

"No." I pressed my palm against his chest again. "I'm going down on you."

His eyes widened, boyish excitement filling them, like the mere idea was unfathomable. He looked like a kid who just got the present he wanted for Christmas.

It reminded me Tate had never been allowed to be a kid.

And that his Christmases likely did not include any pressies.

You took the only person who gave him a sense of family.

Pushing back the guilt, I brought my head down to the crown of his cock.

"Wait," he said breathlessly, scrambling up to his feet. He grabbed the edges of the countertop, staring down at me. His chest moved rapidly, abs constricting into a bulging six-pack each time he exhaled. "Shit. Fuck. Okay. I'm ready now."

He wanted to watch.

I'd never felt more powerful in my entire life.

I wrapped my fist around his shaft and brought my lips to his crown. I didn't want him to know I'd never sucked cock before. I'd done very little in the sex department. Slept with three men, Ashley included. It wasn't an impressive record, but up until a month ago, I'd lived my life mostly tending to my career and my mother.

Winging it, I wrapped my lips around the tip, trailing my gaze up his torso to check his reaction. His eyes were fixed on me, heated with possessiveness. I rubbed my lips around his crown awkwardly, unsure what to do. He seemed content with that.

"Look at you, darling." He reached to cup my cheek, his tone dripping pure affection. "You're taking it so well."

I nearly laughed at that. I barely covered the tip. I slowly inched forward, covering a bit of his shaft. The tip hit the roof of my mouth, filling it with a salty, earthy taste. He was hard but velvety. So velvety. I stopped myself from gagging.

He didn't move, didn't thrust into my mouth like I heard some men did. With the patience of a saint, he allowed me to hold on to his cock and slowly explore the art of oral. "Take as much time as you need," he hissed, sounding in pain. "There's no right or wrong way of doing it."

I pulled his cock out of my mouth and pressed the tip of my tongue to the slit. It was extra salty. I gasped.

"You've never…" He swallowed hard. "You've never sucked cock before, Gia?"

I shook my head, embarrassed.

Tate tipped his head back and cupped his cheeks. "My fucking God, the woman that you are. You can snare me into death, and I'd say fucking thank you."

After that encouraging praise, I tried everything. Suckling, licking, spitting. I suckled his ball sack into my mouth, then decided to take as much of his cock as possible until his tip hit the back of my throat. That really got him going. His breathing quickened.

"You can come in my mouth if you want," I murmured around his cock.

"Nice try, sweetheart." He gently pulled his penis from my mouth and offered me his hand. I took it. I followed him into my bedroom. "On the edge of the bed on all fours," he instructed.

I did as I was told, crawling onto the plush linen. The mattress dipped as he climbed onto it behind me. It suddenly struck me that despite the fact that we'd been messing around for a while now, we'd never done it in a proper bed and never missionary style. Our hookups always had a filthy, tainted feel to them. We didn't make love. We made hate filled with desire. He never allowed for my soul to touch his. For our heartbeats to crash against one another.

"Three strokes." Tate's gravelly tenor pierced my thoughts. His cock slid into me effortlessly despite its size, gliding through my narrow, sleek channel. "That's how long I'm gonna last." He drew circles with his cock inside me, filling me to the brim and making me whimper. He pushed two fingers into my mouth roughly, fucking it with them. "Your pussy takes my cock so good, and now we'll practice you taking it in the mouth too." He grunted. "You've been a magnificent PA, but this is your best job yet, Apricity."

His fingers relentlessly pushed in and out of my mouth as he took me from behind. Even though my jaw was already raw from sucking him off, I loved how rough he was. How unapologetic and dirty we were together.

"I want to see you when you're inside me," I moaned around his fingers.

He froze, still inside me. For a moment, I thought he hadn't heard me. But then he withdrew his fingers from my mouth. "Why?"

"It's important to me," I admitted. "We're not animals. I want eye contact. I want to feel that you're present."

The discomforting quiet told me this was an issue. Finally, he spoke.

"I've never done it missionary style."

My pulse thrummed between my ears. "Guess we're both experiencing our firsts now."

He pulled out of me, and I rolled onto my back, blinking up at him.

Grimacing, he grabbed himself, guiding his penis back into me like a victim withdrawing cash at gunpoint. I had never seen less enthusiasm from a man putting his cock inside me. Our eyes locked, terror and anxiety swirling inside them. Something about the setting, about this intimacy, set us both on edge. Once he was nestled inside me, he braced one arm next to my ear, using his free hand to tap out his numbers.

I swallowed hard, pretending not to notice. After a few awkward strokes, his movements refined into deep, leisured thrusts. Desperate to provide distraction for him, I pulled his face to mine and kissed him fervently. Nipped and tugged his lower lip. Rolled my hips to meet him halfway. Slowly, his rigid muscles loosened. He stopped tapping and gathered me closer, hooking one hand on the back of my knee and angling my leg across my body. The friction was unbearable. Our bodies melted together into one entity, and he kissed me back, gentle in a way that made tears cling to my lashes, grunting words that bathed me in warmth.

"So gorgeous."

Thrust.

"So perfect."

Thrust.

"So mine."

Thrust.

Heat eddied behind my navel. I twisted and writhed, my lips chasing the sharp planes of his face. I kissed him everywhere. His nose. His cheeks. His throat. And before I knew it, words fell out of my mouth, surprising to my own ears.

"I've always wanted you." I bowed, my full, sensitive breasts pressing against his muscular pecs. "I've wanted you since I walked into Baron Spencer's office for an interview and saw you, terrifying and gorgeous, and I didn't know what to do with myself. And when you reached out..."

Thrust.

Grunt.

Moan.

"Tell me," he urged.

"When you hired me, I thought I'd combust on the spot. I'd never planned to stay in America for this long. A part of me had always foolishly hoped I could get you to like me. That if I was smart enough and brilliant enough and reliable enough, I'd...I don't know, win you over."

"There was no game for you to win." He hit my G-spot, brow furrowed in concentration, his sweat dripping from the tip of his hair into my face. "I took one look at you and knew I was going to bond my destiny with yours, even if it was the last thing I did in this life."

We both came at the same time, holding each other anchored as the storm ripped through our bodies. Panting hard, sweaty, naked, and petrifyingly close. When he tried to pry himself out of my arms, I clung to him harder, refusing to let him leave.

"Stay," I yelped. He was still inside me. "Spend the night."

I wasn't so silly as to hope he'd let me sleep in his bed. But surely, we could share mine?

We went to sleep wrapped in each other that night.

And in the arms of the most dangerous man in the world, I finally felt safe.

I woke up some hours later with a full bladder and a dull ache between my legs.

My bed was empty, my sheets cold in the pitch-black room. I

daftly patted my surroundings, hoping to find my husband splayed next to mine, to no avail.

I was alone.

Padding barefoot to the toilet, I peed, washed my hands, then returned to my bed. The clock showed three thirty, but I knew sleep wouldn't come.

After slipping my nightie back on, I wormed out of my room, deciding to explore the flat I now called my own. I weaved through unlit rooms, taking note of everything. I noticed the room at the end of the vast hallway—Tate's bedroom—had its door open and the lights off. I peered inside. It was empty.

Where did he go?

My pulse pitter-pattered against my breastbone. I moved across the hallway, feeling like an intruder, until I reached his office door. It was slightly ajar, with light pouring from the tiny crack. Fear coated my bones like tar. Sticky and dark. I wasn't even sure why.

I peered through the gap, and what I saw behind it made my breath hitch.

Tate paced around the room like a captive animal, onyx hair tousled, wearing only his joggers. Everything—textbooks, furniture, bookshelves, *walls*—was covered in mathematical equations scribbled in Sharpie. Barely an inch of wall remained not yet covered in numbers.

Tate stopped in the middle of the room. I swallowed a yelp of surprise, wondering if he'd noticed me. Turning his back to me, he hurried to a tiny, blank spot on the wall and jotted another equation, muttering agitatedly to himself.

You did this, a voice inside me accused. *You pushed him over the edge. Made him do something he feared—making love to a woman, staring into her eyes, when he can barely stare at his own reflection in the mirror.*

This wasn't just OCD. I'd met people with the disorder. Many highly functioning individuals I came in contact with were somewhere on the spectrum. No. Something else was going on here, something more. Something bigger—that needed urgent attention.

My husband needed help, and I desperately wanted to support him.

Rolling my shoulders back, I knocked on the door, but only after I saw he'd finished solving his equation. He looked up, eyes glittering predatorily, like a beast in the darkened woods.

His jaw locked.

I wasn't supposed to come here.

"This place is off-limits," he snarled.

"You have OCD," I said matter-of-factly.

"Beautiful *and* perceptive." He chuckled somberly. "Your perfection truly knows no bounds."

"But there's something else too." I ignored his sarcasm, stepping deeper into the room, into the lion's den. "You need to get properly medicated. You need therapy. You need—"

"I need to be left the fuck *alone*."

His roar rattled my bones, and I inhaled, my instincts screaming at me to step back but my pride and stubbornness making me step forward and tilt my chin up.

"No," I said. "Not until I help you."

He tipped his head back and laughed. "I've subjugated the world and brought billionaires and governments to their knees. Send someone else an invitation to your pity party."

"You think I feel sorry for you?" I narrowed my eyes. "You have the world at your feet. You're handsome, filthy rich, and a literal genius. But those things don't produce happiness. Merely more stress and expectations. I want you to be *happy*. You can have everything and still get relief from your condition."

"My OCD gives me an edge." He walked over to a bar cart and poured himself a drink. "Equations clear my mind. My rituals are my time to form new strategies."

"You can function without self-destructing," I said quietly. "The two aren't mutually exclusive."

"If I didn't have my hard-earned power, gained through years of self-inflicted pain, I wouldn't know the sweet taste of that gorgeous cunt of yours, Apricity." He rolled his tongue over his teeth before knocking his drink back. I flinched at his crass words. "You wouldn't be wearing my ring, moaning my name, buying a fucking private plane after a lovers' quarrel."

"But if you try to trea—"

"It'll get me nowhere," he interjected. "My OCD is the least of my issues. I have a cocktail of disorders that'd make Jeffrey Dahmer get FOMO. This is the first and last time we discuss this subject, Gia. I don't want you to tell anyone else about it."

He thought I was going to go around tattling about his mental health struggles? Did he not know me at all?

Dejection choked me like poison. For every step forward we took, Tate was adamant to take three steps back. This was yet another reminder I was just another conquest. An unattainable prize he now managed to get his capable hands on.

"Don't worry, Tate." My tone turned icy, and just like that, I morphed into PA Gia. Professional. Stoic. On guard. "Your secret's safe with me."

"At last, she behaves like a wife." He strode over to his desk, holding his second drink and picking up his Sharpie. He tucked it behind his ear, flipping through a textbook. "Now, unless you want to fuck again, I'm partial to spending the rest of the night separately." His words left welts of heat on my cheeks, his eyes never wavering from his textbook. "After all, you were the one who insisted on keeping this marriage strictly a formal arrangement."

Shaking my head, I turned around and walked away.

CHAPTER THIRTY
TATE

AGE TWELVE

No one knew about Apollo. I made sure of it.

I learned from my past mistakes. The woods weren't far enough. If I wanted a companion, I needed to ensure it was away from school. Away from Andrin.

Which was how I started volunteering at a shelter.

I spent every Wednesday and Friday afternoon with dogs and cats and rabbits. I preferred them to humans. They were kind and grateful. Never judgmental. And considerably better conversationalists.

It all started with the new superintendent, Mrs. Dagmar. She arrived during summer break, quickly understood that I was one of the only students living on the grounds, and decided to give me tasks to keep me busy. She started bringing her puppy, Frankie, to work and asked that I take him on walks and keep him entertained. I played fetch and cuddled with him for hours, secure in the knowledge Andrin wasn't so deranged as to kill his superior's pet.

Mrs. Dagmar brought me books to read. Fun books, not the stuff I could find in the school library. When she found out how good I was with numbers, she put me in charge of doing all her bookkeeping for the school and, in return, gave me small presents. Treats. Her son's old Legos to build. Once, she brought a photographer to take pictures of me to put on an adoption site. I laughed when the old woman insisted I wear a crisp white shirt and knee-high socks. "No one's coming for me," I parroted Andrin's words. "I'm damaged goods. Too old, too twisted."

She cried, and then she did something even more disturbing— she hugged me.

I froze, not hugging her back. I froze, because she was the first grown-up who'd ever touched me in a way that wasn't meant to punish me.

At the beginning of the school year, I'd asked Mrs. Dagmar if I could take the bus to and from the boarding school to the shelter, and she agreed on the condition I took her old phone and texted her each time I arrived at the shelter and back at the dorms. We were breaking a shit ton of protocols, but she didn't seem to mind.

I sometimes thought she suspected Andrin was abusing me. I didn't know if she spoke to him about it, but that year, he came to visit me less frequently at night.

Anyway, back to Apollo.

He was a Flemish giant rabbit. I immediately took a liking to him because he was very old and he limped. He reminded me of *Alice's Adventures in Wonderland's* White Rabbit.

They told me at the shelter he'd been attacked by hound dogs and barely made it.

I always had a soft spot for broken things.

I hung out with him twice a week and dreamed about adopting him. I knew I couldn't. He was ginormous and nearly blind. Besides all that, I didn't have a house. Only a teacher that liked killing animals.

But for a short while, life was better.

I had Mrs. Dagmar and I had Apollo and I had treats and Legos and fun books.

Then one day, everything changed.

Mrs. Dagmar called me into her office. She smiled big, and

my heart accelerated, because for the first time in my life, I knew someone who smiled when they had positive news to tell me and not because they wanted to taunt me.

"You are being adopted," she announced, her eyes bright with tears.

I said nothing at first. I didn't move. Didn't breathe. I was scared. Scared that she was pranking me.

Scared that she was not pranking me too. Because what if this was real, and my adoptive parents were worse than the boarding school? At least in the confines of this place, Andrin couldn't kill me.

"He is American, like you. He is a very important man. I met him twice. You will like him. Very kind. Very excited to meet you."

So many questions ran through my head. I didn't know where to start.

"What do you mean, he? There's only one parent?"

She laughed, shaking her head. "Yes. It's just him. But one parent is more than enough if it's the right one."

"He wants to adopt me without meeting me first?"

She nodded. "He saw your grades. Your accomplishments in math. Your pictures. He loves math too."

I forced my heart rate to slow down. I didn't want to feel too hopeful.

"But…why me?" I frowned.

"He doesn't want a small child. No nappies and bottles for him. He wants an heir he can teach the ropes of his business."

"Did you tell him that I'm weird? That I don't have any friends?" I demanded, almost angry at her now. I was sick with anxiety that once he met me, he'd return me like an expired can from the supermarket.

"I told him all about you." Another tender smile. "Let's just say this gentleman is…similar to you in that he doesn't like crowds. Or people in general."

I couldn't help it anymore. I got excited. Just a little bit. I had no delusions about cozy Christmas days and family bingo nights. But having someone to understand me, to not be cruel to me...

"It is really happening." Her hands moved across her desk, clutching my own. "He is coming to get you in two weeks. You'll live in New York. He has a big apartment. You will have an Xbox and a PlayStation, with a pool in your building. Aunts and cousins too. This is the beginning of your new life."

The next two weeks, I walked on clouds. Mrs. Dagmar offered me pieces of information about my adoptive father like morsels of chocolate, each of them bringing me to new heights.

He studied math in college.

His work took him all over the world.

He loved playing chess and planned to take me on vacation to Italy after he picked me up from the boarding school to sightsee before we went to America, so we could get to know each other.

For the first time, I didn't think about death. I thought about life. And it was both exciting and frightening.

My last night at the dorms, I heard Andrin's footsteps down the hall. It was five in the morning, and I wasn't asleep. Too much adrenaline coursing through my body every time I glanced at the big suitcase that stood by my door.

Three months had passed since Andrin had last come to me. I was hoping he'd forgotten all about me.

My body turned to stone. I stopped breathing when I heard the door whining open. I squinted my eyes shut, pretending to be asleep. Though he made no noise, I felt his dark energy swirling around the room, gaining momentum, like a hurricane. My bed creaked when his shins pressed against the wooden frame. He hovered over me.

"Oh, Boy, you'll want to open your eyes for this one." He sounded smug. So of course, I had to open my eyes. "I have a parting gift."

Andrin's face was clasped between the shadows.

"Look what I brought this time."

I blinked my vision into focus, sitting up. Scraps of sunlight grazed my pupils. I squinted at Andrin's hand. He was holding a gun.

I choked, coughing on my saliva.

He was going to kill me. I wasn't even surprised. Somehow, I always knew I'd never live to see a good day. My mysterious adoptive dad was a standard deviation. An isolated error.

"Don't worry, Boy. It's not your brain I'm going to blow off. Get up." He balled the collar of my shirt, wrenching me to my desk.

I landed on the edge of my wooden chair and got a good hit in the nuts but was too stunned to register the pain.

"Grab a pencil. I have an equation for you to solve." Andrin rummaged through the front pocket of his slacks, his other hand digging the barrel of the gun into my right temple. My heart nearly tore out of my chest it beat so hard.

Guns were for pussies, I decided then and there. If I ever had the privilege of killing the bastard, I would do it with my bare hands.

"There we are." He produced a small, folded note, unfurling and planting it in front of me on the desk.

Cold sweat dripped into my eyes. It was a not an equation, per se. It was…

"Fermat's last theorem," Andrin finished the thought for me. "There are three positive integers, a, b, c, that satisfy. Get going."

I stared at the problem, pulse throbbing against my eyelids. My palms were slick with sweat. The metal mouth of the gun burrowed harder into my flesh.

"How long do I have?" I cleared my throat.

"Ten minutes."

"And if I don't find the solution?"

His hand that held the gun sailed from my head to the window. I craned my neck, and then I saw it.

Apollo.

He was tied to a tree not too far from my room, running in circles, yanking at the chain, staring at my window. He heard when

Andrin tapped the gun on the window. He flinched and blinked to express his terror at being chained. Begged me to come help him. My heart dropped.

Fuck, fuck, fuck.

"Picked him up last night. He thought he was being adopted." Andrin laughed, like an old pet's hope was amusing. "Rabbits are such stupid creatures."

"He can have a heart attack and die." My voice was so shaky and fragile I wanted to punch my own face.

"Hmm." Andrin stroked his chin. "Better get on with your task before he does then."

Anger swirled inside me. I was sick with it. It grew and festered within me like wildfire. I thought I might combust. But I bit my tongue. For Apollo.

"Your time starts now." Andrin smacked the clock on my desk, and it started ticking down the seconds.

I grabbed the pencil and started working.

The clock ticked in an uneven rhythm, I noticed.

Two, six, two.

Two, six, two.

Two, six, two.

It was broken. It was slightly late. That afforded me, I calculated, forty extra seconds. Almost an entire minute.

I threw everything into the problem. This was the last fucking time. That was why he came here. To get his pound of flesh before I was gone. To encourage myself, I tapped the side of my leg, reminding myself I had all the time in the world to get things right.

Two, six, two.

Two, six, two.

Two, six, two.

And then I got it. I got the answer.

"Here." I looked up and handed him the paper. The clock said I had thirty seconds left. Which meant the broken clock had saved me. Saved Apollo. "Integers a, b, and c can't exist for n greater than two. Anyone who understands elliptic curves and modular forms can crack this," I said excitedly. My new father was due to be here in a couple hours, and I really wanted to see him for the first time while not going through a massive meltdown. "Now let Apollo go."

Andrin picked up the paper, his pupils running over the solved problem. His lips rubbed together agitatedly. "Where was that brain of yours when I paraded you through math competitions?" He slammed the paper on my desk, causing me to flinch.

I didn't answer. I didn't want to anger him. Not because of me—I was used to the pain. Because of Apollo.

"Speak, Boy." He banged his fist over my desk.

I didn't move.

He was screaming. Not being careful. This was a first.

"You can hit me. You can drag me through the woods. You can…I don't know, do whatever you want with the rest of the time I have here," I said quietly. "But let me take Apollo back to the shelter first."

"No." He used the hand that held his gun to wipe his forehead.

"Andrin, I—"

He angled himself fully to the window, raised his arm, and released a bullet. Apollo's anguished running and yanking ceased at once. He collapsed backward, his pristine white fur painted red.

My vision went white. My ears rang.

No, no, no, no.

I leapt from my seat, jumping out the broken window and falling flat on my face. I didn't care.

I scrambled up and started running to the rabbit. He was dead. Lying on the ground, still, eyes open, horrified, shocked, and… human. So human.

A scream ripped from my throat.

I gathered him in my arms, clutching his fur, crying. I kept convincing myself this was all a bad dream.

Somewhere in the back of my head, I knew my face was bleeding from the fall, that I was barefoot, that it was cold, that I had to grab my things and go to the communal bathrooms, make myself presentable for my adoptive father. But I couldn't do anything but hug Apollo and mumble the word sorry over and over and over again. I was so nauseous with grief, there wasn't even room for the rage I should have felt for Andrin.

A hand fell on my shoulder after a few long moments. Heavy, with a foreign weight to it. It wasn't Andrin. I recognized sensations, one of the first things I learned from living in the dark.

I swiveled my head, looking back at a stranger's face. He had a wide-set forehead, a hawkish nose, and bushy eyebrows. He looked like an old bear in a suit.

"Gabriel?" he asked.

I understood immediately that this was my adoptive father, but I couldn't bring myself to speak. I was too devastated to give a shit about what he thought of seeing me clutching a dead rabbit at the edge of the woods.

"Gabriel, what happened?" He clutched my arms, his hold firm but not punishing, his gaze swinging between the rabbit and me.

"Andrin," I yelped. Narcing on him was satisfying. I wanted him to pay. I wanted him to suffer. "Andrin did it. My teacher." The words rushed out. So did the tears as I wiped my snot with the back of my arm, like a loser. "He's been abusing me. He kills my pets. All of them. If I don't solve the math problems he gives me. But this time, I did solve it! And in less than ten minutes." I was rambling.

He fell to his knees, grabbed the back of my head, and pushed me into his chest. It took me a second to realize he was hugging me. Another three or four to reciprocate and pretend I was fine with the touch.

"Where is Andrin, son?" His chest rumbled against my face when he spoke.

Son. I liked the sound of it. And I liked that he smelled nice.

That the fabric of his shirt was soft. I liked that he was from home, from America, even though I remembered nothing about it.

"I think in my room, still."

"Son. I want you to look at me." He pulled away from me, clasping my shoulders, still on one knee. He was early. He came before the time he was supposed to meet Mrs. Dagmar and me. He was eager to see me. Someone in this world wanted my company.

"This was the last time someone will harm you. No more. I will make sure Andrin pays for what he did to you. For what he did to all your animals. No more heartbreak, Gabriel."

I flinched. He frowned. "What's wrong?"

"No one calls me that."

"What, Gabriel?" He seemed surprised. "Why? Do you not like your name?"

Shrugging, I admitted, "It's not that. It's just that…there are a lot of kids here. Sometimes for only a year or two as part of exchange programs. No one's ever bothered remembering my name. Andrin calls me Boy. Mrs. Dagmar calls me Child sometimes, but in a nice way."

"And your friends?"

"My friends…" I trailed off, picking at a scab on my knee. "Uh, well, I don't have any, exactly."

His frown turned into a smile. "Good. Me neither. More time to spend together."

It was like he lifted a heavy stone from my shoulders. And this time, I smiled too.

"I have something for you." He reached into his pocket, taking out a pocket watch. He handed it to me. "Mrs. Dagmar told me you like *Alice's Adventures in Wonderland*. So do I. This is a family heirloom I think you'd enjoy."

He steered me away from the dead animal, walking closely beside me back toward the dorms. I felt safe next to him. Andrin couldn't burst out of the building and drag me into the woods anymore.

"Gabriel, would you like to choose your own name to mark your new start?" he asked. "You don't have to take mine. You'll find out quickly that my house runs with very few rules, but the ones I have are good ones."

I liked the sound of it. So much so I felt sickeningly guilty for being happy so soon after what happened to Apollo.

"Yeah. I want to choose something good. Something…dark."

"I'll help. Maybe we can catch an opera in Milan. They tend to have fucked-up stories. It'll give us inspiration."

My gaze snapped up to him.

He chuckled. "Oh yeah. Our household is very tolerant when it comes to profanity. You can use it in moderation."

I drew a deep breath. We reached the building just as Andrin tried to slip out the main door.

Daniel Hastings, my new father, blocked his way with his much larger frame. "You're not going anywhere," he said dryly. "Your next stop is the police station."

And I knew, at last, I was finally safe.

CHAPTER THIRTY-ONE
TATE

A few days after my wife asked that I seek help for my numerous conditions, I left Gia with the idiot sandwich that were Enzo and Filippo. It was a necessary evil, since I couldn't watch her twenty-four seven, but I was still in a foul mood about it.

Enzo was a jokester, a brat, and, on top of all those shortcomings, more fucking attractive than any man had a right to be.

My mood further spoiled when I got a call from an encrypted number. The only people who were able to reach me had to go through a four-step verification and enter two separate codes, so I figured it wasn't some cold caller trying to talk me into a pyramid scheme.

I swiped my phone's screen, returning my attention to the road as my gunmetal Lamborghini zipped its way to the Hamptons.

"Heard your wife's a particularly lovely creature," a rugged voice with a playful Irish lilt greeted.

Tiernan.

"Long lashes, soft lips…" he mused, sounding both poetic and diabolic. "My, my, my, but I do love me some pretty things."

"And I heard your sister is almost as pretty. Tierney, right?" I didn't let the anger bleed into my tone. "Red hair. Big green eyes. Not a hard sell either if you want to make a fast buck."

The silence on the other end told me Tiernan was no fan of the scenario of his precious twin being smuggled onto a superyacht and sold to the highest bidder.

I was surprised he called. Then again, I'd been told he was unpredictable. A wild card. Totally unhinged.

"If you so much as google my sister again, I'll make sure it's the last thing you do with your fingers," Tiernan said cheerfully.

"Didn't have to google her. She made herself known by cheating at the craps tables at the Ferrantes' underground casino a few years back. I think she took one of their lowly soldiers back home that night too. Real classy gal."

"If you think you're walking out of this unharmed, I applaud your optimism," he replied in a low, steady voice that for sure frightened everyone around him. "You killed four of my men."

"How about you land a paper cut before throwing more empty threats in the air?" I suggested. "So far, I managed to single-handedly deal with everyone you sent my way without even breaking a sweat. I've no interest in your sister if you leave my wife alone. This is between us."

"Up until now, I sent low-grade traffickers to feel you out. If I wanted you dead, I'd have been pissing on your grave daily for a month now. The only reason the NYPD is not collecting your body parts with tweezers and a magnifying glass is because I'd love to blackmail you."

"Yeah? What's the holdup?"

"Haven't decided what I want from you yet."

"I'm on pins and needles." I enjoyed the winding green scenery of the Hamptons.

"Won't keep you long. For now, I'd advise this killing spree stops now while your debt to me is still manageable."

I appreciated a good, unhinged personality. The fact that he thought he was in a bargaining position was adorable. Truly.

"Sure thing. Right after I kill Nash Moore." I lit myself a cigarette, rolling down a window. "Who's in my trunk now, by the way."

At the sound of his name, Nash, the last man on my hit list, banged the top of the trunk with his cuffed wrists, thrashing and kicking. His screams were muffled by the metal barrier between us. Oh, and the crusty used underwear I shoved into his mouth to shut him up.

"He's making a lot of noise," I groused. "You think it's because I stuffed him in a two-hundred-thirty-liter space in the nose of the car?"

Tiernan offered a harsh chuckle. "I told him to make himself scarce. Can't fix stupid."

"No, you can't," I agreed.

"We should sit down and see how we solve this predicament with your head still attached to your neck."

I wasn't opposed to negotiations. Not necessarily for striking a deal, but it was always good to gauge my opponents.

"Sure. I'll be indisposed for the next few hours, but you can call my PA and ask for a meeting."

Rebecca was still less capable than a rotten tuna sandwich discarded at the bottom of a third grader's backpack, but this was an example for an event I *wanted* her to fuck up and not put in my calendar.

Tiernan was about to mouth me off, but I had already killed the call and tossed my phone onto the passenger seat.

Andrin used to say I never learned from past mistakes, but I disagreed.

This time, I was going to kill Nash Moore deep in the woods.

Red didn't go well with the dark green wallpaper of my property.

CHAPTER THIRTY-TWO
GIA

Tate made himself unavailable to me the week after I broached the subject of his disorders. He went both to the Hamptons and on a mysterious trip abroad. I was left with Enzo, Filippo, and a million unanswered questions. Oh, an ailing mother who was still in a medically induced coma.

The fun just never stopped for yours truly.

In lieu of a husband, I threw myself into visiting Mum, making arrangements for her hospice transfer, and work. All my colleagues were wondering why the big, hulking men in suits followed me everywhere. Even though I worked diligently on forming a union, most of them still didn't approach me.

My five-day streak of not seeing my husband was coming to an end, though. Tate had texted earlier today he would be picking me up for a mysterious meeting.

Tate: We're leaving the office at four today. Meeting in Brooklyn. Be ready.

I was.

So were the twenty people sitting in my office, serving as the organizing committee of our freshly formed workers' union.

Tate arrived on the HR floor half an hour before we were scheduled to leave, accompanied by his two bodyguards and Rebecca. Seeing her next to him made my heart squeeze with jealousy. He entered my office poker-faced, as though being ambushed by twenty of his employees was nothing out of the ordinary.

"You unionized the staff." He reached to give me a cold peck on the lips. The gesture caught me by surprise.

I swallowed down the ball of wariness in my throat. "What makes you think that?"

"You haven't fired anyone in two weeks." He shouldered off his coat, ignoring everyone, eyes trained on me. "And haven't done anything to ruin my life in almost a week. I was starting to get worried."

Rebecca tutted in disapproval, shaking her head. The gesture forced me to turn my attention to her. I had worked with her back when I was assisting Tate full-time. She never wore skirts this skimpy before. And knowing she was openly flirting with him bothered me, I realized. A lot.

It also didn't help that my husband had been ignoring me for five days. My confidence in our shaky marriage had hit rock bottom. She was still propositioning him, I'd bet. Her attire was only appropriate for brothels and a Victoria's Secret runway.

Tate followed my line of vision. He nodded swiftly. "I see. Rebecca?"

"Yeah?" she purred behind his back.

"You're fired."

She gasped. "What?"

He tossed a glance at her over his shoulder. "Fired. Discharged. Laid off. Done-zo. Can't think of other synonyms."

"I believe ousted is also an appropriate term." I cleared my throat demurely. It wasn't like me to be gleeful of another person's woes. "Exiled is a bit of an overkill but also a fitting substitute."

"Yes." Tate grinned at me with open admiration, and my whole body blossomed with warmth. "That. Anyway." He waved a hand. "Goodbye. Apricity, find me a replacement."

After five days of being deserted, the last thing I wanted to do was help him, but I needed to put myself aside for my passion project.

I nodded. "Stay tuned."

"Now, tell me what all this is about." He gestured to the room full of people, who watched the entire spectacle with their mouths agape.

"We want you to recognize our union and start negotiating better health care and working conditions." I stood up straight.

"You're violating your employee's textbook," he shot drily.

"I retained a lawyer who found a loophole," I countered, bracing myself for a bitter argument.

"Fine."

"If you don't agree, we'll file an election petition with the NLRB offi—wait, what?" I cocked my head sideways.

"I said fine." He rolled his sleeves up his elbows and took a seat at my desk, picking up the forty-page folder I prepared with our demands. "I have twenty minutes to look at your asks. I'll get back to you by the end of the month with an official counteroffer once legal tears it apart."

Everyone in the room was stunned into silence. A few people whispered in shock. Hank, an elderly employee, looked like he was about to faint.

"You're not going to balk?" My husband was not a businessman. He was a vulture profiteering from other people's misery.

He flipped through the pages of my demands, grabbing a red Sharpie and making notes on the margins. "Do you want me to?"

"No." A frown kissed my forehead. "You're usually less agreeable, though."

"What can I say? Fucking the woman of my dreams regularly has made me considerably less prickly."

Gasps and giggles erupted from our audience. Enzo smirked from his place by the door, swiveling in an office chair like a child. I wanted to crawl under a rock and hide there forever.

"Tate," I chided, swatting his shoulder.

"Apricity," he answered, looking up to scan the room in boredom. "Don't sound so shocked. We're married, young, and attractive. Why wouldn't we be fucking like rabbits?"

More giggles and awkward laughs.

"You're not that young," I muttered. "And you're sexually harassing the staff right now."

"Bullshit. No one in this room is fuckable to me other than you." He crossed out an entire paragraph about shorter working hours and possible remote work.

"How am I supposed to look these people in the eye after what they heard?" I leaned into his space, whisper-shouting.

"If it's an issue, I can fire all of them and hire oth—"

"You know what? Just concentrate on my proposal."

I let him read through the rest of the document silently, afraid he'd divulge more information about our private life. You know, like give me pointers about oral sex in front of the entire HR department. Tate was quick and eagle-eyed.

"Anything else?" He stood up, offering me back the folder with his comments.

I plucked it from between his fingers. "No."

"Scan this and send it back to me so I can pass it through legal. I'm waiting by the elevator. Congratulations on your union."

Claps erupted in the room. As soon as he walked out of my office, everyone clamored to hug and cheer for me.

"This is going to be such a game changer!" Monica from customer service was in actual tears.

"I can't believe he agreed." George, our senior accountant, squeezed my shoulder. "Now I can finally have some personal time off for my hip replacement and physiotherapy."

"I hadn't realized you had him so wrapped around your little finger." Mariam gnawed on her lower lip thoughtfully, arms folded. "That was…impressive."

"For real." Trisha pouted. "I thought Tate's love language was glaring. He didn't seem like the type to…you know, do nice things. Even for his wife."

"And the way he fired Rebecca." Mariam fanned herself. "You've got yourself a keeper."

When I met Tate at the elevators, he didn't tear his gaze from the climbing numbers on the digital screen, back to ignoring my existence.

"A few weeks ago, you forced me to fire people for a living," I said quietly. "Now you're letting me start a union. Why the change of heart?"

"First of all, I have no heart. That hasn't changed." He looked down, putting on his leather gloves. "Second, I found something to replace my hobby of pissing you off."

"And what's that?"

"Making you come on my tongue," he answered conversationally, ignoring our bodyguards.

Enzo whistled low, slanting his head. Filippo elbowed him on a chuckle.

"The two don't go hand in hand. I had to pick one," Tate continued. "I chose the pussy."

"No, you chose to disappear for five bloody days."

"I had my reasons."

"Right. Business in Europe, and…? Why were you in the Hamptons?"

He gave me a wry look. "You know very well why I was there and why you couldn't come."

He killed the third and last man.

He avenged his father.

And it made me feel…good for him, somehow. I hoped he'd found his closure.

"Where are we going?" I asked.

"To meet the Callaghans." He swiped invisible lint from his suit. "And the Ferrantes, of course."

"Ceasefire?" I asked hopefully.

The doors slid open. We stepped inside, our bodyguards following suit.

A dangerous grin played on his face. "Ensnarement, my dear."

CHAPTER THIRTY-THREE
TATE

"Why are you bringing me to the lion's den?" Gia broke the silence in the back seat of my Range Rover while Iven cruised the streets of Brooklyn.

"If you stayed at work, the Callaghans would know I wasn't nearby and make a move."

"This shit needs to stop. I'm scared," she admitted, reaching to fumble with her bracelet before remembering it wasn't there anymore.

"You've no reason to be. Tiernan knows what I'll do to his sister if he so much as glances at you the wrong way."

"You'd hurt a woman to get back at someone?" She turned to me, stunned.

"Hey, you were the ones who were hell-bent on being treated equally," I deadpanned.

The truth was I could've executed Nash Moore in two, three, even five weeks, when there wasn't so much heat between the Irish and me. But I needed an excuse to get away from her.

An excuse to stop myself from slipping into her bed and fucking her again while we drowned in each other's eyes.

I had vowed the day Apollo died to never love again and managed to keep my promise to myself, even with Daniel. Gia wasn't about to destroy my perfect streak.

The car stopped in front of a warehouse. We chose a neutral

place to meet, and the Ferrantes suggested they act as mediators for the modest fee of $10K from each party. This was Camorra territory, which meant no one was about to get murdered.

At least tonight.

As soon as Gia and I made it to the door, two burly Camorra soldiers confiscated our phones and gave me a thorough pat down. When they turned toward Gia to do the same, I smiled cordially.

"Touch her, and I'll break your trachea and make her a sustainable coffee straw out of it."

"Leave her be, Primo." Achilles appeared at the entrance, wearing his usual smart combo of a black shirt and matching slacks. Shame about that face, because his style was impeccable. He motioned for us to come in. "The Callaghans are already here."

We walked through a vast, open space to a side door that led to a basement. I grabbed Gia's wrist and held it firmly. She laced her fingers through mine and started tapping her index finger over the back of my hand in a familiar pattern.

Two, six, two.

Two, six, two.

Two, six, two.

A jolt of panic rushed through my spine, followed by immediate orgasmic relief.

She knows.

She understands.

She cooperates.

She soothes.

My muscles loosened. And in that moment, I needed her more than I'd ever needed anything else in my entire fucking life.

At the end of the stairway was a dimly lit room with a long table, a built-in kitchenette, and an overhead lamp. At the table sat Vello, Luca, an older Irish man, Tiernan, and Tierney. I recognized the twins. They both had dark red hair, almost radioactive-green eyes, and sharp, cunning features.

Luca swiftly made the introductions. The older man was Tyrone, the twins' father and the retired boss. It was my understanding Tiernan took the reins some time ago. We all sat down.

"I see you brought your sister along." I lit a cigarette.

"For the same reason you brought your wife." Tiernan's cold gaze could frost over the sun.

"Because you want to wine, dine, and fuck her afterward?" I cocked an eyebrow.

Enzo barked out a corroded laugh.

"Hey, listen, no judgment here. I'm a man of decadent tastes. You do you, buddy."

Tiernan's glare told me we were off to a catastrophic start. *Good.* My strategy for today was to show them there'd be no negotiations. Each of their soldiers who killed my father deserved to die. And anyone in my way to them was destined to a similar fate.

"Tate," Tiernan said easily.

"Tiernan," I answered in earnest.

"How much do you like your Mediterranean yacht?"

My eyes tapered to slits. "No."

Don't tell me he touched *Urania.* I'd only had her for three years.

"Yes," Tiernan tsked gravely. "You know, a lot of bystanders took pictures. It's a very fine thing, watching a superyacht burning to ash inside a large body of water." He flicked his phone, thumbing his screen alive and boomeranging the device across the table to me. "Here. I kept this picture as a souvenir."

Bastard.

And a bastard who cost me fucking two hundred million dollars.

"Blackthorn," Tyrone piped up. "You've killed five of our men."

"Boo-fucking-hoo." I sat back, folding my arms over my chest. "Couldn't have done it without the help of the Ferrante family."

Tiernan speared Luca and Achilles with a bloodcurdling glare.

Achilles shrugged. "Hey, business is business. For the right price, I'd make meatballs out of you. Eat them too. By the way." He reached for his cigarette pack, pulling one out with his lips and lighting it. He pointed at Tierney with the hand that held the lit cigarette. "I always wanted to know, banshee. Does the carpet match the drapes?"

Gia choked on her saliva next to me.

Tierney, however, smiled serenely. "Seeing as you'll never be invited to the house, I'm afraid you'll have to take that mystery to your grave."

Achilles beamed, elated with the challenge. "Never say never. And I'm not planning on dying just yet."

"You sure?" Tierney raised an eyebrow. "Because I'm happy to lend a helping hand."

"I have a good idea where I want that han—"

"Let me know when you're done flirting." I rolled my tongue along my upper teeth. "No pressure, though. I'll wait."

"Look, Blackthorn, we have no use for you as a rival." Tyrone cleared his throat, sticking to the subject. "No territorial or financial disputes. At the same time, letting you walk away from this unharmed would send a terrible message to our enemies."

Vello nodded in agreement.

"With that in mind, what have you got to offer us?" Tyrone asked.

After they burned down my yacht?

"I can offer a *fuck off*." I lit up a cigarette Even that was generous. "See, the three men I set out to kill murdered my father in prison and deserved the slow, violent death I granted them. The second two were collateral for going after my wife, and I'm here to tell you, you'll be out of soldiers if you keep sending people to harm her. You don't want me to start striking back and going after your precious gem." I cast my eyes on Tierney. To her credit, she didn't budge.

Tiernan stood to his impressive height, smashed his tumbler of whiskey on the edge of the table while dripping nonchalance, and pointed a shard at my throat, looming over the table between us. Despite the violent act, he was calm and collected. "You best watch your fucking mouth when you speak about my sister. I'd hate to gut you like a fish in front of your wife."

No, he wouldn't. He'd probably take extreme pleasure in it.

I glared at him dispassionately. "The rumors are true then. You're an angry, useless drunk. What a cliché."

"Sit the fuck down before I put a bullet in your skull." Achilles pointed at Tiernan with his cigarette. "I'm the only one here with a loaded weapon, and I don't take kindly to people threatening my guests on my property, with the shards of a tumbler that cost me two hundred bucks, no less."

Tiernan sank back to his seat slowly, tauntingly, never breaking eye contact.

I caught Gia glaring at me with alarm. This wasn't going how she'd hoped for.

"Blackthorn." Vello turned to me. "Stop wasting everyone's time. You killed five of their soldiers in less than five months. It's understandable they'd want compensation."

"They burned my yacht."

"You're insured through your ass," Luca deadpanned. "Give them something to work with."

"The best I can do is pay for this asshole over here to get his dick wet in a low-grade whorehouse." I pointed at Tiernan with my cigarette. "Maybe that'll loosen him up."

"Who knew all Tate needed to find his sense of humor was a megalomaniacal Irish mobster?" Enzo gleefully carved a skull into the table with his knife. "He's a hoot tonight."

Tiernan played with the shard of glass in his hand, a small smile on his lips.

"We'll take your three cargo ships. The ones docked here in Brooklyn," Tyrone offered decisively. "We need them for shipments. They're old enough that it's not a financial strain on your end, and peace will be restored."

"Have you lost your plot, Da?" Tiernan impaled him with a glare.

"He should be giving us a spot on the board of GS Properties and a blow job for our troubles."

I knew any reasonable man would accept Tyrone's offer. But I wasn't reasonable. And I definitely wasn't letting his son off the hook after trying to kidnap my wife. *Twice.* It wasn't about Daniel's murderers anymore. It was about Gia. I wanted them to know no one went after my wife.

"You're getting jack shit," I drawled. "I don't respond well to pressure from below."

"We're going in circles." Luca put out his cigarette in an ashtray, immediately lighting another one. "Tiernan, Tyrone—Blackthorn isn't gonna budge on this. I know the man. He's as flexible as a three-day-old corpse."

"And just as charming," Achilles contributed. "You do what you will with this information. But this is his best and final offer."

"His best and final offer is *nothing.*" Tiernan yawned, and I had a feeling he was the same brand of crazy motherfucker as Achilles. Two peas in a fucked-up pod.

"Incorrect." I put out my cigarette. "The alternative is war, and trust me, you don't want to go there. Cut your losses. Move on. Don't ever get near my wife. Great deal."

Tiernan bowed an eyebrow. "You won't win this, Blackthorn. What I lack in resources I make up for in cruelty. I won't be the first to blink."

"Why did you come here if you didn't want to strike any sort of deal?" Tyrone turned his attention to me. He wasn't like his hotheaded son. In another life, we could've gotten along.

"Mainly to piss your son off." I hitched a shoulder up. "See up close where I want to stab him. He wears his heart on his sleeve, and if he isn't careful, that heart is going to end up as taxidermy in my Staindrop cabin."

I was lying, of course.

I didn't have a cabin in Staindrop. It was a shithole.

I had a cabin in Vermont, and I actually did need to decorate that wooden wall.

Tiernan stood up again and leaned across the table until our faces were an inch apart. His eyes glinted with madness. The violence dancing inside them told me he was the worst kind of a crime lord. The type who saw killing as the destination, not a means to an end.

"I want to be clear on one thing." He dropped his voice to a whisper, fingers splayed across the table. "If you walk out of here without giving us a concession, something to show for our trouble, I *will* come after you and all that's yours. That's not a threat, Blackthorn. It's a promise."

I stood up slowly, prolonging the moment. All eyes clung to us.

"Do your worst, Callaghan. I'll do the same. May the best man win."

CHAPTER THIRTY-FOUR
TATE

I was eighteen when I checked on Andrin again. By that time, I was no longer scrawny, awkward Gabriel Doe. I was Tate Blackthorn, lacrosse star, Harvard darling, the mysterious son of a real estate mogul, a prodigy, the most handsome Prince Charming on New York's social roster.

A quick Google search was enough to reveal Andrin's destiny, and it wasn't what I was expecting.

Three months after I moved out of the boarding school, Andrin found his death in a suspiciously unfortunate skiing accident. Suspicious because fucker didn't ski. Even more so because it wasn't an injury that caused his death. The article stated he veered off course onto a secluded mountaintop, where he was mauled by forest animals. The death, the article suggested, was slow and painful and took three or four days. His body—or whatever was left of it—was found scattered a couple of months later.

Peculiar still was the fact that he was found holding a black thorn.

There were no plants or bushes on the snow-covered mountaintops.

I didn't have to ask Daniel about it. I knew.

Because I remembered that three months after I was adopted, Daniel called his mother—Nana Nelly—to watch over me for the weekend as he conducted urgent business in Zurich.

No part of me found it immoral or distressing that Daniel dealt with my abuser.

He did what he had to do. What I'd do for someone else if I ever was stupid enough to allow myself to love.

He took a life so I could live mine peacefully.

CHAPTER THIRTY-FIVE
GIA

"And that's the last of it." Cal waltzed into Mum's hospice room carrying a box of her toiletries.

Dylan was standing next to me, fluffing fresh flowers in a vase. I was tucking Mum's blanket under the mattress. We all pretended like what we did mattered in some way. But it didn't.

My mother was brought back from her medically induced coma but remained unconscious. The infections were finally gone, but her body was deteriorating. My time with what was left of her was limited.

"Cheers for everything." I smiled at them.

"Nonsense, I wish we could do more." Cal unloaded a box onto the shelves in the bathroom, leaving the door open.

"Yeah, like getting rid of these unfriendly men for you." Dylan tossed a hand in Enzo and Filippo's direction. They stood at the doorway, chatting in Italian. It was necessary I had protection now, since my husband blew up the negotiations with the Callaghans. "By the way, are you sure Tate found them at a security company and not the entrance of Abercrombie & Fitch?" Dylan did an appreciative double take.

"Dylan," I reproached. "Don't objectify them!"

"Oh, please. Women have been objectified for at least two millennia." She waved me off. "I'm just trying to even the score."

Enzo and Filippo didn't even acknowledge my friends. Or me for that matter.

"What did Tate do to piss off the Irish so much anyway?" Cal stuck her head out from the bathroom, frowning.

"Oh, screwed them over financially," I lied. It was easier than explaining my husband was a serial killer. "He's working on a solution now, though."

"Is he treating you well?" Dylan turned to look at me, searching my face.

"Yeah," I admitted, biting down on my lip. "He showers me with gifts and orgasms. He leaves me to my own devices at home and at work. It's pretty sweet."

But he also refused to seek help for himself. Refused to stop a bloody war. Worst of all—he refused to truly let me in.

"Is he a freak in bed?" Dylan grinned.

"Dyl!" Cal threw a hand at Mum's bed. "Her *mother* is right here."

"*Unconscious.*" Dylan rolled her eyes. Dylan was going to med school and checked my mother's vitals each time she was here. "Besides, if Telma could hear us, I bet she'd be happy to know her daughter is sexually satisfied."

"Dylan is right," I conceded. "Mum was a sex-positive feminist. She'd want to hear all the sordid details."

"*Is,*" Cal corrected softly.

"Huh?" I patted my wrist, an old habit whenever I wanted to get strength from my bracelet.

"Your mother is still alive, Gia."

This was true, but I knew that the woman who raised me—the woman who shaped me to be who I was today—was no longer there. The grief of family members of people with dementia started before they lost their loved one in body. Because we first lost their souls.

"Promise me one thing." Dylan held my gaze. "Protect your heart." She pressed her palm to my sternum, worry etched onto her features. "You're going through so much right now. If something poses a threat to your mental health, get rid of it. Even if it's your husband. You can't afford more sorrow."

Later that afternoon, one of the hospice's doctors walked in. Short, stocky, middle-aged, with glasses and an exaggerated wig. I squinted at his tag. I always memorized my mother's carers' names, brought them Starbucks gift cards and baked goods. But now I realized there was no point in doing that. Mum wouldn't be here long enough to reach any milestones.

"Mrs. Blackthorn, there you are." He flipped a page on the old-school clipboard in his hand. "My name is Dr. Fields. I'll be your primary contact here. Do you have any questions?"

I was tired and irritable. In over my head. So I asked bluntly, "How long does she have?"

"She's exhibiting signs associated with end of life. Drooping of her nasolabial fold, nonreactive pupils, and periodic breathing. Worst-case scenario will be the next twelve hours. Best-case? I'd say a week."

"Is there a chance she'll wake up?" I held back my tears. I was too exhausted for another big cry.

"Miracles happen, but…" He grimaced. "It's unlikely."

"What do I do?" I blurted out. "It's just…once she's gone, I'll be all alone. And I know that cognitively she hasn't been with me for a while, but even taking care of her kept me together." Remembering myself, I laughed, dabbing the corners of my eyes with tissue. "God, look at me. A sobbing mess. You didn't ask for any of this. You probably see grieving family members all the time and don't have the energy for that."

He put his clipboard down, hesitant. "I entered this field because I wanted to help. I still do. What you're feeling is normal. Grief is a part of letting go." He paused. "It's important to remember to prioritize self-care. We have a bereavement group if you need to talk to someone. Having a strong support system is essential."

I knew what I had to do.

Dylan alluded to that too.

I needed to protect my heart.

To leave Tate behind.

If I didn't leave now, I'd stay stuck in a loveless marriage, the worst place for a broken person to be.

Only it wasn't so loveless. I *was*, in fact, in love.

With all that he was and all he could be.

The only way to protect my heart was to shield it from the man who could break it.

The man who would hate me if he knew what really happened with his adoptive father that night.

A man who chose pride over happiness.

Money over family.

And war over me.

CHAPTER THIRTY-SIX
GIA

"He's going to kill someone when he finds out." Enzo tossed a chip into his mouth, chewing loudly. "Most likely me."

Surprised, I looked up from the fluffy rom-com I was reading on my Kindle. It was the first time Enzo spoke to me the entire time he was my bodyguard. Filippo was taking a nap in a plush recliner behind us.

"Why?" I reached for my Bloody Mary. We were sitting in my newly purchased private jet, flying out from New York to London. "Because I left the country without telling him, or because I served him with divorce papers?"

"Both," Enzo deadpanned. He was slunk back with one boot propped on the table, playing with his Swiss Army knife and eating kettle chips. His hands were full of cuts. I noticed that whenever he made fresh cuts, he didn't even flinch. Like he was incapable of feeling pain.

I had studied the Ferrantes closely in recent weeks. Luca was the quiet, calculating one. Adequately handsome. Chillingly mysterious. Achilles was the deranged, ferocious one. Scarred from head to toe, tattooed to his last inch. Enzo was the loveliest. As exquisite as fine art. But he seemed so out of place in this world. I could see him partying in Cancun with his fraternity brothers or running in slo-mo in an A & F ad, throwing a Frisbee.

"Well, it shouldn't come as a surprise." I sat up demurely. "Our contract says I can divorce him when my mother dies."

"Last I checked, she ain't dead," he drawled, eyes trained on his fingers as he flipped the knife like quicksilver. "Unless of course he found out you were gone and decided to punish you creatively."

Despite knowing Tate was more than happy to unalive large swaths of people, I wasn't worried about him killing anyone innocent or faultless.

When I didn't answer Enzo, he continued, "He wants to protect you, you know."

"*Protect* me?" I snorted. "Tate is the reason why I'm in danger."

"Yeah." He ran his hand over his hair. "He kinda messed that up."

"He doesn't love me," I snapped.

"Dude, are you for real?" Enzo snorted. "No man I know would go through all this convoluted bullshit for a piece of ass."

"Convoluted bullshit?" I narrowed my eyes. "It's not like *I* trapped *him* into marrying me."

He shrugged. "The sick mother. That experimental trial thingy. The contract. The bodyguards. The shopping sprees. The sass. Admit it, Gia, you've got baggage."

"Everyone's got baggage," I snapped.

"Sure. But plenty of people are willing to hide theirs to bag someone like Blackthorn. Not your ass. No. You keep it real."

Was there a compliment hiding somewhere in his sentence?

"You give him hell, and he gives you back heaven. Why do you wanna call this?"

"Obsession," I said crisply. "And I don't know...karma for something terrible I did in the past?"

"I can see why he's drawn to you." He ran his tongue over his upper lip wolfishly. "I like a woman with a smart mouth. I always wonder what other impressive tricks she can do with it."

I shook my head, looking out the window. A fluffy sheet of white clouds stretched beneath us like linen.

Enzo was dead wrong about Tate's feelings for me. Anyway, I didn't want to talk about it. The Ferrantes already had a front-row seat to the dumpster fire we called our marriage.

"So…how did you do it?" I piped up, glare still fixed on the sky.

"How did I do what?" He shook the crisps bag, staring into it.

"Kill someone when you were inducted. Tate told me about Luca and Achilles. He said you brothers like to top one another. Make it as gory and frightening as possible so your reputation will precede you. How old were you, and what'd you do?" I couldn't picture Enzo hurting a fly.

"I was fifteen." He tucked his knife into his pocket, aware his next words would frighten me. "A late bloomer. Luca was inducted at fourteen, Achilles at thirteen. Fucker couldn't wait to draw blood." Another tug of his hair. "My brothers, they're real sociopaths. Me, I like to think of myself as a pacifist. But one who doesn't mind bending his own rules if it means inheriting an empire. I needed to prove myself. I wanted to do something that required both skill and imagination. You know, show off my moves."

I swallowed hard, adrenaline pumping through my body. "Yes?"

"I decided to flay my victim while he was fully conscious." He examined his outstretched, cut fingers as though they were a work of ancient art. "I skinned him from ankles to neck before he died of hypothermia, but it took several days and a large number of infusions. When it was over, I managed to keep his entire skin intact."

My stomach roiled. "H-how…"

"I was a STEM dude at school. Even did a year of premed."

"What happened?"

"Uh, my dad happened?" He laughed humorlessly. "Have you met the guy? He doesn't leave much room for agency. It's cool, though. I made peace with what I do."

"What did the man do to deserve it?"

"He killed an underboss's wife and the baby in her belly. Stabbed her in the stomach several times. Then killed the underboss too."

A beat of silence followed. "The underboss was my godfather. The man who killed them was one of our own. He wanted to rise up in ranks quickly. Thought he wouldn't get caught."

"What did you do with his skin?" I didn't know why I asked. I didn't want to know.

"I made myself a nice, warm leather coat. I'm wearing it now, actually."

My gaze shot to his black leather jacket, and my eyes flared.

"Oh my God, look at your face. I'm just fucking with you. What kind of sick bastard do you think I am?" Enzo chuckled good-naturedly. "No, but I did make a few knife sheaths with it."

I massaged my temples. "I don't know how I found myself surrounded by such bad men."

"Ah, that's an easy one." Enzo untucked his knife, playing with it again. "You fell in love."

I made one quick stop at a newsagent's on my way to the cemetery to visit Dad's and Elliott's graves. They were buried side by side. Mum and I had to pay a convenience fee for their proximity, which felt utterly ridiculous. Nothing felt convenient about losing two of your loved ones.

"Hi, lads." I lined up their favorite snacks and drinks by their gravestones. "There we are. Elliott—your scratchings, peanut M&Ms, and...Irn-Bru." I shuddered at the radioactive-looking drink. My brother never had the chance to outgrow the criminally sweet soda. "Daddy, here's your prawn cocktail Skips and Bounty bar." I always brought them their favorite snacks. They were so serious about their food. "Sorry it's been a minute. I've been taking care of Mum."

My eyes stung from tears and the cold, and I knew Enzo and Filippo were standing behind me, probably wondering if I was mental.

"Don't worry, though." I sniffled, wiping at my runny nose. "She'll be fine. I'm taking good care of her. I—"

I stopped, shaking my head and squeezing my lips together.

"Who am I kidding?" I let my head fall between my shoulders. "She's not going to be fine. She'll be joining you soon, and I'm scared, and I'm sad and angry, *so* angry." I fell to my knees in front of their graves, my entire body shaking. "They say there are five stages to grief, but I think mine hit me all at once. The pain is everywhere. I can't escape it."

The graves didn't answer, but they did listen. I knew, because some of the agony rolled off my shoulders.

"I tried everything I could." I wiped my eyes and nose with the end of my sleeve. "I broke the law. I made a deal with the devil. Married him too. All in order to save her. You'd be disappointed if you were alive, Dad. And to top it all, I lost the bracelet. *Our* bracelet. A bad man took it with him to his grave."

I couldn't stop the tears from rolling. My entire life, I had tried my hardest to be the person I thought others needed me to be. And what I got in return was a senseless car accident that took Dad and Elliott away from me because some pissed wanker decided to get behind the wheel and drive. When the loss of them brought me to my knees, I'd clung to the only person I had left—Mum. But she'd been ripped from me too.

That bracelet wasn't just a piece of jewelry. It symbolized another part of my life I'd never get back.

"Please forgive my self-pity." I dabbed at my eyes again. "I love you so much. Both of you. Elliott—I miss our banter. And our late nights binge-eating biscuits in front of *EastEnders*. Sorry, Dad. Yes, it was us who ate your digestives, which, by the way, are still junk food. Just because they have the words 'whole wheat' on them doesn't make them healthy."

I snorted out an ungraceful laugh.

"I miss kicking your arse at Wii. And you kicking my arse at tennis. And the practical jokes we pulled on each other. And how you were so attuned to my feelings, you once took my goldfish to the vet because it was unwell and actually managed to save it." I clamped my mouth shut, looking down at the damp, loose ground. "And, Dad, I miss your advice. Geeking out with math riddles. I miss the unconditional love I took for granted my entire childhood. I have recently come to realize that no matter how grand and all-consuming love can be, nothing can match the love between a parent and a child."

I stood up and turned around, surprised to see my husband leaning against a black SUV. He waited a few feet away from Enzo, staring at me quietly, his pocket watch in hand.

How long had he been here? How much did he see?

I slinked toward him. Twilight draped over the cemetery, the crows standing on bare branches in the shadows our only audience. I stopped six feet away from him. "How long have you been here?"

"My flight left twenty-five minutes after yours."

My gaze immediately shot to Enzo, who gestured to his face. "I think we can both agree I am far too beautiful to be beheaded."

"You betrayed me." I narrowed my eyes.

"I was never loyal to you to begin with," Enzo corrected softly.

Tate unbuttoned his coat, producing the divorce papers from his breast pocket. "Thought I'd do this in person." He proceeded to tear the papers in front of me, tossing them between us. They sailed to the ground like confetti.

To have Tate fight for me, right when I was about to lose my last relative on earth, felt reassuring. But he wouldn't feel the same if he knew the whole story.

"She's dying," I said.

"Not dead yet," Tate countered.

"You're no good for me," I said.

"I can change. I *have* changed."

"I'm no good for *you*," I tried again.

"Let me be the fucking judge of that." His eyes burned with determination.

"Tate…" I hesitated.

Guilt devoured me like a hungry pack of wolves, tearing at my flesh. I knew the truth would make him hate me.

He deserved to know the truth. And *I* deserved to be set free.

"It wasn't Daniel," I blurted out, the bitter wind slapping my face.

"What do you mean?"

"That night. The man your father killed. Leon Gorga. He didn't kill him…" I closed my eyes, not wanting to see his expression when he finally heard the truth. "I did."

Silence. Thick and sticky and suffocating. I opened my eyes. He stared at me, his eyes suspiciously bright, red-rimmed, matching his ruddy cheekbones.

"Gonna need more than that."

"Leon Gorga killed my father and brother. He was the other driver. Gorga was on holiday in London and pissed out of his arse. But he got away with two vehicular manslaughter charges because he was powerful and wealthy, the son of a senator. His solicitors managed to exclude incriminating evidence and argued rubbish premedical conditions. I'm sure the fact that my father was driving a Vauxhall, not a Ferrari, played into the trial. Point is Gorga didn't spend a day in prison for what he'd done. And…and…"

"You couldn't bear it," Tate finished for me. "The injustice."

I had obsessively searched every detail about Gorga after the accident.

Where he lived: Westchester, New York. Where he worked: Wall Street. Who he was: a twice-divorced wealth management playboy with a pink cocaine habit.

"You're not the only one with fixations," I croaked out. "I was obsessed with Gorga for a very long time. When I finished my A-levels, I chose to go to college in New York so I could follow him, even at the price of moving away from Mum. In hindsight, it was probably what finished her."

Mum was young—still in her late forties—suddenly widowed and without the prized teenage son and husband she adored so much. Her daughter, me, moved across the pond, leaving her to lick her wounds alone. It was, in her doctors' opinion, the catalyst of her early-onset dementia. So in a way, Gorga didn't only take Elliott and Dad—he also took Mum.

"It helped that I got a full ride through my tennis. I stalked him every waking moment I wasn't studying or playing. I knew where he took his lunch. Where he dined. The clubs he frequented. Which hotels in the city he took his hookups to."

Enzo stood far enough from us that he couldn't hear, but I knew I was being foolish, admitting this to another living soul.

"I never meant to kill him," I whispered.

Tate's hands circled my upper arms, steadying me. "Tell me exactly what happened."

I hiccupped. "I was always so careful about putting enough space between us when I followed him, but this time, I got too close." I dropped my gaze to my feet. "Every Friday, when he got off work, he went to the Forbidden Fruit Club. I'd follow him and wait outside. He'd sit on the balcony with his mates, chain-smoking and drinking champagne. I didn't know why I did it to myself, but I got addicted to watching him live his life so carelessly after killing half my family. I was punishing myself. That night was different because he drove to the club in his Ferrari."

My lower lip trembled.

"I watched from across the street as he polished off bottle after bottle of champagne and snorted cocaine. I knew he'd get behind the wheel and kill someone else, and it made me furious. So I confronted him."

I was shaking so badly, Tate had to physically keep me upright. I'd never uttered this out loud to anyone, and speaking the truth, relaying it, made me face what happened for the first time. Tate motioned for Thierry to get out of the driver's seat and tucked me into the back seat of the car, closing the door so it was just the two of us.

"Continue," he instructed.

"You're going to hate me."

But wasn't that what I wanted? A way out of this marriage before my mother's death?

"I could never hate you," he muttered grimly.

Worrying my lip, I soldiered through. "I followed him to his car. I just wanted to stop him from driving. It was dark and isolated in the parking lot. He confronted me and said he knew I'd been following him. I told him who I was—that it was my family he struck and killed."

Tate's hands were pressed firmly on my shoulders, anchoring me to the leather seat.

"He laughed in my face, Tate. He *laughed*." I gulped. "He told me I needed to move on. That *shit happens*. He said he'd been cleared, I wasn't supposed to be harassing him, and that he could call the police and get me deported."

"Fuck." Tate's lips barely moved.

"He had no remorse and laughed in my face, so I picked up a loose brick from the ground and hurled it his way. I honestly underestimated my swing." I sighed. "The brick smashed his head in. I remember seeing part of his skull caving in. He collapsed, and I knew immediately he didn't survive that injury. I panicked. I didn't know what to do. When I turned around, Daniel was there."

"He used to frequent the Forbidden Fruit's gambling tables," Tate grumbled.

"Daniel gathered me in his arms and put me back together." My voice cracked. "He helped me calm down. I told him what happened, why I did it. Told him I didn't mean to. Then we got into an argument."

"He wanted to take the fall for you," Tate guessed, his voice dull.

"Yeah, because I had a motive to kill, not injure. And I wanted to call the cops, to turn myself in." I licked my lips. "Daniel wanted me to run and pretend it never happened. Sirens blared in the distance. The cops were getting closer. He told me to admit nothing. Said it would jeopardize my visa and my school. That Gorga wasn't worth my future. He wouldn't have to serve time, and if he did, it would be minimal."

I fell silent, staring at my fingers.

"Your father didn't kill Gorga, Tate. I did."

I should have been the one who went to prison. If not for me, Tate would still have his adoptive father. I ruined everything for him.

Tate was quiet, digesting my confession, before he said, "In the trial, Daniel said Gorga tried to attack you. That your top was torn. That was why he threw that brick."

"That never happened," I admitted. "Moments before the police arrived, Daniel ripped my top so the story would track in case I was found."

"And you went along with his plan?"

I jerked my head guiltily. "I did, yes. He seemed sure he'd get out of it fairly quickly. Gorga was obviously intoxicated. He said he'd plead self-defense. He told me not to check on him, not to contact him, to protect both of us."

And I didn't, staying true to my word.

"W-what happened after, Tate?"

"He was taken to Rikers but got out on bail the following night." Tate stroked his jawline. "The self-defense case was strong. Gorga had a violent past, with several aggravated assault charges, and the autopsy showed insane amounts of alcohol and cocaine in his system. Dad, by contrast, had no past records, was a legitimate businessman, and adopted a son. He was serving a measly amount of time. I was supposed to see him a few weeks before he was murdered."

"I took away the most precious thing you've ever had." My voice broke. "The father you neede—"

"That wasn't your fault," he snapped. "That was Callaghan's soldiers. Besides, there's a fucked-up symmetry in this story if you look closely." A rueful smirk teased his lips. "My father helped you get revenge on the man who killed your father. That's what family does."

"Why aren't you more upset? I just told you I kept a secret from you. Betrayed your confidence."

"You did what you had to do at the time," he said emotionlessly. "I'd do the same. It's easier to forgive mistakes than lies. Because mistakes are never malicious. Lies are. Now, is there anything else you are hiding from me? Any more secrets?"

I shook my head.

"Good." He nodded, rolled down the window, and snapped his fingers. "Thierry, take us to the airport."

CHAPTER THIRTY-SEVEN
TATE

Gia was silent during the flight back home.

She thought coming clean about what happened with Daniel would make me dump her. Wishful thinking or guilty conscience? Either way, she severely underestimated how invested I was in our endeavor.

When I got the call from Enzo that they were boarding a plane to England, fifteen minutes after I was served divorce papers, my knee-jerk reaction was to drag her back kicking and screaming and remind her that not only was her mother still alive, but I was the only thing standing between her and Tiernan Callaghan putting a bullet in that pretty head of hers. But when I got to the cemetery and saw how sad she was, something stirred in me. An uncomfortable feeling that landed somewhere between acute anxiety and deep concern.

"Will you let me go once my mother dies?" Gia was sprawled on the seat across from me.

Enzo and Filippo sat at the back of the aircraft, playing cards.

"No," I answered frankly, not lifting my eyes from my paperwork.

"You keep whining about me not fulfilling my end of the bargain, but you refuse to adhere to the rules yourself?"

"Correct." I flipped a page. "Since you can't honor the terms of the arrangement, neither will I."

"Tate." She closed her eyes, drawing in a breath. "Please, if you have any shred of humanity in you, release me from this marriage. We both know you'll never love me, and I desperately need love."

"I care for you." My eyes skimmed a particularly tricky clause in the contract.

"You're infatuated with me," she corrected. "I'm a prize to you. You'll get bored of me. The fascination will wear off. Then what?"

I looked up from the contract, putting my pen down. She was honest with me. I might as well reciprocate. Maybe if she understood why I could never love her, she'd learn to accept what I had to offer.

"I was wired not to love from day one." I lounged back, lacing my fingers together. "Even at our height, after Daniel saved me, nourished me, helped me become who I am today, I still cannot say I truly loved him. Not loving you protects you more than it does me. Trust me."

"What happened to you at that boarding school?" Her brow knitted.

I told her what I didn't even tell Daniel in detail. What no other soul in the world knew. About Andrin. About Ares and Apollo and Zeus. About sleepless nights in thick, cold woods. Weaving my way back to safety in the dark, barefoot.

By the time I was done, she was crying. On paper, it was something that would piss me off. In reality, it didn't. I liked her softness.

"Andrin taught me an important lesson. Everything I love is destined to die. My ultimate way to shield you is not to love you." I leaned forward, taking her hand in mine, pressing a kiss to her palm. "I don't know how to love."

"Bullshit, Tate." Her eyes flew to me. "Maybe the child whose name I don't know wasn't capable of love. But my husband *is*. I'm sorry no one protected you when you needed it most." She put her hand on my cheek. "However, my children won't inherit my trauma, nor yours. They deserve a clean slate. A functional home."

"I can simulate normal very well," I said slowly. "I've managed to fool everyone for years."

She faked a smile, but I could see the pain through it. Worse than that, I seemed to *feel* it on my skin.

My wife stood up, picking up her purse. She strode over to the back of the aircraft, stopping suddenly, glancing at me over her shoulder. "You know what hurts the most?"

I stared at her silently.

"I'm falling in love with you, and I don't even know your name."

My jaw ticked, and I dragged my gaze back to the contract in front of me. She was being overtly expressive.

The only thing worth loving in me was sitting in my bank account and investment portfolio.

This was purely her emotional meltdown speaking. Nothing more.

"In the future, you are not to leave New York without giving me notice." I scribbled on the margins of the contract, my voice ice-cold. I tapped my numbers with my free hand. "If Tiernan manages to put his hands on you, I won't be responsible for my reaction."

An hour later, Enzo plopped on the seat in front of me. The clown was playing with his stupid knife again. "What did you say to her?"

"Why?" I was now on my laptop, catching up on emails. "Is she crying?"

He fell onto the seat in front of me. "Try aggressively online shopping. She just bought meals for every pet in every shelter on the East Coast and vowed to rebuild a few hurricane-stricken counties in South Carolina."

"Seems on brand." I clicked the laptop shut and gave him an annoyed glance. "Why the fuck are you here, Enzo? I push a call button when I need to summon the help."

Enzo rolled his eyes. He reached for my charcuterie board and popped a grape into his mouth. "There's a third option."

"Third?" My mouth curved with a scowl. "I didn't even know about the first two."

"The first option is you win in your power play. The second is that Tiernan wins," Enzo explained.

"And the third?"

"The third is you let the poor girl go, and none of this shit matters. She's too innocent for the life you've carved out for her. If you divorce her, he won't touch her. Have you considered that?"

"No," I said flatly. "I'm not giving her up."

"Interesting. I didn't peg you for a leftovers kinda guy." Enzo chuckled darkly.

"Meaning?"

"I've seen Tiernan in action. If he gets his hands on Gia, he would put out a message. To you. To the rest of his enemies. Before he bargains over her, he'd let his soldiers have their fun."

My blood charred in my veins. I sank my fingers into the leather of my lounger to prevent myself from tapping my numbers. I needed my equations. No. Fuck the equations. Even they weren't enough right now.

I needed…I didn't *know* what I needed.

If I was being honest with myself, numbers were becoming less effective since Gia moved into my apartment. Old rituals became redundant. I felt like I was on the edge of something big.

"I am no less capable than he is," I said shortly.

"Agreed." Enzo slammed his palm against the table between us, fingers splayed, and started snicking his knife between them. "But Tiernan's cruelty is his business card. Now that you've killed the men who murdered your father, you have nothing to gain and everything to lose by continuing this feud. You can end this with minimal financial damage and put it behind you."

"He doesn't deserve to be compensated."

"Better to be smart than to be right." He tapped his temple. "You're usually not a dumbass, so I'm gonna go ahead and assume you're the equivalent of a dumbass."

"What the fuck is that?"

"*In love.* Either way, if you aren't going to strike a deal with them, I highly recommend you let her go. The time will come when my brothers need me for an actual assignment, and all she'll have left are simple musclemen to protect her. Tiernan will outsmart them."

CHAPTER THIRTY-EIGHT
GIA

Tate and I retired to our respective rooms as soon as we arrived at the flat. I was exhausted and humiliated. I told my husband I was falling in love with him, and in return, he told me to sod off.

Not in so many words, but the message was clear.

After calling the nurse on shift at the hospice and checking in on Mum, I went through my night routine, put on a nightie, and slipped into bed.

Sometime after I fell asleep, I felt my body being scooped from my bed. My legs dangled in the air. My eyes fluttered open and settled on Tate's hard jaw. He sailed across the corridor in the pitch black, carrying me honeymoon-style. He moved with predatory grace.

"What's happening?" I asked groggily.

"Nothing."

"Is it the Irish?"

"Relax. It's not the Irish."

"What's going on then?" I yawned.

"You're to sleep in my bed from now on."

That woke me up instantly. I rubbed the sleep from my eyes. "You don't let anyone sleep in your bed."

"You're not anyone. You're my wife."

"You hate me."

He didn't answer until he draped me gently across his bed.

"Just as I am incapable of loving you, I am also incapable of hating you. You could ruin my whole damn life, and I would still want you. Nothing you do or say could ever turn me away from you."

He slipped under the blanket beside me, turning his back to me.

I closed my eyes, too exhausted to try to extract an explanation. But when I tried to slide back into sleep, I felt his fingers tapping numbers across his leg under the covers.

I shouldn't have any sympathy for the man, considering what he put me through. Still, something compelled me to swivel and press myself against his back. I kissed his bare shoulder, dragging my fingers through his hair. I needed his body, even if I could not have his heart. He turned around and searched my face in the dark. His thumb trailed the outline of my forehead, rolling down to my chin.

"What do you need?" he croaked, grabbing my wrist and placing a kiss against my palm.

"*You.*"

"Do you want a quick, dirty fuck? Slow, missionary-style sex?"

"Rough and hard." My thumb traced the shape of his thick eyebrow.

We both needed the distraction.

His lips crashed against mine, tongue belligerently dominating my mouth. Tate wrenched the top of my nightie down, tugging hard, stretching and ripping the fabric against my skin.

Twisted, sick possessiveness took him over. He kicked the duvet off us, clawing my pj's from my body. The fabric stood no chance. I fumbled with his joggers, pushing them down. His cock sprang out, thick, veiny, and erect.

Grabbing both my wrists, he pinned them to the headboard above me. "Move, and I deny you an orgasm. Clear?"

I nodded.

He planted his knees on either side of my waist, hiking himself up, angling his engorged, dripping cock into my mouth. He scooted along my body until his thighs trapped my shoulders, his glistening crown in my face.

"Gonna check how good you worked on that gag reflex."

I nodded again. I was so excited I could feel my pulse between my thighs.

"Understand, Apricity, that I'm about to fuck your face. Are you prepared for that?"

"*Yes*," I said slowly. "I understand. Fuck my face already. I'm about to fall back to slee—"

He shoved his cock into my mouth in one go. I immediately gagged, my eyes watering as I inhaled through my nose. Oh God. He was thick. To make matters worse, he braced one hand over the headboard, using his free one to grab the back of my neck. He thrust into my mouth, hard.

"That's right. Take it like a good girl."

I had the distinct feeling he was trying to mark me somehow. He pulled back, then thrust his cock into my mouth again, and I saw stars, my mouth dripping with saliva as I held my breath. He fucked my face mercilessly, without rhythm or tempo, his balls hitting my chin each time he drove home. I resisted the urge to reach and play with myself while he hit the back of my throat again and again, using his hand on my neck to pull me into him, making his entire shaft disappear inside my throat until I felt it curve into my bloody neck. I couldn't risk not getting an orgasm. I knew this one would be earth-shattering.

"No. No. I'm not coming in your mouth," he muttered to himself, pulling out of me all at once. He rolled me to my stomach and braced his knees on either side of my bum, locking me in place. He was quivering a little, and I knew it was because he was breaking his own rules, having me in his kingdom, in his bed. "How's the mouth?" He scowled.

"I'll survive," I said around a big ball of nothing. *Maybe*. If he didn't dislocate my jaw.

His knuckles slid down my ass, a finger dipping into my pussy.

I slapped his hand away, my face buried in his pillows. "No," I said, my breathing choppy. "Fuck me. Use me. Drown in me. You want this to be loveless? So be it."

With a growl, he spat on his cock, sheathing it with saliva by stroking it up and down, then wedged the crown into my opening. My thighs were squeezed together, which made the friction unbearably hot, and when he pushed inside, he discovered I was already wet for him.

A guttural sound came from the bottom of his lungs, and he leaned forward, his teeth sinking into the side of my neck as he began thrusting into me, hard and deep, still caging my legs shut for maximum resistance. My eyes rolled inside their sockets. Each time he pushed into me, the momentum jerked me forward, making my head bang against the headboard and my clit chafe the mattress. My tits bounced, my nipples grazing the sheets, creating delicious friction. Heat spread inside my core.

My pulse became erratic, mirroring his fitful thrusts. I pushed to my forearms, arching my back. This allowed him to drive deeper into me. But it was almost too good. I was going to come soon, and I wanted to prolong this sensation. The sound of our flesh slapping together mixed with the scent of our juices filling the air. We panted and grunted and clawed at each other's skin, like we were at war. Each time he slammed into me, I felt like he was tipping me over the edge of a tall, looming cliff.

He reached around my waist, massaging my clit and stroking my labia. My orgasm gathered in the pit of my stomach like a tsunami gaining momentum before rising above surface.

"Don't come until I tell you to." His mouth grazed my ear.

I slid into a cat/cow pose as I kept dangling my arse in offering to him. I wanted him to claim all of me. I wanted to come to terms with what we were.

Forbidden.

Wrong.

A lie.

He caught up with my wordless invitation. His lips nibbled the shell of my ear. "Is this an offering?" His palm dragged from my waist to my ass, massaging my glutes with confident strokes.

"No," I hissed. "It's a demand."

"There's my little killer." We were both killers. No matter how much I tried to excuse my own past. "Why?"

"Because the more pieces of me I give you, the less I feel guilty for what I've done to you."

"I've already forgiven you the day you agreed to be my wife." He slid out of my pussy and bent between my legs. Thumbing my arse cheeks and spreading them open, he dragged his hot, flat tongue from my clit along the slit of my pussy, all the way up to my tight hole. He licked and nibbled, causing me to shudder with pleasure, before spitting into my rectum and repositioning himself on his knees. "Besides, I could never get enough of you." The head of his cock kissed my taut hole. "Not too late to change your mind."

"Fuck me like I'm one of your nameless conquests."

The push inside was painful and exhilarating. He kissed my damp, sweaty spine, stroking my ribs tenderly. "Fuck, Apricity. Fuck."

When he was finally inside me all the way and started moving, I thought he would tear me apart I was stretched so wide. He dipped two fingers into my pussy, and I felt both uncomfortably full and elated. I erected my spine, my body wanting to run away from the pain and the pleasure. My back was flat against his pecs, and I wrapped an arm around his neck. We kissed and fucked, slow and sensual, his cock in my arse and his fingers in my cunt, playing, stroking, rewarding.

I was close. So close I could cry. Trembling on unsteady knees. Tate's hand moved from my waist to my tit, playing with my sensitive nipple.

"Please," I moaned. "Let me come."

"Come," he ordered ruggedly.

We both did. I felt a rush of heat zipping through me, like thunder, my entire body spasming, and his thick, warm liquid gathering inside me. I went down like a wrecking ball, falling face-first into a pillow, convulsing. When he pulled out of me, my bum was full of his cum. It dripped down the curve of my arse onto my inner thighs. Tate kissed my cheek from behind, planting a firm hand on the base of my back to keep me from standing up.

"Sleep like this, Apricity." He collapsed next to me. "I want you to wake up tomorrow remembering you are full of my cum."

We fell asleep tangled in each other, in a messy bed reeking of sex, breaking all his rules.

And all of mine.

CHAPTER THIRTY-NINE
GIA

"She's in a coma. There's nothing more we can do," the doctor said. "Your mother is now in a state we call unresponsive wakefulness syndrome. UWS for short. The life support keeps her going, but she won't regain consciousness."

I clutched my purse to my chest as though it could shield me from further bad news.

"It was the lack of oxygen to the brain as we battled her numerous infections." He took off his reading glasses, cleaning them with the hem of his shirt. "We had to put out a lot of fires all at the same time."

"But she's not brain-dead?" My voice was steady, dignified.

"No. She can breathe independently but is otherwise not responding to outside stimulation. Aside from breathing on her own, she's in complete brain atrophy."

"Okay." I licked my lips. "What do we do?"

"Well, your mother is not a registered organ donor in the U.S., and even if she was, most of her internal organs are in decline. Once we remove the feeding tube, salts, and electrolytes, she will pass away within days."

"Starving her to death? That sounds rather cruel."

Dr. Fields met my gaze head-on. "She won't feel a thing, Gia. Hunger, thirst, those are things she can no longer experience.

Palliative pain management will be administered. She'll be as comfortable as one can be considering the circumstances."

"You will let her diminish slowly," I countered. I wasn't sure why I was arguing with him. I hadn't the greenest clue about this procedure.

"She can't *feel*. Not pain. Not hunger. Not thirst. None of it."

I nodded. "Okay." I inhaled. "Okay."

"Would you like to take her off the feeding tube?"

"Yes." I didn't stutter. I knew my mother. She wouldn't want to exist like this. "Yes, I would."

"Do you want to be present when we remove her?"

"Yes." No hesitation there either.

"Would you like to call your husband or a loved one when we take off her tubes?"

I thought about it briefly. Cal was in London. Dylan was in med school. Tate was busy running an empire and fighting the crime lords. He didn't have time for this. Besides, he'd be irritable and selfish, knowing her death meant the dissolution of our marriage.

"No." I smiled politely. "I don't need anyone with me. I'll do it alone."

CHAPTER FORTY
GIA

"This woman is the baddest bitch I've ever known," Dylan announced ten days later, bursting into Mum's room with coffees and cider donuts.

I sat at my mother's side, stroking her hair. It had been over a week since they removed the G-tube and IV hydration, and she was still very much alive and even urinated yesterday. Dr. Fields was puzzled but assured me she wasn't suffering.

"Ten days without a feeding tube. I mean…wow." Cal plucked the coffees from their holder, squinting at the names on them and handing me my oat milk cinnamon latte. "It's gotta be some kind of record, right?"

"It's surreal to actively wait for your parent to pass away." I took a sip of my coffee. "I'll need to extend my leave from work."

"You don't owe anyone an explanation." Dylan plopped on a small blue couch in the corner of the room, pulling her legs into a crisscross. "You *are* fucking your boss."

Enzo stood by the door, reading a K-drama on his phone. Well, he *claimed* it was a book. To me, it looked like straight-up manga porn. "Tsk. Always a lady."

"You got a problem with my language?" Dylan whirled sideways, pointing at him. "Keep your judgment to yourself, and fuck the patriarchy."

"What a coincidence. My middle name is Patriarchy." Enzo smirked. "Wanna go somewhere private?"

"She's happily married." I wagged a finger at him. "Don't flirt."

"He can flirt, but he's not getting any," Dylan announced. "I *did* get him coffee, though."

"You don't know how I take my coffee." Enzo's grin broadened. He was letting more of his personality slip past the exterior.

"Okay, guys? We're in the presence of a spirit who's currently transitioning to a higher place." Cal rubbed my back in circles, glaring between them accusingly.

"Her spirit ain't going nowhere." Dylan took a pull of her coffee. "This woman is stronger than all of us combined."

I fluffed Mum's pillow behind her, checked that her fuzzy socks were pulled up, and put another coat of lip balm on her dry lips. "This can't be comfortable for her."

I'd already spoken to a funeral home in Wimbledon. Everything was ready. And as horrible as it sounded, so was I. I had barely left my mother's side since Dr. Fields took out her tubes. Only briefly to sleep at home. I slept in Tate's room but didn't share her condition with him. He didn't ask.

"Is there any way to accelerate the procedure?" Cal asked softly.

Dylan threw Enzo a sassy look. "Why don't we ask him? He's the expert."

"Stop picking a fight with my bodyguard," I reprimanded my friend. "And no, unfortunately, there isn't much we can do. She wasn't supposed to…last this long."

Dylan chewed on her lower lip, contemplating.

I turned to them. "This can't go for much longer, can it? I mean, how long can you last without any food or liquids?"

Cal checked on her phone. "Eight to twelve weeks, according to Google."

"Jesus Christ." I massaged my temples. "Mum is stubborn. I'm sure she'll wait until the very last minute."

"What's her full name?" Dylan's thumbs flew over her phone screen. "I'll ask my mother to pray. She's a devout Catholic. Super tight with God."

"How do you know?" I smiled.

"She prayed I'd find a man who'd love me exactly the way I am, and I did. That *must* be higher intervention."

I gave her my mother's full name.

"That's not a bad idea." Cal flashed a tender smile. "We do need a miracle."

I dug the bases of my palms into my eye sockets. "What we need is an exorcist."

"That's unnecessarily harsh. I just got here." Tate's voice made me jump out of my skin. He strode through the door, holding bags of takeout.

Blasé and draped in his Kiton work suit, no one would guess the same man had taken five lives over the past four months.

"I was talking about my mother." Heat spread across my cheeks. "She is comatose."

Dylan and Cal exchanged confused looks, surprised he didn't already know.

He put the takeout down on a credenza. It was Cuban; I could tell by the smell of ropa vieja, lechon asado, and yuca con mojo. Some of Mum's favorites. He walked over to me and placed a kiss on my forehead. "Why an exorcist?"

Worming out of his embrace, I cleared my throat. "We disconnected her from her feeding tubes ten days ago, but she's still hanging on."

Tate's gaze dragged along my mother's ashen face. Anger sizzled in my veins. Couldn't he at least *fake* concern? I was his wife. The least he could do was pretend to give a crap.

Tate jerked his chin once. "I'll see what I can do."

"I haven't asked for your help," I bit out. "Trust me, I know you wouldn't mind relieving her of her existence."

I immediately regretted my words. Did I just out my husband as a murderer?

"I mean…because you're a first-rate arsehole," I mumbled.

Not a muscle in Tate's face moved. "Clearly."

"Okay, I know this is bad timing but…" Dylan picked up her bag, checking her wristwatch. "I have to go study." She walked over to give me a hug. "Call me if you need anything."

"Thank you."

"I need to pick Serafina and Gravity up from preschool." Cal embraced me quickly, suddenly eager to leave too. "Please let me know if there are any updates. Row will drop by again with food for you and the staff."

"That's so generous of you both, Cal."

"Enzo." My husband turned to my bodyguard. "Get out."

"Can't. I'm on the job." Enzo shrugged.

"You'll have *no* job if you don't obey me," Tate clarified. "I am perfectly capable of protecting my wife."

"She's not the one in need of protection. You, on the other hand, look like you're about to get ripped a new one."

Tate gave him a stare that'd make Satan shrivel under a rock.

"Whatever. I still need to catch up on episode four hundred and twelve on my totally-not-porn manga story." Enzo shrugged, fishing for the phone in his pocket. "I'm wearing green to your funeral, by the way."

"That's my least favorite color."

"I know." He left the room.

Just the three of us remained in the room: Tate, my mother, and me. I refluffed her pillow for the hundredth time. Tate's gaze seared the back of my neck.

"You didn't tell me your mother was comatose."

"You didn't ask." I picked up my coffee. Anger bubbled up in my stomach like bile. "In fact, you've never once asked about my mother since we got married."

"Not because I don't care."

"Oh no?" I turned to look at him skeptically.

"No." His eyes bore into mine.

"Then why?"

"Because I was too fucking terrified what the answer meant for *us*. I've shared my deepest, darkest secrets with you," Tate said slowly. "And you didn't even tell me how dire your mother's condition is?"

For the first time since I'd known him, he looked genuinely hurt. Not irritated. Not inconvenienced. *Hurt*. It gave me a glimpse of Tate as a child. Gray, glittering eyes that refused to blink from fear of shedding a tear. And lips pressed together from fear a scream would escape.

"What do you want me to say, Tate?" I sighed. "I told you I was falling in love with you, and in return, you wagged your finger at me, gave me the silent treatment, and then fucked me in the ass."

Tate glanced at my mother, elevating an eyebrow.

I rolled my eyes. "She can't hear us."

"*I* can," he countered. "And what you just said was total bullshit."

"Excuse me?"

"*You* ran away." Tate pointed at me. "As usual. And I chased, *also* as usual. I have spent the better half of this decade following you like a lovesick puppy. Yes, you told me you were falling for me, but those are just *words*."

"Just words?" I spluttered, eyes nearly bugging out of their sockets.

"Just words." His nostrils flared, a thick vein pulsating in his temple. "I chased you. I sheltered you. I moved fucking oceans and continents to get your mother a spot in the experimental program. I visited her. Often. I read to her, because I knew it was important to you."

The memory of *Alice's Adventures in Wonderland* assaulted my mind. He was telling the truth.

"I *killed* for you." His lips twisted around the confession. "And

I'd do it all over again without a second thought. Killing. Dying. Stealing. Torturing. There is not a red line in this world I wouldn't cross for you."

The confessions were ripped from his mouth and thrown at my feet like a sacrifice at an altar.

"You are so fixated with love as a concept." He shook his head. "You have completely forgotten what it looks like."

"If you love me," I said quietly, "stop the war with Callaghan. Put me first."

"Just because you said those fucking words doesn't mean I care any less than you do. By the way." He ignored my words, rummaging through his front pocket, producing something small and shiny. He tossed it to me. I caught it between my palms, uncurling my fingers.

I stopped breathing altogether. Something lodged inside my throat, and I was pretty sure it was my heart.

"But how…why…"

"I found this shell the week I finished off Moore."

A perfect *Scaphella junonia* shell bracelet was in my palm The same one I thought I'd lost. Only shinier, prettier, the bracelet now studded with tiny, glittery pink diamonds.

"Flew to Jamaica—same beach you and your family went to—to find an identical shell."

My eyes snapped up to his face. "This is not the original bracelet?"

He shook his head. "It was lost on the way to the coroner's office. I checked."

"So how did you—"

"I knelt down in the sand like a fucking toddler and looked for a similar seashell. Took seven hours."

"How did you remember exactly what it looked like?" The shell was a dead ringer to the one I'd had.

"Because I remember every fucking thing about you, Gia."

"Thank you," I whispered, draping the bracelet over my wrist. He stepped forward to help me clasp it. I wasn't quite ready to apologize for not keeping him updated on my mother's condition, but I wasn't livid with him anymore. The man flew to Jamaica and searched its beaches to find me a seashell. To imagine him crouching in his suit on the loose white sand, burying his fingers in it to fish for one of the rarest shells in the world, made me feel fuzzy.

As though reading my mind, Tate grumbled, "And yes, I wore a suit."

"God." I placed a hand on his cheek, biting down on a smile. "Now Cal and Dylan think our marriage is a mess."

"Our marriage *is* a mess." He stared at me incredulously.

"I know." I laughed tiredly. "But…it's not bad all the time. It's just that their relationships are so…*normal*. They're perfectly in tune with their husbands."

"It hasn't always been like this." Tate brushed my cheeks with his thumbs, cupping my face. "I remember when Calla ran away from Row five hundred times because she was scared of her own shadow. Rhyland and Dylan alternated between boning and trying to kill one another publicly. Relationships are messy. It takes time to find your groove."

"What a profound observation." I curled my arms around his waist, drawing him close.

"Thanks. I stole it from a Hallmark movie."

"Tatum Blackthorn, I'd bet every penny to my name you've never watched a Hallmark film."

"Please don't do that. We have a joint account, and you'd lose." He kissed the tip of my nose. "I did, once, while flying commercial. Only one channel was available due to a technical problem. Everyone on the plane had to watch it. It's what drove me to make enough money to buy my own plane."

I laughed. I couldn't help it. It was the first smile I had on my face since we took Mum off her tubes.

"Also, to set the record straight, *you* were the one to suggest anal." He stole another peck, this time on my lips.

"You literally asked me!" I swatted his chest.

"Because *you* literally pushed that sweet little asshole onto my dick," he retorted. "I was being polite. Contrary to popular belief, I take social cues well."

Nothing was right between us. Nothing but the notion we needed each other in this fucked-up, toxic way. And Tate was right—the blame didn't sit squarely on him. I'd been dodging, avoiding, and omitting too.

"Oh yeah?" I raised an eyebrow.

"Yeah."

"Then shut up and kiss me."

CHAPTER FORTY-ONE

From: Dr. Arjun Patel, MD
(arjunpatel@stjohnsmedical.com)

To: Tate Blackthorn
(willnotanswerunsolicitedemails@GSproperties.com)

Subject: Follow up.

Tate.

I have been following the news closely.
  I'm worried.
  Please get back to me.

CHAPTER FORTY-TWO
TATE

Three more days passed, and Telma Bennett was still alive.

I was torn. On the one hand, as long as she survived, so did my marriage to her daughter.

On the other, it took its toll on Gia. She was exhausted whenever I saw her, which wasn't often. She sat vigil day in and day out at the hospice while her mother straddled the gates of life and death.

Strictly from a practical point of view, Gia was safe as long as she was there. Tiernan wasn't dumb enough to raid a fucking hospice. And me? Well, let's just say I used my Gia-less time doing a deep dive in his sister's life. I knew where she lived, who she fucked, and how often.

Row and Rhyland decided to take me out for a few pints tonight to keep me occupied while Gia was with her mother. Even before I got to the bar, I'd decided they were two boring fucks going stale, and I'd called Achilles and Luca to tag along.

Rhyland and Row kept their poker faces on when I strolled into the Forbidden Fruit Club with two full-blown gangsters. The club was Ferrante territory, so I didn't get what the big deal was. The table was filled with appetizers and expensive spirits.

"Casablancas. Thank you for catering my engagement party. We received nothing but compliments." Luca offered Row his hand to shake.

"That's probably because your family makes Al Capone look like a kitty, but I'll take it." Row squeezed his palm. "When's the wedding?"

"Hopefully never." Luca knocked a shot back, slamming the glass on the table. "But in all probability, next summer."

"How are the Callaghans?" I turned to Achilles. I didn't mind talking shop in front of Row and Rhyland. They were straitlaced but discreet. Also, I had both by the balls financially through different endeavors.

"Lying low." Achilles adjusted the shoulder holster under his suit. Asshole arrived with enough weapons to start a full-fledged war. "They've been beefing with the Bratva, so you're not their first priority."

"Maybe Tyrone talked some sense into his cuntbag of a son," I hedged.

"Oh, my sweet summer child." Luca chuckled, tossing his arms on the back of the leather sofa. "Tiernan answers to no one. I've seen him burn down entire neighborhoods for much less."

"He sounds like a liability."

"Not necessarily." Achilles cocked his head. "Crazy is unpredictable. No one wants to fuck with crazy. I'll take a smart, pragmatic enemy over a deranged one any day of the week."

I put a hand to my chest. "I'm touched but also taken."

"Not for long, according to Dylan." Rhyland reached for his pint of Guinness, draining half of it.

"Releasing Gia from the contract when her mother dies? What is this, amateur hour? You're usually a much better negotiator."

"My head wasn't doing the negotiations," I drawled into the rim of my whiskey tumbler. "My dick was in charge."

Row snorted. "How's her mother doing anyway?"

"Still alive," I said. "Tomorrow it'll be two full weeks since they took her off the feeding tube."

"Shit," Achilles muttered.

"Yeah." I tsked. "Gia's in shambles. I'm half tempted to finish her off myself. It's probably what she'd want too."

Row raised his hands. "Hey, if I'm brain-dead with no hope for recovery, do me a favor, and shoot me between the eyes."

"Gladly." Rhyland bowed his head.

"Thanks, bro." Row and Rhyland fist-bumped.

"Shut up and show some respect, or I'll voluntarily relieve both of you of your miserable lives," I warned.

"Her mother's Cuban, right?" Luca turned to me.

I nodded.

"Catholic?"

"Yeah." I ran my knuckles over my stubble.

"You should hire a Santeria priest," Luca suggested. "You know, they're kind of like psychics. Or mediums. Someone to connect with her spirit. Ask her what's the holdup."

I stared at him like he just suggested I fuck my own ass. He didn't strike me as the spiritual type. People who slaughtered others for a living rarely were. "You gonna sit here with a straight face and tell me you believe in spirits?"

"I'm telling you that your wife might." Luca's eyes were hard on mine.

A half waitress, half escort plopped her ass on Luca's thigh, grinning at him. She had deep cleavage and wore a black-and-white French maid mini dress.

"You know, I think I might be able to help." Row rubbed the back of his neck. "One of my sous-chefs comes from a semi-celebrity family. His mom is a medium. A very popular one. She's on TV and shit. Lives in Miami."

"I want her number," I said.

Row picked up his phone. "Texting him right now."

"So, Tate." Achilles drew my attention, signaling for service without even looking in their direction. Two waitresses bolted toward him like bullets, each taking a seat in his lap. "I have bad news."

I cocked an eyebrow.

"We're transferring Enzo to another job."

Fuck.

"How come?" I asked.

"He's needed in Crimson Key." Achilles ignored the two women, each kissing a side of his neck, until their mouths met one another for a passionate play of tongues.

Crimson Key was a private island, a stone's throw away from southeast Florida. The Ferrantes had purchased it decades ago and turned it into a billionaires' playground. A place to fulfil their shadiest and most debauched fantasies, a dark net of cities, a poisoned paradise for playboys.

"Give me a month," I drawled. "By then, I'll have brought Callaghan to his knees."

"No can do." Achilles shook his head. "There's a mole on the island. Someone's working with the feds. He needs to dig around and find them before shit hits the fan."

"The rest of your men are too dumb." I motioned to a waitress to bring another round of drinks. The women entertaining Luca and Achilles were well into oral sex territory, all three of them slowly sliding down the table to pleasure their bosses. I was far from a prude, but I also wasn't a fan of making eye contact with a man who was getting his balls vacuumed while we spoke. "I'll hire through a security company."

Achilles shrugged. "He's flying out on Friday."

"That's less than a week from now," I seethed.

Achilles threw me a laconic once-over. "So the rumors are true. You *are* good at math."

"Don't worry." Luca spoke with a cigarette dangling from the side of his mouth. "I'll tell Filippo to pay extra attention in the meantime."

The Ferrante brothers eventually retired to fuck their escorts in the champagne parlor, and Rhyland and Row took the opportunity to remind me I needed to let Gia go.

"It's the right thing to do," Rhyland, whose saintly conscience was nowhere to be seen when he fucked older women for a living before he got together with Dylan, preached to me.

Tiernan had been too quiet for too long, and I was growing edgier. We were both sitting on the sidelines, waiting to see who would be the first to blink.

Luca and Achilles reemerged. Achilles looked suspiciously tranquil. I hoped he only fucked his employees, not killed them.

"Shall we?" Luca jerked his head toward the exit.

We slipped out of the booth, pushing through sweaty, perfumed, half-naked bodies grinding on the dance floor.

"Do you need a ride home?" Row turned to shout into my ear. He knew I asked Iven to stay outside the hospice in case Gia needed a ride.

I shook my head. "Brought my Ferrari."

"You know, you can say thank you when someone offers to do you a favor."

I pushed the heavy doors open. "Me having to spend more time with your ass negates the favor part."

The five of us tore through the early spring air before my ears rang with a deafening explosion.

Blazing, suffocating heat scorched the edges of my face. Someone slammed into me midrun, yelped, then continued ripping through the pavement. Behind them, a few more people ran for shelter.

I turned my head to the source of the heat. Flames engulfed my Ferrari, which was parked across the street. The orange and yellow fire curled through the windows, climbing higher, dancing upward, reaching for the sky. Charred, black rubber smoke ribboned off the burning wheels.

"*Fuck*," Rhyland rasped as a second blast erupted from the car. The doors flew, sailing through the air before dragging across the cement, landing right at our feet.

"Well." Achilles stopped next to me, producing a cigarette and crouching down to light the tip with the still-burning flame that devoured the door of my car. "Guess we know what Tiernan's been up to lately."

"You either pay him or you gut him." Luca clapped my shoulder. "But you should do one or the other in the next few days, because you won't have the stomach for what happens next."

"I'm guessing you changed your mind about that ride, Mr. Instant Karma." Row looped his keys over his finger.

I gave him a curt nod.

In this game of Russian roulette, Tiernan was the first to pull the trigger.

CHAPTER FORTY-THREE
GIA

"If this woman doesn't die in the next few hours, I swear to God, I will." I leaned forward to coat my mother's lips with another layer of Lypsyl.

She was going through them like candy, and every time I applied it to her broken, parched lips, her mouth moved as if she was trying to eat it.

I swiveled toward Dr. Fields, narrowing my eyes. "Are you sure she's not trying to communicate with us?"

He shook his head. "It's a reflex. We're monitoring her daily. No neuroactivity is showing on the scans."

"It's been eighteen days." I capped the Lypsyl and dumped it on the nightstand, pacing across the room. "Something's wrong. You need to look into her condition."

"You already received second and third opinions."

I did. Each one of them supported his prognosis. But this state, of watching my mother suspended above the chasm between life and death, her fingers slipping one millimeter at a time, was pure torture. My entire existence shrank to this room, to this hospital bed, to the empty, withering shell of a once vital woman who danced like no one was looking, read poetry, taught me how to bake cookies, braided my hair, and shaped me to be who I was today.

"Maybe we should reinsert the G-tube," I said.

My college friends Alix and Sadie both stood up from the couch, about to argue with me, but Fields beat them to it.

"How about I finish doing my morning rounds, and we can discuss it?" His voice was sympathetic.

I nodded distractedly. He left.

"Gia, she's on death's door." Alix put her hand on my shoulder.

"Alix, then she's got the wrong bloody address," I sighed.

Tate ambled into the room. My hollow, depleted heart picked up speed at the sight of him. My spine uncurled. He came to visit me every day, and I still arrived home every night to sleep, but we barely spent time together.

He stalked over to me, ignoring my two friends. "Hanging in there?"

"For the most part."

"I brought someone here." He stepped away from me. His hand reached into his pocket, and I knew he was tapping his numbers. I studied him in confusion.

"Oh." I forced out a smile. "You move fast. Who's the lucky lady?"

"Lina McCain," he provided just as the door opened again and an impeccably dressed, middle-aged woman swanned into the room.

"Okay…"

"She's a medium and has come to help find out what the holdup is with your mother." Tate tried to keep a straight face, but I knew better than anyone that this heathen did not believe in the afterlife, souls, or anything else that wasn't firmly backed by science.

"Gia." The woman reached over to kiss both my cheeks and give me a hug. "Your husband is very concerned about you. He brought me over on his private plane. I had to cancel a big, *big* event to be here. I can never turn my back on a family emergency."

I continued staring at her, too perplexed to speak.

"I'm sure you must be going through hell. Well, let me tell you a little bit about what I do." Lina proceeded to explain that she specialized in communicating with people in comas who were on life support or had severe brain damage. She said she connected with the spirit guides of her clients—me or the person in a coma—to better understand what caused them to get stuck in limbo.

"Sometimes people are trapped in the in-between because things that are left unfinished are bothering them. I once communicated with a woman on life support who told me her astral cord was still attached to her body, but she hadn't yet decided whether she wanted to die or not. Her father pushed her off the balcony and pretended to be concerned for her, staying in the room with her day and night. I was able to alert her distraught son who'd hired me, and the father was arrested. Shortly after he was sentenced to life in prison, she passed away."

I shot Mum another look. I was skeptical about spirit guides, but I was also at a point where I'd try anything.

"You don't have to do anything if you don't want to," Tate interjected. "Just say the word, and I'll send Ms. McCain packing."

"You should do it," Alix squeaked from the couch.

"Yeah," Sadie added, biting down on her lip. "Telma was very mystical. She believed in spirits."

I pressed my lips together, nodding. "Let's do it."

"I'll get to work right away." Lina approached Mum.

I watched helplessly, my breath bunched together like a ball deep inside my throat.

Tate clasped my shoulders. "You need a break. Let's go to the cafeteria. Alix and Sadie can monitor Lina."

"We'll be here the entire time," Alix reassured me. "Go."

"Hold on a minute. How did you know their names?" I frowned at Tate.

Alix winced, exchanging glances with a deeply red Sadie.

"Tell her," Sadie whispered.

"No, you tell her." Sadie elbowed Alix.

I swear, if one of them had sex with Tate before we hooked up, I would have to attend more than one funeral this week.

"Well?" I narrowed my eyes between the three of them.

"So you know our 'girls only' weekend we do once a year?" Alix scratched her neck.

My face relaxed. "Yes. Shall we do Cancun this year? Or perhaps Key West? I will need some relaxa—"

"And remember how Alix always pays for it because her dad is loaded?" Sadie cleared her throat.

"Yes?"

"My dad is, in fact, loaded," Alix rushed to say. "But he never paid for our vacations. Tate did."

I swung my gaze to my husband. He paid for my holidays before we were even together. Why?

He erected a warning finger between us, scowling. "You were wound too tight. Always complaining about how overwhelmed you were. Sending you off once a year was a pleasure. I didn't have to suffer through your huffing and three hundred Post-it notes."

"It's okay, sweetie." I patted his shoulder, a teasing smile on my face. "I would secretly love me too if I were you."

He ushered me out of the room and left Lina and Mum with my friends. Our walk to the cafeteria was silent. I bought a cup of coffee and a sandwich I had no intention of eating. The scent of impending death made food unappealing altogether. We settled in the corner of the busy room.

"How are things going with Tiernan?" I dropped my voice to a whisper, since the place was swarming with families and patients.

Tate immediately started tapping his side. His pupils moved in a way that let me know he was solving equations in his head to calm himself down. "He blew up my Ferrari the other day."

I gasped. "Jesus."

"I know. Getting another one customized is going to take *months*. He couldn't blow up the standard Rover? *Prick*."

I gave him a chiding look.

"Also." He cracked his neck and knuckles. "I had a bit of an episode and might've scribbled all over the bedroom a few days ago."

I hadn't even noticed.

"Negotiate peace with him," I demanded.

"Fine."

"Really?" I arched an eyebrow.

"Really." He sat back. "I evened the score after the Ferrari incident, so as far as I'm concerned, we're squared away."

"What did you do now?" Dread filled my lungs like a toxic fume.

"Don't worry about it."

"Spill it." I jerked my chair forward, the sound of its legs scratching the floor startling everyone in the room. All heads spun to us. "You dragged me into your mess, Tate. The least you can do is keep me in the loop."

"Burned down his underground fight club."

"Enzo mentioned it was huge. A UFC feeder." I frowned. "It must be an important source of income for them."

"Their main financial pipeline, yeah."

"Jesus, Tate," I whisper-shouted, drawing more curious glances. "I get it. Conflict is your favorite hobby. But I haven't asked for any of this. Tiernan is going to do terrible things to me if he catches me."

A spark of wrath flickered in his eyes. "*If* is the operative word. I won't let it happen."

"Yeah. Me either. Because I'll divorce you." I stood up abruptly.

He followed suit. "Don't be a hypocrite. You and I are cut from the same cloth, little Apricity." He caught my wrist like a thief in the dark, his fingers wrapping around my own. "The only difference is that I don't want to change to appease the world. *You* do."

"I'm not like you." I tugged my hand away, every nerve ending in my body on fire. "Yes, I don't care when bad people die, but I'd never put you at risk to solve my own problems. If you want this to work, you need to break bread with the Callaghans. I *will* leave you," I warned. "I love you, Tate. But I love me too."

Tate closed his eyes, releasing a ragged breath. He gripped the edges of the table between us, his knuckles bone-white. A storm was brewing inside him. Between the man he was—cruel, careless, vindictive, bloodthirsty—and the man he needed to be to have me. I waited for a full minute, maybe two, before my husband spoke again.

"Very well. For you, Apricity, I'll stop this war."

CHAPTER FORTY-FOUR
GIA

When we returned to Mum's room, Lina looked like she'd seen a ghost. Which probably *was* the case, considering her line of work. I stiffly moved toward the blue couch that had become an integral part of my life. Alix and Sadie muttered their quick goodbyes and scurried along, giving me privacy.

Lina took the recliner opposite me, and Tate sat beside me.

"I've spoken with your mother, Gia. Not with her spirit guide but directly with *her*."

I blinked, not really sure what that meant.

"This is rare," she explained. "I didn't expect it."

"How come?" I tucked my hands under my bum.

"I can usually make a connection directly with people only after they are deceased. This means your mother's soul is almost fully detached from her body. The two are barely integrated anymore. Because her soul is no longer trapped inside her body, I was able to speak directly to it."

"Does this mean she's dead?"

"Almost." Lina glanced over her shoulder at Mum as if contemplating something. "Our line of connection was very strong. Probably the strongest I've had in my entire career."

"Mum has always been chatty."

"We spoke in Spanish," Lina said. "I told her I speak it. I spent a few summers in Spain. She missed speaking Spanish."

I smiled softly. Mum spoke Spanish whenever she could. Elliott and I spoke it with her.

"She told me you lost your father and your brother a few years ago. It was why she struggled with letting go and leaving Earth. She was very worried about you."

My gaze snapped to Tate in shock. Did he tell her the details of my family's tragedy? He shook his head, understanding my unspoken question.

If he didn't tell her, how did she know? This information wasn't readily available. Still, I was skeptical. She must've found out somehow. Maybe Alix and Sadie said something while I was gone.

"She said you've always taken care of everyone around you," Lina continued. "That you stayed in this job so you could take care of her and send money to her sister, who is struggling financially."

"Yes. My aunt has a chronic illness."

Dread made way for panic. If this was legitimate, what else did this Lina woman find out?

"Gia, your mother has been ready to leave for months now," Lina said quietly. "She stayed because of you."

"What made her change her mind?" I sniffled. "To disconnect her soul from her body?"

"She said things are different now." Lina's eyes darted to Tate. "One of the things she mentioned was that she found out you had a husband. She approves of him. She said he takes care of you. She trusts him to pick up the pieces she'll leave behind."

My face heated. I still didn't know what to believe. This could all be a setup by Tate.

"You think I'm a fraud, don't you?" Lina studied me with a small, knowing smile. She didn't seem upset by her own observation.

"I'm more of a science girl." I smiled apologetically. "Numbers. Physics. That sort of thing. Mum was the spiritual one."

"Ah yes." Lina smiled. "She mentioned that. In fact, she told me you would probably be very skeptical. Which was why she told me to tell you…" She looked down at her hands. "Al mal tiempo, buena cara."

To bad weather, a good face.

An expression my mother often used when life was difficult. The general meaning was to stay positive. To have hope.

Just survive this, and all will be well.

My heart flapped in my chest like a fish out of water. I believed Lina. I didn't know who she was talking to really. Maybe her own intuition. But I found my mother in that conversation.

Scooting forward on the couch, I gasped. "Why is she still clinging to life then? Obviously, she saw that I'm married and taken care of."

"Well, of course, she doesn't want to die in this drab robe!" Lina threw a hand in Mum's general direction, her expression scandalized. "She wants to go fashionably. To die the way she lived. She gave me instructions. Write this down."

She snapped her fingers, and I sprang into action, taking out my phone and opening my notepad.

"She wants to go a certain way. And by the way, she is *horrified* that you've let so many strangers see her looking like this." Lina clucked her tongue disapprovingly. "She wants you to put her in the asymmetric Zimmermann organza silk dress, the one with the Havana, and the buckled silk Manolo Blahniks."

I typed her instructions fast. I was now 100 percent sure this wasn't a setup. Mum *loved* pairing the two together. They were the same shade of rose gold.

"What else?" I looked up from my phone.

"She wants you to color her hair. She doesn't want any grays when she passes on to the next life, and for heaven's sake, style it. Her hair is frizzy from all the times you brushed it!"

Laughter burst out of me, and my eyes brimmed with tears. "Okay. Got that down. No more brushing. What else?"

"Full face of makeup, of course."

"What shade of lipstick?" I asked. Mum had about twenty of them, all a different hue of red.

"Gucci's ruby."

I nodded. "Good choice. Anything else?"

"That's mostly it." Lina tapped her lower lip with a French-manicured fingernail. "She wants this to happen sooner rather than later. She's ready, Gia. I think she's been ready for longer than you can imagine. She pushed through for you. But you are okay now. You have someone to take care of you." Her eyes crinkled, sweeping to Tate. "Someone who would go to great lengths for you."

Tate's expression was impenetrable. He stared forward rigidly, like a queen's guard.

The weight of her words pressed like a boot against my solar plexus.

Could someone broken put another person together?

I guessed we had to wait and see.

Five hours later, my mother was clad in her favorite attire. Her makeup was flawlessly done the way she liked it—applied meticulously by yours truly—and her shiny coal hair was swept and pinned into elegant perfection, still oozing the pungent scent of ammonia hydroxide.

She looked beautiful, and I was glad she asked for this. It gave me a chance to take one last look at her as the woman I adored. Since she was already made up fully as per her instructions, I had time to ask Filippo to go to Walgreens and get me clear nail polish.

I didn't miss Enzo's gaze or the way he played with that knife so expertly, reminding me he could make a Birkin out of my skin without batting an eyelash. "Dude, you knocked it outta the park. She's beautiful."

Tate did not leave my side. We operated in silence, him watching my every move and me clasping Mum's cold hand in mine, painting her nails, which were thin, overgrown, and stacked with vertical ridges.

My back was to my husband when he said, "When was the last time you saw her chest move?"

I lifted my head from the third coat of nail polish I was applying. "Pardon?"

"Her chest." He swung his gaze from his phone, perched on the incliner. "She hasn't inhaled in over a minute."

"You've been…monitoring?"

"My marriage kind of depends on it."

I placed two fingers to Mum's cold throat, where her pulse should thrum. I waited, the silence in the room thumping between my ears.

"I feel nothing," I swallowed.

"Welcome to my world," he murmured.

"No, Tate, I think she's…" I couldn't utter the rest. "Come look."

He placed his phone on the arm of the recliner and stood. His fingers gently brushed mine as he checked my mother's pulse grimly. I stared up at him, tears clinging to my lower lashes.

One second chased the other. I knew he wasn't feeling any pulse. Finally, he removed his fingers from her neck. Closed her eyes with a gentleness I didn't think he possessed. Produced his pocket watch to check the time. "I'm sorry, Gia."

I buried my face in the rich layers of organza in her lap, heaving a panicked yelp. She was well and truly gone.

I wept in Mum's lap while Tate stood quietly behind me. Every now and again, I thought about how, not too long ago, he'd lost a parent too and didn't have the privilege of hugging him one last time. I'd played a big part in him losing the only human who ever loved him, and he graciously forgave me for that.

Dr. Fields peered through the crack in the door, accompanied by a nurse. He rapped gently. "I promised you a checkup…"

He didn't complete the sentence.

Tate invited them in, relaying the last few hours' events with Lina. They spoke about the arrangements ahead, and I was glad my husband was there, because I couldn't produce one word.

Mum was wheeled out of the room looking like an old-school movie star. A grand finale worthy of the dazzling woman she was.

Tate made some calls but kept one eye on me.

The drive back home was a blur as I came to terms with my new reality.

I was alone, my entire family was gone, and the only person whose destiny was tied with mine was a coldhearted murderer.

Till death do us part.

CHAPTER FORTY-FIVE
TATE

Tate: Tell Tiernan I want to see him.

Tate: This weekend.

Achilles: Am I wearing a pencil skirt and please-fuck-me-daddy lipstick?

Tate: I hope not. You don't have the ass to pull it off.

Achilles: Then stop treating me like I'm your fucking secretary.

Tate: This bullshit needs to stop.

Achilles: You just burned down his CLUB. It's his move.

Tate: Gia's mother passed away. She doesn't need to worry about this shit. Set up a meeting.

Achilles: He's not going to let you off the hook.

Tate: I'll hand over the damn vessels and eat the loss.

Achilles: That was never gonna cut it.

Tate: Would 200M do?

Achilles: I'll see what I can do.

When we got back home, Gia went straight to her old room and locked herself in the bathroom.

I paced back and forth, listening to the shower spray on the other side, punctuated by her sobs. I felt a lot of inconvenient feelings, and I wanted them all gone.

Annoyance. Dread. Exhaustion. Terror. Sadness. Goddamn *sadness* for someone I didn't even know and who meant nothing to me.

"Gia," I growled every half an hour through the door, just to confirm she was still alive. She'd hiccup by way of response, and I'd return to my pacing. This went on for three hours. It was late, and she hadn't eaten all day.

I asked her through the door what she wanted to eat, but there was no answer. Deciding not to inconvenience her further with mundane questions, I DoorDashed from seventeen different restaurants to cover my bases. Would she be in the mood for a double cheeseburger or black truffle risotto? Fuck knew.

Eager to relieve my wife from administrative duties, I assigned Edith, my new secretary, to deal with the funeral preparations. It helped that Edith was entirely focused on doing her job and not on trying to get me to fuck her.

At around ten thirty, Gia finally left the bathroom. She wore an ivory satin robe; her eyes were swollen and glassy.

"I bought you food," I clipped out, unable to soften my tone. It wasn't anger. It was anxiety. A combination of not being able to tend to my daily rituals and the looming idea of losing her.

"I'm not hungry." She sniffled. "Cheers, though. What did you order?"

"Everything."

She elevated a doubtful brow. Clearly, she underestimated my level of unhinged.

"I wasn't sure what you'd like. So I ordered Italian, Greek, Thai, Chinese, Cuban, Mexican, Japanese, Vietnamese, McDonald's, Indian, Peruvian, soul food, sushirito, salad, and a few more things I can't recall." I frowned. "Pretty sure we're still waiting on the Tex-Mex, but the elevators are jammed because of all the delivery guys."

She looked exhausted. I was losing her, and I had no way to pull her back to me. I was a fantastic fuck with a deep wallet, but I fucked this up so many times with her. Before we even got together.

She needed comfort and stability. Not a complete maniac who scribbled equations all over the walls and was subject to sudden bursts of violence.

I'd deteriorated in recent weeks.

"I really appreciate it, Tate. But I have no appetite."

"Okay." I ran my tongue over my upper teeth. *Don't fucking snap. This isn't about you. It's about her.* "What *do* you want to do?"

Her usually hooded, feline eyes looked tiny after all the crying. "What is there to do?"

Think, asshole, think. What do couples do that doesn't include sex? You watched enough TV in your lifetime. Surely, you can come up with something.

"Anything." I snarled, but at least managed not to show my teeth this time. "Watch a movie. Play Monopoly. Chess. Cards. Take a walk." *Take a walk? What is she, a fucking Pomeranian?* "I could take you to Paris. Maybe to London for a pint." *I could buy you the London Eye if it makes you happy.* "Look, you can fucking shoot me for shits and giggles. My pain threshold is incredibly high. Just tell me what to do."

My wife didn't seem impressed with my suggestions. I wondered how long I'd be able to call her my wife before she'd turn into my *ex*-wife. Those, I had plenty of. Only they never truly felt like wives to me. Humans, I found, were a currency, like money.

Except for Gia. But she wasn't a human. She was a goddess.

"I think I'll just go to bed if that's okay." Gia looked around her, hugging her midriff.

I stepped sideways to give her access to the door. "I have a weighted blanket somewhere. Would you like me to bring it to our bed?"

"I'd like to sleep here if that's okay." She licked her lips. "*Alone.*"

I'd been shot before. Once. In the ass. It happened when wife number two caught me in bed with her sister. Or maybe it was her cousin. Anyway, they bore adequate similarities, and by the time I realized I was fucking the wrong person, I was too close to the finish line to stop.

I was running stark naked from the French chateau where it happened when she decided to aim a vintage rifle at me from her Juliet balcony. The bullet not only grazed my ass, it took out a nice chunk of it. At the time, I thought nothing could be more painful or humbling than to have my ass stitched together sans painkiller while a judgmental doctor listened to my ex-wife animatedly explain how the accident occurred.

But I was wrong.

This was worse.

Far worse.

More painful. More humiliating. More *everything*.

"Alone," I repeated. "Of course. Can I get you anything before I leave? Water? Tea? Some Advil?"

She shook her head. "I just want to rest. I haven't really slept well since they transferred Mum to hospice. I kept waking up every hour to check my phone."

I evacuated myself from her room, stalking off to my office. An office that currently looked like a math book vomited all over it. Every inch was covered in numbers. I cracked open some books. I did my equations. I tapped. I counted hardcovers on shelves. Grains in an hourglass. Tiles on floors. I read *Alice's Adventures in Wonderland* in English.

And Flemish.

And French.

Nothing helped. I wanted to claw my skin off my fucking body.

It was never about my OCD. It was all the other stuff Dr. Patel diagnosed me with. The things I ran away from. The mood swings. The chemical deficit. What were his exact words? Oh yeah—*the antisocial personality disorder you struggle with, paired with your cognitive distortion and traumatic past, is the equivalent of sitting on a barrel full of dynamite and playing with matches. I strongly recommend psychotherapy, keeping up with your mood stabilizers, and cognitive behavioral therapy. Consistency is key.*

I was sick.

I had been sick for a very long time.

I'd had no one to get better for.

Until now.

I'd been selfish, I realized. Selfish in pursuing my revenge, in putting Gia at risk. Selfish for not taking care of my mental health, my issues, my shortcomings, and letting everyone around me bear the consequences.

I would never be a good man.

But I *would* be a good husband.

I logged into my email and was about to answer Dr. Patel. Then, thinking better of it, I called him. It was one in the morning, but he'd survive.

"Tate," Dr. Patel answered on the first ring. Talk about a fucking fanboy.

"Arjun."

Silence ensued before I managed to push the words out of my mouth. The last time we spoke, it ended with me stalking out of his office in a blaze of fury.

"I got married."

"Congratulations." His voice was neutral and belied his true feelings. "I'm guessing Gia Bennett is the lucky bride."

"Yes."

He knew, because in our last session, I'd foolishly told him why I hired her. About how I made her life a living hell.

And thought about her every time I fucked someone.

And dreamed about her every single moment she wasn't next to me.

He pleaded with me to get evaluated for a bunch of other shit. I refused. He told me I was emotionally harassing her because I resented her for stirring emotions in me. That I was in *love* with her.

I told him he was high and needed to have his license revoked. Things got...*heated.* I left.

I left, because I thought I knew better.

But I didn't. And now here I was.

"I need to get better." I swallowed. "For her."

"For both of you," he corrected softly. "When can I see you?"

"Tomorrow," I said. I knew he was booked out a year, but he'd find time for me. "I'll pay you double to meet me at an unorthodox hour."

"No need for that. How about ten thirty p.m.?"

"Yes."

I killed the call and fell to my knees, surrendering to the new, foreign feeling I had been trying to run away from for the past few weeks.

For the past few years.

For my entire life.

Love.

CHAPTER FORTY-SIX
GIA

It was four fifteen in the morning when I woke up.

The red numbers on the digital clock stared back at me defiantly, daring me to try to go back to sleep. My whole body felt drained and deflated. My stomach growled. I couldn't remember the last time I'd eaten.

I rolled to the edge of the bed, about to plant my feet on the floor, when I noticed a large, dark shadow draped across it. I squinted. It looked like a piece of furniture, or maybe...

Tate.

It was my husband. He was sleeping on the floor next to my bed. But...why?

Because you told him you wanted to sleep alone, and he respected that, but he also didn't want to be away from you.

My heart cracked in two, warmth flooding my chest. Tatum Blackthorn, the most formidable man in all of New York, was curled into a fetal position on the floor by my bed, like a gentle Great Dane protecting its owner.

Reaching down, I placed my palm on his shoulder so not to startle him. Tate was a light sleeper.

He rolled over and blinked up to me in the darkness.

"Do you, uh, want me to leave?" His voice was thick and raspy. "I thought it was okay, since I'm not technically in your bed."

"No," I said softly. "I was just about to get myself something to eat. Come to bed. I'll join you in a bit."

He straightened, sitting up with his back pressed against the nightstand. "What do you want? I'll bring it to you."

My knee-jerk reaction was to tell him I could do things for myself. But I knew Tate derived pleasure from doing things for me. It made him feel better. He could never love me, but he *could* take care of me.

"You know, what I'd really like is beans on toast. I have a few Heinz cans in the pantry."

"Stay here." He scurried out of the room, and I sat up against the headboard, praying that he wouldn't burn down the kitchen. Tate wasn't what I called a natural nurturer.

He came back fifteen minutes later with two charred pieces of bread, unevenly warmed beans, and a glass bottle of Diet Coke. I thanked him and ate in my bed. He took a seat on the edge, watching me. I turned on a bedside lamp.

"I'll make things right with Callaghan," he said out of nowhere. "I'll stop the bloodshed. I'll seek therapy. I'll go on meds. I'll do anything." He paused. "Just please don't leave."

I put the burnt toast back on the tray. I'd already made up my mind to stay. I would take the cheap, sugar substitute for love he offered me—the synthetic sweetener—if it meant being by his side.

Cal and Dylan were right. Tate and I had always been inevitable.

I put the tray on the nightstand and crept forward on my knees to where he sat. He watched me through half-lidded eyes. I pressed my lips to his collarbone, then kissed my way down his bare torso. I wanted warm flesh against my own, to feel his heartbeat, the vitality of his nimble muscles. I wanted to remind myself I was still alive and that I had much to live for.

His black joggers tented, his cock jerking against the fabric, demanding to be freed. I tugged his waistband and bent down to give it a lick, root to tip. He threw his head back, hissing.

"I want you to fuck me so hard and so dirty that I forget my own name," I rasped against his velvety shaft, enjoying the goose bumps that chased one another to the heat of my breath against his muscular thighs. My lips skimmed back up his abs, catching his lips. "I want you to treat me like a nobody," I murmured as he gobbled down my voice. Tears streamed down my cheeks as I spoke.

He gave me a shove, pinning me down to the mattress. I gasped as he pulled at the knot on my robe. His eyes glazed over, empty and hard.

He was going to deliver on my request. First, because he always fucked me rough. But also because he never denied me anything I'd requested from him.

After unknotting my robe, he flicked it open so I was bare in front of him, then scooped up my wrists, pinning them against the headboard. He shoved his face in mine, holding my wrists tight in one hand, taking his cock in the other, angling it between my legs.

Then he froze completely. "You're crying."

"Ignore it." I rolled my hips. My center met his throbbing, hard cock.

"Can't." His hold on my wrists loosened. He cupped my face instead. Firmly but gently.

"My tears have nothing to do with sex," I argued. "I want—"

"I can't treat you like a whore," he growled in my face. "Even if I wanted to."

I huffed. "You always fuck me raw."

"Yes, and tomorrow, I can still fuck you like a whore if that's what you want." He kicked his pants down roughly, crushing me under his weight. "But tonight, I'm going to make love to you. Whether you like it or not. Because that's what you need."

I was about to protest when he buried himself inside me. I arched my back, moaning, but the sound was swallowed in a sweet, tender kiss. His mouth followed mine, licking, biting, exploring. He started moving inside me in one, smooth, never-ending wave, caressing my body from head to toe. He touched me everywhere, so affectionately I wanted to scream.

My thighs. My breasts. My back. My *soul*.

Tears continued running down my cheeks. Tate chased them away with his tongue.

"Don't cry."

Kiss.

"I'll do anything to make you happy."

Kiss.

"Rearrange constellations."

Kiss.

"Pluck the moon from the sky."

Kiss.

"I'll buy you the fucking sun, Apricity."

Kiss.

He hooked his hand around the back of my right knee, slinging my leg over his shoulder, kissing the inside of my ankle while maintaining eye contact with me, his pupils blazing with heat. I shuddered when he swirled his tongue along the sensitive spot of my medial malleolus. He brushed his fingers gently over my outer thigh, leaving tingling sensations everywhere.

I shook uncontrollably as his thrusts grew deeper and more erratic. He hit my G-spot again and again. It felt different. Not as chaotic and depraved but no less intense. The way we stared at each other, with hunger and anger, with cloying desperation, felt like we were conceiving something new and whole that made us intertwined forever.

The climax climbed up my body like a vine, gripping me by the toes, all the way to the crown of my head. Our bodies melted into one another, and it was exactly what I needed. This skin-to-skin reminder of my own mortality—and the vibrancy of my existence.

I can smell.

I can see.

I can hear.

I can touch.

I can *feel*.

Tate dipped his mouth to meet mine, catching my bottom lip between his teeth.

"My real name is Gabriel," he croaked, his silken voice coming from the depth of his soul.

My heart stopped.

"Gabriel Doe. And he—I—*we* love you. We've loved you from the first moment we saw you."

Sweet, tantalizing delirium seized me. I was a flame, soaring up in the air, dancing in the wind, climbing impossible heights.

Gabriel.

My body tightened, my breath catching. My climax felt different this time. Not like a tsunami thrashing me into the deep sea but like gentle waves rocking me to sleep. I could feel all of my husband now. The vein throbbing in his cock as he spilled his seed into me. The sweat gluing our bodies together like two pages in a book.

The pleasure was unbearable. I tried wriggling away. He pinned me down with his entire weight, forcing me to ride the orgasm until the end, kissing my lashes, the tip of my nose, my pulse thrumming in my neck.

"I love you so fucking much," he said. Sadly. Dejectedly. Like he'd fought a war and lost it. "It *sickens* me." He ripped himself away from me at once, scurrying to the end of the bed like I'd caught on fire. His back was to me, bare and moving wildly with his breaths. He gripped his hair, elbows pressed against his knees. "I can't stand it. When I love someone, I lose them. I can't lose you."

"You *won't* lose me." I flattened my palm to his damp back. "I mean…you will, eventually, to death, I suppose."

"Don't be so sure," he muttered. "You'd be surprised at the sum I'm willing to pay to make sure you're immortal."

His words spread across my body, warming my bones.

"Tate?" I asked.

"Apricity?" His back was still to me.

"How do you know it's love and not obsession?" I perched my chin on his shoulder, peering into his face. "What's the difference?"

"Because I used to put my happiness before yours and thought I'd never let you go. I am now willing to let you go if it's what makes you happy." His head hung between his shoulders. "Your happiness comes before mine. You can leave if it suits you. I won't stop you. I'll sign the papers."

It felt like I was choking on my own heart, I was so overwhelmed with emotions.

I felt his cum drip down my inner thigh as I kissed his shoulder. I wrapped my arms around his neck. His eyes met mine.

"I love you." I held his jaw in my hands, enunciating each word slowly. "I've always loved you. You are my White Rabbit. I'll follow you to the ends of the earth and back, no matter how terrible and awful the world you led me to is. I think there's something wrong with me. Because even when I tried to convince myself I hated you, I never could walk away."

"And you're my Alice." A rueful smirk tilted his lips. "Brave, adaptable, curious, confident. I knew it from the beginning, but hating you was so much easier than loving you. Because loving you meant admitting I might not get the one thing I ever truly wanted."

He pressed his lips to my forehead, and I closed my eyes, relishing the moment.

"No more pretending." Tate clasped my chin. "This twisted game of cat and mouse stops here. You're my wife. You understand?"

I did. Like *Through the Looking-Glass*, the tide had turned. The shift had completed. Fates had been made.

CHAPTER FORTY-SEVEN
GIA

I spent the next week and a half crying and making love to my husband. Often times simultaneously. Dazzling bouquets of flowers arrived at our doorstep, dozens or so every hour. I wasn't ready for company yet. Luckily, Tate had a talent for kicking people out.

"She's not accepting visitors," I heard him drawl at Cal and Dylan one day while I was buried under my blankets, crying my eyes out.

"Listen, honey, the only time I care about a man's opinion is when he praises me in bed." Dylan tried to push through him. "She's our best friend. We want to see her."

"She's my *wife*," he deadpanned. "And she'll be ready to see people at the funeral. You wanna see her? Go look at a fucking picture."

"We can't even do that. You crashed all the servers that hosted pictures of her from events and social media!" Cal whined.

"She said she needed a social media break," Tate said dryly. "And I am nothing if not thorough."

"That's such a weird way to pronounce obsessive. Anyway, since when did you take the role of the doting, caring husband?" Dylan lamented.

"We're a real couple now. Guess you're not as close as you thought if you're this far out of the loop."

Dylan huffed and puffed, but eventually they left. I clutched my stomach, curled in a fetal position. I'd see all of them at the funeral. I needed a few more hours to lick my wounds alone.

Tate returned after a few moments, arms laden with treats and flowers.

"You want me to send the flowers to the nearest hospital and the food to the soup kitchen like last time?"

"If you can." I sat up in our bed, smoothing over my dressing gown. We were both ignoring the other glaring reason neither of us wanted visitors. Which had to do with the equations covering nearly every surface.

"Tate?" I asked.

"Apricity?" He stopped on his way out of the room.

"Does it ever get better?"

He kissed my forehead. "No. But you learn to live with the pain."

Ten days after my mother's passing, she was put to rest in Wimbledon Cemetery, next to Dad and Elliott.

Tate purchased an elegant coffin and potted plants. He'd been on edge the entire week, barking orders at Edith to get everything right. At some point, I had to remind him that my mother wasn't here to appreciate the gesture.

To which he answered, "So? She communicated with that Lina woman and said I was doing a good job. You think I don't know I'm on probation?"

Now, we were walking toward her grave, arms linked. Medieval angels, crosses, and saintly maidens spotted the lush, green grounds around us. Stony and assessing pebbled eyes of statues followed us. I had the acute, unrelenting feeling I was being watched by other *alive* beings, but I chalked it up to stress.

My husband promised me he'd take care of the Tiernan issue, and I believed him.

I stopped when I spotted the thick crowd of mourners gathered around the empty grave where Mum's casket would be tucked. They swarmed like bees, all sheathed in black, not in the dozens but the hundreds. Not just Mum's friends and former colleagues but also my friends from home and a staggering number of my colleagues. Anywhere between one hundred and one hundred and fifty GS Properties workers arrived from London and New York combined.

"I hadn't realized you chartered flights for the New York branch of GS Properties." I cleared my throat.

"I didn't." Tate plucked his leather gloves off. "They purchased their own tickets, using their personal time off."

My heart dipped, and I did a double take at the rows of seats in front of the open grave as they filled with people. Everyone was here. Kevin and Mariam and Trisha. The entire HR department. Cal, Dylan, their spouses, and Kieran. Alix and Sadie too.

Among the familiar faces I also detected the Ferrante brothers. A chill rolled down my spine when my eyes landed on Achilles's bored, soulless gaze. He surveyed the crowd like a predator picking his next meal.

"Gia." Kevin barreled toward me, pink-cheeked. He eyeballed Tate apprehensively before asking, "May I hug your wife, sir?"

"Sure, if you don't feel too attached to your limbs." Tate's ice cube voice trickled down my spine.

I rolled my eyes, reaching to embrace Kevin warmly. "Thanks for being here, Kev. How's your mum?"

"Better!" He perked. "Ever since the new health insurance kicked in, I've been able to get her more therapy sessions and access to better treatment. She started going to the gym. She's even crocheting."

"That's amazing."

"Gia." Trisha hobbled to my side on her high heels, jerking me into a hug. "I'm so sorry for your loss."

"Thank you."

Trisha bit on her lower lip, waiting for Kevin and Tate to disperse by the prolonged glare she gave them. Kevin shuffled along quickly enough, but Tate stayed by my side, awarding her with an expression twice as cold.

"Go ahead," my husband said. "If you wait for me to leave, you'll hit menopause before that happens."

We really needed to work on his attitude.

Trisha swiveled to me. "I just wanted to apologize, for how I… Well, I wasn't very nice to you when you first arrived at HR."

"To put it mildly," I agreed.

"I made some judgments. We all did, but we shouldn't have. The union you started has improved so many lives, secured so many incomes. You made the biggest impact since I started working at GS Properties over nine years ago. So…thank you."

I smiled. "All water under the bridge. Let's focus on bettering people's lives, yeah?"

"And making me richer," Tate noted clinically.

When Trisha left, I turned to my husband and dropped a kiss on his shoulder, the only place I could reach without rising up on my toes. "I'm sorry about the union, but it was very important to me. I know how much the idea of being good and helpful to others pains you."

"It truly does." He resumed our walk toward the seats in front of Mum's grave. "Of course, the union bumped GS Properties up to the number one spot on *Forbes* America's Best Employers list, thereby allowing me to recruit the crème de la crème of Ivy League interns for half the price my competitors pay. They now think we have an altruistic cause. A *movement*. We managed to attract the sharpest minds in the business without lifting a finger."

An anxious blade grazed my spine. My legs froze midstride. "You set this up, didn't you?" I whispered, squinting at him. "You knew I'd riot as soon as I witnessed how dire things were at HR."

He transferred me to human resources because he realized I wouldn't last more than five seconds firing people and wanted someone to start a union so his company would look great. He played the long, sophisticated game and won. Every single time.

"Shh, the service is almost starting. Let's focus on the here and now."

He placed a firm hand on the small of my back, ushering me into the thick crowd of grievers.

CHAPTER FORTY-EIGHT
TATE

I always maintained it'd be a cold day in hell when I left the Upper East Side for anything that didn't include an airport.

Well, it appeared that the netherworld's residents were in need of a warm coat today.

I found myself descending to the lowly sewers of New York, also known as Hunts Point, Callaghan's measly territory. The Ferrantes had no use for run-down neighborhoods full of drug users and particularly didn't want to be linked to petty crime, prostitution, and violent burglaries, so they left the Irish the leftovers of the Big Apple.

More specifically, I was in front of Fermanagh's, a pub kissing the edge of the Bronx River in a particularly underprivileged area. Though the street left much to be desired—namely, a bathtub full of bleach—the place itself was oddly charming. A medieval church converted into a pub. There was something inherently European about it. Like it'd been plucked from a green Irish cliff and screwed right into the grit and filth of the Bronx.

It was a little after noon, and when I pushed the red wooden door open, the place was packed. The Irish flag covered the majority of the shit-brown ceiling. The gray walls were exposed brick. The wooden floor creaked under my wingtips. The stench of stale stout beer, cigarettes, and sweat hung in the air like dirty laundry.

I headed directly to the bar, where I knew I'd find Fintan, the twins' older brother. It wasn't hard to recognize him. He had the same shade of flame-licked hair as his brother and sister. He was dressed in a sharp suit and looked considerably less unhinged than his siblings.

"Ay, mate. What can I get ya?" He turned toward me, drying the inside of a Guinness pint with a towel. He was a jack-of-all-trades, helping his father and brother run their various establishments around South Bronx.

"Your baby brother's head on a platter." I slid onto a stool at the bar, keeping my hands in my pockets. "But since the fucker is hard to track down—he's been dodging the Ferrantes' calls—I'll settle for a word with him here."

Fintan's face was unreadable. Not unfriendly but far from alarmed. "Tiernan's not here."

"We both know that he is." I peered around, taking in the old, scruffy crowd. A mix of retired alcoholics and transients. "And I'd absolutely hate to shut down this place too. You'd be strapped for cash in no time."

"Liar. You'd love it." A smoke-strained voice, highly entertained by the sound of it, chuckled from behind me. I swiveled to find Tiernan sitting at a rickety wooden table, nursing a half-finished pint of Guinness. Splayed in front of him were various old-school maps. A joint hung from the side of his mouth. "What brings a pretty, spoiled boy like you to this kip of mine?"

"You know damn well the answer to that question." I slid off the stool and took the seat opposite him. A waitress rushed to place a freshly poured Guinness in front of me. I pushed it aside. "Thank you, but I'd rather lick the inside of a toilet at Penn Station than put my lips on anything here."

She recoiled, tossing her hair back as she tromped away. Tiernan laughed quietly.

"The Ferrantes are pissed at you," I said.

Tiernan's eyes lit with amusement. "Fuck me, and I haven't even given them a good reason yet."

Yet. The man had a death wish. I'd be doing him a favor by finishing him off before those evil fuckers got their hands on him. The only thing stopping me was the knowledge he fully deserved to die at the hands of the Camorra.

"We need to end this feud." I sat with my legs spread open, hands balled into the pockets of my peacoat. I did not tap my numbers. Dr. Patel had prescribed me antidepressants and an antipsychotic to help relieve my symptoms. He also referred me to a shrink I was to start seeing twice a week.

"Do we now?" Tiernan lit his joint, contemplating my words. "Bit convenient, wouldn't you say? Ending this feud after you destroyed my six-figure-a-day fight club," he said around the weed stick, dropping his lighter into his coat's pocket.

"I'm willing to make concessions."

"What's changed?"

I finally pulled my head out of my ass and admitted to myself that I'm in love with my wife.

Of course, giving him this type of leverage would be the height of idiocy.

I shrugged. "Not a fan of having my place crawling with bodyguards. I prefer to leave my roommate days in college."

"You lived in a seventeen-million-dollar mansion in Wellesley while attending Harvard." Tiernan took a sip of his pint. He did his homework. I wasn't surprised. He had more ambition in his fingernail than most businessmen I knew had in their entire bodies. "Tired of bodyguards? That's your excuse?" His green eyes gleamed like a silver blade. "Don't insult my intelligence."

"Should I insult your personality instead?"

"Not helping your cause, lover boy."

"Name your price."

He tapped his chin, making a show of mulling it over. "Janey Mack, but I genuinely can't think of anything I want more than seeing you on your knees, begging for mercy."

I cracked a wry smile. "Lesson number one, boy. Don't let your enemies get that deep under your skin. Feelings are a weakness in your line of work."

"Just because you're old doesn't mean that you're smart." He downed the rest of his Guinness, wiping his mouth with the back of his hand. "Now, offer me something interesting."

"The vessels your father was after," I said. "They're yours if the feud ends here."

A hostile smile slashed his face. "Nice try. That was just my old man punching under his weight. Not me. I have standards, you see." He put out his joint on a spot on the map that was circled. "And that was *before* you killed my main source of income."

I knew the art of negotiation. Nothing I'd offer would please this motherfucker. His empire was built on the skeletons of his enemies. He wasn't an arbitrary creature.

"However..." He rolled his tongue over his teeth. "I'm willing to let you retain your miserable life *if*..."

I arched an eyebrow.

"You convince your little friends to give me their territory north of the park."

I simply stared.

He continued, mistaking my disbelief for attention. "I want Harlem, Spanish Harlem, and the Heights. Everything north of 110th Street."

"That's not mine to give." I stared at him incredulously. He wanted the Ferrante territory? That was stunningly ambitious. Not to mention dumb. They owned everything from Philly to Boston on the East Coast, with the exception of a few shitholes like this one.

"Not yours, but you can bargain with them on those terrains. You have the capital and their ear."

"A territory is not just about money. It's about prestige," I spat out.

"Precisely." Tiernan flashed that canine, deranged smirk of

his. "And currently I have very little of it. We need to establish ourselves."

"You are established here," I argued. "The Irish Mafia in New York is called the NYPD. Sometimes the FDNY."

"You have a sense of humor, Tate. I appreciate that. The Ferrantes own Crimson Key, also known as billionaires' Vegas. They can give me their New York City scraps."

That wasn't going to happen. But at least now I had an open channel to bring the Ferrantes and Callaghans back to the negotiating table and talk some sense into Tiernan.

Who knows? Maybe once Achilles and Luca found out what Tiernan was up to, they'd kill him for me.

"Let me run this by the brothers." I rapped the table between us, standing up.

Tiernan remained seated, inhumanly still and completely unfazed. "You do that, old man."

I leaned across the table to loom over him, knuckles digging into the rotten old wood. "In the meantime, you stop following my wife. You back the fuck off and let her live her life, you hear me?"

He cocked his head, tsking. "A wise man once told me not to let people get deep under your skin. It's a weakness in your line of work, see."

God-fucking-dammit with this asshole. "Your *word*, Tiernan." I bared my teeth.

Tiernan's eyes blazed with something I'd never seen before. Not even on Andrin. This unabashed, gleeful hunger for chaos.

"And they say romance is dead." He put a hand to his heart. It was the first time I took inventory of his attire and realized he was armed to the teeth. His holster held two Glocks, and he had a knife strapped to his thigh.

"Don't mess with me." I bunched the collar of his shirt, yanking him so that our noses smashed together. A spray of blood erupted from his nostrils at the sudden, rough contact. "Give me your word."

"I'm surprised it'd mean anything to you," he mused, tongue darting to lick a trail of his own blood, a smirk on his face.

I'd almost broken his nose, and he didn't give half a fuck. Between us, I felt the mouth of his gun digging into my sternum, warning me to back off.

"It does."

"I give you my word then."

I released him.

He sat back down unhurriedly, an amused smirk on his face. "You can go on your merry way now, Blackthorn. Do my bidding for me." He raised a fresh pint of Guinness the same waitress who approached me put in front of him, angling the drink to me in salute. "You have forty-eight hours. Use them well."

CHAPTER FORTY-NINE
TATE

It was my twenty-first birthday when Daniel and I got drunk in Vienna.

He took me to an interesting destination each birthday. Europe was our favorite spot, since it was relatively close and drenched with history and art, both of which we were fond of.

"Have you ever wondered"—Daniel raised his fourth glass of whiskey to his mouth, mumbling around the rim—"why Andrin did what he did to you?"

I froze midsip, slowly putting my drink down. We never discussed Andrin. I never asked Daniel about my abuser's peculiar skiing accident. I figured he would never fess up if he did anything. And frankly, I knew I'd be disappointed if Daniel denied it.

I wanted to think the last person Andrin ever saw promised him a slow and painful death.

"I did." I cleared my throat. "All the time, in fact."

"Why didn't you check then?" Daniel asked. We were in a traditional Austrian pub, where the beer was leisurely crafted, the furniture carved of raw wood, and the lights were golden and creamy. Most of the people around us were locals. They were too wrapped up in their own conversations to pay attention to the two drunk Americans.

"Because I knew how much it'd trigger me," I admitted. By then,

I understood I had ten tons of baggage. That my sanity was held together by a thin, brittle string. And that looking into Andrin—really looking into him—may snap that string and become my undoing.

I didn't want to fall apart.

Didn't want Andrin to win, even if it was from his grave.

Daniel stared into his whiskey, rolling his knuckles over his white whiskers. He was growing older. Old enough that I was a little panicky. I always had the inkling Daniel, in fact, was the very string keeping me together.

"Well, I did." My father put his drink down. "I conducted thorough research. I wanted to know why he—" He stopped, glancing sideways to catch my expression.

I kept it blank and glacial. It was bad enough to admit to myself how much power Andrin, dead or not, had over me. No need to act hysterically.

"Carry on," I said, realizing that I wanted to know. Was desperate to unveil why this man had tortured me the way he did.

"Why he did what he did to you," Daniel finished. "So I hired a security company that ran an investigation on him. It was crucial I knew everything about him before…" He stopped again.

I reached across the table, squeezing his hand in mine. "Yes, I know."

Our gazes locked, and something passed between us. An unspoken promise. A vow. Daniel killed for me, and I would kill for him. No questions asked. It was the least I could do for the man who saved my life.

"So." I withdrew my hand from his, still unaccustomed to affectionate touches. "What did you find out?"

"I looked into what made him take such a risk. Torture you and jeopardize his life. His career. He was born in a small village in Switzerland. Lived there his whole life…until university. That was when he moved to Zurich. And during his time at ETH Zurich, he took a semester in New York."

"Okay."

"In New York, he met someone. A lovely woman named Fiona. They had an affair. It is my understanding they tried to do the long-distance thing for a while. A year or two. Then she moved to Switzerland, because this was where his career took off. But eventually—after about seven years—they got a divorce. Fiona returned to America, and he stayed in Switzerland. They were childless."

"So far, so fucking boring." I yawned into the back of my hand. "What does it have to do with me?"

"A few years after Fiona and Andrin got divorced, she met someone else—a man named Robert—and they entered a relationship. The relationship produced one son." Daniel paused, staring down at the wooden table. "The child's name was Gabriel."

My entire fucking universe tumbled down like a house of cards. To hear about my parents—that they were, in fact, in existence at some point—seemed so trivial. Everybody had biological parents. Yet I never fully registered it before today.

I swallowed hard. "Tell me more."

"Andrin found out about you when you were less than a year old. He was angry, upset. He had hoped Fiona would reconcile with him eventually, I guess. And there was something more. This, I didn't find out through the investigators, but it was just an inkling. It is my belief that Andrin couldn't have any children. Otherwise, why would Fiona conceive almost immediately upon meeting Robert? She wanted children."

I nodded, transfixed. "She did." It was stupid. I didn't know her. Wasn't aware of her existence until a second ago. And still, I knew. "She wanted children."

She wanted me.

"Andrin arrived in the States and confronted Fiona and Robert. The police report said that Robert and Fiona died in a burglary gone wrong. The killer was never caught."

I closed my eyes. Took a deep breath.

"When I met Andrin shortly before his death, I made him tell me the entire story. He killed them, Tate," Daniel slurred, tears making his eyes glitter.

Normally, I would be uncomfortable with this extravagant show of emotions. Yet I felt just as raw as Daniel. Actually, ten times more.

"He told me Fiona and Robert protected you with their bodies. It was you Andrin wanted to hurt. They fought for you. Begged for your life. Threw themselves at Andrin so you wouldn't get hurt. He killed them first with the intention of killing you, but by the time he got to you, the police were coming. He heard the sirens. He took you and ran away."

Everything clicked together. How I showed up at a Swiss boarding school of all places. How I knew so little about my parents. How no one claimed me—my family thought I was dead, along with my parents. How someone seemed to foot the bill for that expensive school—that was Andrin himself.

He hid me so he could fuck with me.

I was his dirty little secret.

Instead of killing me fast, like he did my parents, he killed me slowly, until there was nothing left of my soul and hope.

Daniel spent the night telling me everything. About the so-called skiing accident Andrin had. The confessions he managed to rip from his mouth. The shreds of information he had about my parents. We didn't sleep. We didn't drink any more. We just talked and talked until our mouths were parched and our eyes stung.

And even though I recognized that my life was tragic and horrifying to most people, I couldn't help but think I was the luckiest boy alive.

Because I lost my biological parents.

But I gained a father.

CHAPTER FIFTY
GIA

"I booked your annual vacation with Alix and Sadie," Tate announced from his spot next to me in the back seat of the Escalade, his arm slung over my shoulder, his other hand scrolling through stocks on his phone. "Figured you could use some girl time."

"Where am I going?" I nuzzled into his neck. He'd been my rock since Mum passed away. It was thanks to his unrelenting devotion that I was able to slide back into reality rather than crumble into it. We drove to work together every day, took lunch together, and went back home together. He'd been good at distracting me, getting us Broadway tickets, taking me to restaurants I'd always wanted to try, and binge-watching highly acclaimed foreign movies with me, even though I knew their slow pace and nuanced topics drove him mad.

"Havana." His eyes warmed, but his face remained cavalier. "In honor of your mother. I figured you could take off from our house in Crimson Key. It's close to Miami."

Our house. I'd never even visited it, but Tate considered what was his also to be mine.

"Thank you." I pressed my lips to the curve of his jaw. "It's the best gift. *You're* the best gift," I corrected.

An overwhelming urge to treat *him* slammed into me.

"Darling," I said, "I want to make dinner for you tonight."

He whipped his head my way, surprised. "You know how to cook?"

"Yes." I smiled brightly. He was in for a pleasant surprise. I was somewhat of an amateur chef. "I do. And you know how to eat." As he'd demonstrated throughout our short marriage.

A wolfish grin tugged the corners of his lips. "That I do."

"Anything specific you have in mind?"

"Never met a good steak I didn't like."

"Potatoes?" I asked.

He shook his head. "Broccoli. I haven't had a starch in five years."

My expression probably gave away my shock and alarm at that information.

He chuckled, stealing a quick kiss as the vehicle reached the entrance of GS Properties. "I know, Apricity. It's hard to understand when you are a twenty-six-year-old former athlete and have the metabolism of a hummingbird. But your thirties bring with them a whole new level of maintenance. There's an entire decade between us."

I scrunched my nose. "Sometimes I forget I'm shagging an old man."

He tipped back his head, barking out a delighted laugh and scooping me into his arms in a tsunami of kisses. "Then how about I remind you why it's worth it."

After holding meetings with union members all day and tending to my administrative duties, I got off work at four to have adequate time to prepare a romantic dinner. I only had one bodyguard now—Filippo. We got along well, although I kind of missed Enzo's sunshine energy and funny jokes.

We started out at the farmers' market, where I purchased flowers and three boneless rib eyes—yes, Filippo needed to eat too—along with some broccoli florets and other greens for a fresh salad.

"So when did you join the Camorra?" I tried to use the time

shopping to get to know him better as we strolled side by side. I doubted we'd be spending a lot of time together now that Tate was working diligently to make peace with the Callaghans. "Enzo mentioned you are not a Ferrante by blood."

The young, brawny man considered his words, weeding through what he wanted to tell me and what he wished to keep to himself. "Yes, we're not technically blood, but we're much more than that. Back in Napoli." He scratched the back of his neck, his cheeks flushing. "My mother was a prostitute, and my father was a drunk. My father used to do some work for Vello in his Ischia summer house, so he knew the don. He sent me off to work for the Ferrantes to pay a debt. I could've ended up in a very bad spot, but the family took a liking to me because I was a hard worker, a fast learner. Achilles especially." He ran his teeth over his lower lip. "They let me live in their shed, not with all their other laborers in the motel they own in Jersey City. In time, they even let me have a place at their dinner table."

"Achilles doesn't seem like the type to just dole out friendship," I noted, striding along the stalls sprouting colorful bouquets of flowers, freshly baked goods, and handmade mittens. We were edging out of the farmers' market and toward the car park. It was surrounded by low, industrial, red-bricked buildings, with a narrow one-way road leading out to the main street.

"He can be terrible," Filippo agreed. "But he is always fair."

"Is he?" I asked doubtfully.

Filippo nodded. "In our world, it is better to be cruel than to be weak. Whatever punishments he gives people, they always deserve it."

"Did his baby brother deserve having his girlfriend shagged to make a point?" I couldn't help but snap out. What a load of rubbish.

"This wasn't a punishment, vita mia. It was a favor." Filippo frowned, his eyes constantly scanning our surroundings, hyperaware we were in a public though secluded place. "And a lesson too. Enzo has a lot to learn about himself."

I wondered what that meant.

I thought about Filippo's life. How his choices were taken away from him at such a young age. I wanted to help him if I could.

"Filippo, would you rather—"

The rest of my words were drowned in a sharp, loud noise. Filippo jerked forward suddenly, landing face down on the pavement. Gunpowder scorched my nostrils, so smoky and peppery I could taste it on my tongue. My eyes darted to his crumpled form. Horror quickly flooded through my veins. His raven hair was wet and matted to his skull, and blood gushed from his wound, down the slope of his ear, in a river of deep maroon.

His eye was missing. Either it exploded or rolled off somewhere.

I shrieked, dropping the brown paper bags I held to my chest. I whirled around, my eyes flaring when I spotted Tiernan Callaghan standing about twelve feet from me, a Cheshire Cat smirk on his lips. He was holding a gun with a silencer, spinning the trigger on his index finger. Behind him were three scary-looking men.

"Hello, *Gia*."

I started running before I had time to think about what I was doing, my heart pumping so hard I felt my pulse thrusting against every inch of my skin. I had never run so fast in my life.

"Bring her to me," Tiernan ordered in an indifferent tone. "I want her alive and well. Mostly anyway."

The side street was empty, so I tore across the pavement as quickly as my legs could carry me, looping around streetlamps and stop signs to slow down the three men at my heel. Their feet pounded on the cement, reverberating through my spine as they inched closer.

I spotted two overflowing plastic bins. Whirling behind them, I pushed them hard against the three men, unleashing a dam of garbage on them. They tumbled backward, cursing and growling. It bought me a few precious seconds, which I took to turn onto Fifth Avenue. There, I'd be able to disappear amid the throng of people. My lungs were burning and my muscles shaking, but I kept running.

As soon as I made the sharp turn, the fog of catastrophe clouded my vision.

The street was closed for construction. Thick, long wooden boards blocked my way.

I'd hit a dead end.

The sound of thrashing boots grew louder, closer. They were snarling, swearing under their breath. Hurling garbage at them obviously only angered them further.

I stopped in front of the barrier, calculating whether I could smash through it. I yanked my phone from my pocket and tried to slide the screen to unlock it, but my fingers shook too badly. Tiernan's soldiers materialized from the corner of the street, circling in on me as they spread across the narrow alleyway. They stalked toward me. My nerves finally gave in. I dropped my phone between the bars of a water drain. *Bollocks.*

I was completely screwed.

"Ah, there she is, the little spitfire." The burliest man out of the three advanced in my direction, cracking his knuckles, his friends following close behind him. The three of them were brawny and pale, dressed in inconspicuous black jackets and dark denim.

My gaze danced between them, trying to come up with a game plan.

"Here, kitty kitty." The leader of the pack rubbed the pads of his fingers together as though I was an alley cat. "C'mere now, you little—"

I pounced on him with a snarl, scratching his eyes out with my fingernails. Maybe I was going down, but I wasn't doing it without a fight.

"Fuck!" He stumbled backward, falling flat on his arse. "This pussy has claws."

The other two men tackled me, one of them pulling out a knife and pointing it toward me. "Tiernan said *mostly* well," he reminded me, flashing rancid, yellow teeth. "He wouldn't mind a few shallow cuts, and man, wouldn't I love a taste of a proper lady."

My back was pressed against the boards. I heaved, knowing the only way out was through. I could let them take me...

But as Tate graciously pointed out countless times, I was never good at taking orders.

Drawing a deep breath, I gained momentum and started running straight into the men, hurling myself between them. For a moment, I thought I could actually escape them. But then one of them grabbed me by my pearl choker, yanking me back. My head slammed against the ground. My ears rang. Liquid heat spread across the back of my skull. I was bleeding.

A cloth was pressed against my face, and my eyes snapped open, flaring in horror. *Chloroform.*

Thinking on my feet, I pressed my mouth shut and stopped breathing. Losing consciousness was a terrible idea. I fluttered my eyes shut after a few seconds while holding my breath until I felt the hand that pressed the cloth to my face loosening around my nose.

"Finally," one of them spat on the floor. "Fucking bitch. Do you wanna have a go?"

"Nah," another one sighed. "Her husband is killing people left and right. She's gorgeous, but no pussy's worth it."

My eyes were closed, and my head was dizzy, but I wasn't passed out. Someone grabbed my feet. Then a second pair of hands scooped me by the wrists. They dragged my back over the pavement on their way to the vehicle purposely, leaving painful welts of raw skin.

They tossed me into a waiting van. Tiernan's face peered down at me, wearing his victorious expression like a crown of vipers. I watched him through half-closed eyes, still feigning unconsciousness.

"If it isn't Tatum Blackthorn's one and only weakness, in the flesh," he rasped. "Oh, what lovely plans I've waiting for you."

CHAPTER FIFTY-ONE
TATE

Some people smashed glass ceilings.

I smashed a thirty-five-hundred-year-old, eighty-million-dollar vase I'd bought at an auction.

"Kidnapped her!" I grabbed the edge of my office desk and flipped it over. That shit was at least two hundred pounds of solid wood. "He fucking managed to kidnap her. I'm impressed with your incompetence. I've met broken condoms with better security."

Achilles, Luca, and Enzo stood in my office, solemnly taking the verbal berating. As soon as the three of them walked in together, I knew things were dire. It had been forty minutes since they gave me the rundown of where we stood, and I still wasn't over their bullshit service.

"It was a miscalculation on our part." Luca's jaw ticked. "But as I said, we have a plan and collateral."

"He gave me his *word*." I screamed so hard my throat gave out.

"Dude, his word is worth jack shit." Enzo flicked his knife open, squeezing it in his palm until blood oozed out. "He's got no honor. No code of conduct. He's a loose cannon."

"Well, no fucking shit." I tore my jacket apart, feeling too hot to breathe all of a sudden. I stalked out of my office.

The brothers followed me stoically through my apartment. I was going to execute their so-called plan and inflict maximum pain on everyone involved.

"Filippo proved to be fucking useless," I spat out, ripping my coat from the hanger in the mudroom and putting it on.

"Tiernan killed him." Achilles's throat worked, and I thought I saw a flash of something that wasn't undiluted crazy going through his face. "Shot him in the back of the head."

I yanked the entrance door open and stormed to the elevator bank. Panic ran through my veins. Callaghan was obviously insane and capable of anything. Gia was a small, unarmed woman, but that didn't mean he'd spare her. And she had a very smart mouth, something I usually worshipped but that, in this situation, gave me a lot of anxiety. She'd sass back even with a gun to her head.

Especially with a gun to her head.

"I'm going to kill him," Luca muttered.

"Get in line, motherfucker," Enzo protested. "You dragged my ass from Crimson Key to take care of this hiccup. The least I can do is—"

"He killed Filippo," Achilles cut both of them off savagely. "I'll be the one killing him, and I'll be doing it very slowly, over the course of a fucking week. Death will be an unattainable fantasy when I get my hands on him."

"No one is touching a hair on his head until I have my wife back, safe and sound," I informed them. "This is no longer a pissing contest. I—"

My phone buzzed in my hand. I glowered at it. It was Callaghan. I knew, because I had the foresight to save his number in my contacts last time he called, when Nash Moore was in my trunk.

Oh, how the tables had turned. I slid a finger across the screen and put him on speaker as we all stepped into the elevator.

"Blackthorn," Tiernan greeted merrily. "What's the craic?"

I wanted to lash out at him. To threaten and yell and beg and bargain. But doing so would put Gia in even more danger. Pretending to have my shit together was crucial if I wanted to get her back.

By the looks Luca, Achilles, and Enzo gave me, they too were worried I'd go down on my knees and start bawling like a little bitch.

"Been better, been worse," I said calmly. "Yourself?"

"Grand. I have a visitor. Would you like to say hello?"

I closed my eyes, swallowing down the scream wedged in my throat. I had never felt so out of control. I started tapping my numbers, not giving a fuck about Dr. Patel or the Ferrantes.

Two, six, two.

Two six, two.

TWO. SIX. FUCKING TWO.

"If you insist," I croaked finally, sick to my stomach about my own manufactured tranquility.

"Here she is," Tiernan said gleefully.

I heard a soft groan, followed by my wife clearing her throat. "Sorry, love. Rain check on that steak I was going to make for you tonight."

Gia.

She sounded even-keeled. Blasé. Put together.

I loved her, even more than usual, for that. She was playing the game. Fucking with Tiernan's mind, having him second-guess the card he held in his hand. Tears pricked my eyes. I couldn't recall crying since Andrin killed my rabbit, but I came close now.

"That's okay. I had a big lunch." I fought to keep my tone conversational. "Are you hurt?"

"A mild head injury, I think." She paused. I heard her take a slow, deliberate sip from a bottle. "Otherwise, I'm just terribly inconvenienced. He only has Aquafina here," she added regretfully. "Would you mind negotiating for Essentia Alkaline? There's really no need for these inhumane conditions."

Exhaling through my nose, I bit down on a smirk. What a badass. I couldn't wait to have children with this woman. "Consider it done. I'm sorry for this, sweetheart."

"Uh-huh. Very touching. Anyway." Tiernan cut the conversation off. "How about what I asked for? The territories I want from the Ferrantes. Put a dent in that yet?"

I shot a glare at the three brothers. Their faces were blank. We had discussed it after my visit to Callaghan, and Luca and Achilles said they'd take care of it. Unfortunately, both sides secured their collateral at the same time. If Tiernan had just waited a few hours, none of this shit would have happened.

"You're not getting an inch of their land, but we can negotiate not having your sister's throat slit by a high-profile billionaire mogul with a taste for violence," I answered.

"You can't get to Tierney." Tiernan laughed. "I made sure she was far away from harm before I came for your wife."

"Is that right?" I mused.

"Yes," Tiernan said with conviction. "She's in an underground bunker in an undisclosed location."

"She was in a rural Colorado basement in your buddy's vacation house." Achilles barked out a laugh. "Forget organized crime, Tiernan. I see a bright future for you in fiction."

The elevator dinged and slid open, and the four of us barreled toward my Escalade.

Achilles snapped his fingers. "Oh. By the way, we have her now." His rusty laugh grated my nerves like nails on a blackboard. "Your precious Tierney."

The silence on the other line told me what I already knew. We had hit a nerve.

"No," Tiernan said finally. "*No.*"

"Yes," I countered, unlocking my vehicle and sliding into the driver's seat. "And unlike Gia, she actually has a lot of interesting information about your less than kosher antics. I wonder what'd make her sing…" I revved the engine, clucking my tongue. "Or purr. Let me assure you, I can be *very* persuasive when I want to be."

"Where is she?" Tiernan spat out.

I yawned in his ear by way of an answer.

"I'm going to slit your wife's thro—"

"Relax there, buddy. No one's going to harm anyone. You know damn well the minute you give Gia as much as a paper cut, I drain your sister, then make a nice high-end sex doll from her deflated corpse. We both have too much to lose. So how about we cut to the chase?"

"How do I know you're not lying?" he demanded.

I sighed, flipping through my phone gallery while shaking my head. I hadn't started driving to Tierney's place of hiding yet. "Because unlike you, my word actually means something. Here." I hit Send with my thumb.

A second later, I could hear the video Achilles had taken of Tierney playing in Callaghan's background.

"Today is March fifteenth, and I can confirm that I, Tierney Callaghan, am in the hands of the Ferrante family. I'm safe, in good health, and well." She was made to follow a generic script. "Stop this shit now, brother." Her voice did not waver, did not break. "Enough is enough. There are other ways to conquer the world. If they touch me, if something bad happens to me..." She obviously veered off script, which was just as well, because it entertained the shit out of Achilles when he took the video. "I'm going to murder them and then *you*. Fix this shit now, Tiernan."

The video came to an end.

I sighed, "Is she always so poetic?"

"What do you want?" Tiernan asked after a pause, resigned.

"You know what I want. I want my wife," I said simply. "Unscathed. And a promise this thing between us is put to bed. This time, your word won't be enough, though. I'd want a third party to ensure both sides keep their end of the bargain."

"The Ferrant—" Tiernan began as I kicked the vehicle into drive.

Luca was quick to interject. "Are fucking pissed. You killed Filippo. He was our family. You don't *really* think we'll work with you again, do you?"

"Of course you will. Greed is a potent stimulus. Besides, it was nothing personal." Tiernan yawned offhandedly. "Merely business. I do believe you were the ones who pointed Blackthorn to the whereabouts of my soldiers, and I don't remember holding it against you. Nolan was Fintan's godfather, I'll have you know."

"You're not powerful enough to hold grudges," Achilles said. "We decide who lives and who dies in this city."

"And what's the verdict?" Tiernan sounded more amused than concerned.

"Undecided," Luca lied. There was no other way to lure him in. "How about we exchange hostages and sleep on it?"

"Sure."

For the first time since Gia was kidnapped, I took a deep breath. Oxygen hit my lungs, and I became almost lightheaded.

"How about we go somewhere picturesque?" Tiernan suggested. "Set the mood."

"Not gonna fuck you either way, but knock yourself out," Achilles muttered as we drove out of my building's garage and toward the place where they were holding Tierney. It was guarded to the teeth, so we weren't worried about being followed. "What do you have in mind?"

"The Palisades."

I shared a quick look with Luca, who jerked his chin in a nod. "We'll spread our men evenly around the place. I know it well."

"Sounds good," I said into the phone.

"Excellent." Tiernan clapped his hands together. "Tell my sister I'm fixing everything. And forget about water. Give her champagne."

"Don't push it, asshole. Oh, and, Callaghan?"

"Yes, Blackthorn?"

"If I find out you as much as sneezed in Gia's direction, you will be grateful I can only kill you once."

CHAPTER FIFTY-TWO
TATE

I hit the red button on my phone for the millionth time, focusing on the road ahead.

"Dr. Patel better be your fucking mistress, or you'll have some explaining to do about all the phone calls you refuse to answer." Achilles lit himself a cigarette in the seat next to me.

Dr. Patel wasn't happy I skipped my therapy visit today. Well, he'd have to deal. I had more pressing matters to tend to.

The growing list of assholes blowing up my phone also included Dylan, Calla, Sadie, and Alix. They all presumably tried to get ahold of Gia with no success.

"He's far too obsessed with his wife for a mistress." Tierney had the audacity to chip in to the conversation from her place wedged between Enzo and Luca in the back seat. She examined her long fingernails with her hands perched in her lap, wrists zip-tied tightly. "It's probably his shrink. I'm guessing he has at least two on the payroll."

She was good.

I regarded her coolly through the rearview mirror. She'd been running her mouth like it was training for a marathon since she got into my vehicle. Just like Gia, she didn't let big men in expensive suits intimidate her, even those with a habit of killing people.

Tierney pouted, stretching her long legs and crossing her

ankles. "Or maybe you're in search of a mistress? I could use a sugar daddy."

"No, thanks," I hissed out. "Your idea of sugar is probably rat poison."

The men in the car laughed.

"You know, I never really understood why men join the Mafia of their own accord. It's so…childish."

Achilles looked like he'd prefer a lobotomy over listening to her, shaking his head and taking a long drag of his cigarette.

Tierney continued, undeterred. "If you want to do a bunch of terrible things for your own profit, why not become a politician? There's less of a chance you'd spend time behind bars if you get caught."

"There's a *very* good chance I'll hurl you right out the fucking window and off the bridge if you don't zip it," Achilles announced.

"Speaking of fucking, a little birdie told me Achilles had a thing with Enzo's sweetheart to get back at him for a failed mission." Tierney swiveled her head to Enzo, arching a speculative brow. "But you don't seem too broken about it. Wonder why that is?"

Enzo stiffened beside her, flattening his lips. "What do you want me to do, cry into a pillow?"

Tierney was in on a secret. And Enzo was obviously shitting bricks, not wanting her to spill it out.

"I did him a favor," Achilles said coolly. "Any woman willing to open her legs for her longtime boyfriend's brother is not worth putting a ring on."

"Nice mental gymnastics." Tierney gave him a thumbs-up, her wrists chafing together. "Are you also this flexible in bed?"

Achilles twisted toward Luca. "Permission to cut off one of her fingers?" he inquired dryly. "The bitch is having way too much fun in our captivity."

"And you care because?" Luca sneered.

"She's ruining my reputation. Not to mention my fucking eardrums."

Luca glanced at his Cartier. "Just ten more minutes, and she'll be back to being Callaghan's problem. Along with the others he created for himself."

"I wouldn't mind parting ways with just one finger if it saves your fragile ego." Tierney twirled a scarlet lock of hair around her finger.

"Oh, but I'll make sure it's the one you use to get yourself off." Achilles showed her his teeth.

This made Tierney blush, which I assumed was a world fucking record.

"*Anyway*," Tierney singsonged, recovering quickly. "I *personally* wouldn't forgive a sibling for screwing my partner, but that's just me."

"One more word," Achilles said slowly as I zipped over the bridge crossing into New Jersey, "and I *will* harm you, piccola fiamma. It's in Tate's best interest that you arrive unharmed, but I couldn't give two shits about what condition you'll be in."

Dipshit just gave her a nickname.

I hoped we were close, because at this rate, they'd be having babies in my back seat before we got there.

Dr. Patel called again. His sixth time. The call went to voicemail. Then all was quiet for half a second. I groaned, relishing the momentary silence.

Achilles's shoulders unknotted, and he reached to turn on the radio. "18 and Life" by Skid Row blasted through the speakers.

"Did you know…" Tierney shoved herself between Achilles and me, looking between us with a smirk. "This song is inspired by guitarist Dave Sabo's brother, Rick, who didn't kill anyone, but his life was changed forever when he came back from the Vietnam Wa—"

Achilles grabbed ahold of the steering wheel, jolting it sharply toward the shoulder of the road. The car skidded and screeched. I pumped the brake lightly so as not to throw us all off the bridge.

It swiveled a couple times anyway, careening with momentum. The scent of burned rubber singed my nostrils.

Tierney let out a piercing cry. Luca muttered an exasperated "for fuck's sake," and I contemplated killing all these assholes right after I secured Gia.

The Escalade stopped an inch away from the metal framing the concrete. Smoke erupted from the engine, curling skyward. "Fuck." I slammed my fist against the steering wheel. I didn't want to be late because the evil twin from hell decided to rile up American Psycho over here.

Achilles threw his door open, strode outside, opened the back door, and plucked Tierney out as though she weighed nothing. He tossed her over his shoulder savagely, breezing his way to the edge of the bridge and flinging her kicking and thrashing body out over the barrier. For a moment, my heart stopped inside my chest. I couldn't give half a shit about Tierney's life, but she was my currency to get my wife back.

I unbuckled and threw my door open.

Luca clamped a hand over my shoulder from behind. "Trust the process, Blackthorn."

"He *threw* her into the fucking Hudson." And now I had to jump in and retrieve the mouthy bitch.

"No, he didn't."

Sure enough, I noticed Achilles was leaning over the edge, holding Tierney by the...

"He's sustaining her by her *heel*." I punched the steering wheel again. "Goddammit."

"It's a good heel. Those Jimmy Choos are sturdy as fuck," Enzo mumbled.

Luca threw him a look.

"Or so I heard." Enzo raised his palms innocently.

"He just wanted to look up her skirt," Luca reassured me. "She's probably wet from the foreplay, and he's taunting her for it."

"Why would he do that?"

"This is his idea of flirting."

These people were far too messed up, even by my standards.

Achilles and Tierney seemed to be doing some negotiations. He seemed calm, and shockingly, from what I could tell, so was she. The entire ordeal took no more than five minutes before he tugged her back up, hurling her across the asphalt. She fell flat on her ass. Rather than help her up, Achilles walked briskly back to the car, slipped into the passenger seat, and slammed the door.

"Problem solved." He wiped his palms.

Tierney steadied herself on her heels, limping to the car.

"What'd you tell her?" Luca drawled.

"It's a secret." Achilles smirked.

Tierney got back inside.

She didn't say a word for the rest of the journey.

Ten minutes later, we were standing on a cliff overlooking the Hudson River. The wind whipped at my face. Tierney wasn't wearing a jacket, and although I would have liked nothing more than to toss her off the cliff, I wanted her in pristine condition when her brother arrived. Her lips were a little blue, her eyes pink-rimmed.

"Here," I barked, tearing off my peacoat. "Cover yourself." I handed it to her.

Tierney took my coat without saying thank you and stomped over to the edge on those impossible heels, no doubt to piss everyone off.

"Stay close to us." My tone bore no room for argument.

Ignoring me, she balanced herself on one leg, peering down the cliff. She still hadn't uttered one word since Achilles almost flung her off the bridge.

I wasn't in the mood for this bullshit.

"I'm not liable for the next thing I do if she doesn't listen." I pointed at her, turning to the Ferrante brothers.

"Tierney," Achilles barked. "Get the fuck back here."

She stopped twirling along the pebbles, shooting him a murderous look. She didn't move.

"*Sit.*" He pointed at the ground. "Or we're gonna have a problem."

"I'm not your bitch." She finally opened her mouth. "So don't treat me like a dog. If you want me to come over, say *please* and say it nicely. If you make it convincing enough, I just might meet you halfway."

"Being my bitch is an accomplishment too prestigious for you to reach," Achilles drawled. "Come here now, or I'll make good on my threat on the bridge."

I had no idea what they were talking about, and fuck if I gave a shit. I just wanted my wife. Luckily, the sound of tires rolling over pebbles assaulted my ears. Callaghan was almost here. The Ferrante soldiers who drove behind us were also strategically scattered along the route. They alerted Luca they were coming.

"Oh, look." Tierney raised her zip-tied wrists, checking an imaginary watch. "If it isn't I-don't-give-a-shite o'clo—" Then she purposefully threw herself right off the cliff, the fucking banshee that she was.

I pounced toward her, but Achilles was quicker. He leapt through the air, reaching her just in time, and yanked her back in record speed. Tierney fell on her face and knees, laughing at the two panting men above her.

Crazy obviously ran in the family. I hoped they weren't going to reproduce.

I was about to stop Achilles from kicking her in the gut—he looked like he was about to—when an armored Mercedes-Benz AMG G 63 parked next to my Escalade. First, two Callaghan soldiers came out. Following them was Tiernan…and *Gia*.

My wife looked disoriented and exhausted. The collar of her

shirt was bloodstained. I slammed my teeth to stop myself from cursing. I was pissed at myself for giving Tierney my jacket. What she deserved was to nurse a month-long bout of pneumonia.

Gia was tied by the wrists, just like Tierney, but unlike the Irish banshee, her clothes were torn, and it was obvious she had put up a fight. Tiernan had his arm wrapped around Gia's throat as he led her in front of him, holding the muzzle of his gun to her temple as he prowled over to us, her body shielding his.

I tugged Tierney up to her feet by her hair. She groaned but kept her composure.

"What, no gun?" Tiernan elevated a mocking eyebrow when I lassoed my arm around his sister's neck.

I couldn't see past the red mist of fury covering my vision.

"I'll break her neck with my bare hands." I shrugged. "And I'll make it slow, so don't try me."

"All right, I have more pressing matters to attend to. Let's get this show on the road." Tiernan yawned provocatively, settling himself and Gia on the edge of the cliff.

I had so many things I wanted to tell her. So many things I wanted to do.

"You lay your asks, I'll do the same, and we'll see where we land."

"I'll let your sister go if you let Gia go first as an act of goodwill, since you shat all over your word to me. You're not to pursue revenge on us. You are not to contact us. You will not touch us, follow us, or make any claim of compensation toward me at any point in the future," I warned. "This ends here. And all this is contingent and subject to change if I find out Gia was harmed in any way. Your turn."

"I'd slow clap if I wasn't holding such a hefty prize." Tiernan chuckled deviously.

Gia's head bobbed in his headlock, and I wanted to kill him so much my bones actually hurt. I despised a lot of people, but not half as much as I did Tiernan Callaghan.

"Who would've thought? Neither money nor power could bring the great Tatum Blackthorn down in the end but merely delicious pussy."

"Your terms," Achilles enunciated to Tiernan. He wasn't in the mood for laughter after losing Filippo. "Before I put a bullet between your bitch sister's eyes. I'm not Blackthorn. I don't give a shit if you feed Gia to the sharks."

"Cheers," Gia muttered sarcastically.

"Sharks in the Hudson?" Tierney screwed her nose. "You dumb fuck."

"First things first—sorry, darlin' sister, I swear you're next in my priorities—I want the Ferrantes' word that offing their little errand boy, Philip, is not going to be retaliated against." Tiernan rightened his hold on Gia's neck.

"It's Filippo," Achilles spat out. "And I'm not—"

"We won't kill you," Luca cut into his speech. I noticed he didn't say they wouldn't retaliate.

Achilles threw his brother a heated look.

Luca shrugged. "He's unhinged. He'll do something else to piss us off and get himself killed. Give it a few weeks."

"There's no fucking way—" Achilles burst out, but Enzo put his hand on his shoulder.

"Respectfully—and I have no fucking respect for you after what happened with Alianna—you have no say in this. Luca is second to the don. You can bitch about it when we get home."

"Good, good. Second, I want Tierney returned to me safely."

"It'd be my pleasure," I said sincerely. "The woman is a pest. Next."

"I want *you*, Blackthorn, to promise me you won't go after my throat. We start a blank page, right here, right now."

"This'll never be a blank page," Achilles announced. "Too much blood has run through the streets of New York for peace. But I do have a contingency."

"Of course you do." Callaghan smiled. "What is it?"

"Your sister," Achilles said. "I choose who she marries."

"I'm never going to marr—" Tierney erupted like a volcano, writhing and pulling out of my headlock. I squeezed her neck, crushing her windpipe to shut her up.

"Quiet." Tiernan raised his palm in annoyance, a deep frown engraved on his face.

I wasn't particularly hot on the idea of linking this tit-for-tat deal to Achilles's idiotic whim, but if he wanted to play with her, he damn fucking could. Tiernan made too many mistakes along the way, and it was time he paid for them.

"Tiernan, *no*," Tierney growled heatedly, clawing me as she tried to pry my hands off. "Don't you fucking dare."

Tiernan turned to Achilles. "First, you tell me why."

"I don't owe you an explanation." Achilles laughed metallically. "You burned too many bridges. Take it or leave it, but if you leave it, beware, because the entire Camorra is after you, and I'll do what I please with this mouthy little thing anyway."

Tiernan's nostrils flared. "If you're going to do with my sister as you please, why are you asking for my permission?"

"Oh, that's simple. Because by saving your ass, you will have to betray her. You'll never come back from that."

Tierney let out a feral string of profanity. I laughed.

Tiernan turned to Achilles. "Whoever you choose to be her husband won't be violent toward her."

Achilles jerked his chin in a nod.

"And he won't be beneath her in rank. You're not handing her off to one of your errand boys."

"Fine."

"She's an expensive habit."

Achilles smiled calmly. "Her groom can handle it."

"And another thing." Tiernan's nostrils flared. "It can't be *you*."

Achilles grinned from ear to ear. "She's not up to my standard.

She definitely won't do. I might take her as a mistress for those hard, long days I want it rough and dirty. But it won't be me. Now, release Blackthorn's missus."

Tierney sounded like an injured animal, her tears flying in the wind, her fingernails desperately trying to claw away my hold. She broke a couple of them in the process. Gia, on the other hand, remained stoic and patient, stood tall, and managed not to cry.

I was going to save her.

To wrap her in something warm.

To lick the tears that'd come away.

And to make it all up to her.

"*Tiernan*," Tierney cried. "I'll never forgive you."

He ignored her. "Promise me that no matter what, if I release Gia, no harm will come to my sister."

"Promise," I said, almost too eagerly.

"Promise," Enzo said.

"Promise," said Luca.

Achilles took a second, mulling it over. He loved keeping people on their toes. "I guess."

Tiernan released Gia. She staggered to me, silent tears running down her cheeks.

I immediately tossed Tierney into Achilles's hold and bundled Gia in my arms, kissing her tears, the tip of her nose. "I'm sorry. I'm so sorry. Are you okay?"

She nodded, unable to produce words.

My stomach rumbled with rage. She was far from okay, and recovering from this experience was going to take time. I turned to yank the coat from Tierney's shoulders and wrap it around my wife. I buried her head in my chest and praised her in hushed, gentle whispers. Telling her how brave she was, how strong, how graceful.

"Now, may I please have my sister?" Tiernan opened his arms wide, smiling.

"No need," Tierney said coldly, slapping away Achilles's hold but standing by his side. "You already gave up my right to choose. I have nothing to gain under your protection. I'm staying with the Ferrantes."

Achilles snorted. "Hadn't realized we offered to house you."

Tiernan's expression thundered. "Cut the bullshit, Tier."

"Do as he says," I instructed. "I don't have time for these theatrics. I need to take Gia home."

They could all die on the spot, and I wouldn't even attend their goddamn funerals. All I wanted was to take care of the woman who almost paid for my mistakes with her life.

"No." Tierney folded her arms. "I'm not coming."

"We'll see about that," Achilles muttered. He was fucking with her. If he was smart, he wouldn't fuck *her*, though. She seemed like a headache no Advil could fix.

"Fine." Tiernan tossed a careless hand. "As you wish."

He was about to turn around and make his way back to the Mercedes when Achilles gave Tierney a push forward, making her stumble all the way to her brother's arms.

"I've no use for her now." Achilles shrugged. "She's another mouth to feed. Keep her safe and those legs closed. If I hear she's been fucked, I'll chop off the guy's cock. Pass it on. I'll find her an appropriate match when I feel like it."

The heartfelt union came to an abrupt end when Tierney punched her brother's face, giving him a prominent shiner. She stomped to the car, cursing up and down the entire Callaghan ancestry.

I turned to the Ferrante brothers. "Ride with your soldiers." It was an order, not a request. "I'm taking my wife home."

"Hey, Gia, you good?" Enzo's eyes were soft.

She nodded, trying to smile.

I crouched down to pick Gia up and carried her to the Escalade. The journey home was quiet. I didn't dare speak. I didn't dare *breathe*. She warned me this could happen. I failed to protect her. No matter what happened from this point forward, I would always remember this failure.

She stared straight ahead, her jaw tipped up regally, her eyes heavy-lidded. "They tried to drug me when they caught me." Her sweet, soft voice pierced through the condensed silence. "When they thought I was knocked out, I heard them talking. They're planning a bloodbath. Killing the Russians, up and down the ranks, and taking over."

I was so wrapped up in her I couldn't even give a shit. If the Irish wanted to start shit, this was Achilles and Luca's problem. As far as I was concerned, I was done with this world.

When we reached the first traffic light in Manhattan, I turned to look at her fully. The back of her head continued to bleed. It trickled down in a steady stream, running down the seat all the way into her lap. She didn't even notice.

"Apricity." I tried to sound calm. "You're bleeding."

"I am?" She reached to the back of her head. Her fingers shook when she brought them in front of her face and noticed how bloodied they were. Her mouth dropped open.

"I'm taking you to the hospital." I made an illegal sharp turn south and floored it all the way there.

CHAPTER FIFTY-THREE
GIA

"…typically takes a few days to come out of a coma, right?" Rhyland's familiar baritone seeped into my ears.

"Not if you're married to the Antichrist and the only thing that waits for you on the other side is his sorry ass and another half-baked apology," Row's voice groused.

Slowly, I came to, my mind numb, my body feeling rusty. My skin was pebbled from the manufactured air-con chill. My veins felt poked and hooked to tubes.

Hospital. I was in the hospital. But why?

Because of my head injury, of course. Tiernan Callaghan never saw to it that I was treated. I only spent a few hours with the Irish wanker, but he made each minute agonizing.

But…I survived.

Tate did what he had to do, like I knew he would.

I was here. I was safe. It was over. Truly over this time.

"Now's not the time to taunt Tate," Cal scolded the men in the room.

How many people were here? I finally understood my mother's spirit bitching through the medium about allowing complete strangers to see her in a hospital gown.

"No such thing as a bad time to taunt Tate." Rhyland clucked his tongue. "It's a universally enjoyable pleasure, second only to nutting in your wife's rect—"

"You really shouldn't finish that sentence if you plan on giving your daughter a sibling," Row's voice warned, the sound of a shoulder being slapped filling the air. "That wife of yours is my sister."

"I think her eyelids moved," Tate croaked.

"Only her eyelids?" Rhyland snorted. "Dude, when I get entrance privileges, her entire body is—"

"I'm talking about Gia, you waste of environmental resources," Tate barked.

At this point, I was fully awake and fighting a smile. I'd been through hell and back in the past few weeks, but I couldn't deny the joy I derived from knowing I was surrounded by people who loved me.

And that included my cruel and domineering husband.

"She's waking up. Everybody, get the fuck out," Tate ordered, his chair scraping the floor. "I want to be the first face she sees when she opens her eyes."

"Hasn't the poor woman been through enough?" Dylan murmured.

I swallowed down a giggle.

"I'm staying here. I'm filling out my renewal forms for the student organization membership. This is the one spot in the hospital that's not horrible for Wi-Fi."

My eyelids seemed heavy, a crust of sleep gluing them together, but I couldn't resist granting Tate his wish and waited until I heard the door closing behind our friends.

"Apricity." Tate's hand scooped mine, warm and large against my cold, dry one. The mattress dipped as he shifted onto my hospital bed. He brought the back of my hand to his mouth, his lips brushing my skin. "*Gia*. Sweetheart. Wake up. Even in *Alice's Adventures in Wonderland*, she wakes up from her dream. She came back," he croaked brokenly. "My love. Please come back to me. I'll be better. No, that's not good enough. I'll be *perfect*. I'll dedicate my life to worshipping you. You will have anything your heart desires. More airplanes. And islands. And…and…union perks!" he offered breathlessly. "Let's take everyone on a vacation. My treat. You pick the location. I'll be nice to company employees. I'll even…do those team-building activities you tried to rope me into in the past. Just wake up. Please. I need you."

Tears pulled behind my eyelids, moistening the crust keeping them closed.

"Dylan," I croaked, my eyes snapping open. "Are you still here?"

Tate's lips parted against my hand.

"Yes." I could hear amusement in her voice as well as her fingers punching her laptop's keyboard.

"Did you hear Mr. Blackthorn's promises?"

"Loud and clear."

"About the union perks?"

"Yup," Dylan said, popping the *p*. "Started filming the entire thing when it was obvious he was gonna bawl."

"And about the company's vacation?" I singsonged.

"Heard that too," Dylan confirmed.

"Oh, lovey." I placed my hand on Tate's cheek, even though my head pounded angrily, and I was freezing despite being bundled in several blankets.

He leaned into my touch instinctively.

"I contemplated dying, but the need to give you shit for all you've put me through won out in the end." My voice was so brittle, so thin, it reminded me of a crème brûlée, ready to crack under the slightest pressure.

My husband was a wreck, his dark hair unkempt and curling around his ears and forehead chaotically. He was pale, his cheeks sunken, with dark circles around his eyes. His lips were chapped, and he was wearing the same suit he'd brought me to the hospital in. I blinked, taking him all in.

For a moment, he simply stared as though I were a mirage,

something he couldn't trust to be real. Then he grabbed my cold hands in his warm ones, rubbing my skin back and forth with his thumbs, tears pooling in his eyes.

"Apricity." His voice was fractured. "You're never allowed to leave me for this long again."

"How long have I been out?"

"Four days."

He hadn't showered in four days? Hadn't left my side? Hadn't brushed his teeth?

That was…adorable.

Unsanitary too.

"W-what happened to me?"

"Internal bleeding. They managed to stop it in time. Just about." His jaw ticked, his gunmetal eyes darkening, and I knew exactly what was going through his head.

"No, Tate." My fingers wrapped around his. "No more revenge. No more Callaghans. I beg you. I told you I'd leave. I meant it." The mere thought of going through this vicious cycle again made me even more exhausted than I was, which seemed impossible. "I love you, Tate. More than I love myself. But never more than I'd love our children. I won't stay with a vigilante who prioritizes his thirst for blood over his family."

Tate buried his head in my lap, breathing me in with a groan.

"I was serious when I said I was done," Tate clarified. "I promise you, my dealings with Tiernan Callaghan are over."

"Can you give me your word?" I asked.

"I give you my word."

"Then you'll consider the next thing I need to ask you…"

It was a big ask, I knew. An ask that would change both our lives forever. Something so far out of his comfort zone, I never thought he'd agree to it. And still, I wanted it. For my safety. For *his*. For a fresh start and hope. For a chance at normalcy.

When I told him what it was, he didn't even blink.

Didn't even take a moment to think about it.

"I'll do it, Gia, for you," he promised. "Everything I do is for you."

CHAPTER FIFTY-FOUR
GIA

"Okay, am I gonna be the one to say it out loud?" Dylan looked up from her burrito bowl, sucking the straw of her skinny margarita. "Gia, you have no business looking this good three days after you woke up from a freaking *coma* after being kidnapped by Hottie McBadson and almost thrown off a cliff."

Snorting, I covered my mouth to prevent myself from shooting refried beans directly into her lap.

"Did you just call my captor handsome?"

"What? I didn't say he was nice or anything." Dylan pouted. "And I've a feeling the Ferrantes are going to punish him. But *objectively speaking*, yes, Tiernan Callaghan is not a chore to look at."

We were sitting at a small Mexican place in the Bronx, and it was the first time in a long time I didn't have bodyguards hovering over my head. I could say whatever I wanted without feeling embarrassed. The feeling was almost akin to being reborn. I could totally be myself again.

When I insisted on meeting Cal and Dyl for brunch in public and without security, Tate had objected but later relented when I told him I was desperate to get my life back to normal.

"Normal went out the window the moment you married America's most loathed human." He had gestured at himself as I fastened my Tiffany earrings—my hospital discharge gift—after slipping into a lemon-patterned summer dress.

"Please, love. You're not even in the top five." I had rolled my eyes, smiling. "President Keaton? Cillian Fitzpatrick? Baron Spencer?" I named just a few of America's favorite corporate and political villains.

"That makes me fourth. I'm definitely in the top five. And I don't think Keaton is doing that bad. Forty-eight percent approval rating is better than most." He made a scandalized face, alarmed at the prospect of not being positively loathed by the better half of this continent. "That's top four for you. I earned that hatred fair and square. I might not be drilling every inch of the world for oil and fracking away entire ecosystems, but I'll have you know I've fucked over plenty of hardworking fellas."

I'd won that argument, and here I was with my friends, sipping cocktails, eating too many tortilla chips, and it all felt almost... *normal*. Like the good old days.

With the exception that during the good old days, I didn't sport a 1.2-million-dollar diamond ring on my finger and didn't have particularly exciting news to share that'd change my whole life.

"So..." Cal licked the rim of her skinny margarita, collecting coarse salt. "What did you want to tell us?"

"Please don't let it be a surprise pregnancy." Dylan held her hand up. "There are only so many tropes you can cram into your life these days, and villain-gets-the-girl is a hard act to follow."

I raised an eyebrow. "Are you saying you won't be happy for me if I'm pregnant?"

"Oh, don't get me wrong. I'd be *thrilled*," she amended. "I'll support you and be happy for you no matter what, but you have to admit this relationship progressed superfast."

"I'm not pregnant." I rolled my eyes, suppressing a smile. Dyl was right. It *was* too soon for a baby. I hadn't even had a chance to properly enjoy my husband. At the same time, I was oddly comfortable with the idea of having children with Tate considering the fact that our marriage almost cost me my life.

Oh, and that we both had committed murder. In his case, *plural*.

"Thank God. I still need to catch up on episodes: Gia Almost Got Killed, Gia Got Kidnapped, and Tate Gives Great Oral." Dylan wiped invisible sweat from her forehead.

"I gave you all the CliffsNotes." I laughed.

I didn't share what Tate had done to land himself in a Mafia war. Just explained that he screwed Tiernan over on a business deal. This was ridiculously easy for Cal and Dylan to believe, since both their husbands had been fucked over financially by Tate.

"*Hardly.*" Dylan made a face, mounting guac on her tortilla chip and tossing it into her mouth. "You left so much information out."

"Such as?"

"Is Tiernan Callaghan as hot up close as he is in the pictures?"

"This is your second strike," Cal gasped. "Stop salivating over this asshole."

"Don't pretend." Dylan gave Cal a playful shove. "You were there with me when I conducted the, um, my research on him."

"He is ruggedly handsome," I admitted. "That whole mass murderer bit, though, takes him down from a ten to a seven."

"Twelve in my books." Dylan tossed her hair back. "Anyway, you were saying?"

"I was saying…" I lowered my fork and sat back, looking between my two friends with a huge grin on my face. "We're moving."

"On from this episode?" Dylan asked hopefully.

"No, physically, from the city."

"Moving where?" Cal took another mouthful of her burrito bowl.

"England."

She proceeded to choke on her bite, coughing uncontrollably and reaching for her glass of water.

"*New* England?" Cal cleared her throat.

"No. Old England. The one with the castles and king and *real* football."

"I'm sorry." Dylan raised a hand. "It might be the accent. I think you pronounced 'Westchester' wrong."

"No, Dyl." I offered her a rueful smile. "We're moving to England. Permanently. I asked Tate before I got discharged."

"But…why?" Dylan grumbled. "Cal'll have you because she splits her time between NYC and London, but what about *me*?"

"I'll come visit often, and of course, you're always welcome to stay over with your family as much as you'd like!" I assured her. Although if I were completely honest, I wasn't entirely sure my husband was a fan of guests. Or small children. Or…humans in general. "We decided to start over somewhere new, with a slower pace of life. We're moving to the country. Kent, more specifically."

Moving back home was important to me. I wanted to start somewhere fresh, putting our pasts, our anguish, and our animosity behind us. New York was drenched in trauma. The city reminded me of hectic mornings picking up strewn thongs from Tate's desk and clearing his schedule on a whim because he decided to go ruin someone's small business. Not to mention now, New York reminded me of my mother's death. Of the Callaghans and the Ferrantes and the most frightening time in my life.

I'd been a caregiver my entire life. An assistant. A daughter. A fake wife. A real wife. It was time I started doing things for myself, even if it meant others needed to adjust their lives around me. It was a process, and one I was working with alongside a virtual therapist I started to see weekly.

I needed this. *We* needed this to heal.

"And Tate is going along with it?" Cal's eyebrows flew to her forehead, her jaw going slack. "To living in Kent?"

"Yeah. Why?"

"Row said he oftentimes looks down at anywhere in America that isn't New York City and compares living in the suburbs to having a voluntary lobotomy."

I cringed. My husband really was an acquired taste, wasn't he? "Tate is very fond of New York, but he's willing to compromise."

But he wasn't compromising. He was going right along with everything I wanted. And perhaps it was selfish of me, but I needed at least a year to recuperate from the first few weeks of our marriage. Who knew? Maybe after I put time and space between myself and everything that had happened, I'd want to come back to New York.

All I knew was that I'd spent my entire adult life doing whatever Tate Blackthorn wanted me to do. It was time I made decisions for myself too.

"It's the end of an era." The corners of Dylan's mouth pulled down in sadness. "You were there when I needed you the most. When Grav got kidnapped by Tucker. When Rhyland and I started out and I needed someone to help me make sense of everything."

"I'll still be there," I assured her. "I will *always* be there for you. Through thick and thin. Promise."

So this was my story then. Imperfect, messy, and filled with way too much bloodshed for my liking. But this happy ending was completely mine. And at the end of it, I found something beautiful.

I found a family that loved me by choice, not by blood.

A man who would pluck all the stars from the sky just to make my life brighter.

A partner who chose me every day, even through hardship.

And that wasn't just enough.

It was *everything*.

EPILOGUE
GIA

"Another mocktail?" My husband dragged a pink beverage in a fancy cup across the table, embellished with a pretty straw and a slice of pineapple. He took a slow sip of his brandy, squinting at the sun as it dipped into the ocean. We'd escaped to a Jamaican white-sand beach where we sat at a restaurant overlooking the sea.

Summer heat licked at my skin, the briny, fresh air caressed my face, and I was content and full of delicious dishes and desserts.

"Oh, sod off." I pushed the mocktail back to him.

Tate smirked wryly. "I think sodding me was what got you into this predicament in the first place."

Another wave of nausea washed over me, this time a milder one. The mornings were the worst. Which was why Tate had decided to distract me by taking me on a seven-month babymoon around the world, checking off every place I'd wanted to visit before we welcomed the new addition to our family.

The house in Kent was supposed to be ready shortly before the baby arrived. We were gutting it and starting over from scratch since Tate didn't see the same quaint, nostalgic magic I did in the thirty-year-old kitchen and dated wallpaper.

"I'm still incredibly happy to be pregnant," I clarified. "I just don't like mocktails. They're basically kiddie juice with garnishes."

Tate nodded, taking another sip of his brandy.

"And if *I* don't get to drink during this pregnancy, neither does the man who impregnated me."

With the same smooth finesse with which he sipped his drink, Tate tossed the glass off the balcony of the beach restaurant, unblinking. "Done."

"Same goes for cold meats." I didn't know why I was giving him hell. Perhaps because my stomach was way too bloated for eight weeks of pregnancy.

"Yes, Apricity."

"And I want a big *Notting Hill* bench in our garden."

Tate grinned, bringing a glass of water to his mouth. "Got no idea what the fuck that is, but consider it done."

"You should really be more assertive with me." I raised an eyebrow. "Our child will walk all over you if you give them everything they want."

"It's one law for Blackthorn Junior and another one for you." He put the glass down. "No one can wrestle these many concessions out of me."

"You might feel differently when they arrive."

He shook his head. "I'll love them more than I do myself. But nothing and no one will ever compare to how I treat you. I worship at your altar."

His phone beeped, and I knew who it was before Tate had the chance to glance at it.

"Dr. Patel reminding you that you have a therapy session in fifteen minutes, huh?" I smiled.

Tate's psychiatrist worked closely with the therapist Tate spoke to twice a week to ensure he was making progress. And he was. He now solved mathematical problems for fun, maybe once a week, and sometimes he forgot to do them altogether. He stopped writing on walls and furniture. He stopped tap-tap-tapping his numbers whenever he felt anxious. He still followed some OCD routines, but they were mild and didn't interrupt his daily life.

He still checked that all the lights were off before we left the house. Only stepped through doors and into elevators with his right leg. Read the *Financial Times* in a peculiar order that was not chronological and made sense only to him.

"The man is relentless." Tate shook his head, standing up and giving me an apologetic grimace. "You'd think he'd get the hint when I told him I was married, yet there he is, blowing up my DMs like a fangirl." Tate offered me his hand to help me to my feet from across our table.

Smiling indulgently, I shook my head. "The weather is lovely. I think I'll stay here a bit more."

He stiffened for a moment, and I knew what he was thinking. Even though the past six months had been blissfully eventless in the Ferrante and Callaghan department, Tate was still reluctant to let me out of his sight. He had PTSD. So did I, I supposed. But it only made me fight my fears even more.

"You know..." Tate trailed off. "I can always skip today's session. I've been doing it twice a week for seven months now. Nothi—"

"Respectfully, love, I'd like some time alone." I arched a pointed brow.

He looked ready to argue—in love or not, arguing was my husband's favorite cardio right after having sex—but he inclined his head, reminding me he was one phone call away.

"Bill's been taken care of. So has the tip." He leaned to place a hot kiss on my lips, whispering, "But I haven't touched dessert, so if you could open those legs for me when you get back, I'd much appreciate it."

Now that I was alone, I took the mocktail and brought it to my lips, closing my eyes. I couldn't wait to feel the baby growing and kicking inside me. Couldn't wait to raise them in England, far away from the mayhem and insanity.

My eyes trailed the pearly white sand. Brightly colored houses in turquoise and pink and green sprouted along the shore, with arched balconies and red roofs. The waves gently teased the smooth sand, and I hugged my arms, relishing my tranquility. My eyes trailed the edge of the shore, where I spotted a young family enjoying the last rays of sunshine. The couple was sitting in their swimwear by the water, toes curled in the sand, deep in conversation. Next to them was a girl, maybe five or six years old, with dark skin and a mermaid metallic swimming costume in purples, silvers, and pinks. She was holding a bucket in her hand, picking up a seashell, squinting at it, then tossing it back in the sand. I smiled privately. *A perfectionist.*

Something about her reminded me of myself, and an acute desire to help her overcame me. I stood up, my legs carrying me to her. She was tossing another seashell back to the ocean with a heavy sigh when I reached her.

"Hi," I said.

She looked up, her face a mask of confusion. "Um, hi?"

"Are you looking for a particular seashell?" I asked.

Her parents stopped talking and looked over at us, probably to make sure I wasn't trying to kidnap their daughter.

"Yes." She nodded briskly. "The *Scaphella junonia* shell." She had an American accent and a bossy, no-bullshit attitude I adored. I was right. She *did* remind me of myself. "It's so rare that they can be worth thousands of dollars, but on this beach, people have found them. I asked my mommy and daddy to come here." The words rushed out of her mouth. "For my birthday. Because I wanted it. But now I don't think I'll find it. They only wash up in powerful storms. It's our last night here, and I've been looking every day, and, well..." She trailed off, shoulders slumping, her gaze dropping to her sand-covered toes.

"Is it something like this?" I thrust my wrist in her direction, exhibiting the studded bracelet Tate had given me.

"Yes!" The girl's face opened, brightening at once. "Exactly like this one! Wow. So cool. Where'd you find it?" Her fingers twitched, struggling not to reach for it.

"You can touch it if you want."

She did, rolling it between her small fingers, careful not to touch me. Her parents looked on, unsure what to make of it but perhaps rightly not wanting to cut off what looked like an innocent exchange.

"And to your question, it was my husband who found this one for me. See, I had an identical one when I was younger too. My dad and I found it, on this very beach actually. And when I lost it, I was so sad, my husband flew here all the way from New York to find one."

"Wow." Her eyes were as big as saucers, gaping at me. "He must really love you. Mommy gets excited when Daddy gets her surprise Sephora bags for no reason."

I laughed, and so did her parents. I shook my head. "I don't know what it is about this particular seashell, but it's always been more than a pretty shell to me. It represents hope and love and…something else important. Believing in myself." I loosened the bracelet from my wrist, unlocking it before extending my open palm to the girl. "It's yours."

The little girl's mouth hung open. She looked up at me like this was a practical joke. A test her parents put me to. She whipped her head in question toward her parents.

"No." Her mother stood up, rushing toward us. "We can't. Thank you, but this is too much."

"Not at all," I said. "I want her to have it."

"But…why?" The mother studied me.

Al mal tiempo, buena cara.

"Because." I put a hand on my belly. "Once upon a time, I was much like her, standing on this beach, looking for something pretty, and this seashell that I found…it would be a part of my story for many years to come. It was my good luck charm, and now I no longer need it. I got my happy ending. Now I want her to have hers."

Gingerly, the girl took the bracelet from me. The moment her skin touched mine, her fingers lifting the shell and the diamonds and the weight of the bracelet, I understood the power of giving back once your cup has been filled.

I got my happy ending.

Now it was time for another happily ever after to be written.

TATE

FOUR MONTHS LATER

"Love? Are you coming with the coriander?" My wife's voice singsonged from the tea room of our six-hundred-fucking-year-old country mansion in Kent. It was a black-and-white Tudor-style house, sprawling over who knows how many fucking acres, and had a water garden, a meadow, stables, a servants' house, and other old-as-shit features Gia found charming.

Me, the only thing I found delightful here was my wife's pussy. Fortunately, that was enough to keep me content. What was the word my shrink used the other day? *Happiness.* I was happy. Not in a fleeting kind of way but in a *fuck, I've been doing this life thing all wrong the entire time* way.

I crouched, narrowing my eyes at our impressive vegetable garden, trying to find the...what was it?

"Did you find it?" Gia called from inside again.

"Found what?"

"The coriander."

"Is this a fancy word for something else? Like when you call an eggplant aubergine?"

"Do you want me to send Brayden to help?" she sighed.

Eh, yes. Not only was I becoming a father, but I also adopted

Brayden, the kid I won at a poker night at the Ferrantes' casino. Ultimately, I wanted to leave him behind when I moved to the UK, but Gia said it was inhumane. So I figured I could be someone else's Daniel. Minus the getting killed in prison part.

"No. Just tell me," I insisted.

"Oh, hold on. Let me google it." She was quiet for a second. "Cilantro."

"Ah, cilantro. Why didn't you say?"

I stared at the dozens of different leafy greens in front of me. Of course I had no idea what cilantro was. Might as well stay coriander.

"What does it look like?" I groaned.

"Sort of like parsley but with a wider leaf. Try and taste it. If it tastes like something you put in dishes, it's cilantro. If it tastes like something you put in a salad or for garnishing, it's parsley."

I glowered at the greens for a few seconds before Row tromped his way into my garden. He and Cal were visiting us, and he volunteered to cook. "Jesus fuck, how useless can you be out of the board room?" He shouldered me out of the way, crouching down and plucking a wag of green shit and burying his nose inside it. "Smells good. Gia has a green thumb."

"And I have a lethal fist, so shut the fuck up about my woman's body."

Row stared at me, aghast. "You're insane."

Maybe, but I was up to the gills in pills and therapy sessions these days, so I didn't feel that way so much anymore.

We made our way back to the house. Inside, Cal and Gia were cooing and adoring each other's pregnant bellies. They were just a few weeks apart and, to my dismay, insisted on spending a lot of time together.

Serafina, their older daughter, was running around the house, breaking shit. If this was life as a parent, I didn't get the fascination, but if Gia wanted kids, I'd give them to her.

If Gia wanted fucking Mars, we'd move there in a heartbeat.

"Tate! How good to see you," Cal greeted, giving me a forced hug.

"No need to lie. My wife wouldn't let me kick you out even if I wanted to. Something about etiquette." I patted her back, wishing she'd pull away sooner rather than later.

"Are you ready?" Row turned to Gia, already chopping the cori-whatever-the-fuck on a thick wooden board. "I'm going to show you how to make the garnish."

Whatever they were making smelled divine. I could see fish and stew and herbed potatoes.

"Yes!" Gia said excitedly, clapping her hands as she advanced toward him. Her crème woolly dress enhanced her gorgeous curves and pregnant belly. "I'm all ears."

"I'm going to find Serafina." Cal jerked her thumb toward the corridor. "Make sure she didn't break too many things and, if she did, that they're Tate's things."

"Thank you," I said evenly.

Forty minutes later, we were all at the table, enjoying a hearty meal in front of my stunning English garden. Brayden was enthusiastically telling us he got accepted to a lacrosse team at his public school while shoving bread into his mouth like it was some eating competition. His eyes sparkled with enthusi-asm. I liked that I put that glint there. That I gave someone the second chance I had desperately needed when I was about his age.

In the middle of dinner, my phone danced in my pocket with an incoming call. I pulled it out. Achilles Ferrante's name was on the screen.

I stayed in touch with the Ferrantes and visited them from time to time. We had business together, but it was all legitimate these days.

"I need to take this." I tossed my napkin onto the table and stood up, waltzing outside so I could have some privacy. I stopped in front of the king's pond pool, which reminded me fondly of my very first murder, and swiped the screen.

"Yes?" I drawled.

"Tatum," Achilles said.

I followed two swans with my gaze as they sliced through a nearby lake, just on the edge of my property.

"I fucking know my own name. Anything else you got?"

Achilles's laugh filled my ear. It sounded eerily like a nail rolling over a blackboard. "I have a piece of news I think would make you very happy."

"Doubt it."

Only one thing made me happy, and it was currently in the house, cooing over Calla Litvin's incredibly boring story about a pie she burned yesterday.

"Tiernan Callaghan."

The name alone made my skin crawl. He was the first and only man I did not finish off completely after he crossed me. And not from lack of desire. We both had too much on the line.

I could play with my own life but never Gia's. Never our baby's.

"What about him?"

"He fucked up again." Achilles sounded significantly less dead inside, uplifted by the news. "Our last promise to leave him alive has officially expired."

"What'd the bastard do?"

"Killed a Las Vegas pakhan right under our noses. In our territory." There was a pause. "And dumped his body at our doorstep." Another pregnant silence. "Most of it anyway."

"Is that so?" I crouched down and moved an ancient stone, revealing the pack of cigarettes I kept hidden there. I only smoked once every few weeks. Gia didn't like it but learned to live with it. I was still, at my core, a man accustomed to and enamored with darkness. I lit myself a cigarette, blowing out smoke. "And what are you telling me this for? You know damn fucking well I'm not participating in this war. I would never jeopardize my wife's safety."

"We're not asking you to, but there's something else…" He trailed off.

"I'm listening."

"If we were to retaliate, we might need an ironclad alibi."

God bless burner phones. Fucker didn't even miss a beat when he asked this.

"You don't think he'll snitch?" I had no respect whatsoever for that cunt, but even I knew he wouldn't breathe a word if the Ferrantes rearranged his facial features.

"Not him," Achilles tsked. "His sister, I'm not so sure about."

I was quiet for a moment.

"Sure. You were all at my estate at the time. I'll have my guy forge CCTV footage," I said. "Just as long as there's no blowback coming for my family." I wasn't going to actively kill Tiernan, but I was happy to give his fate a much-needed push. I inhaled my cigarette, smirking. "So you've got a death warrant with his name on it?"

"Vello wants him alive, but just barely," Achilles groused with annoyance. "I'm going to pluck a few body parts, though."

"Good. Give him a DIY circumcision, and be generous about it."

Achilles laughed.

"Won't it mess with your ability to choose the mouthy sister a husband?"

"Nah, I have big plans for her."

"I'd ask what they were, but I truly don't care. Oh, and, Achilles?"

"Yeah?"

"If this backfires in any way and makes its way to my doorstep, I am going to personally kill you, your brothers, your entire family, and the Callaghans combined. Make it clean, you hear me? I don't want my wife to be saddled with any more bodyguards."

"Loud and clear, lover boy."

I killed the call and tossed the still-lit cigarette into the mud, making my way back into the house. I assumed my place next to my wife, who made a face that let me know she could smell the cigarette on me. Nonetheless, she placed a reassuring hand on my back.

"Gia and I were just talking designs for the nursery," Cal informed me.

"Oh yeah?" I leaned to kiss my wife's cheek. "Apricity, do you have a color in mind yet?"

"Red," she said without looking at me, taking a spoonful of her stew. "It reminds me of you."

I grinned.

My phone pinged again. Dr. Patel.

From: Dr. Arjun Patel, MD
(arjunpatel@stjohnsmedical.com)

To: Tate Blackthorn
(willnotanswerunsolicitedemails@GSproperties.com)

Subject: Success

Tate, I am happy to inform you I am delighted with your progress and mental health.

I believe you are no longer in need of my weekly service and that a three-month checkup to monitor medicine/dosage is sufficient from this point forward.

I applaud your hard work and your determination to get better.

Warmly, Dr. Patel.

"You look happy," Row accused, frowning like this was bad news all around.

"I am," I confirmed, looking up from the email. "Because I just got my happy ending, perfect and tied in a satin bow."

THE END

WANT MORE L.J. SHEN?
READ ON FOR A SNEAK PEEK AT THE FIRST BOOK IN THE SINNERS OF SAINT SERIES

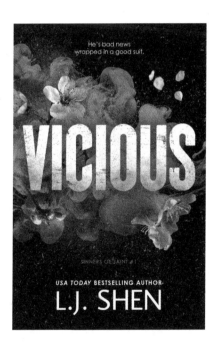

CHAPTER ONE
EMILIA

My grandmama once told me that love and hate are the same feelings experienced under different circumstances. The passion is the same. The pain is the same. That weird thing that bubbles in your chest? Same. I didn't believe her until I met Baron Spencer and he became my nightmare.

Then my nightmare became my reality.

I thought I'd escaped him. I was even stupid enough to think he'd forgotten I ever existed.

But when he came back, he hit harder than I ever thought possible.

And just like a domino—I fell.

TEN YEARS AGO

I'd only been inside the mansion once before, when my family first came to Todos Santos. That was two months ago. That day, I stood rooted in place on the same ironwood flooring that never creaked.

That first time, Mama had elbowed my ribs. "You know this is the toughest floor in the world?"

She failed to mention it belonged to the man with the toughest heart in the world.

I couldn't for the life of me understand why people with so much money would spend it on such a depressing house. Ten bedrooms. Thirteen bathrooms. An indoor gym and a dramatic staircase. The best amenities money could buy...and except for the tennis court and sixty-five-foot pool, they were all in black.

Black choked out every pleasant feeling you might possibly have as soon as you walked through the big iron-studded doors. The interior designer must've been a medieval vampire, judging from the cold, lifeless colors and the giant iron chandeliers hanging from the ceilings. Even the floor was so dark that it looked like I was hovering over an abyss, a fraction of a second from falling into nothingness.

A ten-bedroom house, three people living in it—two of them barely ever there—and the Spencers had decided to house my family in the servants' apartment near the garage. It was bigger than our clapboard rental in Richmond, Virginia, but until that moment, it had still rubbed me the wrong way.

Not anymore.

Everything about the Spencer mansion was designed to intimidate. Rich and wealthy yet poor in so many ways. *These are not happy people*, I thought.

I stared at my shoes—the tattered white Vans lookalikes I doodled colorful flowers on to hide the fact that they were knockoffs—and swallowed, feeling insignificant even before *he* had belittled me. Before I even knew *him*.

"I wonder where he is?" Mama whispered.

As we stood in the hallway, I shivered at the echo that bounced off the bare walls. She wanted to ask if we could get paid two days early because we needed to buy medicine for my younger sister, Rosie.

"I hear something coming from that room." Mama pointed to a

door on the opposite side of the vaulted foyer. "You go knock. I'll go back to the kitchen to wait."

"*Me? Why me?*"

"Because," she said, pinning me with a stare that stabbed at my conscience, "Rosie's sick, and his parents are out of town. You're his age. He'll listen to you."

I did as I was told—not for Mama, for Rosie—without understanding the consequences. The next few minutes cost me my whole senior year and were the reason why I was ripped from my family at the age of eighteen.

Vicious thought I knew his secret.

I didn't.

All I remember was trudging toward the threshold of another dark door, my fist hovering inches from it before I heard the deep rasp of an old man.

"You know the drill, Baron."

A man. A smoker, probably.

"My sister told me you're giving her trouble again." The man slurred his words before raising his voice and slapping his palm against a hard surface. "I've had enough of you disrespecting her."

"Fuck you." I heard the composed voice of a younger man. He sounded…amused? "And fuck her too. Wait, is that why you're here, Daryl? You want a piece of your sister too? The good news is that she's open for business, if you have the buck to pay."

"Look at the mouth on you, you little cunt." *Slap.* "Your mother would've been proud."

Silence, and then, "Say another word about my mother, and I'll give you a real reason to get those dental implants you were talking about with my dad." The younger man's voice dripped venom, which made me think he might not be as young as Mama thought.

"Stay away," the younger voice warned. "I can beat the shit out of you now. As a matter of fact, I'm pretty tempted to do so. All. The. fucking. Time. I'm done with your shit."

"And what the hell makes you think you have a choice?" The older man chuckled darkly.

I felt his voice in my bones, like poison eating at my skeleton.

"Haven't you heard?" the younger man gritted out. "I like to fight. I like the pain. Maybe because it makes it so much easier for me to come to terms with the fact that I'm going to kill you one day. And I will, Daryl. One day, I will kill you."

I gasped, too stunned to move. I heard a loud smack, then someone tumbling down, dragging some items with him as he fell to the floor.

I was about to run—this conversation obviously wasn't meant for me to hear—but he caught me off guard. Before I knew what was happening, the door swung open, and I came face-to-face with a boy around my age. I say *a boy*, but there was nothing boyish about him.

The older man stood behind him, panting hard, hunched with his hands flat against a desk. Books were scattered around his feet, and his lip was cut and bleeding.

The room was a library. Soaring floor-to-ceiling walnut shelves full of hardbacks lined the walls. I felt a pang in my chest because I somehow knew there wasn't any way I'd ever be allowed in there again.

"What the fuck?" the teenage boy seethed. His eyes narrowed. They felt like the sights of a rifle aimed at me.

Seventeen? Eighteen? The fact that we were about the same age somehow made everything about the situation worse. I ducked my head, my cheeks flaming with enough heat to burn down the whole house.

"Have you been listening?" His jaw twitched.

I frantically shook my head no, but that was a lie. I'd always been a terrible liar.

"I didn't hear a thing, I swear." I choked on my words. "My mama works here. I was looking for her." Another lie.

I'd never been a scaredy-cat. I was always the brave one. But I didn't feel so brave at that moment. After all, I wasn't supposed to be there, in his house, and I definitely wasn't supposed to be listening to their argument.

The young man took a step closer, and I took a step back. His eyes were dead, but his lips were red, full, and very much alive. *This guy is going to break my heart if I let him.* The voice came from somewhere inside my head, and the thought stunned me because it made no sense at all. I'd never fallen in love before, and I was too anxious to even register his eye color or hairstyle, let alone the notion of ever having any feelings for the guy.

"What's your name?" he demanded. He smelled delicious—a masculine spice of boy-man, sweet sweat, sour hormones, and the faint trace of clean laundry, one of my mama's many chores.

"Emilia." I cleared my throat and extended my hand. "My friends call me Millie. Y'all can too."

His expression revealed zero emotion. "You're fucking done, *Emilia.*" He drawled my name, mocking my Southern accent and not even acknowledging my hand with a glance.

I withdrew it quickly, embarrassment flaming my cheeks again.

"Wrong fucking place and wrong fucking time. Next time I find you anywhere inside my house, bring a body bag because you won't be leaving alive." He thundered past me, his muscular arm brushing my shoulder.

I choked on my breath. My gaze bolted to the older man, and our eyes locked. He shook his head and grinned in a way that made me want to fold into myself and disappear. Blood dripped from his lip onto his leather boot—black like his worn MC jacket. What was he doing in a place like this, anyway? He just stared at me, making no move to clean up the blood.

I turned around and ran, feeling the bile burning in my throat, threatening to spill over.

Needless to say, Rosie had to make do without her medicine that week, and my parents were paid not a minute earlier than when they were scheduled to be.

That was two months ago.

Today, when I walked through the kitchen and climbed the stairs, I had no choice.

I knocked on Vicious's bedroom door. His room was on the second floor at the end of the wide curved hallway, the door facing the floating stone staircase of the cave-like mansion.

I'd never been near Vicious's room, and I wished I could keep it that way. Unfortunately, my calculus book had been stolen. Whoever broke into my locker had wiped it clean of my stuff and left garbage inside. Empty soda cans, cleaning supplies, and condom wrappers spilled out the moment I opened the locker door.

Just another not-so-clever yet effective way for the students at All Saints High to remind me that I was nothing but the cheap help around here. By that point, I was so used to it I barely reddened at all. When all eyes in the hallway darted to me, snickers and chuckles rising out of every throat, I tilted my chin up and marched straight to my next class.

All Saints High was a school full of spoiled, overprivileged sinners. A school where if you failed to dress or act a certain way, you didn't belong. Rosie blended in better than I did, thank the Lord. But with a Southern drawl, offbeat style, and one of the most popular guys at school—that being Vicious Spencer—hating my guts, I didn't fit in.

What made it worse was that I didn't *want* to fit in. These kids didn't impress me. They weren't kind or welcoming or even very smart. They didn't possess any of the qualities I looked for in friends.

But I needed my textbook badly if I ever wanted to escape this place.

I knocked three times on the mahogany door of Vicious's bedroom. Rolling my lower lip between my fingers, I tried to suck in as much oxygen as I could, but it did nothing to calm the throbbing pulse in my neck.

Please don't be there…

Please don't be an ass…

Please…

A soft noise seeped from the crack under the door, and my body tensed.

Giggling.

Vicious never giggled. Heck, he hardly ever chuckled. Even his smiles were few and far between. No. The sound was undoubtedly female.

I heard him whisper in his raspy tone something inaudible that made her moan. My ears seared, and I anxiously rubbed my hands on the yellow cutoff denim shorts covering my thighs. Out of all the scenarios I could have imagined, this was by far the worst.

Him.

With another girl.

Who I hated before I even knew her name.

It didn't make any sense, yet I felt ridiculously angry.

But he was clearly there, and I was a girl on a mission.

"Vicious?" I called out, trying to steady my voice. I straightened my spine, even though he couldn't see me. "It's Millie. Sorry to interrupt y'all. I just wanted to borrow your calc book. Mine's lost, and I really need to get ready for that exam we have tomorrow." *God forbid you ever study for our exam yourself.* I took a silent breath.

He didn't answer, but I heard a sharp intake of breath—*the girl*—and the rustle of fabric and the noise of a zipper rolling. Down, I had no doubt.

I squeezed my eyes shut and pressed my forehead against the cool wood of his door.

Bite the bullet. Swallow your pride. This wouldn't matter in a few years. Vicious and his stupid antics would be a distant memory, the snooty town of Todos Santos just a dust-covered part of my past.

My parents had jumped at the chance when Josephine Spencer offered them jobs. They'd dragged us across the country to California because the health care was better and we didn't even need to pay rent. Mama was the Spencers' cook/housekeeper, and Daddy was part gardener and handyman. The previous live-in couple had quit, and it was no wonder. Pretty sure my parents weren't so keen on the jobs either. But opportunities like these were rare, and Josephine Spencer's mama was friends with my great-aunt, which was how they'd gotten the job.

I was planning on getting out of here soon. As soon as I got accepted to the first out-of-state college I'd applied to, to be exact. In order to do so, though, I needed a scholarship.

For a scholarship, I needed kick-ass grades.

And for kick-ass grades, I needed this textbook.

"Vicious," I ground out his stupid nickname. I knew he hated his real name, and for reasons beyond my grasp, I didn't want to upset him. "I'll grab the book and copy the formulas I need real quick. I won't borrow it long. Please." I gulped down the ball of frustration twisting in my throat. It was bad enough I'd had my stuff stolen—*again*—without having to ask Vicious for favors.

The giggling escalated. The high, screechy pitch sawed through my ears. My fingers tingled to push the door open and launch at him with my fists.

I heard his groan of pleasure and knew it had nothing to do with the girl he was with. He loved taunting me. Ever since our first encounter outside his library two months ago, he'd been hell-bent on reminding me that I wasn't good enough.

Not good enough for his mansion.

Not good enough for his school.

Not good enough for *his town*.

Worst part? It wasn't a figure of speech. It really *was* his town. Baron Spencer Jr.—dubbed Vicious for his cold, ruthless behavior—was the heir to one of the biggest family-owned fortunes in California. The Spencers owned a pipeline company, half of downtown Todos Santos—including the mall—and three corporate office parks. Vicious had enough money to take care of the next ten generations of his family.

But I didn't.

My parents were servants. We had to work for every penny. I didn't expect him to understand. Trust-fund kids never did. But I presumed he'd at least pretend, like the rest of them.

Education mattered to me, and at that moment, I felt robbed of it.

Because rich people had stolen my books.

Because this particular rich kid wouldn't even open the door to his room so I could borrow his textbook really quickly.

"Vicious!" My frustration got the better of me, and I slammed my palm flat against his door. Ignoring the throb it sent up my wrist, I continued, exasperated, "C'mon!"

I was close to turning around and walking away. Even if it meant I had to take my bike and ride all the way across town to borrow Sydney's books. Sydney was my only friend at All Saints High and the one person I liked in class.

But then I heard Vicious chuckling, and I knew the joke was on me. "I love to see you crawl. Beg for it, baby, and I'll give it to you," he said.

Not to the girl in his room.

To me.

I lost it. Even though I knew it was wrong. That he was winning.

I thrust the door open and barged into his room, strangling the handle with my fist, my knuckles white and burning.

My eyes darted to his king-size bed, barely stopping to take in the gorgeous mural above it—four white horses galloping into the darkness—or the elegant dark furniture. His bed looked like a throne, sitting in the middle of the room, big and high and draped in soft black satin. He was perched on the edge of his mattress, a girl who was in my PE class in his lap. Her name was Georgia, and her grandparents owned half the vineyards upstate in Carmel Valley. Georgia's long blond hair veiled one of his broad shoulders, and her Caribbean tan looked perfect and smooth against Vicious's pale complexion.

His dark-blue eyes—so dark they were almost black—locked on mine as he continued to kiss her ravenously—his tongue making several appearances—like she was made of cotton candy. I needed to look away but couldn't. I was trapped in his gaze, completely immobilized from the eyes down, so I arched an eyebrow, showing him that I didn't care.

Only I did. I cared a lot.

I cared so much, in fact, that I continued to stare at them shamelessly. At his hollowed cheeks as he inserted his tongue deep into her mouth, his burning, taunting glare never leaving mine, gauging me for a reaction. I felt my body buzzing in an unfamiliar way, falling under his spell. A sweet, pungent fog. It was sexual, unwelcome, yet completely inescapable. I wanted to break free, but for the life of me, I couldn't.

My grip on the door handle tightened, and I swallowed, my eyes dropping to his hand as he grabbed her waist and squeezed playfully. I squeezed my own waist through the fabric of my yellow-and-white sunflower top.

What the hell was wrong with me? Watching him kiss another girl was unbearable but also weirdly fascinating.

I wanted to see it.

I didn't want to see it.

Either way, I couldn't *unsee* it.

Admitting defeat, I blinked, shifting my gaze to a black Raiders cap hung over the headrest of his desk chair.

"Your textbook, Vicious. I need it," I repeated. "I'm not leaving your room without it."

"Get the fuck out, Help," he said into Georgia's giggling mouth.

A thorn twisted in my heart, jealousy filling my chest. I couldn't wrap my head around this physical reaction. The pain. The shame. The *lust*. I hated Vicious. He was hard, heartless, and hateful. I'd heard his mother had died when he was nine, but he was eighteen now and had a nice stepmother who let him do whatever he wanted. Josephine seemed sweet and caring.

AUTHOR'S NOTE

This book was my most ambitious in recent years, because it dealt with sensitive topics and delved into personality and cognitive disorders, which required sensitivity readers as well as professional guidance from medical experts.

The subject of disorders is one that is close to my heart as an ADHD person who is married to an OCD person. (And I don't just mean in the offhanded way people say they have ADHD and OCD. This has affected many facets of our lives from childhood through adulthood.)

It's a privilege to explore and familiarize readers with the struggles of obsessive-compulsive disorder (or as my husband refers to it "Obsessive-compulsive order. There is nothing disorderly about me").

On another note, while this is the third and final book in the Forbidden Love series, the universe will continue to expand with my brand-new, seven-book series, Society of Villains. You'll get the Ferrantes' and Callaghans' stories and so much more.

Book one in the series, *Bad Bishop*, will see Tiernan Callaghan as the hero. If you think you hate him now, you just wait.

More to come soon, so please make sure you subscribe to my newsletter: Design emails people love to get. (flodesk.com)

ACKNOWLEDGMENTS

As always, this book couldn't have happened without the help and support of many, many people to whom I owe my thanks.

To the Books & Moods' incredible artists, including Julie and Mary, for the gorgeous covers, stunning teasers, and announcement graphics. Thank you for making every release an experience.

To my editors, Mara White and Paige Maroney Smith. Special thank you goes to my Bloom Books editor, Christa Désir, for being an incredible craftswoman and human. I am in awe of who and what you are every day. My infinite gratitude also goes to Siena, Madison, and the entire Bloom PR team.

Big thank-you to my beta readers who always show up, even though I am (also always) late—Liah Barros, Vanessa Villegas, author besties Ava Harrison and Parker S. Huntington, Kelly Allenby (who ensured Gia's British English is on point), as well as my beta/sensitivity readers for this book, who graciously took the time to help me (hopefully) get it right—Tijuana Turner (also known as Momager), Rebecca Davis, and Zaji-Kali Galan.

Special thanks to the person without whom I wouldn't be able to tackle such sensitive subjects, including OCD, cognitive distortion, and ableism—Terry Young, thank you for the time and expertise. Please note that any and all inaccuracies or mistakes of cognitive distortion in this book are my own.

And to Maria Gobo, who graciously agreed to share with me her mother's story and allowed me to draw inspiration from it.

Another big shout-out goes to Stacey Blake for the incredible formatting and Literally Yours (Gabby, Sarah, Lori) and the Author Agency (Becca and Shauna) for spreading the word about my books.

My deepest gratitude goes to my agent, Kimberly Brower at Park, Fine & Brower, as well as my Facebook group, the Sassy Sparrows, my influencer group, creatively named LJ's Influencers' Group, and any blogger, bookstagrammer, or booktoker who took the time to read, review, and recommend these books to their fellow readers.

If you reached this far and enjoyed the story, please consider leaving a brief, honest review on Amazon so others can decide whether the book is for them or not.

Tate and Gia got their hard-earned HEA, but there are many characters in this Ljverse that are going to absolutely shock and delight you.

Buckle up and stay tuned.

All my love,
L.J. xoxo

ABOUT THE AUTHOR

L.J. Shen is a *New York Times*, *USA Today*, *Wall Street Journal*, *Washington Post*, and #1 Amazon Kindle Store bestselling author of contemporary romance books. She writes angsty books, unredeemable antiheroes, and sassy heroines who bring them to their knees (for more reasons than one). HEAs and groveling are guaranteed. She lives in Florida with her husband, three sons, and a disturbingly active imagination.

Website: authorljshen.com
Facebook: authorljshen
Instagram: @authorljshen
Twitter: @lj_shen
TikTok: @authorljshen
Pinterest: @authorljshen